MURDER AT HOLLY HOUSE

www.penguin.co.uk

By Denzil Meyrick

The DCI Daley Thrillers
Whisky from Small Glasses
The Last Witness
Dark Suits and Sad Songs
The Rat Stone Serenade
Well of the Winds
The Relentless Tide
A Breath on Dying Embers
Jeremiah's Bell
For Any Other Truth
The Death of Remembrance
No Sweet Sorrow

Kinloch Novellas
A Large Measure of Snow
A Toast to the Old Stones
Ghosts in the Gloaming

Short Story Collections
One Last Dram Before Midnight

Standalones
Terms of Restitution

MURDER AT HOLLY HOUSE

The Memoirs of Inspector
Frank Grasby

DENZIL MEYRICK

bantam

TRANSWORLD PUBLISHERS
Penguin Random House, One Embassy Gardens,
8 Viaduct Gardens, London SW11 7BW
www.penguin.co.uk

Transworld is part of the Penguin Random House group of companies
whose addresses can be found at global.penguinrandomhouse.com

First published in Great Britain in 2023 by Bantam
an imprint of Transworld Publishers

A CIP catalogue record for this book
is available from the British Library.

ISBN 9781787637184

Typeset in 12.75/16pt Minion Pro by Jouve (UK), Milton Keynes
Printed and bound in Great Britain by Clays Ltd, Elcograf S.p.A.

The authorized representative in the EEA is Penguin Random House Ireland,
Morrison Chambers, 32 Nassau Street, Dublin DO2 YH68.

Penguin Random House is committed to a sustainable
future for our business, our readers and our planet. This book
is made from Forest Stewardship Council® certified paper.

For my late grandfather, Cyril Pinkney.
A Yorkshireman to his bootstraps.

PROLOGUE

It's odd how little bits and pieces find their way, almost indiscriminately, to this person or that.

In my case, though I'd heard tell of Frank Grasby – a distant cousin on my mother's side – all I knew for sure was that he'd been a police officer in Yorkshire, roughly from the end of the Second World War until some time in the late sixties.

He was one of the lesser names in her family canon; therefore, it is safe to assume that my mother relegated him to a mere mention now and again because of a flaw in character or deed. Until then, it didn't appear to me as though he'd lived a particularly noble, interesting, or even worthy existence. But when two small wooden crates were sent to me as part of the goods and chattels left over after my parents died, my interest was piqued.

On opening these crates, I discovered that, not only did they contain Frank Grasby's self-penned memoir, but also a positive archive, consisting of police reports, telexes, statements, meeting notes and many other little gems, all pertaining to cases he'd investigated. I include these sparingly, though I hope they add to the context of it all.

I was also pleasantly surprised at the fine condition of the many notebooks that form the story of the inspector's career, and was most surprised that, despite Grasby's challenging handwriting, I seemed to be able to decipher it quite easily. Perhaps it's a family thing. But nothing is perfect in this world, and the odd ripped-out or water-damaged page sometimes appears at the most inopportune of moments. It was fun, though, to piece together the evidence at hand, and recreate these lost passages – almost as though one were in Grasby's head at the time.

Frank Grasby is a good writer, born entertainer and storyteller. His tendency to head off at a tangent, however, has required me to trim here and there. I've tried to do this with the minimum of interference possible.

What follows is virtually as written. I've taken the precaution of changing some names in order to protect the reputations of those mentioned, living or dead (most are the latter). I've also toned down some of the more 'explicit' content, be it bad language or some of the author's more colourful adventures. In essence, I've done my best to curate them in a manner more suited to these modern times and sensibilities.

The memoir leaps backwards and forwards in time. I chose this as his first published case, as I think it best sums up the great fellow. Also, it's as he intended (see Grasby's note below).

But, to all intents and purposes, please find herein a glimpse into the extraordinary life of Inspector Frank Grasby.

Original Note from the Author

Dear Reader,

Welcome to my jumbled, scattered remembrances. I begin, not at the beginning, but with a case into which I was flung unwittingly. It turned out to be pivotal, not just as far as my career was concerned, but as regards the course of my whole life. A fine place to start, as you'll see.

It's so often the way, one crashes into situations unprepared and ill-informed. When sent by then Superintendent Arthur Juggers to the village of Elderby, I wish I'd been given sight of this police report. Unfortunately, it came into my possession after the fact. It contains, albeit obliquely, information that may have influenced my decisions and conduct on arrival in the village. But being wise after the event is one of my little foibles.

I found it in the old police archives, just as I was completing this volume of my memoirs. I enclose it for reference, and as a nod to the absolute peril into which I was unwittingly stepping.

I hope you will find interest in the life story of this old chap.

Frank Grasby
York, March 1975

*****

North Yorkshire Police Report: 17th May 1949

*****

By Telex: 1050 hrs

On the evening of 16th May 1949, at about 2000 hrs, a call was received by Elderby Police from the Hanging Beggar public house in the village. A complaint regarding rowdy customers refusing to leave the premises was made by staff.

Being the duty officer, Inspector D. P. Moore took the call at his domicile and attended the Hanging Beggar at around 2015 hrs.

On his arrival, he apparently found the public house to be quiet and all in order. However, following protocol to the letter, Inspector Moore stayed behind to take statements from staff and customers, and ensure that the miscreants did not return.

This duty complete, Inspector Moore left the Hanging Beggar at approximately 2215 hrs, his intention being to return to his domicile.

Though on a re-rostered rest day, I answered a call from Division at approximately 2355 hrs that same evening, 16th May. Mrs Moore, the Inspector's spouse,

informed the night shift at Pickering by
telephone that her husband had failed to
return home and she was worried as to his
whereabouts. She told them of his leaving
the public house and intention to return
home.

Shortly after midnight, I made a cursory
search of the area, including Elderby
police station, in case Inspector Moore had
returned to write a report on the matter
and perhaps fallen asleep after what had
been, by all accounts, a busy day.

There being no sign of Inspector Moore at
Elderby police station, or in the environs
of the village, I called Division and
officially reported him missing at 0222 hrs
on the morning of 17th May.

I and seven officers from Pickering
mustered at 0500 hrs on the morning of 17th
May in order to prepare a search,
commencing at first light, approximately
0620 hrs.

At approximately 0745 hrs, a member of
the public, one Andrew Moleston, a man
local to the village and of sound
character, approached officers from
Pickering to say that he had observed
something odd while angling on the River
Lise, at the weir. This is a location
approximately two miles east of Elderby.

Attending, Constables Rickmansworth and
Hastie discovered the body of Inspector
Moore at 0824 hrs. The remains had become

entangled in weeds in a shallow part of the river.

Following a brief examination on the riverside, at which I attended, commencing at 0931 hrs by Force Doctor Terrance Clancy MD, life was officially pronounced extinct. The time was 0935 hrs.

Inspector Moore's remains were removed to Pickering for post-mortem examination at 1005 hrs, under my supervision.

Sgt. E. M. P. Bleakly
Elderby Police Station

1

York, December 1952

Each day of the week has its own feel – or so I think. Mondays are universally loathed, whilst Fridays bring a spring to the step. For me, a Sunday heralds a nagging echo of my lost piety. Gone is the angelic choirboy, the youth who seriously considered following his father and grandfather into the Church. I still feel guilty that I only attend around this time of year or other high days, holidays, weddings and funerals; I've seen far too many of the latter.

I suppose my job as a police inspector offers some mitigation, but never enough to quell the wrath of my prelate father. In fact, hell hath no fury like a village vicar spurned by the bishops of the Church in which he serves.

But with Christmas on the way, I've decided that it's high time I try to improve my form as far as church attendance is concerned. If I'm honest, I need all the help I can get being, yet again, in hot water.

I try not to think about it as I walk along the smoky corridors of police headquarters in York. The senior officer who's about to drag me across the coals bears more than a little resemblance to the man who gave me life; not physically, though. While the Reverend Cyril Grasby is tall, thin and grey – almost as though he is in the process of fading away – Superintendent Arthur Juggers is squat and florid. He is very much of this earthly realm, a true corporeal reality wrought in blood, bone, pipe tobacco and ale. He's the kind of man one thinks could stand in front of a solid wall and will it to collapse by sheer force of personality alone. I'm sure you know the type. But we get on passably well – sometimes.

I straighten my tie and stub out a cigarette on a nearby ashtray as I stand before his stout oaken door. I'm reminded of his presence by a shining brass plaque bearing his name and rank.

'Who's hovering out there?' he bellows in the thick brogue of the county. 'Everyone knows I can't abide bloody hoverers.'

It is as though he possesses the aural qualities of a large bat – a querulous, malicious one, at that.

I knock; hear him grunt admission, and enter. His office is as you might expect: much wood panelling, old photographs, various citations for bravery and other achievements. The pungent but strangely pleasing odour of pipe tobacco and a hint of stale beer is never far away. Behind him on the wall is a painting of the pavilion at Headingley. Thankfully, cricket is the one thing we have in common. I aim to use this in my defence. Had it not been for the intervention of the Second World War, being a rather late starter and having an unfortunate predilection for getting out to wide balls on the leg side, I would be turning out for Yorkshire now, instead of pursuing an ever-growing list of miscreants and ne'er-do-wells. But life can be cruel, as we all know.

'Don't sit down,' he says without looking up from the newspaper he's reading.

I do as I'm bid, then embark on my strategy. 'I saw young Trueman this morning, sir.' I feel this foray in the direction of Yorkshire County Cricket Club has had the desired effect, as he lifts his eyes from the paper and stares at me over the rim of his half-moon spectacles.

'No small-talk, Grasby – not this time. If you'd not been so bloody feckless you could be out there. Even though you're at the veteran stage now. Can't be worse with a bat than you are with a notebook, mark you.'

'Sir?' I enquire disingenuously, as though I have no idea of what he's about to say.

'Lady bloody Winthorpe. Does that ring a bell?'

'Ah.'

'You go out to Admere House to bring a light-fingered servant to justice, but before you can say "How's he?", twenty of the best thoroughbred horses in England are running free across the county.' The newspaper is cast aside. 'Seven are still missing!'

'Just a confusion between myself and the groom, sir.'

'Confusion? You arrested the groom and forgot to lock the stable door. Bloody classic stupidity, is that.'

'In all fairness, sir, Constable Armley was also present. He should have been paying attention to such minor details.'

'He was handcuffed to the prisoner – this groom chap. You expected him to secure the stable block too?'

'Well . . .'

'If we don't find these bloody ho'ses His Lordship's going to sue the chief constable. How do you feel about that?'

I ponder on which response is most suitable, deciding that a grimace should do the job.

'No wonder you're pulling a face, Grasby. I'm all that's

between you and the dole. You can't go messing with the aristocracy. We'll have the young queen at the door next, no doubt demanding your head. Aye, and I'll give her it an' all – on a plate. She's got enough to worry about, poor lass, without fretting on inept Yorkshire detectives.'

There follows a dire list of consequences, all of which leave me more and more alarmed, as the superintendent's face turns an increasingly unhealthy beetroot colour. No doubt feeling as though his head is about to explode, he reaches for the solace of his pipe. As he's tamping down tobacco, I'm worrying I may be forcibly transferred to East Yorkshire, envisioning a wet Tuesday night on the docks in Hull. It's happened before, you know. Mumford, an old colleague of mine when we were detective sergeants, ended up walking the beat as a bobby on Hessle Road. Not for the faint-hearted, let me tell you.

'Do you want me to go and search for the horses, sir?' I offer.

'Abso-bloody-lutely not! The boss would have a fit. No, Grasby, it's been one calamity too many for you.'

Oh no, it's Hessle Road! I feel my knees weaken.

'He wants you out of the way for a while. Until this all blows over.'

'But my record, sir. I've brought a good few to justice since coming back from the war.'

He stands, his belly popping out over the waistband of his uniform trousers. 'You have, of that there is no doubt. But you've had more than your fair share of problems along the way.'

'No more than most, I'd say. Horses apart, that is.'

He prods his stubby finger at me. 'What about old Mrs Smelt?'

'Ah, the quote in the *Yorkshire Post*.'

'Oh aye: "When asked for a response to the suspicious death, Inspector Grasby of York Police said: 'Grandma Smelt, we wonder why?'"'

'An unfortunate comment, I admit. I was just trying to introduce some levity into the proceedings.'

As though he hadn't heard this plea of mitigation, Juggers continues. 'And what about the lord mayor's daughter, eh?'

'A tricky business, sir.'

'You had her locked up for being drunk and disorderly.'

'She was rolling about on the floor in the Minster Inn!'

'She was having an epileptic fit!'

'To be fair, that was only confirmed later by the force doctor. I don't think anyone present thought otherwise – including the publican.'

Superintendent Juggers shakes his head, jowls following slightly behind the rest of his face. 'Tell me about James Thomas Goss.'

'A breach of trust, sir. Honour amongst thieves is a thing of the past, quite clearly.'

'But your stupidity most certainly isn't. You get to London with one of the most persistent and elusive burglars the Metropolitan Police has ever encountered, and you simply let him run free.' Juggers's face is crimson again.

'Tardiness, sir. They were supposed to take custody of him at Euston. They were late.'

'And you needed to answer a call of nature because you'd been swigging beer with this reprobate all the way to London.'

'We had a refreshment – it was a hot day, sir.'

'You should have taken him with you to the bathroom. Handcuffed the bugger to something whilst you were relieving yourself.'

I'm not sure that the superintendent has chosen the

right words here, but nonetheless I persist. 'It's very off-putting, to be honest. I find it almost impossible to go under such circumstances, sir.' I feel that most men must appreciate this little foible, or at least have experienced such a problem in a busy gents' toilet. Juggers clearly doesn't agree.

'Bloody jessie! No, your solution is to have him go to the bar and buy a couple more beers while you're indisposed. Of course, he buggers off into the throng.'

'With the ten-bob note I'd given him, into the bargain!'

'What did you think he was going to do?'

'Keep his word, like a man.'

'He's a bloody criminal! What would you do if you were facing ten years inside and some clot gave you the opportunity to abscond, not to mention providing the bus fare to freedom?'

'They found him – eventually.'

'It took two bloody years! During which time he broke into houses all over the place.'

I feel this conversation has definitely taken a turn for the worse. I pray he doesn't think of any more of my misdemeanours. But just in case he does, I decide to rest my defence. It's only making things worse. But, as it turns out, he's already come to sentencing.

'No, the die is cast, Grasby – though I'll be sad to lose you, despite everything. When you're not being utterly stupid, you can be an inspired detective.'

'Not Hull, sir. Please, for old times' sake, at least.' I'm ready to go down on bended knee at this point. But I realize such an action is more likely to inflame the situation. Instead, I adopt a pleading look, desperately searching for Juggers's better nature. My thoughts are now dominated by the sight and sounds of Hull's worst drinking establishments on a

Friday night when the trawlers come back to port. The very notion makes me shudder. Plus, these ridiculous helmets constables are forced to wear have never suited me. I've inherited my father's tall, lean frame; I look like a lamp post in a uniform. People laugh.

'Elderby, that's where you're headed.'

'Sir?' I'm wracking my brains in a desperate attempt to work out where Elderby is located. They're planning to build new council estates in Hull; I hope this isn't one of them.

'It's far enough away from the chief constable, in case you're wondering. On the North York Moors. You're on secondment for the foreseeable.' Juggers turns to the window and gazes out as light snow flutters down on passing traffic and pedestrians, the good folk of the city going about their business. 'You were good with a bat. Decent right-arm spinner into the bargain.' He nods sagely, no doubt playing one of my many great innings for Yorkshire's second eleven back in his mind's eye. 'Shame about them legside balls, eh? You could never get your head round them.'

Damn.

'You'll keep your rank and your job as a detective. Don't thank me.'

'Thank you,' I say without thinking.

He turns on his heel and glares at me with those piggy eyes. 'There's been a spate of thefts from farms in the area around Elderby. We owe it to them to be of mutual assistance. They don't have our manpower or resources. Anyhow, most of these farms belong to Lord Damnish.'

Bugger, the bloody aristocracy again.

'You sort this out, bring the culprit or culprits to justice speedily, and I'll have a chance to plead on your behalf. Get you back here once all the fuss has died down. And them ho'ses are found, of course.'

My mind is working overtime now. You know, the various domestic consequences of such a move, like where will I lay my head and how will I get there? Plus, what will I do on Christmas Day? It's not that far away, but when it snows on the North York Moors, it really *snows*, if you know what I mean.

As though he's read my mind, Juggers sits back behind his big desk and shuffles through his papers. 'We've found you digs with a Mrs Hetty Gaunt. She'll make sure you're comfortable over the festive period.' He glares at me over his spectacles again. 'She's a widow of a certain age, so don't let your mind wander to things of a base nature, Grasby. You're one of the only single men in the CID. With sufficient rank and experience to deal with Damnish, at any rate. Can't send a young lad with a new suit, can I?'

'Indeed not, sir. The very thought.' In saying this, I could have hoped for a more delectable landlady. A young widow would have done nicely. There are plenty about since the war. I've yet to settle, you see. And with my fortieth birthday calling from not too far away, I fear I may become a confirmed bachelor. Mrs Gaunt sounds formidable, and above all, old. However, with a miserable Yuletide in prospect, and only my father for company . . . well, a change doesn't sound too bad.

'Take the rest of the day off and get your things together. Stubby Watts will give you a car from the pool. It's a nice little village, if a bit remote.' Juggers picks up his newspaper again. 'And don't make a backside of it. Next time it will be Hessle Road!'

So, that was it. I resolve to find a map.

2

Stubby Watts, a short man in dungarees, removes his oily cap and scratches the pale skin on his bald head. He's a mechanic, and in charge of all the vehicles used by the police in York. He has rather a curmudgeonly reputation, but today appears to be in reasonably good, mid-season form.

'We don't have much doing, lad.' He scans the big garage, a place where cars come to die, by the looks of it. 'There's this Austin A30, mind you, though it's been in the wars.'

He leads me to a typically battered-looking green car. I say typically because that's the way of things with police cars, marked or unmarked. The dolts that drive them do so with very little care and attention. This results in bashes, scrapes, cigarette burns on the upholstery, etc., etc.

'How does she run?' I ask hopefully.

'Not as good as when we got her. Been in a smash, you see.'

'But you've fixed her up?'

'I'm a mechanic, not a bloody magician. But aye, I've done my best.'

I peer through the window and am pleasantly surprised by the absence of old fag packets or greasy fish-and-chip newspapers. He hands me the keys and I rev the engine. The car chugs into life in a throaty, unhealthy way.

'Doesn't sound too good, Stubby.'

'Well, it's as good as you're going to get, young man. I've nowt else to spare. You'll be glad o' it in a blizzard. Aye, and they're on the way, trust me.'

I ignore the snow warning and jump in. When you're tall, small cars have the unfortunate habit of making one feel packed, like a sardine. My knees appear to be unnaturally close to my ears, but I suppose that's just me. The car decides to backfire, sending a cloud of black smoke into the air, accompanied by a sharp pop that reminds me too much of my experiences during the war. Loud bangs make my face prickle, which is a most unpleasant sensation. I spent my entire service in the East Yorks with that uncomfortable prickling for company.

'Does it do that a lot?'

'No, I wouldn't think so. Like as not she just needs a good run to blow out the cobwebs, lad.'

I'm always suspicious when men of the machine like Stubby are driven to describe the exigencies of one vehicle or another using non-mechanical terms. 'Blow out the cobwebs' is a perfect example. I'm even more disturbed when, as I rev the engine again, the same happens in a puff of smoke and a sharp report.

'Aye, just needs a good run, that's all.' But Stubby Watts strokes his chin with an expression on his face that says otherwise.

Never trust a mechanic. It's a motto that will handily see you through life.

But, as I have no choice in the matter, I drive out of the garage. In the wing mirror, I see Stubby mouthing something.

No doubt a friendly farewell. I wave my hand out of the open window by way of acknowledgement.

It's only a short drive home. When I say home, I really mean my father's domicile, a small cottage just to the north of York. It's the place the Church of England found for him to while away his declining years after being forcibly retired. Of course, nothing comes free in this life, and as part of his tenancy he's compelled to fill in for members of the clergy in the area who are sick or off on holiday. They have a name for this, but I can never remember it.

Suffice it to say, he hates being handed a parish for a few days or weeks, so behaves in an utterly shameful way by scaring his peripatetic flock half to death with the kind of fire and brimstone last practised by the Roundheads. It's his way of getting back at the Church that rewarded him with a pittance of a pension and little more than expenses for these little chores. I'm sure when the incumbent vicar returns to post, he finds himself down a few punters.

I find him staring up at the guttering from the tiny front garden as I arrive in a thick cloud of black smoke and a small explosion. He's dressed in a long overcoat which belongs to me. Though I am by no means broad-shouldered, it hangs off him like a choirboy's surplice. I stare at this man who looks like a scarecrow with advanced malnutrition. You see, though I had a good flat in town, I felt it only right that I abandon it when my mother died. I knew he would be glad of the company, despite his protestations.

'I'd rather share a house with Abimelech,' I remember he said at the time.

Thankfully, this arcane biblical reference is lost on me. And I'm sure he's happy to have his son about the place, really.

'What's this?' he enquires, taking in the Austin with a leery eye. He drives a rather grander car: an ancient Bentley, left to him by his father, my grandfather – a bishop, no less.

'I have news!' I announce breezily.

'Oh.' The reply is typical of his understated manner.

'I have to push off for a while, I'm afraid. Don't know how long for, to be honest. Sorry about Christmas and all that.'

'Are you going to prison?' he offers less than charitably.

'No, it's a special secondment to the North York Moors. A place called Elderby.'

'They've found you out at last and want you out of the way, more than likely.'

My father can be unnervingly prescient at times. It's a quality of which I've never been fond.

'No, absolutely not.' I raise my chin nobly – I'm good at that, incidentally. 'I've been sent to solve a crime for Lord Damnish, actually.'

'Huh.' He wipes away a drip from his nose on the sleeve of my overcoat. 'I hope you make a better job of it than you did with Lady Winthorpe's horses. That was in the *Post*, you know.'

I decide to mumble something about a misunderstanding and make my way into the house for some respite. But my father is like a very thin dog with a bone – an elderly Lurcher, perhaps. He follows me inside.

'I know you think you're *simpatico* with these dreadful people. That damned school your mother insisted we send you to is responsible for that. But let me assure you, to them you're nothing but an annoying smut on a white collar.'

My dear father is referring to my time at Hymers

College, a minor public school situated in Hull. I know and fear so much about the place, let me tell you. On the plus side, it helped my cricket no end; but it also left me with a rather *toffee* accent. On the whole, though, this has been to my great advantage in life. I very much doubt I'd have made the rank of inspector were it not for the old school tie. Mind you, it made for some ribbing from the lads when I first joined up. But when they noted my capacity for strong drink, we soon mucked in rather well. I also propelled the station's cricket team to unknown heights, which always raises morale and the number of friends one manages to accumulate.

Yes, I do remember telling you that I haven't been able to settle down. But it hasn't been for want of trying. I'd like to say that I've never found the right girl. But that would be disingenuous. It's more honest to say that, when a nice girl finds me and eventually gets my measure, she usually runs off at a pace that would challenge Roger Bannister. The sad truth is that women find me feckless. My love for the sport of kings, and all that accompanies it, can also be a stumbling block. It often leaves me rather out of pocket. Heigh-ho. I live in hope.

Unfortunately for me, the new chief constable, being the son of a fisherman from Whitby, cannot abide anyone without a glottal stop. So, public schoolboy or not, I find myself in my current predicament.

My father also hates privilege. Years ago, he seemingly had a run-in with King George V over some matter theological. It did nothing for his standing in the Church and left him hating anyone with a hint of blue blood. I suffer by default because of what he sees as my received affectations. But what can a chap do? They sent me to the bloody place. It was a kind of scholarship scheme reserved for promising sons of the clergy. They called me the Archbishop of York for the first three terms, but I didn't mind. I am blessed with a sunny disposition, in the main, you know.

I decide to ignore him and make my way to the miserable garret that is my bedroom. I've learned, by dint of regular bumps and bashes, to lower my head when I go in. The ceiling is impossibly low, you see. Designed when the good burghers of York were a great deal smaller than they are now, I reckon.

With a view to my new assignment, I pack my other suit and a few bits and pieces into an old suitcase that once belonged to my mother. I always feel more than a twinge of sadness when I think of her. A caring woman, always willing to inform her only son about the world and its many wonders. She always encouraged me too, making sure my love of cricket was catered for, despite my father's distaste for the game. I miss her still, and she's been in my thoughts every day since she passed away seven years ago. It's especially poignant at this time of year. Another good reason to bugger off to the moors, methinks.

Leaving these sad thoughts behind, I trundle down the old staircase in search of supper. I'm delighted to discover that we have company. So caught up was I in the process of packing, and anticipation of my trip to this Elderby, all to the background of the burbling wireless, I've completely missed the arrival of Lord Parsley – Mitch, as he's been to me since I was a little snapper.

Lord Parsley is of the purple because of his stellar career in the army. He and my father grew up together, and though they appear polar opposites in so many ways, have remained friends. Mitch is small, red and rotund. He's involved in the Army Intelligence Corps these days. He hasn't ever said much about it, which is absolutely in line with chaps who follow that path, in my experience. Makes sense, of course. Don't want every Tom, Dick and Frank knowing official secrets.

Dear Daddy towers over him as they stand in the kitchen, pouring some of his notoriously powerful home-brewed elderberry wine into a glass for his guest.

'Now, young Francis,' says Parsley, insisting on the proper form of my name as always. 'I hear you're off to the back of beyond.' He smiles with his accustomed warmth.

'Indeed, Mitch. I couldn't stand by and see the married chaps separated from their families at this time of year. I took a step forward on this one,' I say, lying through my teeth.

'Jolly good. You've always been a good egg, that way.'

'Rotten egg,' says my father, rather typically.

'Ignore him, Francis. Hopefully you'll manage to find a wife up in the hills. One needs a wife, you know. I'd be in a right bloody fix without Jess, I can tell you. You'll enjoy it, I'm sure.'

'I don't know much about the place, to be honest, Mitch,' say I.

Somehow, I think he gives me an odd look. I'm sure his expression darkens for a moment. But in a flash he's back to his cheery self. 'Here's to you and Elderby!' He raises his glass, as my father reluctantly pours me a drink.

For all his many faults, my father cooks well. This is possibly down to the unfortunate fact that my mother could burn a salad. Anyhow, he's dished up lemon sole in a nut-butter sauce, with some potatoes and garden peas. Rather good, given the lingering rationing restrictions we still suffer.

Despite being a bishop's son and growing up in some splendour, my father has working-class pretensions. So we don't have a good Sancerre or even a decent red Burgundy with our meal. No, it's another large glass of elderberry wine. Now, I'm not saying my father's skills in this regard are to be sniffed at: he uses honey to sweeten his alcoholic outpourings, so they are pleasant to taste. Rather too pleasant, in fact. The honey hides any real sensation of imbibing dangerously, but one is, nonetheless.

So, after a few glasses or so, and some most companionable chatter, I find myself three sheets to the wind, as do my father and Parsley. In a while, he checks his lordly watch and expresses surprise at the time. 'My driver is due in ten minutes. Time does fly in good company, you know.' He makes to get up, sits back down sharply and bursts into a fit of the giggles.

'Still can't take your drink, I see,' slurs my father as he searches for a potato on the table rather than his plate.

'On the contrary,' says Lord Parsley. 'Regular consumption of your home brew over the years has left me with a fine tolerance for anything that's served in the mess.'

And it's true. Having had a liberal mother, I've been knocking this concoction or something like it back since I was about ten years old. She always felt it best I be exposed to alcohol as soon as possible. Many a sore head I've had since. But, by goodness, I can hold my booze.

'Elderby, you say?' At the end of the table the thin grey man that is my father squints at me over the rim of his glass.

'Yes, on the moors, Father,' I reply.

'Saint Thomas's-on-the-Edge.'

'Is he? That's bloody bad luck,' say I, making Parsley chortle again.

'No, you fool. That's the name of the church in Elderby.'

'Oh, bit of a strange moniker, isn't it?'

My father smiles in a way that is scarily familiar to me.

'You've been there, Father?'

'Not recently,' he says, returning enigmatically to the last of his fish.

I know this approach. He's done it all my life. It's in the expression, his manner. He knows something about this outpost to which I'm being exiled, but he's not going to say what. I used to try to probe him on such details but have long since learned not to bother.

'Well, I'm looking forward to it. It'll be a nice change to get out in the countryside.'

'I say, Francis,' says Parsley. 'Be a good chap and give me a hand off the chair, would you?'

I do as I'm bid, pulling his compact but solid frame up and fetching his greatcoat. He thanks my father for dinner, they share one last joke, and I show him out to get his car. Sure enough, with the expected military precision, it's sitting there, the driver ramrod-straight behind the wheel.

Mitch Parsley fumbles in his pocket, and for a terrible moment I fear he's that drunk he's going to give me five bob for my trouble. But instead he hands me his card, all military insignia and suchlike. 'You take care up there, young Francis.' He taps his nose and belches loudly. 'Remember, you can call this number at any time.' With that, he staggers towards the car, his driver emerging just in time to grab his arm and usher him on to the back seat safely.

As they drive off, he's still tapping his nose. It feels very odd. Why is everyone being so enigmatically guarded about Elderby? But on we go.

When I return to the kitchen, my father is busy stubbing out a cigarette in his wine glass. He mumbles something incomprehensible, then leans slowly forward, his mouth gaping open. He's been doing this for years, getting tipsy and falling asleep. It happens in a breath. He'll wake up in a few hours and head off to bed as though nothing is amiss. In the meantime, I grab his arm and we stumble through to the small living room. I deposit his thin frame on the cracked leather of the old chesterfield and cover him with a blanket.

This is our habitual evening routine. We have supper, drink a few glasses, and I take him for a lie-down in order to sleep it off. I'm glad he has some good friends like Mitch Parsley around. Suddenly he looks very old to me, curled up there on the couch. Age is a terrible thing, to be sure.

I take Lord Parsley's card from my pocket and examine it. There are two telephone numbers, as well as the address of his office in Catterick Barracks. I wonder again why he's given it to me, putting it down to his state of insobriety.

I too must sober up, for tomorrow I drive to Elderby.

3

The journey north from York to the moors would have been a pleasant one had it not been for my car's frequent alarming need to backfire, plus the lack of a heater in a heavy snowfall. Stubby Watts – as I suspected – had been wrong to predict that all the vehicle needed was 'a good run'. In fact, as I meander past fields of cows and sheep quickly being adorned by a white sheet, and carefully negotiate the pretty hamlets and villages, all being rendered almost identical by the snow, the vehicle appears to sense the optimum moment to issue forth with a tremendous blast and puffs of unhealthy black smoke.

The residents of both Thirsk and Helmsley are treated to relatively minor discharges. But as we progress through Pickering – a little town I've always admired since having a fling there – my Austin A30 chooses to discharge most spectacularly, leaving an elderly woman clutching her chest, whilst a man with a distinctly agricultural aspect waves his crook at me in a less than friendly fashion.

Welcome to the North York Moors, thinks I. I must admit to being a tad worried about the lady who'd managed a decent impersonation of someone in the throes of a coronary, so I ease my foot on to the accelerator and leave Pickering behind.

I'm also concerned whether I'll make it to my destination. The snow is beginning to lie heavily on the road, but as I tootle up on to the moors the scenery becomes stark and beautiful. I've always felt as though I'm skirting the top of the world as I take this single-track road. The ubiquitous heather is now a huddle of tiny mounds under a white blanket. It resembles a luxurious wedding cake. A bird of prey hovers above a tiny hillock before diving to catch something. I'm rather glad to say that it comes up empty-handed – or -clawed, in this case. I reason that it must be of Grasby descent, as I'm sure it bears an almost resigned look as it flies off with an empty stomach. I've lost count of how many times I've experienced similar emotions.

Still, my spirits are high, and I decide to pull in to have one of the ham sandwiches I'd hastily assembled earlier that morning. My father, having consumed the fruits of his own brewing skills to the full the previous evening, didn't get up to bid me a fond farewell. Rather, he lifted his head a couple of inches from the pillow and warned me not to use the last of the milk. He's never been a very demonstrative man when it comes to family, friends – almost anyone, in fact. I've never seen him perform a christening where the unfortunate child in arms doesn't erupt into paroxysms of desperate hysterics and protestations at his cold grip and stern visage.

But, as he would no doubt say himself, it isn't as though I'm following in the footsteps of Doctor Livingstone. I aim to be back in York as soon as I can; I'm desperately hoping Juggers will be able to round up the rest of these damned horses and I can solve these thefts with relative ease.

As it turns out, the ham in my sandwich has seen better days, being rather slimy and accompanied by a whiff of something not exactly palatable. I nibble at a few corners before pitching it into the field beside the car. I hope the unlucky Grasby falcon, or whatever type of bird it is, will happen upon the discarded snack in the snow. Everyone needs a break now and again – even birds, I dare say.

According to my notes from the map, I must turn left in a couple of miles. I'm on the moor road to Whitby, so I should reach my destination soon. It'll be nice to meet my new colleagues in the village police station – not to mention my chatelaine, the formidable-sounding Mrs Gaunt. My intention is to view this as a kind of sabbatical – a change of scene, a Christmas break from the humdrum of policing in York and frequent visits to Superintendent Juggers's office.

And yes, as I breathe in the cold air through the crack of the window, open to dispel much cigarette smoke, the discernible hint of the sea reminds me that things could be infinitely worse. In another world, yours truly could be on the way to Hull instead of Elderby. It's always handy to extract whatever good one can from a situation. I should know, I've spent a lifetime doing it.

I continue my journey, and true to form, despite my notes, almost miss the turn-off to the village. Mind you, I could be forgiven, as the rusting iron sign was almost impossible to decipher as it's caked in snow. Though I know better, I can easily picture Dark Age metal workers staring up at it, proud of their handiwork. Certainly, it hasn't been renewed since the road was laid, and that must be aeons ago.

Now, 'road' is a term I use loosely here. I soon find out why the good people at the Automobile Association saw fit only to execute it with broken lines on the map I studied so closely earlier in the day. Picture the worst farm road you've ever experienced, then imagine it's worse than that in a blizzard. I proceed at a snail's pace along a surface akin to that of mountain scree, punctuated by deep potholes neatly disguised by huge brown, slushy puddles. This must be what the Himalayas are like, I ponder. Amazingly, as though it is deep in concentration, no doubt in a desperate attempt to survive the road to Elderby, my A30 is as quiet as a mouse. Hopefully, this is the type of 'run' Stubby has in mind in order to clear the engine of whatever cobweb is blocking it.

I reason that if any miscreant tries to escape justice in a getaway car from Elderby, they'll have bugger all chance of doing so, given the state of the roads and the elements.

See, there's my optimistic, sunny nature at work again.

After what seems like hours of jolting, thumping, creaking, careering discomfort, I see a long ridge ahead. Poking its head just above this geological feature through the snow is the very tip of a spire. Doubtlessly the church of St Thomas's-on-the-Edge. I wonder again how my father knows of this place, but soon discount the thought based upon the knowledge that I'll almost certainly never find out.

If it isn't bad enough, the snow-covered, rutted, rubble-strewn, potholed road rises in front of me steeply. I embark upon the upward direction of travel that leads to the village of Elderby with no little trepidation. Not only is my car lurching alarmingly from side to side, it has developed the kind of whine familiar to all those unfortunate souls harried by Stuka dive-bombers during the war.

I can see another ancient signpost at the top the hill, and though I can't read it yet, I judge it must be *in situ* to announce the entrance to the village proper. However, a good two hundred yards short of this, Elderby still out of sight in the sheets of white, my car sighs, judders and comes to a grinding halt.

Though I pull on the handbrake, I'm fearful, given the dramatic incline and conditions, that the vehicle will flip head-over-tail and cartwheel me back the way I've come. So, with beads of perspiration breaking out on my forehead (this happens when I find myself in difficult, especially potentially life-threatening situations), I turn the engine over, only to be greeted with a tired sigh and a rattle akin to a dying man's last breath.

Damn!

Hard-won experience of all things mechanical tells me that the rest of the journey must be made *au pied*. So, with this in mind, I take off my trilby and manage to push my useless car on to the side of the road. I drag my dear mother's suitcase from the boot and embark upon the steep rise to Elderby.

This part of the journey is remarkable in that, once I've taken to the verge, I'm able to walk considerably faster than the car had been able to travel, albeit being careful not to slip or get bogged down in a drift. I'm forced to rethink my strategy regarding fleeing criminals, calculating that if they can muster a decent gallop they'll be back on the main road long before anyone in pursuit on wheels can possibly catch up. In fact, I wish I'd left the damned car on the moor road and taken the track – for that's all it is – on foot to begin with.

You see, this is the problem with the modern world. We all assume that progress will take us further and faster than what came before. When in actual fact a fleet-footed stallion would have made this journey in jig time. I'm no Luddite by any means. But I do wonder how things will go in the future. I read that the indigenous population of

North America have prophesied dire consequences should we carry on the path to modernization embarked upon since the dawn of the Industrial Revolution. Having tucked into my fair share of cowboy novels, I always find that these chaps know a thing or two. You know the thing, the Sioux or whoever are quietly mulling over the situation with the odd puff on a long peace-pipe, while the cowboys are getting well and truly mashed on rye whiskey. Booze doesn't make for sound thinking, in my experience. The next thing you know, it's four blokes hiding behind a rock surrounded by the tribe. Good on them, say I! What business we had taking over their country, I don't know.

Turning round to look at the heap of useless metal that I managed to encourage on to the snowy roadside, I can't help but wonder if everything we think we've achieved may well bring us down in the end. It's a sobering thought.

Just as my knees are beginning to protest and my feet throb with cold, I reach the top of the hill and there below, at last, I spy a road bordered by shops, houses and other nondescript buildings. Smoke is spiralling into the leaden sky from a few dozen chimneys. This must be Elderby, nestling beneath the escarpment like the homes of peasants under a medieval castle. And sure enough, just below the summit of the rise is a church: St Thomas's is truly on the edge. A funny place to build a house of worship, if you ask me. This makes me even more suspicious of my father and his past connections with this place. He seems to know it too well.

I make my way down the hill with somewhat of a spring in my step and a slip or two. 'Hail the Conquering Hero', comes to mind. I hum the theme to myself whilst seeking out Elderby police station. My first job will be to phone Stubby Watts and give him a piece of my mind.

I bolster my confidence with the knowledge that the good citizens of this North Yorkshire village will be able to sleep more soundly in their beds when they realize Grasby is now on the case. Though, for some reason, as I stride through the village of Elderby, a street lined with houses and shops, I'm gripped by fleeting anxiety. It's as though there are eyes – many eyes – on me, boring into my soul. I put this down to another imminent brush with the aristocracy, and a religious upbringing, so carry on.

*****

North Riding of Yorkshire Constabulary
Report: 18th December 1952
*****

Attention: DIV HQ 09277345: 1031 hrs

Call received at 1015 hrs to Elderby office
from Holly House, Elderby.
  Reports of intruder at domicile of Lord
Damnish.
  Am attending. Will report in due course.

Sgt E. M. P. Bleakly
Elderby Police Station

4

At first, it is as though the population of the village are still tucked up with teddy; there's not a soul to be seen. It's like one of these villages in Spain or the south of France one reads about, when the heat of the midday sun sends everyone scurrying for a nap. But it can't be the case here. I mean, it's only gone half ten.

Thankfully, as I near a cluster of little shops – you know, the type boasting mullioned windows decorated in anticipation of Christmas – I see a young woman, with blonde hair and a confident cant to her, head out of Fletcher the butcher's shop and trot off ahead of me.

I stand still for a minute, trying to find my bearings. The shops all look well cared for and presented, with bold signs announcing both owners and wares. The butcher is next to Vine's the greengrocer, which, in turn, abuts Swaddles, a little post office doubling as a newsagent. My heart sinks when I read the *Yorkshire Post* headlines, hastily penned on a snow-caked board standing on the pavement outside the shop.

Still No Sign of Thoroughbred Horses.

But this is a new day, and I'm sure the good folk of Elderby aren't remotely interested in such things.

'Are thee lost?' This voice comes from a ruddy, thickset

man in a blood-stained butcher's apron, standing in the doorway of Fletcher's.

'Well, not a great deal to get lost in,' say I. 'You'll be Mr Fletcher, I presume.'

'No, he's dead. I'm Braithwaite.' He eyes me suspiciously, one eye closed, the other open, as though he's about to take aim. 'You'll be the new copper.' The man delivers what he has to say in a flat, deadpan, disgruntled fashion, which alongside his appearance instantly brings Superintendent Juggers to mind.

No secrets in Elderby, clearly. 'Yes, in a way, I suppose I am.'

Braithwaite, the *new* butcher, eyes me up and down, shakes his head, turns on his heel in smart, almost military fashion, and disappears back into his shop.

Hearing the click of high heels from behind, I turn to face a woman of middle age squeezed into a thick, black coat over a floral dress. She has very red hair, matching her bright red lipstick.

'Bert's his usual self, I see,' she says in between puffs of a cigarette. 'Not half the butcher his predecessor was. You'll be the new man, then?'

It's becoming obvious that news of my arrival is widespread. I offer her my hand. 'Inspector Grasby. Pleased to meet you.'

'Most polite, I must say. Makes a change round here. I'm Ethel, Ethel Robson, landlady of the pub over there.' She gestures over her shoulder and across the street.

Though this public house looks picturesque enough, nicely painted, its bay windows edged with snow, the name is rather off-putting. I mean, I like a drink with the best of them. But 'Let's go down the Hanging Beggar for a couple of jars' isn't the kind of invitation likely to inspire the flinging on of a coat and a light tread.

'Don't say it, Inspector Grasby. It's a bloody awful name, I know. But we inherited it with the place. We talked about a change, but there'd only be a revolt.'

At least she's more welcoming than the new butcher. 'I'm sure it has its own charm.'

'Aye, it's the Hanging Beggar, and that's it. Though I refuse to put that original sign back up, end of story.' Ethel looks determined.

'I assume it depicts a hanging beggar,' say I.

'It does. And to make matters worse, there's a crowd of smiling, happy locals laughing and joking all round him as he's in his death throes. I'm telling you, it speaks volumes, it does. The place used to be called the Merry Ploughman, so they say. Changed it when some poor bugger got hung. It's been that way ever since.' She makes a face.

'Can I ask you a favour?'

'Of course, dear.'

'The whereabouts of your police station, if you please?'

'Copper don't even know where he's going. You'll fit in fine with the rest of them.'

'Oh,' say I, trying not to picture my new colleagues.

'Down the street, turn right. You can't miss it.'

'Much obliged, thank you.'

'You'll pop in after work, I hope? I pull a fine pint, and it's always nice to see a handsome man in Elderby. Aye, and if this snow continues, we'll have a good crowd. They love watching the snow with a pint. Odd ways, here, I tell you.' She smiles, winks, then goes into the butcher's.

As I wander down Elderby Main Street, I scrutinize the row of little shops. Just what everyone needs. As well as a pub, butcher, greengrocer and newsagent, there's the baker, a fishmonger (no doubt due to the proximity to Whitby), ironmonger, a doctor's surgery, next door to the veterinary surgery, and – somewhat incongruously – what appears to be a milliner. Add to this a branch of Martins Bank and a police station and, well, it's a fine wee place, as my mother would have said. And to keep the spiritual welfare of the community healthy, there's St Thomas's-on-the-Edge.

I also note, contrary to my first impression of the place as being infinitesimally small, that there are little lanes off Main Street, where more of the good folk of Elderby live in stout-looking cottages and the like. So, all in all, it looks like a thriving little place. Just the ticket for yours truly.

Thoughts of Hull are now far away.

If it weren't for the ubiquitous blue lamp attached to the front of the dark sandstone building, there would be little to identify Elderby's police station as such. It could just as easily be a domicile.

However, I trot up three steps and find myself in a cramped front-bar office. A young man in uniform is busy on the phone. He appears quite animated, managing speeds of at least six words a second in a thick dialect I can barely understand. Though I do pick up on the fact that he wants a car back at the station as quickly as possible.

As my colleague is paying me no heed, I cough surreptitiously. When he still doesn't respond, I have no other option than a full-bodied 'Hello!'

The man manages to tilt his head in my direction, puts his hand over the receiver and grunts. Quite what he's said is a mystery, but I respond by announcing myself, and asking for the senior officer on duty.

Most of what he utters in response is incomprehensible, but I'm quick-witted enough to decipher that he wants me to take the door to my right. I thank him for very little as I make my way into a corridor that takes a sharp turn to the left at its end. It smells just like every police station I've ever been in, the heady odour of disinfectant, tobacco, old wood and perspiration. Though I'm yet to be convinced that anyone here has managed to get a good sweat on for years.

This notion is confirmed when I find a door on the right marked 'Sergeants'. Hoping to encounter someone that can at least speak, I knock and enter. After all, I am an inspector, so I have every right.

I see a figure leaning on folded arms, fast asleep. His grey hair is slicked back, a loose strand of it almost touching the table. I can see nothing of his face. He's snoring gently, pipe sitting in an ashtray, still smouldering, a copy of the *Daily Sketch* and a half-empty tin mug by its side.

Again, I go through the polite dance of coughing and shuffling noisily about. I'm well brought up, you see. But I now suspect that every officer in Elderby police station is deaf. So I resort once more to a loud 'Hello!'

This slumbering figure raises its head, mashing away at a dry mouth in a most disconcerting fashion. Sergeant's stripes are revealed, so at least I've found someone of rank.

'What the bloody hell is it now, Lumpwold? I told you, get yourself down to Holly House!' A long-faced man of late middle years squints at me, appearing momentarily bewildered. He then produces a pair of spectacles from a pocket and looks me up and down. 'Who on earth are you?' He blinks.

'Inspector Frank Grasby – you know, on secondment from York CID. I'm here to help bring these thefts from farms to an end.' I'm quietly astonished that whilst most of the village appear to know who I am, the officers with whom I'm to work seem to have no idea.

'Oh, aye. Right. I do remember getting the memo. Grasby, that's right, isn't it?'

'Yes, *Inspector* Grasby.' Time to assert my authority. I've yet to hear a *sir*.

'But you're not due until tomorrow. This is the seventeenth.'

'Sorry, old boy. But it's the eighteenth.'

'Bloody Lumpwold! He's not changed the date again.' He nods to a wooden-framed calendar with '17' written in bold, red Arabic numerals. 'I don't know how many times I've told him about it. I've a memory like a bloody sieve, me. I must have reminders about the place. Don't you find that helps?'

'Is Constable Lumpwold the officer at the front desk?'

'Yes. And he should be off to investigate an intruder at Holly House. Not the brightest light in the cave, Inspector.'

At last, my rank!

'He appears to be searching for a car. Sorry, I don't think you told me your name, Sergeant?'

He has a think for a moment, as though recalling his own name is somewhat of a struggle. 'Bleakly, Elphinstone Bleakly. I know, my mother was a scholar, hence the Christian name.'

I shrug in empathy with his problematic nomenclature. Grasby isn't a common name, and I've always taken a ribbing for it, one way or another. Parents should engage the old grey matter before deciding to foist unusual names upon their children, no matter how exotically appealing they think them to be. Of course, Grasby is my surname. But I did know a chap – Larry, decent right-hand seamer – whose father changed the family name from Ramsbottom to Brown so his offspring wouldn't be lumbered with it. Sadly, his sister – a dreadful snob – decided that wasn't a good move and changed it back without losing her new adopted surname. In her mind at least, a double-barrelled job was just the ticket. And with that, the alluringly titled Miss Prunella Brown-Ramsbottom did embark upon adulthood. I often wonder what became of her.

Bleakly picks up the phone hitherto hidden by his side and dials a single digit.

'Lumpwold, why aren't you with Lord Damnish?' Bleakly stares at the phone with a pained expression and demands his constable gets down to this Damnish's sharpish. 'I swear, I can hardly understand a word that lad says.' He shakes his head. 'You only get the bottom of the barrel here, sir.' He thinks for a moment. 'Present company excepted, of course.'

He opens a drawer in his desk and produces three manilla files. Ah, at last, the stock-in-trade of every detective: the file!

'We'll have us a cup of tea, then take a look at these, Inspector Grasby. I must say, it's bloody odd. This place is normally free of crime – apart from the odd scuffle down at the Beggar when the young farmers have too much ale. But Lumpwold and his partner in crime, Constable Withers, get that sorted in no time.'

'How many of there are you here in Elderby?'

'Me and two constables. Normally more than plenty. But this thievery has me beat. Apart from shopkeepers, most hereabouts work on the land. They don't steal from their own – doesn't make sense.'

'I take it that you think the thefts are being perpetrated by outsiders?'

'Have to be.'

I sit myself down on a chair across the table from Bleakly. Apart from finding him asleep, and the only person for miles around who isn't expecting me, I've taken to him instantly. I'm a notoriously good judge of character – well, apart from that Goss swine who absconded from Euston station with my money and professional pride. It must be a real sickener when a cosy little number like this is ruined by the arrival of light-fingered types. Though I'm not sure I agree with his assumption that it isn't the work of a local or locals. No, in my experience, those closest to you are the most dangerous, whether it be the misappropriation of a shovel or murder most foul.

'Grasby, eh?' Suddenly Bleakly is deep in thought. 'You're not the one that lost all these ho'ses, are you? It was in the *Yorkshire Post*, you know.'

Quickly, I begin to reassess my unfortunate tendency of expeditious character assessments. This local plod likely hasn't collared a wrong 'un for decades.

But as I brood on missing horses, the room lights up with the arrival of tea. No, not because of the Neanderthal Lumpwold, but via the unexpected appearance of one of the prettiest women I've ever seen.

5

I think it only natural to remove my trilby, run a hand over my hair and sit up a bit straighter when a young lady appears, goddess-like, as though from nowhere. As I'm doing this, she smiles winningly at me with big, cornflower-blue eyes.

'Now then, Inspector.' This to me. Then turning to the young lady. 'What is it you are, again?' says Bleakly.

'I'm an intern. Golly, how many times?'

I'm not sure whether it's her irreverence or the fact she has an American accent that most surprises me. In a trice I'm on my feet, offering an incline of the head and my hand.

'How gallant, Inspector Grasby.' She shakes my out-stretched paw enthusiastically.

'Sorry, Inspector. Meet Miss Daisy Dean,' says Bleakly wearily.

'But you can call me Deedee,' says she.

My goodness, she has dimples and everything. My father always says that God has a plan for everyone apart from me. And that I've been discarded by the supreme deity for lack of application and general worthlessness. Though, I must admit, to date, there's been little evidence to the con-trary, things have taken a distinct turn for the better. To think, this is supposed to be a punishment! Clearly, I've been doing it wrong all the time. I should have misplaced as many horses as possible during the course of my career. I'd likely be the chief constable by now.

'Well, *Deedee*, very pleased to meet you,' say I with my winning smile. 'Please tell me, this *intern* business. I've heard the word before, of course. But not in the context of the English police.'

In truth, I only have the vaguest idea as to the meaning of the word. Right now, I'm just glad it exists.

As Bleakly sighs, the delectable Deedee leans on the table.

'Oh, it's quite the done thing "across the pond". I'm studying at Yale – my field is criminology.'

At this point I hope she will keep going, as I have no notion of what criminology is either. But she just stares at me hopefully, no doubt waiting for suitable congratulations for this great educational feat. Mind you, I'm not stupid, and quickly break the word down into its constituent parts. Crim-in-ology. And as Deedee finds herself in a Yorkshire police office, I rapidly calculate that she must be studying something to do with criminals. I deduce in a flash that her course is not based on how to be a successful one – though the Americans do have some odd notions – so it must be the study of crime.

'Ah, yes. A delve into the criminal mind, most interesting. Something sadly lacking in our universities, I'm sorry to say.'

'Wow! You know about my subject. You're the first person I've met in England that does.'

'Oh, you know.' Had I an available moustache, I'd now be twirling it with alacrity. 'Where are you from, Deedee?'

'New York – the Upper East Side of Manhattan. I miss it sometimes, but England is so beautiful. And it's snowing. I can't wait.'

'You'll not be saying that when you're knee-deep in the stuff, stuck here for the duration,' says Bleakly. He's a cheery soul.

'Never had the pleasure of a visit to the States. I must rectify that,' say I. As soon as possible, if they're all stunners like you.

'All I can say is they stay in school for far too long over there. She's almost thirty, sir. If this is the way things are going, folks will be finishing their education and stepping straight into retirement.' Bleakly slurps his tea like an elephant going at a pool.

'This is my doctorate. I have a master's, too.' Deedee looks almost indignant.

'Now, there's a thing. Well done, you.' I pull down my eyelid and point my face in Deedee's direction. 'I must admit, I find these veins on my eyeballs a tad troubling. Have you any idea what they are?'

'Oh, I'm sorry. I have no idea. Old age, maybe? I think my father has them.'

Deedee sinks – only slightly, mark you – in my estimation. Clearly, becoming a doctor in the USA can be achieved without any knowledge of the eye. But still, not a bad effort.

'Miss Dean also has a doctorate in politics, sir. Something of minor genius, I'm told.' Bleakly's words are warm, but his baleful gaze isn't.

I now feel like a bit of a nit. Again, it's time for a Grasby get-out-of-jail joke. 'I'm just kidding, of course. I always do that when I come across a doctor that isn't actually a doctor. I do apologize.'

'Not at all. How quaint.' Deedee smiles weakly. 'And you and I are to be housemates, Inspector.'

Oh, how wrong can you be, Father? It's all I can do to stop myself from punching the air as though I've copped a century. 'Oh, really?' say I, all calm and collected. 'How do you find Mrs Gaunt?'

Deedee smiles sweetly this time. 'Very kind. A well-doing old lady.' She bites her lip.

I'm always struck by how polite Americans are. I think you'd have to murder a granny or two in order to see them whipped up into a state of condemnation. 'Do I sense a *but* coming?'

'It's the raven. I know it's none of my business, but I do find it a bit strange.'

'Raven?'

'The old dear is as mad as a basket of gulls. Walks about with a crow on her shoulder,' offers Bleakly. 'Mind you, she's smart when it comes to the darker things,' he continues ominously.

'I think it is a raven, Sergeant,' says Deedee chidingly.

'We'll settle on a Corvus of some description,' I suggest. It's in my nature to quell disagreement – not inherited from my father.

'I better leave you both to it,' says Deedee as she turns to walk from the room, taking all the light of the day with her – or so it seems. She stops in the doorway. 'I'll see you at dinner, if not before, Inspector Grasby.'

As Bleakly wipes the residue of tea from his lips with his sleeve, I adopt a serious expression and lean on my hand. He's about to brief me on these agricultural thefts and I want him to know there's more to me than the odd fleeing horse.

'Nice young lady,' I say absently.

'I don't know what to do with her, to be honest, sir. She arrived a month ago. Her father's a bigwig over in New York. Bags of money, or so they tell me at Pickering.'

'Well, I dare say I could use an extra pair of hands finding these farm thieves. I know she's not been here for long, but Deedee will still have a better handle on the place than I have.'

Bleakly nods non-committally at this idea. It's clear that he thinks himself in charge. Time to disabuse him of that.

'Good,' say I jauntily. 'That's agreed. Miss Dean can assist me. Now, I'd like the briefing on these robberies. No time like the present, old boy.'

Confident that I've made my position clear, I notice Bleakly adopting a distant look. His eyes are suddenly losing focus, his head just lolls forward, and he looks dead to the world.

Now, I realize that this is a sleepy little village where very little happens. But one at least expects one's colleagues to manage to stay awake during working hours. This is most definitely not the done thing.

'Sergeant Bleakly!' There's no response. Shaking him vigorously by the shoulder is having absolutely no effect either.

I've seen my fair share of death, you know. But given the recent incident with Lady Winthorpe's horses, it's hard to imagine that I'll survive killing off Elderby's station sergeant within minutes of my arrival. Juggers's jowly face is prominently before my mind's eye as I rush into the corridor wailing for assistance.

Thankfully, the delectable Deedee appears from nowhere yet again.

'What on earth's the matter, Inspector Grasby?'

'It's Bleakly. I think the poor chap's bought it.'

Though I'm yet again dazzled by Miss Dean's smile, I

think it inappropriate. I'm not sure how Americans greet events like sudden death, but they have obviously travelled a long way in the wrong direction since 1776 if this is their accepted norm, certainly as far as tragedy is concerned.

'He has narcolepsy – or something like it – poor man,' says Deedee.

'What? I damn well hope it's not catching,' say I, taking a moment to feel my forehead just in case my temperature has shot up in the intervening seconds. One can't be too careful when it comes to health, you know.

Gently, she's taking my hand in an effort to lead me back into the office and the afflicted sergeant.

She's a strong lass, I must admit. But not strong enough to resist the Grasby fear of illness – a trait inherited from my father. He regularly requires parishioners to vacate the church if they have the slightest cough.

Deedee is looking back at me, seeming less than impressed at my reluctance.

'It's a sleep disorder. And you can't catch it, Inspector. We have to bring him round gently.'

'Gosh,' say I. 'Damned bad luck.'

Together, now I'm reassured that I'm not about to catch some awful affliction, we are back in the office.

After a few moments, thanks to Deedee's oh-so-gentle cajoling, Bleakly's eyelids flicker and open. He looks bemused for a second, but – no doubt used to these sudden attacks of sleep – carries on as though nothing had happened. This, despite there being one more person in the room than there was when he was last conscious.

'Now, back to these files. I think it's likely easier to do this in conjunction with our map.' He gets slowly to his feet and meanders over to a large map of the locale hanging on the wall. He's taller than I expected, almost my height.

Deedee grimaces, no doubt at his affliction.

'I say, he doesn't fall asleep on his feet, does he?' I whisper, instantly tapping into her thoughts.

'Sometimes.'

I resolve to stand as far away from Bleakly as I can without seeming detached. I don't want a great lump of police sergeant landing on me unexpectedly.

'Now,' says he, looking reasonably *compos mentis*, if still a little bleary-eyed. Hopes of him staying upright during this briefing are rising. 'I'll give you an overall sense of the place. Here we see the two roads into Elderby. Though nobody is mad enough to use the old one.'

'It's impassable,' says Deedee.

'Hang on,' says I. 'What do you mean "two roads"?'

Bleakly points his finger at the map. 'This, here, is the old one. And here,' he points to a section along the main Pickering to Whitby road, 'is the one they laid just before the war. Still don't have the new signpost back up. Took it down during the war for the metal, you know.'

I'm mulling over whether I should say anything or not. It's clear I took the old road. But I swear I didn't see the other, nor was it marked on my map, never mind the absence of a signpost. Mind you, I didn't take the time to look at the age of said map. Normally, little changes in this part of the world, and one doesn't expect to have to check the vintage of one's cartography before setting off.

I'm calculating what to say at this juncture. I'll have to arrange for the car to be picked up at some point. This is a problem. I don't want to look like a fool.

Inspired, I speak. 'At this point, I have some rather disappointing news. On the way here, I stopped for a squint at the map. I think this was the place,' say I, pointing to a lay-by. 'Well, damn me, once I'd come back from a short walk – you know, to get my bearings – the damned car was gone.'

'I'm not sure the lay-by is still there,' says Deedee.

You can go off someone.

I attempt to look suitably perplexed. 'Near there, then.'

'Now, there's a thing,' says Bleakly. 'We had a bike stolen a while back – 1947, I think it was. But we've never had a stolen car.' He points. 'Can you show me again where this was, roughly, sir?'

Damn.

'Now, let me see.' I look at this huge map on the wall, desperately try to think of something. I've always been a bit foxed by maps, if I'm honest. Why they can't make them more pictorial, like the old days, I don't know. I mean, it's easy enough to find a church or a forest, for instance, they draw the bally things on there. But all these meaningless lines, squiggles and numbers – well, it's confusing.

'Could it be here?' says Deedee, pointing at a suitable location that I wish I'd found.

Don't rush, I reckon. Take your time, Francis. I finger the tip of one ear to facilitate this pause, and squint at the area she's indicated. 'You know, I do believe you're right, Miss Dean. Jolly well done!'

Good. This means I can absolutely abdicate all responsibility for being stupid enough to take the road from hell. I know it's a bit of a fib, but it's a harmless one. It's not as though they'll catch the miscreant, because there isn't one. But – hopefully – they'll find the car. Game, set and match!

Bleakly resolves to set his finest constables on the job. I can tell by the look on Deedee's face that this fills absolutely no one with any confidence. Judging by my encounter with the incomprehensible Constable Throb, or whatever he's called, it's highly unlikely he could find a fish tea in the

CID office at York Central. And let me tell you now, that is by no means an impossible task – at any time of the day.

My car problems now dealt with, Bleakly points to farms here and there on the map, and then turns his attention to the relevant files to match these agricultural thefts.

But just as he's about to bore me rigid, the phone on his desk rings.

Bleakly answers it unenthusiastically. Suddenly this attitude changes. 'Oh, Your Lordship,' says he, with a look on his face like a well-slapped kipper. 'I assure you my men were dispatched immediately following your call.' He holds the phone from his ear.

Deedee looks at me with a grimace, as the chuntering of an irate peer sounds distantly on the other end.

When Bleakly puts the phone down, it's obvious that Lord Damnish ended the exchange in a most perfunctory manner, affording our poor sergeant no time to wish him good day.

'Bugger, I'll have to go myself,' says Bleakly. 'I'll roast that pair when I get back,' he adds, referring to his two errant constables.

Now, I'm no lover of aristocrats, as you know. But this might be the opportunity to get on the right side of one, for once.

'I'll go,' say I. 'Miss Dean can accompany me. It'll be good for her to see a proper detective at work.'

Though Bleakly looks rather unhappy at this assertion, there's nothing he can do. I'm his superior, and the decision is made. But he's wise enough to agree, no doubt working on the basis that he'll be made as welcome at His Lordship's house as Robespierre.

'You better take my car. It's the dark blue Rover at the back.' He fishes into his pocket and hands me the keys.

They're warm from being cossetted next to his leg, which gives me a moment's revulsion. It strikes me as rather unfair that I'm driving about in a car a clown would turn his nose up at, while this country sergeant has a Rover at his disposal.

'Right, you can show me the way, Miss Dean,' say I.

6

I'm even more jealous of Bleakly's car when I get into it. All leather seats and walnut dashboard. And not a hint of a backfire when I start it up. Seems I should have plighted my troth to North Yorkshire Constabulary rather than York. Heigh-ho, not the first mistake I've made in my life.

With Deedee's directions, we drive through the village and soon find ourselves on a road bordered by the stark winter aspect of oak and elm. To my right, a reasonably sized hill is revealed through the trees. Deedee informs me it's called Withernshaw Fell. I take a mental note of this for later, not knowing how relevant it will prove.

We head down a long driveway, almost an essential when it comes to stately homes. Though it has stopped snowing, the sky remains that odd shade, a bit like mother of pearl, I always think. So, there's more on the way. At least someone has seen fit to clear His Lordship's drive, leaving it much easier to navigate than the road. But you become accustomed to snow in Yorkshire.

Amongst the jagged fingers of trees, stripped bare of leaf by this season's cold hand, we find Holly House. I'm pleased to see large holly bushes, dotted with their bright red berries, all frosted with snow as we arrive at the big, oaken front door. It is Christmas week, after all. I do so love this time of year and all that goes with it, despite missing my poor mother. But life must go on.

Holly House itself is a good-sized mansion, with none of the martial pretensions often seen in the great halls of the ruling classes. Deedee tells me that the old hall was demolished, and this building erected by Damnish. Not popular with the locals, by all accounts. More of which later.

'I've seen old photographs. Quite austere, it was,' she says. 'All stark and forbidding, if you know what I mean. I kinda wish it was still here.'

This, in my experience, is typical of Americans. They expect dear old England to remain frozen in time, unlike their young, thrusting nation. Despite my yearning for an authentic past and my dislike of the interference with our history by the nouveau riche, if I was Lord D, I'd certainly prefer life in Holly House to some draughty old pile, with an accumulation of the dust and funk of centuries. Half of this country still get along with outside toilets. Show an outside toilet to an American and they'd likely have a fit and cry foul.

I park the car at the front steps leading up to the great doors, taking the opportunity to ask Deedee what this Damnish is like before I meet him. Forewarned is forearmed, in my book.

'Oh, he's – well, you know.'

Though she shrugs disarmingly, I'm left with no insight into the aristocrat's personality. I'm sure this will be revealed soon enough.

We take the stairs, and rather than knock, I find one of those pull-style bells. When I do the necessary, though, I hear no insistent chime. I'm about to resort to a firm policeman's knock, when one half of the door creaks open. Before us is the classic-looking butler, tall, with tails and a haughty look. As I'm also reasonably gangling, he has to address me eye-to-eye, rather than down his long nose.

'May I be of assistance?' he asks, narrowing his eyes.

'Inspector Grasby. This is my *intern*, Miss Dean.'

I'm delighted to note that he looks as confused as I was at her description. He nods just the same.

'May I ask where Sergeant Bleakly is?' he says.

None of your damned business, thinks I. 'As his superior, I thought I should be the one to deal with His Lordship's report,' I say. I'm damned if I'll be questioned by the hired help.

Almost reluctantly, I feel, he shows us down a long hallway, adorned by paintings of grand-looking folk. The carpet is so thick I almost trip a couple of times. The wallpaper is striped and expensive, there are ornaments, chandeliers and dainty pieces of furniture placed hither and yon. It's clear no expense has been spared at Holly House. The place fairly reeks of cash.

We reach another oaken door. The butler stands, straightens his long back and knocks three times, a bit like Black Rod. A distant reply indicates that entrance is permitted. He asks us to wait, then enters the room and announces our presence.

'Inspector Grasby of the Elderby Constabulary, and his *intern*, Miss Dean.' He coughs, placing a white-gloved hand to his mouth.

When I enter the room, I see why. The place is shrouded in a film of smoke. Three figures sit on two rather magnificent couches, or whatever it is one would call these chintzy articles. A stout man and a thin, middle-aged woman occupy one, while a spare youth with floppy hair lounges on another, as young people are wont to do these days. I spot a very large Christmas tree, its lights shining dimly through the grey smoke.

The stout man, bursting out of a tweed suit, stands and greets us with hands behind his back rather than a shake of the paw.

'Now, good to see you've managed to take a break in your busy schedule to investigate our prowler.' He exudes sarcasm. 'Where on earth is Bleakly?'

I repeat the calumny that I attend his pleasure because of my elevated rank.

'Ah, yes. The new man. You've been sent to stop these thefts.' He regards me with great enmity then calls the butler. 'Harrison, make sure you don't let the inspector near the stables, there's a good chap.' He laughs, making a curl of greasy dark hair fall over his brow.

Damn you, thinks I. Has everyone heard of these bloody horses? I'm delighted when he bursts into a paroxysm of coughing, no doubt caused by the smoke.

'Harrison, attend that fire. Something's lodged up the damned chimney, I'll wager.'

'It'll be the snow, Father,' says the youngster, a lad in his late teens.

'Do wait until you're spoken to, Beauregard,' says the woman I presume to be Lady Damnish. 'You know how your father hates to be interrupted.'

She's as thin as her husband is fat. A tiny, bird-like woman with a sharp nose and small, darting eyes. Her son shakes his head and continues to lounge.

Though the fire appears to be out, smoke is still billowing round the fireplace.

'I told you it was a bad idea to pour water on the damned thing, Harrison,' says Damnish, doing a fine impersonation of Mr Toad.

The butler hurries over to the fireplace, looking helpless.

'Now, Gribley, or whatever your name is . . .'

'Grasby, sir.'

'A chap was spotted last night by one of my gamekeepers. Looked as though he was trying to climb a drainpipe. This is most troublesome. I shall have my staff at the ready. But this house boasts some fine art, pottery, and other bloody expensive items. I'll be damned if some sneak-thief is going to be off with them. I want to see the local police do their bit – unlike their progress with all this stealing from farms. Same bloody chap, I reckon.'

Before I can reply, there's a clatter from the fireplace. Harrison the butler swears under his breath and does his best to clean one of his white gloves, now stained black with soot.

Now, this just happens to be one of my fields of expertise. As a nipper, we lived in an assortment of ancient rectories. Without fail, chimneys would be blocked by birds' nests, loose bricks and other detritus. My father, having no head for heights, regularly tasked me with climbing on the roof to poke a long pole down said chimneys. Admittedly, we never possessed a grand fireplace like this, huge, set in its inglenook. However, in an unashamed attempt to ingratiate myself with Damnish, I offer my services.

'I'll have a look, Your Lordship. I'll bet it's something very simple.'

'Do you moonlight as a chimney sweep, Gately?' says Damnish, once more getting my name wrong.

I ignore this manfully, and proceed to the fireplace, where I have to fairly elbow Harrison out of the way. It's big, quite room enough for three men to stand comfortably abreast – if they wanted to be roasted alive, that is. It's tall, too. I only have to duck slightly to stick my head up the chimney.

It's damnably smoky, so I cover my mouth and nose with a hanky – thankfully clean this morning – and squint heavenwards. I'm sure, through the smoke and my watering eyes, I can see the shadow of something above my head. I reach out, and sure enough, my hand rubs against some foreign body.

I duck back out of the fireplace. 'Something up there, blocking the damned thing. Might be a bird, sir. I've heard tell of geese getting trapped down chimneys.'

'Oh, how awful,' says Deedee, yet again displaying what a fine, caring lass she is.

I lean back underneath the great mantel shelf and reach up above my head. I grip something solid but evasively familiar.

To this day, I don't know why I didn't realize what was lodged there. The lack of context, I suppose. I pull, and feel the obstruction dislodge.

Quickly, I step out from the chimney just in time for the body of a man to fall on to the ruined fire with a clatter. He's accompanied by a great billow of soot, which covers me, then moves out into the wider room.

'What on earth!' shouts Damnish, as Lady D shrieks.

I'm wiping soot from my eyes, when Damnish Junior sees fit to comment.

'My goodness, Santa Claus appears to have got it terribly wrong this year.'

7

For a moment, everyone is frozen in shock. Of course, being the solid chap I am, I'm first to react, telling Harrison to call the station quick-smart and get Bleakly and the constables here. I then suggest that Lady Damnish and her son depart the scene. Not pleasant, seeing a soot-covered corpse in one's lounge or whatever this place is. Deedee, I note, shows no sign of upset. In fact, she looks positively intrigued by the whole turn of events.

I bend down and remove some of the soot from the deceased's face with my now-filthy hanky. He looks to be about my age, though, from what I can tell, with a stockier, more muscular build. Not the kind of chap who should attempt chimney-scaling.

'He must have made it on to the roof and tried to access the place via the chimney. I've never seen the like,' says Damnish. I get the feeling he's more concerned by the break-in, rather than the fact there's a dead man in his fireplace.

Gently, I pull the dead man's head up. Though it's still sooty, I've managed to remove some of the stuff from his face. His eyes are set well apart, he has a broad nose and a jutting chin. Quite easy to identify, I think. 'Do you know this chap, My Lord?' says I.

Damnish looks at me as though I've just burst into a few sentences of Swahili.

'What?' says he brusquely.

'This gentleman, sir. Do you recognize him?'

'How on earth would I be able to recognize him? You don't think he's one of my friends, do you?'

'No, of course not. Just thought you might have seen him in the village, around and about, you know.'

'No, I've never seen this man in my life. In fact, I want him removed immediately. Harrison!' he shouts at the top of his voice.

'Yes, sir,' says the butler, appearing from nowhere.

'Get some lads together and have this thief taken away. Deliver him to Elderby police station.' He turns to me. 'Your problem now, Grantley.'

'I'm sorry, Lord Damnish. But I must insist that the dead man remain here until I've contacted my superiors. Not every day one comes across such circumstances, and I must seek their advice.'

Damnish looks for a moment as though he'll boil over. 'Do as you must. But I want this criminal out of my home by lunchtime, got it?' He storms out, no doubt to find his wife and son.

There's a telephone on a little scallop table. I make my way to it and lift the handset to my ear.

'You'll have to ask His Lordship's permission before you make a call,' says Harrison snottily.

'Police business, can't wait,' say I, then tell the operator to put me through to York Central police station, 'Superintendent Juggers, please.' I tell her who is calling and hang on. I've already had to leave town once because of the aristocracy. I'm damned if I'll make the same mistake again. I wait through the usual clatter of clicks and pops, as operators do their jobs. Mercifully, I soon hear Juggers's strangely reassuring voice on the other end.

'What's to do, Grasby? I'm taking Mrs Juggers out to lunch and some shopping soon. Still don't have a bird yet.' He sounds agitated – normal, in other words.

I explain the circumstances and their lead-up to my superior. The line appears dead, and for a moment I'm about to ask if he's there. He is.

'Bloody hell, Grasby!' he wails. 'You're like a one-man wrecking ball. Do you have something against the ennobled?'

'No, sir!' Time to sound outraged myself, methinks. 'You can't blame me for some chap throwing himself down a chimney, sir.'

'Aye, but it's not just any chimney, is it? Bloody Lord Damnish.' There's a pause. 'You've only been there for an hour or so, by my calculations. I'm going to have to tell the chief constable, thou knows. That won't be pleasant. No, not at all. Shouldn't be surprised if he wants me to sack you on the spot!'

When he stops ranting, I manage to get through to him that we need to do something with the deceased. I mean, we can't just leave him here.

'Are you sure he's dead, Grasby?'

'Rather, sir. I have seen my fair share of dead people. I was a soldier during a world war, after all.'

'Don't get lippy, young man,' says he. 'Get a local doctor to do the necessary. I'll get the mortuary out to pick him up.'

'Shouldn't we send him to Northallerton, sir? It is their patch, after all,' says I, foolishly.

'What are they going to do there, put him in a cell? Do as you're told. Get this Bleakly on the job. You get back and await my instructions.' My boss decides not to say good-bye, ending the call with a thud and a crackle.

Thankfully, Bleakly arrives with Constable Throb. I leave him to await the mortuary van from York, and deal with Damnish, as well as the dead man in the fireplace. I instruct the constable to take a look on the roof of Holly House to see if anything's to do. Bleakly can also interview anyone pertinent at the house to ascertain what, if anything, they saw or heard. It's time he was doing something productive.

It may be mere instinct, but as I stare at the sooty features of the deceased, I can sense in his expression that he died in great pain. I revisit the corpse and gently run my hand down his spine then up on to his neck and the back of his head.

Of course, though my hand is covered with soot when I examine it, there's a smear of something that can only be blood. Now, perhaps this is a consequence of his fall. But I'm disquieted. Let the mortuary clean up and examine this poor chap. They'll make a conclusion as to the cause of his demise, and the investigation will flow from there. I take a mental note of my findings, just the same.

Deedee, who had observed all this quietly from the back of the room, suggests she drive me to my new digs.

'You sure are a mess, Inspector,' she counsels, eyeing me up and down. 'You need to get cleaned up.'

As we're leaving Holly House, I see a man standing in the grounds, a shotgun broken over the crook of his arm. He glares at me, all gimlet-eyed.

'Who's that?' I ask Deedee as she settles into the driver's seat.

'Oh, that's McGill the head gamekeeper. I've seen him at the Beggar a couple of times. He's not a guy I want to meet on a dark night. Bit of a bully, if you ask me.'

8

I'm not a chap who enjoys walking too much. As a young buck, when locating a flat in York, I made sure there was a handy public house across the road, and my place of work, the police station, was just round the corner. With a fish and chip shop and a bookmaker also close by, these were the perfect surroundings for yours truly. Slope home from a shift, a quick flutter on the gee-gees, a pint or three of Sollop's Gurgler, all rounded off with good old fish and chips.

As we drive through Elderby, I'm pleased to note how compact it all is. I won't have too many problems getting from the pub to where I'm to lay my head. This is important. The snow has stayed off, though the sky is still lowering.

As I mentioned, there are little lanes off the village's main thoroughfare, and Deedee, all cheery chat and bubble, turns suddenly on to one. There are three houses on what is in effect a cul-de-sac. First, two smart little brick bungalows, one on either side of the lane, then at the end what I can only describe as a dolorous building, wrought from dark stone with a steep peaked roof, straight out of an Edgar Allan Poe story. The garden to the front of the property looks like a jungle, unkempt and untamed. The wooden gate that leads to the house is hanging off its hinges and permanently stuck against a great clump of snow-covered grass. We head up a small path to a black door with flaking paint.

'Home sweet home?' I offer.

'Yes.' She lowers her voice. 'It's not as bad as it looks.'

'It looks like the ghost of the Duke of Buckingham could lean his head out of the window and demand satisfaction.' I'm not a fussy man, but gosh, this takes the whole biscuit barrel, and then some.

'Gee, you do have an active imagination, Inspector.' Deedee presses a button on the front door jamb, and after a pause I hear a clang akin to a dread ship's bell tolling on a stormy sea.

'Things are improving by the minute,' say I. This place has leached all joy from the day, and I suffer from an involuntary shiver as footsteps sound behind the door.

As it swings open, a large black shape shoots over my head in a flurry of wings and feathers, almost dislodging my trilby. Instinctively, I shrink into my own shoulders; an act common to this day amongst chaps who saw service during the war. It's hard to shake off certain habits, especially when they were originally in place to save one's skin.

A small woman is framed in the doorway, dressed from head to toe in what, to my admittedly untrained eye, is black lace. Somewhat unusually, she sports a black bowler hat, you know the kind with the very narrow brim popular amongst certain sorts, decades ago. On the headband is the only splash of colour in her eccentric outfit: a red feather. Probably because of being named Mrs Gaunt, I had in my mind's eye an elderly lady with hollowed, grey cheeks, sunken eyes and a bun. Not so. Mrs Gaunt has leathery, tanned skin, with eyes of such a piercing pale blue they are disconcerting.

I step forward and offer her my hand.

She stares at me. 'What on earth happened to you? You look as though you've just struggled out of the pit.'

I tell her we've had some trouble with a blocked chimney. No need to mention the dead man. In a trice, she grabs my left hand and begins to trace her finger up its lines.

With a bishop for a grandpa and a vicar father, I'm not keen on the occult, however benignly it is treated these days. Do you know, they even have a fortune teller on the seafront in Scarborough? Not at all what you'd expect of the place. Blackpool, yes, absolutely; but not Scarborough. Anyhow, I've always given divination a wide berth. Not least because I'm notoriously superstitious.

Mrs Gaunt discards my hand and stares into my face with her icy eyes.

'From York, are you?'

I nod, fearful of some presage of doom.

'Aye, that makes sense. You and Miss Dean better come in, I suppose.'

Her voice is husky, almost as though it's made up of a number of individual whispers.

I feel positively glum now. Gloomsville is where I'm to lay my head for the foreseeable. Mind you, as I've managed to kill somebody already, the chief constable may well decide that I should be sent to France, or some such awful place.

I step through the door and instantly feel further oppressed by the darkness and strange paintings adorning the walls. They're not of anything discernible, merely splashes of colour, mainly dark blues, reds and bright greens, all on black backgrounds.

'You like my paintings?' enquires my landlady, noticing my gaping mouth as I stare at them.

'Yes, very interesting – really original.' Well, what's a chap to say when faced with this ghoulish trash? I really want to say, 'Bin these and stick up a couple of nice Turner prints, or that one of the little urchin holding the dog.' But that would be impolite and certainly not the way to win over one's chatelaine, however temporary the arrangement.

We're led into a parlour. I say parlour because it reminds me of the funeral variety. There's no doubting that Mrs Gaunt is fond of black: it's everywhere, leavened only by the odd red cushion. As with the feather in her cap, this only serves to underline the unsettling nature of it all and reminds me of blood and death.

'Just thought I'd bring Inspector Grasby along to leave his suitcase in his room and get cleaned up, Mrs Gaunt,' Deedee says brightly, as though we've just walked into a fairground funhouse rather than the chamber of horrors. It's at this moment I spy a large stuffed bat hanging from a contrived tree branch, covered by an inverted glass bell jar.

'Grasby is your name, is it?'

'Yes, unusual, I know.' I'm used to people asking questions about the provenance of my surname. It's of Danish origin, brought over by the Vikings. Though I do find it hard to picture men like my father and grandfather storming up a beach, wielding axes and intent on bloodthirsty murder. I suppose that years of being exposed to England's green and pleasant land has quelled the turbulent blood in these sea raiders' veins. Personally, I hate sand. Horrible irritating stuff that gets between the toes – everywhere, in fact. Having jumped off a longship and stormed along a distant shore, my thoughts would be set on a hot bath rather than pillage and excess. But there you are.

My mother was of Scottish stock – from whence comes my auburn hair. So, I suppose that my ancestors were only happy marauding all over the place. Did you know it's still legal to kill a Scotsman if he's carrying a bow and arrow in York? Every time I pass one of them in the town, I wonder what would happen if a chap ran them through with a sword. An interesting legal conundrum, I don't doubt.

'I met a young curate called Grasby once,' says Mrs Gaunt.

'My father's a vicar. Isn't that a coincidence?' I say this brightly. The old swine does know Elderby, mark you. I'd seen that knowing look, his expression just before he fell asleep in a fug of home brew.

'There's no such thing as coincidence in life, my boy,' says Mrs Gaunt. 'What's happening has happened before. Aye, and it'll go on and on happening until the end of time.'

She's staring into the distance. And I must admit, whilst the very thought of having to live through my many mistakes in life over and over again is daunting, the revival of many happy days might be quite jolly.

'I'll take you to your room presently. But I want to lay down one or two house rules before we get any further.' Her gaze flits between me and Deedee. 'I was young once, and I can still remember the rising of the sap.'

Not promising.

'Young people are driven by the need to copulate. They have their requirements – it's only nature's way.'

I cough with embarrassment, whilst Deedee is blushing delightfully.

'But there will be no congress of the flesh under my roof,' says Mrs Gaunt in the withering way my father speaks to any passing congregation. 'In any case, lovemaking is best enjoyed outdoors under the sky, the sun and the stars. As was the creator's intention.'

She looks wistful at this juncture, taking hardly any weight at all off her feet by sitting down. Thankfully, Deedee intervenes.

'I'm sure that Inspector Grasby has much more on his mind than a congress of the flesh, Mrs Gaunt.'

Well . . .

'In any case, he's middle-aged.' Deedee smiles, though for me this might as well be a dagger to the heart.

'Steady on, Miss Dean,' say I. 'I'm thirty-eight.' Not saying I'm not much older than her.

'Exactly,' she replies.

It's strange how the young always perceive anyone more than five years their senior to be positively ancient. All she has to do is wait. One's late thirties arrive in a trice, let me tell you. One minute you're bagging a brace of wickets for the school eleven, the next you find yourself to be older than most of the masters. It's unfair, really.

'I could do with a bath. Just a dabble, to get this soot off, you know, Mrs Gaunt.'

'Like as not,' she says, easing herself from her wing-backed chair with surprising grace for one so venerable. She's a restless soul.

She leads us to the hall, and up an inevitably creaky stairway on to a narrow landing.

'There's the bathroom.' Mrs Gaunt points to the door at the head of the stairs with a bony finger. 'There's a limited supply of hot water, so it's one bath a week normally. You can have special dispensation because of your present poor state of hygiene. Advance notice is required normally.'

She scowls at me. I am about to quip that we could share, making two baths every seven days. But given her dire warning about covert copulation, I'm sure this would be frowned upon.

We turn to face three other doors.

'The room at the end of the landing is mine. On the left – as we look at it now – is your room, Grasby. On the right, Miss Dean's.'

I'm not too happy being called just 'Grasby'. Now, Mr Grasby – or more appropriately, Inspector – would be much better. My surname spoken in this way makes me sound like a wine waiter or a clerk.

She walks over to what is to be my room, producing a large bunch of mortice keys from the folds of her lace garments.

'In you go,' she says, holding the door open.

I enter and take in my new surroundings. Thankfully, the place is painted white, not the black I had envisaged. There's a metal-framed bed under a single window, and a nightstand on which sits an ancient-looking lamp. At the end of the room are placed a small, thin wardrobe and an equally diminutive chest of drawers. On the other side of the door is a tiny washbasin and a mirror. I feel as though I've walked into a doll's house, everything is so diminutive. It's basic, but what more do you need – apart from perhaps a chance to have a bath when required.

'A week in advance if you're staying for any length of time,' says my landlady.

'Sergeant Bleakly will deal with that, just as he does with my fees,' says Deedee helpfully.

I leave my suitcase on the bed, to unpack my other suit. Only when I look up do I notice a sketch. It's placed some-what unconventionally at the side of the window, beside the musty grey curtains. It depicts the head and shoulders of three people, one young woman between two men of a similar age. My heart leaps into my throat, for the man on the right looks just like old photos I've seen of my father.

'I say, I like your sketch, Mrs G.' I'm reeling her in like a fish. It's an old interrogation technique, but I'm determined to get to the bottom of the mystery of Elderby and my father.

'Delighted, I'm sure,' she offers dryly.

'Can I ask who these people are?'

'No, it's none of your damned business.'

Rather harsh, methinks. I try again, more subtly, this time.

'It's just that the man on the right reminds me of my father.'

'Oh, that's nice, you'll feel at home, then.' With that she turns on her heel and hurries me towards the bathroom. As I'm about to protest, she fishes another two keys from her pocket. They're attached to a rudimentary wooden fob.

'The smaller one is for the front door – in case of emergencies, mind you.' Mrs Gaunt positively glares at me. 'I expect my guests to be in before ten o'clock.'

'I'm sorry,' I reply, already weary of all these rules and regulations. Worse than the bloody army. 'How am I going to find the time to make love under the stars if it's lights out at ten?'

Another glare.

'Just joking. But in my line of work, one can't keep regular hours. Indeed, such are the nature of the crimes I'm here to investigate, I'm sure to be getting a few night shifts under my belt.'

'I'll need a note from Sergeant Bleakly.'

'You'll be in receipt of no such thing,' I retort, much put out. It's time for the high hand. 'I'm Sergeant Bleakly's superior officer, and this isn't school. You'll comply with my requirements or alternative accommodation for myself and Miss Dean will be found, do you hear?'

She stares at me for a few moments that seem like much longer. Her eyes have a terrifyingly hypnotic quality. I feel rooted to the spot, like an unfortunate creature in the headlights of some oncoming vehicle.

'You must do as you see fit, Grasby. But I'll tell you this, you shouldn't be abroad in this village – aye, or hereabouts – after the church clock chimes twelve.' Her eyes are wide now.

'Why on earth not?'

'I tell thee, now. There are dark matters afoot, very dark indeed. More blood will be spilled. You mark my words.' Her bony forefinger is pointed right in my face. 'I'm only trying to protect you both.'

'What poppycock!' I say. But why does she say *more* blood? I know gossip travels fast in villages like this. But not this fast, surely? I decide to make no further comment.

The old woman shrugs. 'You'll see. There are things that you city folks will never understand.'

I'm about to carry on this argument when in another flurry of wings and feathers the damned raven arrives and perches on Mrs Gaunt's shoulder.

'Where did he come from? We closed the front door,' says Deedee.

'He comes and goes as he pleases. There're more than doors that lead into this house, lass.'

I could lecture her on the overall security of the property, but I realize that there would be little point. If birds can enter the house through nooks and crannies, then so can people. And if Elderby is as dangerous as she maintains, well, we're all sure to have our throats cut in the night. Still, she stands in front of me, the huge raven on her shoulder all but dwarfing her. Damn me, though I've had some rum digs over the years, this is the worst by some margin. And I've not even spent a night in the place yet.

Ironically, I know my father would be the very man to disabuse her of this damned divination nonsense. I try to conjure up the image of a younger Mrs Gaunt, but I can't. She appears stuck in time – a bit like the village itself.

'I really must get cleaned up,' say I.

I look at my watch. Time is getting on, and I'm bloody hungry. The way I see it, with Bleakly guarding the corpse until the mortuary van arrives from York, there's little to be done. I'll have to question Damnish and some members of his staff, including the gamekeeper. I don't trust sleepy Bleakly not to miss something. Juggers has told me to stand by for more orders.

I tell Deedee to pop back to the station and tell them to pass on to Juggers that I'm out on urgent investigations and I'll phone him back. Before this show really kicks off, I'll bathe and make my first trip to the Hanging Beggar.

Who knows, there may be information to be subtly gleaned there, and I'm damnably peckish.

9

Thankfully, we're soon free of the clutches of the unsettling Mrs Gaunt. I'm clean and refreshed, and in no time at all I cross the threshold of the Hanging Beggar for the first time.

It is low-ceilinged, with dark rafters and horse brasses, as you'd expect. There is the obligatory Christmas tree, and some sugar-paper streamers hanging off the rafters. There's a surfeit of holly and mistletoe, too. An old Bakelite radio is chuntering away in the background – the Home Service, I think, crackling out some carols. There are a few customers dotted about: two at the bar, an elderly couple at a table picking away at a ploughman's lunch, and a younger man in a cap that's pulled down over his eyes, nursing a pint. He is silhouetted in front of a bay window.

Whilst this place is as poorly lit as Gaunt's fun palace, it exudes an entirely different ambiance. As much as my new digs are cold and uninviting, the pub is – as most pubs tend to be – welcoming and cosy. There's a blazing fire in the hearth. It's there, as every good publican knows, to appeal to the ancient instinct to huddle round and stay there. Also, as on a snowy day not long before Christmas, it makes the Beggar a hard place from which to extricate oneself. But this is a grub dash, as we used to say in the army. I'll be busy once Juggers has decided what to do. Better enjoy it.

'Hello again,' says Ethel, hands grasping two beer pumps as she smiles from under much red lipstick. 'I hoped we'd see you soon, Inspector Grasby.'

'Oh, you've already met?' says Deedee.

'Me and your Inspector here are old pals, aren't we?' She winks conspiratorially.

'Well, we met in passing this morning,' say I. I decide to change the subject quickly. I can already see Deedee looking between me and the landlady as though I just rolled out of her bed this very morning. 'We were looking for a bite of lunch, if that's possible? Do you have a menu? Something quick.'

'Aye, I do have a menu, thanks,' says Ethel, moving not an inch.

'Could we have one, please?' I say.

'It's simple fare, Inspector. We're still struggling with rationing, you know. No need for a fancy menu.' Ethel taps her head. 'It's all up here.'

'I see.'

'You can have a ploughman's: good Wensleydale cheese and a pork pie from the bakery.' She leans forward. 'I'd like to say that I pickle my own onions, but that would be a lie.' Ethel takes this opportunity to give me a knowing look. 'There's the soup of the day, which is, more often than not, lentil.'

'I do like a bowl of lentil soup, good-oh,' say I.

'That's a pity, because it's oxtail today. I didn't say lentil were every day.'

'Oh.'

'There's a choice of sandwiches.'

'And they are?'

'Ham and cheese.'

'And . . . ?'

'No, ham or cheese. That's what I should have said. You can have ham sandwiches or cheese ones – that's the choice.'

'Right. Anything else?' I'm beginning to realize that limited fare is on offer.

'Steak pie, mash and mushy peas.'

Being quite famished, and enjoying my food despite my thin frame, I think this might be for me.

'Only steak pie is off today as Bill's feeling a bit poorly. He was up all night, the poor soul.'

Time to deploy my famous powers of deduction. 'Bill the baker?'

Ethel looks puzzled. 'No, the baker's called Wally.' She looks at me as though I'm short of a few bob upstairs.

'Who's Bill, then?'

'Of course, you don't know. Bill is Wally's red setter. Lovely coat, you know. Same colour as your hair, I fancy. Poor thing was sick all night. Must have eaten one of Wally's pies.' Ethel bursts out laughing at her own joke.

So, my hair's like a dog's. My father's said worse. I ask what other culinary delights might be on offer.

'That's it, lad. It's not Lyons Corner House, thou knows.'

'Just some of your lovely soup,' says Deedee.

'I'll have the same. But I'm famished. Could I have a ham and cheese sandwich please?'

'What do you mean?'

'Well, ham and cheese – you know, in the one sandwich, together, as it were.'

Ethel furrows her brow. 'How many times? It's cheese or ham, on their own, not together!'

What chat there is in the place stops, and everyone

present stares at me as though I've turned up in my birth-day suit. The two men at the bar – working types with leather patches on the elbows of their jackets – look astonished.

Deedee whispers in my ear, 'She only does one or the other, don't ask me why.'

'I see. In that case, I'll have one round of ham and one round of cheese, please.'

'And soup?'

'Yes, and soup.'

'Drinks?'

While Deedee opts for what she calls a soda, I fancy a pint. There are only two pumps on the bar, mild and bitter, made by Dewberry's, a brewery whose wares I've yet to sample.

'Mild, please, a pint.'

Ethel busies herself behind the bar, whilst Deedee and I take a corner table. My goodness, she's a picture. Though her observation as to my being middle-aged still rankles. After all, she's not much younger than me.

'Do tell me about yourself,' I say, by way of a conversation starter.

'Not much to tell, really.'

'Bleakly let slip that your father is fabulously wealthy.' I smile winningly. It's always good to know where one stands with the rich.

Deedee bites her lip. 'I suppose he is. I never think about it. He's heavily into whiskey. It takes up most of his time.' She looks rueful, which conjures up an image of this poor young woman shrinking into her room when Daddy arrives home beastly drunk.

'I'm sad to hear it. Drink is a curse when it gets a grip.' I think of my own father's alcoholic predilections.

She looks bewildered for a moment. 'Oh no, he's not a drinker. He owns distilleries – mostly in Kentucky. That's the business he's in.' She laughs. 'I swear, I'm still getting used to speaking to the English. I know we share a language, but the nuances are all so different.'

I'm feeling like a nit again. I should have realized that the father of this young woman who is doing her doctorate at Yale wouldn't be some lush. It's being a police officer, you know. Instantly makes you think the worst of everyone.

'I'm sure. But don't fret on it. You'll get used to us in a jiffy.' It's a sly move, but I feel to save face I must deflect blame for this misunderstanding her way. It's a face-saver. 'So, where do you live when you're not in Gloom Towers?'

'I still live with my parents. It's really interesting being a scholar, but it doesn't pay much.'

Don't worry, methinks. When Daddy pops off, you'll be worth a fortune.

'The Upper East Side, you said?'

'That's right. How clever of you to remember. We have a summer house on Long Island, also.'

'How lovely.'

'And a place down in Florida.'

'Right.'

'And a big apartment overlooking the bay in San Francisco.'

'I see.'

'Oh, and this beautiful cabin in Aspen. I say cabin, but it has ten bedrooms.'

This is another tendency I've detected in many of the Americans I've met. During the war, everything they had was bigger and better. This pre-luncheon chat has rapidly turned into the North American property guide.

'Not short of places to lay your head, then?' I say more sourly than I intend. I hope I'm not looking scunnered, as my mother would have said. She always warned me that I couldn't hide my feelings. Facial expressions, apparently.

'But all that travelling.' Deedee sighs wearily.

'Yes, must be absolute torture,' say I, picturing a humble existence with my father. I swear, if I have to watch him keel over when he's squiffy one more time, I'll scream.

'What about you?' says Deedee.

'You know, a bit like your dad but without the fortune. Consumed by my job.'

'And your girl?'

'Girl?'

'Young lady – other half – I've heard people say that here in England.'

'Bit of a drought on the young lady front, I'm afraid.' I tell her how my job gets in the way of long-standing relationships. You know the drill, odd hours and the like. Of course, I should be honest and say that as soon as potential partners find me spark out drunk, surrounded by a bundle of torn betting slips, they take off quick-smart. But that would spoil the mood.

Thankfully, just before the going gets too tough and more questions arrive as to why I'm not hitched with a brood of squawkers, Ethel arrives with the soup and sandwiches, all balanced artfully in the crooks of her arms.

'Here, make yourself useful, Inspector, and grab this bowl of soup before I drop these everywhere.' Ethel swings her wares in my direction, and I do as I'm bid. 'That's you. Enjoy your lunch.' Her right hand lingers on my shoulder.

'The drinks?'

'Hold your horses, I've only got the one pair of hands.

Or maybe that's the last thing I should say to you, eh?' She slaps me on the back with a hearty chuckle.

If I hear one more horse comment, I swear, I'll not answer for my actions.

'I think you have an admirer,' says Deedee as Ethel clops off in her stiletto heels.

'Rather too old for me.'

'You think?'

'I do! She must be in her late fifties, if not older.'

'Really? I'm so bad at gauging the age of older people,' says Deedee.

You're not kidding.

'I think once folks get over thirty-five, they all begin to look the same – age-wise, I mean.'

'Steady on,' say I.

'I don't mean really old people – wrinkles, and all.' She slurps at a spoonful of soup and leans into me conspiratorially. 'I had an ethics professor back home. He made a pass at me.'

'Bad form,' I muster. 'Mind you, "The older the fiddle, the sweeter the tune," my mother used to say.'

Deedee bursts into a fit of giggles. 'You're so funny! You remind me of my dad. How he makes me laugh.'

Another icy hand on the heart for yours truly. It's clear this young woman thinks me fit to be sent off to pasture. I'm beginning to doubt myself. Maybe I truly am over the hill. I damn the war; all that wasted time.

Thoughts return to the matter in hand at Holly House. Deedee asks a number of rather juvenile questions about our chimney man, and I'm unsettled. She remained admirably calm when the poor chap fell down the chimney. Rather flew in the face of what I'd have expected.

The meal continues in this fashion, bursts of small-talk

in between a wrestle with luncheon. The soup isn't too bad, but the bread is as hard as the cheese and the ham is chunky and feels as though the life has been wrung out of it in some way.

There's a little bell above the front door of the Beggar. It tinkles as a middle-aged couple appear in our midst. The woman is slim, with long brown hair, dressed in a neat tweed skirt and jacket. The man is of medium height, in a double-breasted suit, brogues and a homburg hat set at a jaunty angle on his head.

'Chuck, how are you?' says Deedee, suddenly animated.

'Why, it's Miss Dean, honey.' This newcomer addresses his companion in a distinctly American accent. I should have known by the placing of the hat. A bit like a Nazi officer, methinks. Never trust a man with jaunty headwear.

'You haven't come round for supper for ages,' says the woman. She's English.

'They do keep me busy at the police station,' says Deedee.

Busy keeping Bleakly awake, methinks.

'You must introduce me,' say I.

'Inspector Grasby, meet Doctor and Mr Starr.'

'Chuck, please.' Starr reaches out to shake my hand firmly.

'And I'm Elizabeth.' She smiles at me and lowers her voice. 'I'm sure you know where I've just come from. Being the local doctor, I mean.'

'Oh yes, how dreadful,' says Deedee.

Hang on, has Deedee made a mistake?

'So, you're the doc?' I ask.

'That's me.' Dr Starr nods her head.

'We met during the war,' says Chuck.

I bet you did. All chewing gum and free nylons, I'll wager.

'That's nice. You're a military man, Chuck?' I'm ready to boast about my wartime service.

'In actual fact, no. I'm a journalist. I was a reporter for the *Chicago Tribune* during the last lot.'

Huh! I hate these euphemisms for war. It's a damned terrifying, bloody messy, hellish business. Typical of a scribbler.

'That must have been a challenge,' say I, not meaning it at all.

'It had its moments. Especially D-Day. Now, that was a thing.'

Quickly, I decide to change the subject. This bloody writer obviously has a heroic tale or two to tell. You can't stop those who use words for a living from telling a story. Damnable bores, the lot of them. I'd rather face Lady Winthorpe and her empty stable than sit through it all. And no doubt, being of the fourth estate, he'll eventually connect my name to missing horses, and I'll have to go through all that again.

'Have you been here long, Elizabeth?' I ask, neatly holing his D-Day story below the waterline.

'Yes. I came here two years ago as a locum. But poor Doctor Clancy passed away while birdwatching on Withernshaw Fell – his holiday – so I've been here ever since.'

Bloody bad luck, thinks I.

'You love it here, don't you, Elizabeth?' Deedee pipes up.

'I do. The people are so friendly.'

Really?

'And the fresh air is good for Chuck.'

Oh no, a gallant injury. Wait for it.

'You must come visit, Inspector Grasby,' says he.

'Frank, and yes, I'd love to,' I lie. I can only imagine an evening filled with tales of derring-do and Purple Hearts – or whatever they call their medals in America.

'It's my afternoon off, Inspector. So, we always come to the Beggar for a couple of drinks,' says the good doctor.

Note to self: don't get ill on a Thursday. The doctor will be plastered.

They excuse themselves and head off to order drinks. But as they depart, I swear I see a look pass between Deedee and Chuck. It's only fleeting, but when you're a trained observer like me, one notices such things. Perhaps young Deedee protests too much about older men. Maybe their mutual ties to the land of the free go somewhat deeper than is appropriate.

The whole thing rather spoils my lunch – such as it was. After another bite of England's worst sandwich, I hear the telephone ring.

'It's for you, Inspector Grasby,' shouts Ethel from behind the bar.

As I head over to the phone, I note that the lad with the cap pulled down over his eyes leaves without a word. It just seems odd, no friendly goodbyes, nothing.

The two working men at the bar edge along towards the phone, as though they're anxious to find out what's being said. Even Ethel lingers in silence. It's the first time she's shut up since we arrived. All told, I get the feeling everyone is watching me again.

'Hello,' say I.

'Aye, hello to you too. There's a man lying dead and you're in the pub!'

It's Juggers. I'd hoped he would have left a message at Elderby police station. Instead, he's tracked me down to the pub.

'It's a line of inquiry, sir.'

'Don't give me that old tosh, lad. D'you think I was born under the last snowflake?'

You must admit, quite poetic.

'Well, with Sergeant Bleakly there waiting for the mortuary van, and you having to consult your superiors, I rather thought it would be appropriate to grab a bite, so to speak.'

'You'll grab a punch on the nose, if you're not careful. I've spoken to the chief constable. Sinned my soul, I did. Just told him we had a man on the spot. If I'd said it was you, he'd likely have had a heart attack. Get back to Holly House. Interview every last Tom, Dick and Harry.' He pauses for a draw of his pipe. 'But pay close attention to the son and the gamekeeper. Don't ask me how I know this. Just do it.' He ends the call in what is rapidly becoming the usual way.

I look round, just in time to see one of the men with the leather patches on his sleeves pick a piece of paper off the bar and put it in his pocket. Damn the man, he's up to something, furtive. I can spot a wrong 'un.

'You, there!' I shout, rushing to his side. 'Give me that piece of paper this minute.'

He shrugs. 'What if I don't bother?'

Ah, he has me rather foxed on the legal front here. But in true Grasby form, I think quickly on my feet. 'It's a matter of national security. I'm sure you know what that means.' I'm glaring at him with all the *gravitas* I can muster.

'If you say so, Constable.' He digs into the inside pocket of his jacket and produces a crumpled piece of paper – one that has been folded many times.

I look at him then grab the note. At first, I think it's

written in code, little marks here and there that make no sense. But I quickly realize his handwriting is atrocious. Once I become accustomed to it, I'm putting some words together: *Bread, milk, ham (check ration book), tea . . .*

'It's me shopping list. Can I have it back now, Constable?' He's sneering at me.

'Let that be a lesson to you,' say I. 'The war might be over, but there are still some rum coves about, d'you hear? And it's *Inspector*, by the way.'

'Rum coves like you, you mean?' he laughs and turns back to his mate at the bar.

I can almost hear my own footsteps as I head back to Deedee at the table. The Hanging Beggar is as quiet as the grave. I'm beginning to understand how the eponymous bloke felt.

'Can't be too careful,' says Starr with a smile.

I can't work out if he's serious or not.

10

We're back off to Holly House. Though I'm glad to be out of the Beggar, I'm not looking forward to another meeting with Lord Damnish.

I enquire of Deedee what she knows about His Lordship.

'I know he's not popular for knocking down Elderby Hall. Locals didn't like that. Even though the roof leaked, and the place was falling to bits.'

Huh, thinks I. What are the British aristocracy all about, if not a bunch of over-privileged chinless wonders, hanging about in draughty old piles looking venerable and interesting? If they're allowed to go about knocking down our heritage, we'll soon find ourselves in a right pickle. 'Not very noble, demolishing the old hall. His Lordship should remember where he came from,' I say.

'Leeds, I think.'

'Sorry?'

'Lord Damnish is a fish buyer from Leeds. Sergeant Bleakly told me.'

'You mean to say he isn't a hereditary peer?'

'No. He earned his title through hard work. Surely that's better than mere accident of birth?' Deedee flushes.

And there we have it. She's a lovely girl but infused with

that colonial chip on the shoulder the Americans have never quite managed to lose. You see, there's more than one way to become ennobled in this country. One can either trace one's ancestors back to old Billy the Conqueror, or you can throw huge sums of money at the Tories, who, in return, will make damn sure you're rewarded with some title or other. Either that or you can approach the chief whip and tell him the prime minister slept with your granny's parlourmaid or something similar. That'll do the trick just as nicely.

We're invited into another good-looking parlour. Though this time, minus a dead man in the fireplace.

It's the same tableau but in a different room. Damnish is sitting like a client king beside his tiny wife. Across from them lounges their son and heir. Looking up, Damnish, less than happy to see us again, begins to babble on about inconvenience and suchlike.

Though I suppose I'm listening more intently this time round, I do detect a little touch of Leeds in his voice.

'Do sit up!' Lady Damnish chides.

Junior, with a sigh, manages to force his thin frame a few inches up the chair.

'I don't think we managed the formalities earlier, Grantly,' says Damnish, getting my name wrong once more. 'My wife, Lady Marion.' He holds his hand out in her direction, just in case we're in any doubt as to who's who. 'And my son, Beauregard Oscar.'

Goodness, he sounds like the bloody phonetic alphabet. Makes Brown-Ramsbottom sound positively elegant. Poor lad.

'Please call me Harry,' says the youngster.

'You'll damn well call yourself by your own name. We'll have none of this bloody Harry business, d'you hear?'

Damnish has the same tendency to flush when angered as my dear old superintendent. It must be something to do with being rather fulsome, if you know what I mean.

'Yes, Father,' says the son, winking in the direction of Deedee with a leery eye.

I have my leery eye on you, young man, thinks I.

'Have you spoken to Bleakly?' says Damnish.

'No, not yet. Isn't he guarding the body?'

'You must have just missed him. Poor man's quite tired out. Spark out on a chair when I last saw him. As for his constable, well, I can't make out a word he's saying. I gave them leave to return to the police station.'

'I'm sorry?' say I.

'They'll be heading back there now. I had cook make them a spot of lunch. Bleakly was ravenous, by all accounts.'

'Your Lordship, you must understand that Sergeant Bleakly had no right to stand down. The order for officers to be placed at the door to the room was given by my superiors.'

'Bah. You're from York, I understand. Your chief constable is a good friend of mine – a *very* good friend,' he emphasizes. 'In any case, I have my gamekeepers up there making sure nothing untoward happens before the mortuary van arrives.'

He doesn't know it, but the mere mention of the chief constable is enough to make me putty in his chubby hands. But I'll have words with our sleepy sergeant the next time I see him.

'Doesn't do to push a man who has distinguished himself for his country the way Bleakly has. He's a war hero, you know. Highly regarded across the Ridings. Fine chap,' says Damnish.

'I need to interview anyone who heard a disturbance last

night, Your Lordship. When will that be possible?' say I, ignoring this veneration of Bleakly.

'Immediately, I should think. Three people spotted this man – damned nuisance. It's just not on. I'll have to have the room cleaned from top to bottom. Soot everywhere.'

Not much regard for the dead chap, thinks I.

'And who were these people, sir?'

'My wife. She'd been out for one of her nocturnal strolls, hadn't you, dear?'

Lady Damnish regards me intently. Small in stature she may be, but she has a formidable stare.

'Yes. I love the evening air, Inspector. I take a wander round the grounds after dinner. Helps digestion, don't you know.'

Her husband may not have been born to the purple, but judging by his wife's accent, she may well have been. Cut glass, indeed.

'And what did you see, Your Ladyship?' say I, pencil and notebook at the ready.

'Am I to give a statement?' She looks at her husband. 'I'm not a criminal!'

'I should bloody well think not, Gantley. You'll take a mental note of her words and remember them!'

This is throwing me off my stride. Of course she should give a statement. But I quickly remember the chief constable, whose good books do not contain the name Inspector Frank Grasby.

'If you could just tell me what you saw, please.' My notebook is returned to a pocket.

'Good.' She composes herself. 'I had been cutting some holly – I had my secateurs with me, a bag and a pair of stout gloves. One must wear good gloves when cutting holly. It does prick so.'

'I see. And what happened next?' say I, anxious to be done with a lecture on holly husbandry.

'I came from the bushes at the west wing. I suppose I was about thirty yards from the front door. I saw a man. He was standing across the lawn under a tree. I don't think he thought I could see him. But there's nothing wrong with my eyesight you know, Inspector.'

'What did he do?'

'Just stood there, stock still. So, I decided to play him at his own game by ignoring him and going into the house to raise the alarm.'

'What time would this be roughly, ma'am?'

'I should say around nine in the evening. I didn't spend long over dinner, Inspector. I'm not a big eater.'

Say it's not true, think I, taking in her tiny frame.

'You raised the alarm, I take it?'

'Of course. With all these thefts, one thought this was a good opportunity to catch the bounder.'

'I roused McGill and his men, and they went off in search,' said Damnish.

'McGill being your gamekeeper, yes?'

'Spot on, Inspector.' He paused. 'What's your name again?'

'Grasby, sir.'

'Ah yes, Grasby.'

'Now, sir. Another two people spotted our man. Who were they?'

Author's note

At this juncture, it's easier to affix a copy of statements given to me at the time and acquired later. Deedee was right: McGill the gamekeeper was a rather disconcerting chap on first meeting. Martha Thornlie, a quiet young chambermaid, seemed overwhelmed by it all.

But with a dead man up a chimney, who wasn't!

More anon,

Frank

North Riding of Yorkshire Constabulary
Witness Statement

Witness: Arthur McGill (41) Holly House,
Elderby, North Yorks.
Locus: Holly House, as above.
Officer: Francis Grasby (Insp. on
secondment, York City)
Case No.: NYE/438/1952
Date: 18th December 1952

I am employed as Head Gamekeeper at Holly
House, Elderby. As such, I am responsible
for looking after the wellbeing and control
of animals, pests, poaching, etc., as well
as general security in and around the
estate. This includes the house and various
outbuildings.

On the evening of 17th December 1952, I
was alerted to an intruder by His Lordship
(Damnish). I undertook to check outside
Holly House, prior to a room-by-room
search. Having noticed footsteps in the
snow beside the front door, I began to
follow them. As I reached the west wing of
the building, I happened upon the figure of
a man trying to climb a drainpipe on the
side of the house. Though it was dark, I
perceived him to be stocky of build,

wearing a country suit, maybe of tweed or similar material. He had a cap pulled down over his eyes.

Before I could apprehend the intruder, he dropped down and ran off into the bushes.

Despite an extensive search of the grounds and inside the house by myself and other members of staff, no further sign of the intruder was discovered.

I attest that this is a true and accurate statement of events.

Arthur McGill
Gamekeeper

North Riding of Yorkshire Constabulary
Witness Statement

Witness: Martha Thornlie (21) Holly
House, Elderby, North Yorks.
Locus: Holly House, as above.
Officer: Francis Grasby (Insp. on
secondment, York City)
Case No.: NYE/438/1952
Date: 18th December 1952

I am employed as a live-in chambermaid at
Holly House in Elderby. My duties include
domestic chores, dressing, running errands,
that kind of thing.

On the evening of 17th December 1952,
just after nine p.m., I was in the family
bedrooms on the second floor, turning down
beds, putting in warming pans, closing
curtains and the like. Young Master Damnish
had asked me to make sure his window was
open a sliver, as he complained of being
stuffy with the cold.

It took time to do this as the sash
windows are stiff, especially in frosty,
cold weather. As I was opening the window,
I noticed a man under a tree beside the
lawn. I got a fright when I spotted Her

Ladyship was walking from the holly bushes on her evening walk.

At the time, I thought they exchanged a few words, before Her Ladyship entered the house via the front door. This made me feel less concerned. However, I later realized I must have been mistaken, as Her Ladyship raised the alarm because of an intruder in the grounds, so this means she couldn't have spoken to the man.

I helped with the search of rooms and corridors on the upper floors along with Rodney, one of the gamekeeper's assistants. Despite being most thorough and taking our time to check every nook and cranny, we found no intruder.

I was in bed by one thirty in the morning.

I attest that this is a true and accurate statement of events.

Martha Thornlie
Chambermaid

Editor's note

Frustratingly, at this point in the journal pages are missing. So, we will never know what Inspector Grasby's feelings were regarding these statements, particularly that of Martha Thornlie.

Now, it's a matter of courtesy that I seek out Lord Damnish again.

It turns out, we find him in his study, indulging in a cigar and a glass of whisky as he pores over some ledger or other. He wipes fallen ash from his waistcoat and curses.

'So, how long will it be until we discover the identity of that bloody rascal?'

I shrug. 'Not sure, sir. He'll be taken to York for a post-mortem. But identification may prove more difficult. There was nothing to identify him in his possessions.'

'Damn. You know I have a suspect of my own as far as these thefts are concerned. A bad lot. Ingleby is his name. He's a tenant at Briarside Farm. Shifty bugger. A bloody Bolshevik, I'm sure of it. The dead man could be one of his accomplices. He's well worth a visit, you know.'

'Why do you suspect him, sir?'

'Oh, no reason in particular, other than he's been a pain in my backside ever since I arrived in this bloody village.' He takes an agitated puff of his cigar. 'Take my word for it, Grantly, he's worth the watching.'

We bid the Damnishes farewell, and are accompanied out of Holly House by Harrison, just as the mortuary van from York arrives. I know one of the chaps, and we pass the time of day. He tells me that one of my old sergeants was found dead in the Shambles back in York this morning. He'd just retired. So much for a life of leisure, thinks I. They go about the grim business of removing the dead man in the fireplace.

We're just out of the gate and a few yards down the drive when I hear my name.

Young Damnish Junior is pelting after us.

'Yes, sir?' I say pleasantly. I detect all is not well between father and son. No bloody wonder after being saddled with such an awful name. I find that where there is division there is opportunity. I shall cultivate this young man for stray information from chez Damnish.

'Just to say, I do apologize for my father. Bloody rude to you – bad form. He's like that, I'm afraid,' says the youngster breathlessly.

I have what is approaching a rather posh accent, but he's full-on Eton, Harrow or somewhere similar.

'Don't worry, Harry,' say I. 'Takes all sorts, and I've met most of them.'

'You're very kind, Inspector.' He smiles broadly. I see little of either of his parents in him – apart from maybe a hint of his mother's sharpness of nose, a trait of this nation's blue-blooded, you know. He may be the spitting image of his father. But it's hard to tell what Damnish Senior looks like, given the blubber that encases him.

'Are you still at school?' I enquire.

'Ah, bit of a sabbatical from Rugby, I'm afraid.'

I knew it.

'Got into a spot of bother. Nothing that Daddy can't fix. But I really wish he wouldn't bother.'

'You don't like Rugby?'

'It's not so bad. But my ambitions lie in a rather different direction, Inspector.'

'Which is?'

'I love the land – this land, you see.' He gazes round-about. 'My father is only interested in stocks, shares, not what's behind the money. He's definitely not interested in people.' He looks rueful.

'You should meet my father,' say I.

He smiles. 'Anyway, thanks for being so gracious about it all. I'll leave you to your business.' Harry shakes me by the hand and fairly bows at Deedee. 'It's a real pleasure to have made your acquaintance, Miss Dean.'

Steady on.

When we part, Deedee is humming a little tune and running her hand through the snow on the bonnet of the car. 'What a sweet young man,' she says.

'He's more than that. He's our main suspect in the farm thefts.'

'What?'

'QED, Deedee,' say I, admiring the instantly constructed tongue twister. 'Young man of some substance, disgrun-tled with his oaf of a father, not to mention that awful name. Fabulous way to get his own back, I'd say.'

I'm pleased to note that this feat of deduction has left Daisy Dean looking bewildered. There's more to detective work than a doctorate or two from Yale, you know.

'But you don't think he's responsible for the dead man, I hope?'

'That's the problem. Everyone and his friend are desper-ate to conflate the thefts from the area with the man dead in the fireplace.'

'And you don't think they're one and the same?'

'I have an open mind. To date, I've seen nothing to prove it either way.'

She's deep in thought as we leave Holly House.

11

By the time we get back to the station I'm expecting reinforcements from York. But none are to be found. Looks like I'm on my own. We were stretched before I left, and I know dear old Juggers wasn't happy that he'd lost another detective. Heigh-ho. I'm feeling dead beat. It's been a long day and, feeling as ancient as Deedee thinks me to be, well, I could do with a kip. In any case, it's too late to do anything else – not practically. And we'll get nothing on the deceased for a while.

I leave Deedee to attend to some filing and go in search of my new colleagues.

Amazingly, when I arrive in Bleakly's office I find him wide awake. He looks rather pleased with himself. Has he cracked the case, I wonder?

'I have good news, Inspector Grasby.' He leans back in his chair with a yawn.

Quite right, old boy, you have a quick forty winks, thinks I.

'Oh, yes?' I say, feigning interest.

'We've found your car. On the old road, of all places. Well, the constables located it, to be exact. I'm sure you'll be delighted.'

'Jolly good!' say I, mustering the appropriate enthusiasm. 'No sign of the blighter who stole it, I'll wager?'

'No, we haven't collared anyone yet. But we do have a suspect.' He stares at me gimlet-eyed.

'You do?' I'm trying not to sound surprised.

He dons his thick spectacles and peers at his notebook. 'Here we are. Mr Wallington – he has a farm just off the Whitby road. He's given us a description.'

Bugger! I should have known some inquisitive yokel would be lurking about just when I was having car trouble.

'Oh?'

'Tall, in a grey suit, overcoat and trilby.'

'Right,' say I, remembering the filthy grey suit now in my room at Mrs Gaunt's.

'Wallington says the man had red hair – colour of the baker's dog Bill, it says here.'

'Ha! An inconsistency straight away. How could he have seen this chap's hair if he was wearing a trilby?'

'Wallington says that this *criminal*,' he emphasizes the word for my benefit, 'had to take off his hat to wipe his brow when shouldering the car on to the ditch. A gentleman thief, quite clearly.'

Now, sometimes when you're caught out in a fib and the odds are against you, it's time to hold up one's hands and think of some mitigation as to why you've lied. This is no such occasion. At the end of the day, it's one man's word against another's.

'Well, this is odd, isn't it?'

'You're right there, sir.' Bleakly shakes his head in mock bewilderment.

'Where was this Wallington chap? In relation to the car, I mean.'

I'd had a good look round for some assistance, I remember. Either this son of the soil was hiding behind a tree, or he was some way off, I'll wager.

'Oh, a good two or three hundred yards away, I reckon.'

'Did he have an eyeglass?'

'Don't think so. Why would he?'

I shrug. 'Wouldn't stand up in court, old boy. What age is this Wallington?'

'I'm not right sure. A bit older than me, I'd say.'

'I take it then that an elderly man, looking from two to three hundred yards away as it's snowing, has been able to absolutely pin down a description of the car thief? No, not good enough, Sergeant. I'll thank the chaps for finding my vehicle, but I don't think we'll ever convict anyone based on this unreliable statement.' I sigh and smile, just so he knows that I know he's pushing his luck. It's like an admission, but not one. Ambiguity is a friend to rogues everywhere. Not that I'm a rogue, mark you.

'Funny thing is this chap seemed to be heading into the village. Now, I know everyone hereabouts. And I don't recognize that description. It's not anyone who lives here.'

He's trying to wheedle his way back into it. That's not happening.

'Who knows, Sergeant? As I say, we will never convict somebody based on Mr Wallington's testimony. Where is the car now?'

'It's outside in the backyard. The lads managed to get the engine fired up. Makes a damnable racket.'

It's a wonder I didn't hear the bloody thing backfire at Holly House. This reminds me that I must get hold of Stubby and give him more than a piece of my mind. That aside, Bleakly is still trying to bait me. It's time to put a stop to it.

'Listen here, Bleakly,' say I. 'I've just had to put my neck on the line with Lord Damnish on your behalf.'

He looks confused. 'What on earth do you mean?'

'He's not chuffed that you've been unable to bring these farm thieves to book.'

'I see.'

'And into the bargain – well, I'm sorry to bring it up. But you do have this sleep problem, don't you know?'

'Aye.' He looks rueful. 'Picked up something in the jungle, the doctor says.'

Sounds like a Thursday diagnosis from Dr Starr.

'Bad luck, old boy. Which jungle?'

'Burma.' He shivers.

'The Chindits?' I ask, mouth gaping. These chaps were the bravest of the brave. They went through hell trying to flush out the Japanese. Under dreadful conditions, too. I think disease killed more than the enemy did. So, that's what Damnish was banging on about.

'Ended up fighting at Wingate's side. Now, there was a man.'

I bet! That's the trouble with your heroic type. They can never go and be heroes on their own – they always have to drag some poor buggers along with them. Unfortunate chaps like Bleakly here, no doubt shaking in his boots the whole way.

'Gosh, did you volunteer?'

Bleakly grimaces. 'Well, yes and no, really. I was a commando, you see – an old soldier. The type he liked around him. Lads with experience. You don't say no to a man like Wingate. I was proud to serve.'

I find myself feeling rather inadequate. Don't get me wrong. I had my moments during the war, but I'll tell you that another time. Of course, when one does cross the path of chaps like these, it's best not to show any signs of deference. In any event, they're usually quiet souls with very little to say, which helps. I now begin to worry that this sleeping sickness might be infectious after all. I take a step or two back, leaving Bleakly lost in his memories.

'I can tell you right now, nobody will gainsay your service when I'm around, Elphinstone.' It's time for the noble tilt of the jaw of the outraged companion. 'I went through it, too. Chaps like Damnish, they don't know the half of it.'

'Thank you, sir, that's true. I'm most obliged to you.'

There we are. All thoughts of this car thief who bears an uncanny resemblance to me forgotten.

'Mind you. Our chief constable is an old colleague of mine. I'm proud to say I saved his life after he caught a Japanese bullet. I'm not too sure he'd listen to the likes of Damnish.'

You fly old bugger. You're in with the bricks here, and you bally well know it, thinks I. Scant reward for dodging guns and disease in the jungle, mark you.

'Well, I'm beat, Elphinstone. We'll mark the car down to bad luck – all's well that ends well. I need something decent to eat, a good book, and bed.'

'She's a good cook is Hetty Gaunt,' opines Bleakly.

'I hope so. The food at the pub is – well, shoddy, to say the least.'

'Aye, Ethel makes some nice lentil soup, but that's about it. Hard with rationing, I imagine.'

'Ham tastes as though it's been wrung through with a mangle.'

'It has, to some extent. That's what's left over when she makes the lentil soup.'

Damn, I should have thought of that.

'I'm a bit worried that Mrs Gaunt is making food out of rats and dead birds.'

'No, she would never do that. She loves birds, hence Cecil the raven.'

'What about the rats?'

He shrugs his shoulders. 'Aye, there is that, mind you. But only one of her guests has ever died during their stay. So, you don't have much to worry about.'

I'm somewhat alarmed by this.

'I'd rather hear that none of her guests have died, to be honest.' I mean, a chap expects to check for testimonials and recommendations when looking for temporary accommodation. You don't really consider contacting a guest house to find out how many people have died there recently.

'He was old. A retired colonel in the Greys. Natural causes.'

Wasn't the bat soup, then. Good-oh.

'Where are my car keys?'

'In the ignition, sir.'

Whether my Austin has taken to life on the North York Moors, or perhaps the run has done it good, I don't know. But there's not a bang or a whimper as I leave Elderby police station, navigate Main Street and then turn into the cul-de-sac and the haunted house that is to be my home, for a while at least.

I park the car on the verge beside the chaos that is Mrs Gaunt's garden, scamper up the path and use my key to access my digs.

Cecil the raven shoots over my head, again brushing my trilby. I'll have to get used to it, I suppose.

Standing in the chamber of horrors that passes for the lounge, calls to my landlady fall on deaf ears. I'm up the stairs in a flash and in my room. My plan is to find the immersion and grab another bath before good old Hetty can say abracadabra. Nothing worse than being around death to make one feel unclean.

Looking round the bathroom, which is neat and tidy, I can't see any sign of the immersion switch. I turn on the hot tap in the bath on the off chance, only to be greeted by a thud from the pipes and a dribble of cold water.

'What are you about?' says Mrs Gaunt, almost shifting my heart. She's framed in the doorway with her arms folded, like a bouncer in a downmarket Soho club.

'Now, listen here, Mrs G,' say I. 'I don't expect you to appear from nowhere to inspect my ablutions. A man needs his privacy, you know.'

'Were you thinking of abluting in the bath? I hope not, for your sake.'

'Steady on. What kind of chap do you think I am?'

'I don't know you, Grasby. I've had some strange guests over the years, you know.'

'I don't doubt it,' say I with feeling.

'If you want a bath I'll have to switch on the immersion. And that will be you for the week, mind.'

It's a hard one, but I had to rush my last bath. There's still soot under my fingernails.

'Yes, please fire up the boiler or whatever it is you're going to do, Mrs G.'

She leans across and pulls at a black cord hanging from the ceiling. I thought this was the light switch. But it's handy to know. If I'm here for any length of time, I'll soon work out her routine and be able to bolt over and grab a bath when she goes out.

'It'll be a good hour before it's heated.'

Positively the Dark Ages.

'Well, that's fine, then. Can I ask, when's dinner?'

'Dinnertime, when do you think?'

'Eight, then?'

'No, seven o'clock and no later. If you miss it, I'll leave yours in a pot to heat up yourself.'

'Very kind. And what's on the menu this fine evening?'

'You'll find out when you get it. But you'll be glad to hear my food beats anything the pub has to offer, as you'll have found out with your soup and sandwiches earlier.' She nods and stomps off. I hear Cecil's wings flap after her as she takes the stairs.

Typical of these small communities. Everyone knows what you're about before you're about it. Mind you, York is nearly as bad. Have a run of bad luck with one bookie, and before you know it, you are *persona non grata* with every turf accountant in the town until you've paid up. Damnable stuff.

I lie down on the bed for a while after my bath. The mattress is on the hard side, but it'll do. My eyes are heavy, so I pull my trilby down cowboy-style over my eyes and have forty winks before dinner.

I wake to the sound of Deedee's light tread on the stairs. As much as Mrs G stomps, Daisy Dean glides like a ballerina. I hear her door close softly, and I sigh. She really is a bonnie lassie, as my mother would have said.

It's just about quarter to six on my Omega watch. The only decent thing the army ever gave me. They tried to spirit them off us when we were discharged, but I don't think they'd much luck. It still has the telltale arrow on the face, indicating that it's property of His Majesty. I suppose it's Her Majesty now. That'll take a bit of getting used to, methinks. Anyhow, I'm sure our new queen has a plentiful supply of watches. Just as well – I won't part with mine.

In the dark dining room, all is set for dinner. One lamp

hangs over it; I'm reminded of a billiards table. The crock-
ery is no slouch, though, all fine china and silver spoons.
Not what I expected. The table is round, meaning nobody
sits at its head. Most egalitarian; my father would approve.

The more I stare at the sketch on my bedroom wall, the
more convinced I become that he is pictured on it. I resolve
to wait for the right moment and ask my host outright,
more ardently, this time.

Deedee appears, instantly lighting up the gloom. She's
changed into a lovely blue frock. It fairly sets off her eyes.
It's as though an angel has landed in our midst. Gosh.

I can hear noises from the kitchen and must admit the
aroma of whatever is to be for dinner is quite heavenly.

When it arrives, it's damned good too. I think it's chicken
in a wine sauce, but Mrs G soon announces that it is, in
fact, rabbit in a wine gravy. No fancy sauces in Elderby, it
appears. There's even wine on the table, in a decanter. I
suspect it's the remnant of what went into the sauce. But
heigh-ho, not what one expects from a country guest
house. It's a good Rhône, I think. Very palatable indeed.

'This sauce is wonderful!' Deedee coos. 'The last time I
ate rabbit was in the Algonquin. It wasn't half as good as
this. You really are a fabulous cook, Mrs Gaunt.'

'Plenty of practice,' says our host. 'Served my time in the
kitchens at the big house. Well, the old place.'

'I hear it was a cold, leaky old pile,' say I. I wish I hadn't
bothered.

Hetty Gaunt points her knife at me. 'Don't talk nonsense, lad. It were a fine place – regal. They say good Queen
Bess stayed there for a couple of nights. Knocking it down
to make way for that pleasure palace was nothing short of
a tragedy.' She scowls at me for a few moments before
returning to her food.

That's me told, thinks I. She doesn't realize that good old Queen Bess stayed in just about every decent house in the country. It saved the royal court a great deal of money and bankrupted many a belted earl.

Just as I'm wondering where Cecil is, I feel the waft of his wings on the top of my head as he lands expertly beside Mrs Gaunt's plate and begins to peck at it.

'Is that quite hygienic?' say I.

'What are you on about?'

'Letting the bird eat from your plate, I mean.' This is spoiling my appetite.

'Don't be daft. There's nothing unclean about my Cecil. How dare you.' The scowl lasts longer this time.

I get my head down and finish my rabbit. It's clear Cecil can do what he jolly well pleases. Good for him. As I push my plate away, only bones left, I swear the bird takes me in with one beady eye. 'Bugger off,' it says in a broad Yorkshire accent. Deedee's giggle turns into a full-blown laugh.

I must admit to being quite shocked. You know, I've never been keen on nature. I think this aversion started at prep school. I was rushed by a sheep when the class visited a farm. Toppled me over, it did. I can remember being terrified before Miss Cowley ushered the great beast of a thing off and dragged me to safety. So, you see, because of this fear of the country and all that's in it, I had no idea that ravens could talk like parrots. My face must be a picture, for I swear Deedee is almost choking with mirth.

You can *really* go off someone, you know.

As I sit looking flabbergasted, Mrs G turns to me. 'And that's you told. Cleverest birds in the world are ravens, you know. Get it on the case of this poor dead bugger. It'll have it solved like that.' She clicks her fingers and excuses herself from the table. Cecil flies off after her.

For a second I'm surprised by her knowledge of the goings-on at Holly House. But I suppose I shouldn't be, in this community.

'Gee, that bird is a riot,' says Deedee, recovering herself and pouring some wine into my glass then her own. 'It told me to do something much worse when I arrived.' She giggles again. 'Mrs Gaunt's great in the kitchen, don't you think? I've had some of the best meals of my life here.'

I must admit, this has come as a pleasant surprise. It's like dining over at Dracula's castle, but the food is fabulous. 'Yes, jolly good,' say I. 'I think it's soup and beer only in the pub from now on.'

'Yes, absolutely.' She leans into me. 'Do you still think Harry is stealing from his father's farms? I mean, it could be significant in our investigations about that poor dead man.'

'First lesson in human nature,' say I. 'Families are murky beasts. All kinds of stuff going on. You know, jealousy, envy – hatred, even. Just because you are related to someone, doesn't mean you'll have each other's best interest at heart.'

'Tell me about it. I have a brother. I can't stand him.'

'Oh, that's a shame.'

It's at times like this I thank my parents for only having managed to copulate once in order to have me. I know it's an odd notion, but I can't picture my father and mother getting down to the jolly old thing. What a ghastly thought.

'What kind of chap is he?'

Deedee looks lost for words for a moment. Then she announces, 'He's a pacifist. He refused to fight in the war. My father managed to get him a pass, but he was so ashamed.' She shakes her blonde locks at the horror of it all.

'Damned bounder,' say I indignantly. But all the time I'm really wondering who's right and who's wrong. If everyone refused to fight, then the politicians would have to slug it out with each other. I fancy Winston would have been a match for anyone in his day. He'd soon have put the Austrian corporal in his place. Don't mess with a man who's survived a public school, I tell you. It's like being flung into gaol as a child. Toughens one up, no doubt about it.

'I try not to think of him,' says Deedee.

It might just be me, but there's a flinty look in her eyes I haven't been aware of thus far. It's as though she has hidden depths. Mark you, which one of us doesn't? Though some are deeper than others. I think mine are just about knee-height, just enough for a good paddle.

Mrs G arrives bearing bowls of plum pudding and custard. She clears away the dinner plates and we tuck in. It's even better than the rabbit. All in all, I think I've rather fallen on my feet again. Yes, it's Gloom Towers, but the grub is top notch, my room is more than fit for purpose and I get to buddy up with Deedee. It could have been Hull, remember.

The meal over, wine drunk, I head to bed. Deedee decides to keep Mrs Gaunt company over a glass of brandy, but I'm too tired.

As I'm donning my pyjamas, my gaze lands on the sketch of the three young people. Damn, I forgot to ask Mrs Gaunt if it was really him. I'm still convinced it is. I've never trusted my father. I remember him being overly friendly with an organist when I was twelve. A lad of that age is beginning to be worldly wise – well, I was, at least. It was something in his smile, the fact they were so close to each other.

It's time to curl up with a book: the new one from Graham Greene, *The End of the Affair.* Having had plenty of those, I hope I'll pick up some tips from the great man.

I read for an hour or so, until I feel tiredness creep up on me again. It must be the country air.

In a jiffy, I'm dreaming about Deedee in a ripe cornfield under a blue sky.

12

I sleep soundly, you know; barely ever wake before seven. So, it is with no little surprise that I find Mrs Gaunt framed in the door of my room. It's still dark outside, so I haven't slept in. If this is a cosy early morning ritual chez Gaunt, she can damn well keep it. It crosses my mind that she's checking I'm still in my own bed.

I sit up and rub the sleep from my eyes.

'What on earth's to do, Mrs G?'

'It's Sergeant Bleakly. He's downstairs. A matter that requires your urgent attention,' says she as Cecil shuffles about on the shoulder of her black dressing gown. No wonder Bleakly falls asleep endlessly, if this is to be the normal course of his day. I tell Mrs Gaunt that I'm on my way. I splash some water on my face at the small sink, drag a comb through my hair, rush on my suit and hasten down the stairs to see what's up with our resident Chindit.

Bleakly's standing in the lounge, his helmet in hand. He's looking around the place like an assessor.

'Good morning, Elphinstone. Have you brought the milk?' say I cheerily. Though I sleep well, once I'm up, I'm awake. Not like some of these moody blokes who mope about for an hour or two after they leave the comfort of their beds. Up and at 'em, that's what I say.

'Good morning, sir. I'm sorry to disturb you this early. We have a bit of a problem, I'm afraid. Normally, I'd have dealt with this myself until they sent someone from Whitby or Pickering. But since you're here, I thought it best you take charge from the off.'

'Not another death, I hope?' I say this in jest, but the look on Bleakly's face isn't encouraging.

'Yes and no, sir. It's a murder for sure this time, I'm pretty certain.'

Gosh, this is a surprise. I've been here for less than twenty-four hours, and already the place is descending into absolute chaos.

'Murder. Are you sure?'

'The man's dead, sir. So, yes.'

'Have you considered natural causes?'

'I did, until I noticed the stab wound under his ribcage.'

I'm galvanized by this information. Your average murder is a messy, unprofessional affair. I've seen poor folk who've been beaten to death, strangled, shot, and the like. But a knife under the ribs is reminiscent of something more practised. It's the way we were taught in the army: approach from behind, hand over the mouth to stop a scream and knife up under the ribs. The classic way of dispatching a sentry.

'I know what you're thinking, sir. It sounds as though it was someone who knows what they're doing.'

'It does. Where did this happen?'

'Just behind the church, up on the ridge, is where the body was found. The vicar, Reverend Croucher, happened upon him, sir. Quite upset, he is.'

'I should think so. We better get up there, quick-smart.'

Just as we're leaving, I hear footsteps on the stairs. It's Deedee's light tread. She's still in her nightdress by the look of things, though bundled up in a coat to protect her modesty.

'Sergeant Bleakly, hello. I heard voices. What's up?'

'No need for you to worry. The inspector and I will deal with the matter.'

'What matter?'

'There's been a murder. I want you to go back upstairs and make sure Mrs Gaunt locks the door. I dare say we'll get reinforcements from the county in due course. But in the meantime, I want you to stay safe. Please pass this on. I'm sure there's nothing to worry about, but at the moment we have a murderer on the loose,' say I.

It's now I notice something unusual. Deedee's legs are filthy – red raw, as though she's been out with the pigs. She follows my gaze and looks down.

'I sleepwalk, Inspector. Have done since I was a child. Hoped I'd grow out of it, but I never have. It's quite embarrassing, sorry.'

'Poor thing. No need to apologize. Mind you, you'll have to wait for the bath roster to get cleaned up.' I smile reassuringly. 'Remember, Grasby's at the wheel, all is well.' Unless you're the dead chaps, that is, I think to myself.

'Do we know the victim?' Deedee asks.

Bleakly shuffles from foot to foot, clears his throat and looks suddenly uncomfortable.

'Come on, Elphinstone. Do we know this poor chap?'

'I'm not sure you do, sir. But Miss Dean does.'

Deedee's jaw drops and she puts a hand to her mouth. 'Who is it, Sergeant?'

'I'm sorry to have to impart this news. I know you've become friends with the family.'

Deedee sits heavily on the stairs, a bewildered look on her face.

'Spit it out, old boy,' say I, feeling quite in the dark.

'It's Mr Starr, sir. He's the local doctor's husband. An American gentleman.' His eyes flick to Deedee, who now has her head in her hands.

'I met them in the pub yesterday lunchtime. How awful.'

'Oh, you didn't say, sir. It also presents us with a problem. Normally, I'd ask Doctor Starr to attend – but that's not appropriate now, is it?'

'Where's the nearest doctor to be found?'

'I suppose we should get someone from one of the other villages. There are some GPs spread about, but I don't have their phone numbers to hand, they're in the office.'

Deedee looks calm now. She's staring ahead, blankly.

'Are you quite all right, old thing?' I put my arm round her shoulder to comfort her.

'I want to come with you.'

'Now, I don't think that's a good idea, Deedee.'

She looks at me and her eyes fairly flash. Her face is set. There's determination behind those peepers; but there's something else too. I just can't put my finger on it. Perhaps it's just the circumstances that have my senses on edge. But over the years, I've learned to trust my instincts. I file away this thought for later.

'I'm not a child, Inspector Grasby. I'm here to gain experience, and that's what I must do.' She turns and hurries up the stairs.

'We should go now, Inspector,' says Bleakly.

'I agree.'

Quietly, we slip out of the front door and make our way to the little Morris Minor, the marked police van in which Bleakly has arrived. Soon we're navigating the dark, snowy streets of Elderby.

*

The way to the church is narrow and steep. The van slides on the frozen road, Bleakly doing well to keep her from the verge. He peers over the wheel like some old biddy. The snow blankets everything. By all accounts, it's been on and off since before I arrived. I shiver at the thought of the man I'd just met a matter of hours ago lying dead up here.

The road stops at the church's lichgate. It sits on a flat piece of ground just under the ridge. Its little roof looks like an iced cake. They've put down some gravel to accommodate parked cars. As churches go, it's set up well enough, with few adornments apart from the odd stone cross here and there, and a big wooden door, arched and studded with large, black nails and matching iron bracing. Through the frost, I can just about make out the words on a little wooden plaque outside the entrance.

St Thomas's-on-the Edge, in the parish of Elderby.

Out of nowhere a slight man in a dog collar appears. He has thin, short, greying hair cut close to his head. He looks wraithlike in this light, wringing his hands as he approaches the car. Bleakly and I get out to make his acquaintance.

'Good morning, Vicar,' say I, holding out a gloved hand. He takes it weakly. 'I'm Inspector Grasby. So sorry you've had to witness this.'

'George Croucher,' he says, looking quite bereft. 'Poor Mr Starr. Such a gentleman. He was at D-Day, you know.'

Here we go.

'Yes, I met him briefly for the first time yesterday. It's just terrible.'

'If you don't mind, Reverend, we better get to the murder scene,' says Bleakly.

'Of course,' says Croucher with a whimper.

'Please stay inside the church,' say I. 'Not the time for wandering off, as I'm sure you appreciate, Your Reverence.'

'I'm going to pray, Inspector Grasby. Might put some whisky in my tea. This has been such a shock.'

Typical of your average clergyman. Can't wait to get some booze down their throats, no matter what the circumstances. You see it all the time. Whether it's a wedding, funeral or baptism, there will be some squiffy man of the cloth hanging about, smiling benignly, drunk as a lord.

'I'll need to speak to you once I've seen the victim. Get a statement and the like. Try not to worry.'

As we make our way round the side of the building, I hear the big front door of the church close and a heavy key turn in a lock.

'Nervous chap,' say I.

'He's a bit highly strung at the best of times,' says Bleakly with the sangfroid to which I'm becoming accustomed. 'Did himself a mischief at a service not so long ago. He was in the middle of the benediction when this great bugger of a rat ran across the floor. He fainted on the spot. Banged his head. Quite nasty, it was.'

'How awful,' say I sympathetically. Of course, I'm really thinking, 'What a clot.'

As we round the corner, I see three figures on the slope leading to the edge of the ridge. Two bobbies, one shorter than the other, are standing beside the body of Charles 'Chuck' Starr, journalist, D-Day veteran and now very, very dead American. He's on his back, arms thrust right out behind his head as though he's flying through the air on a trapeze. Even in this light I can see the frozen grimace of pain on his waxy face. There's also a great black stain on the front of his white shirt. I notice it's torn and muddy.

His hands are half clenched, stiff with death and frost. I see one of his fingernails is missing, and the rest are caked with mud. He's been dragged from somewhere, face down, by the looks of it. It's as though he'd been desperately trying to get purchase on the ground. It's all most odd, ghastly.

I nod to the constables: the Neanderthal I met yesterday who can't speak, and a taller, broad-shouldered lad with a boxer's nose. I take off my trilby, remove my hanky, and unfold it ready to save my trousers from getting filthy on the snowy ground. Another corpse. I'll have to tread carefully, these days they don't like you poking about too much until the body is examined in the mortuary. Poor Starr will have to be examined properly, likely in York again.

I picture he and his wife, full of the joys in the Hanging Beggar not even twenty-four hours ago. I take a pen from my pocket and push aside his collar with it. There's a red band round his neck, rapidly turning black.

'Chap's been strangled,' say I, looking up at Bleakly, whose nose is beginning to turn blue in the cold.

Flatface the bobby is staring at me as though I've just appeared out of nowhere.

'Excuse me, sir, can I ask where you were at around eleven yesterday morning?'

'What?' say I.

'I have a description of a man who stole a car from a police officer yesterday. You fit it perfectly.'

'Shut up!' says Bleakly sharply. 'This is the officer whose car was stolen.'

This oaf looks at me, head tilted like the His Master's Voice dog. 'It's a bit of a coincidence, isn't it, Sergeant?'

Time to put a stop to this, methinks. I heartily regret concocting the car story in the first place. But I don't need Constable Clueless on the case.

'Listen here, whatever your name is. This is a murder scene. If you don't stop this nonsense, you'll find yourself looking for another job. In fact, I'll have you arrested for being an oaf. Do you understand?'

'Aye, I dare say,' he huffs.

'I dare say, *sir*. Now, move off, you're blocking what little light there is. I have my eye on you.' I glare at him appropriately.

That's how to sort 'em. Can't stand uppity junior ranks, especially when they're right.

'You've called this in, Bleakly?' say I.

'Yes, sir. I called Pickering as soon as the body was discovered.'

I'm about to reply when I see a figure climbing towards us. It's Deedee.

'Miss Dean!' Doesn't do to be too familiar, with the constables looking on. 'I told you to stay in the house. You've put yourself at great risk wandering up here by yourself.'

'I didn't wander, I ran. And it was pretty low of you to leave without me.'

She looks down at the remains of Chuck Starr. I expect her to burst into tears, but instead she appears quite dispassionate.

'Did he suffer?' she asks flatly.

'Hard to say,' says Bleakly. 'We'll have to wait for a doctor.'

'And his wife, does she know?'

'No. I was thinking that the inspector would want to take care of that.' He looks to me for a response.

Now, if there's one thing I hate, it's telling some poor relative that their loved one has popped their clogs – especially under these circumstances. I was once sent to a street in York to inform a young woman that her husband had died in an accident. Her name was Smith. I was told the house was at the end of a street near the river. Indeed, there were two houses at the end of the road in question, both facing the Ouse. The first one I came to had *Smith* engraved into a wooden nameplate on the front door.

When the young lady answered my knock, I asked if I could come in. It's only criminals who get jumpy when the constabulary arrive at the door. And like most normal people, she suspected the worst.

'It's my father, isn't it?' she said with a wail.

'No, it's your husband,' said I, with the appropriate *gravitas*.

She screamed and beat my chest with her fists – a common reaction, I'll have you know.

Through her tears, she asked me how this tragedy had happened.

'I'm sorry, but he fell off the footplate of the train he was driving earlier this morning,' I imparted.

She pulled back from me, searching my eyes.

'What was he doing driving a train? He's the manager of a shoe shop.'

Now, it may be reasonable to imagine one's spouse might be slippery enough to get up to all sorts when the other half isn't about. But driving a train when you're not a train driver isn't what you'd expect. It turned out that the neighbours were also named Smith. I had to go through the whole beastly process again next door.

'I'll come with you,' says Deedee. 'After all, we're friends, Elizabeth and I.'

Good-oh. I'll impart the message and Deedee can absorb the grief. Just the job.

I look around the locus. 'I wonder, how did this poor chap get here?'

Bleakly stroked his chin thoughtfully. 'I haven't spoken to the vicar properly. Like as not, we should get that statement now. There's been another snowfall since he were left here, I reckon. Little sign of footprints.'

I order the knuckle-dragging constables to guard the corpse with their lives and we head to the church to see the Reverend Croucher. I ask Deedee to sit in the car, which she does reluctantly. I must say, she's acting strangely, not the way I would expect from a member of the public under such circumstances. But I put it down to a clash of cultures again. I've seen the films. All these ruffians having shoot-outs in the street in America. Violent death must be as common as falling off a log. Though I'm not too sure just how often that happens – unless you're a lumberjack or something similar. I note my mind is working overtime. This isn't unusual when I'm faced with such a case.

Bleakly thumps the door with his gloved fist, and soon we hear footsteps from within the church.

'Who's there?' A timid voice sounds behind the door.

It's the murderer, let me in so I can butcher you, I want to say. Well, such a stupid question.

'It's Inspector Grasby,' I say instead.

The reverend unbolts the church door, and we make our way inside. It's a cosy little church, just the job for a village like Elderby, I think. The usual row of pews, an off-set pulpit and a tiny but nicely carved rood screen under a great stained-glass window. It depicts the figure of a man slouched beside a river, his head propped up by one arm. He looks a bit like that thinker chap in the statue.

'Saint Thomas,' says the vicar. 'Lost in his doubts.' He smiles at the window benignly. I see a trace of sympathy.

My father has told me about this. Since the Great War, it appears some men of the cloth have begun to lose their faith. Of course, they plod on for the salary and the free accommodation. But in essence they don't believe a word they're saying. Personally, I think this is damnable. They should jolly well be given the order of the boot. What next, religious atheists? I'm in accord with my father on such matters; though I rather think he'd have them all burned at the stake.

The Reverend Croucher sits down on a pew. 'I've been praying since I found poor Mr Starr. A terrible thing. Nobody should have to witness such tragedy.' He sobs gently.

From this I conclude that he's more concerned that he stumbled on the unfortunate American than he is for the victim or his family. I saw this type of thing in the war too, you know. 'Oh, why me?', while some poor sod's lying face down in the mud riddled with bullets. It gets my goat, I can tell you.

'It's time to pull yourself together, Vicar,' say I. 'You're the only witness we have, to date. So, you need to tell us everything you heard or saw. Even things that you might not think are of any relevance at all. There's a good chap.'

Croucher looks up at me as though I've just urinated in the font. But I've no time for self-consumed clergymen. I have a murder on my hands.

'Please tell me what you were doing just before you found the body.'

'You are rather brusque,' says the vicar. 'I'm feeling quite fragile, Inspector.'

Huh!

'I understand, but we must think of the victim and his family. So, tell us all about it.' I turn to Bleakly. 'You take this down, Sergeant, if you don't mind.'

I've never quite got the hang of writing on a notebook

without something to lean on. It just turns out to be a dreadful scribble. I've watched many colleagues scratching away with pens and pencils over the years with excellent results. Leaves me quite envious.

Looking as though he's been asked to move the entire church three inches to the left, Bleakly produces his notebook from the top pocket of his tunic, licks the end of his pencil in a less than appealing manner, and coughs. At least he's managed to stay awake, I suppose.

'I arrived here just before four. I try to observe a different part of the Matins service on occasion. It's simply impossible to do the whole thing. One wouldn't get any sleep at all.'

'Lauds, then?'

'Yes, Inspector. How clever of you to know such a thing.'

Lauds is usually at five in the morning. But it's quite normal to have it earlier in the winter.

'Please continue, Vicar.'

'I always walk to the church. I think it's part of the whole thing, you see.'

'Walk from where?'

'From the vicarage in the village.'

'Just behind the butcher shop,' interjects Bleakly.

'Was anyone about, Your Reverence?'

He thinks for a moment. 'I did see Mr Whitmore in his little van. He's the fishmonger, you know. Goes to Whitby very early every morning for fish.'

'Indeed. What then?'

'I walked up the hill to the church with my little torch.'

'Nothing unusual? You didn't see anyone else?'

'Ah, now there was something. I heard some foxes – they get up to all sorts during the hours of darkness. One dreads to think.'

It appears that mating foxes are too much for the vicar. Preserve us.

'You've heard foxes before?'

'Oh yes, many times, Inspector.'

'Where did this noise come from?'

'Up on the ridge. Why do you ask?'

'What time would this be?'

'Around four, I think.'

I look at Bleakly, who makes a face.

'Then what did you do?'

'I went about my devotions. That's why I was here, after all.'

'I'm a bit confused,' say I. 'What made you go outside?'

'I pray with my eyes open, you know. I'm of the belief that closing one's eyes to the Lord isn't a good thing.'

'And what time would this be?'

'I know exactly because I looked at my watch. It was twenty past four.' Croucher bows his head.

'Still doesn't explain why you left the church?'

'I saw the flash of light.' He nods to the stained-glass window. 'At first, I thought it must be lightning. Though I wondered if I was having a deeper experience, if I'm honest.'

'But you weren't.'

'No. But I was sure I heard voices. You must understand, Inspector. The walls of this place are very thick. One only hears sounds from outside at a remove. But I was convinced that I'd heard people talking.'

I thought for a moment.

'Tell me, how often are you here at that time in the morning?'

'Not as often as I should be, I must admit. Maybe four or five times a year, I'm ashamed to say.'

'Any pattern to these early prayers?'

'In what way?'

'I mean, do you have something like a roster, you know, a schedule of some kind?'

'Oh, I see. No, not at all. It all happens when the spirit takes me, if you know what I mean.'

I don't believe a word of it. But one thing is clear: I think the good vicar of Elderby has much to thank the Lord for. It sounds as though he very nearly walked into a murderer – more than one, judging by the voices.

'And these voices were coming from where?'

'Like I say, it's hard to tell. I just went out to have a look around with my torch. There was nothing at the entrance, so I decided to have a wander round the back – up at the edge. Well, you know the rest, Inspector.' He swallowed a sob. 'Then I ran back in and called the police station. We have a phone in the vestry.'

'The operator transfers any calls to my home, sir. Out of hours, and that,' says Bleakly.

'I see. And apart from poor Mr Starr, you saw nothing?'

'I was in a bit of a flap, to be honest.' The vicar puts a large hanky to his nose and blows prodigiously. 'I doubt I'll ever be able to be here alone at night again.'

That's it. He's in floods of tears now. But they're still not for murdered Mr Starr, but rather himself. I suppose all of us are a bit like that. We can only take in the world from our own experience. Empathy is a hard-won quality, don't you think?

I leave Sergeant Bleakly comforting the vicar and go out for a cigarette and to exercise the old grey matter in the biting chill. I find that tobacco is a great aid to detection. It focuses the mind much better than alcohol, the favourite of many of my colleagues. I hear they're harping on that smoking is a dangerous habit. I'm here to tell you, if it hadn't been for cigarettes and tea during the war, Hitler would be parading up the Mall straight into Buckingham Palace. I'm sure of it.

Working things through in my mind, I know that the big guns will arrive shortly. Thankfully, murder is a rare enough occurrence in this part of the world that it merits the attention of senior police officers. But following yesterday's events at Holly House, we'll be knee-deep in superintendents after breakfast, and any onus on yours truly will be at an end. Just the ticket.

I think back to my meeting with Dr and Mr Starr. Apart from him being an American, they seemed quite a normal couple.

Nothing much will happen here until reinforcements arrive. So, I decide to wander over to the van and ask Deedee more about the American. But when I get there, there is nobody in the van. Deedee has gone.

13

It doesn't take me long to conclude that Deedee will have taken it upon herself to tell Dr Starr that her husband has died. That's bad form, you know. And I can't say I'm happy about it. Remembering that Bleakly told me where the Starrs live, I start the van and am soon off down the slippery hill. I know our sergeant won't be pleased but he's doing a sterling job comforting Croucher, so his work isn't in vain.

Back on little Main Street, it doesn't take me long to locate the lane where the Starrs have made their home. And it's idyllic, too. A picture-perfect cottage, with a little trellis round the door where no doubt roses grow in the summer, a thatched roof deep in snow, mullioned windows frosted like something from a Dickens novel. If you happen to be a chocolate manufacturer, get someone to paint this place for one of your boxes. Absolutely charming.

I walk to the door and am about to knock when Deedee appears from behind it.

'Gee, I'm sorry, Inspector Grasby. I couldn't bear the thought of Elizabeth not knowing what has happened.'

In all honesty, I'm quite relieved that she took it upon herself to break this dreadful news to Dr Starr. But she's overstepped the mark, and I must point that out.

'Now, listen here, Miss Dean,' I say in my official voice. 'You're still a student, and I don't know what happens in New York, but here in England we have protocols, and you've just breached them.'

She smiles at me sadly with her great blue eyes. 'I know, please forgive me.'

'Forgiven.' But I can't give in to a pretty face. 'And I hope you've learned your lesson. Don't be running off half-cocked again. I want to speak with Doctor Starr. How's she taking it?'

Deedee steps aside and I make my way into the hall.

'Oh, you know. I think you call it the stiff upper lip.'

That makes sense. Outward signs of emotion are frowned upon in this country. I remember a young captain during the war surrounded by dead colleagues. He tried to rally us with the kind of thing the skipper would say to a flagging cricket team: 'Come on, chaps, one more push.'

Deedee leads me through to a cosy little lounge. There are books in every nook and cranny, and a hint of rose blossom in the air. Elizabeth Starr is working a handkerchief between both hands, clearly distressed. She's wearing a red silk dressing gown. A small electric fire buzzes at her feet. I see the stain of tears on her face.

'I'm so sorry, Doctor Starr. You have my sincere condolences.' I have my trilby in one hand. It's still bloody awkward, even though Deedee has broken the bad news.

'Please, take a seat, Inspector,' says Dr Starr. She looks bewildered, and no wonder. 'Can I get you some tea?'

I could do with a cup, I must admit. But it would be a rum do to expect the grieving widow to jump to and get the kettle on. I'm not that insensitive, you know.

'I'll make tea,' volunteers Deedee.

'Good. In that case, two sugars and just a splash of milk

for me, please,' say I. Well, it's already been a difficult, cold morning.

As my American intern dashes off on tea duty, Dr Starr smiles at me wanly. I'm lodged in an armchair, and it's a comfy one too. Some chairs you just sink into, but this one is nicely supportive without being uncomfortable. I'm fed up of slouching on my father's antiquated chesterfield suite. But I manage to refrain from asking the newly widowed doctor where she bought it.

'I can't take it in, Inspector.' She's looking in my direction, but straight through me at the same time.

'Tragic, just tragic,' I say with all the empathy I can muster. It's hard for police officers in these circumstances. On a human level, of course I feel for her. But one gets so used to this stuff it becomes second nature.

'My husband was a complex man.'

'Was he? In what way?' I ask. Normally, I have to tease information like this from a victim's family. But it seems the good doctor is ready to talk.

'I suppose it was the war.'

'It made an impression on us all.'

'But you managed to move on. I'm sad to say that Chuck was never able to do that.'

'Why was that?'

'He simply couldn't get over it. It's all he thought about. He was writing a book, you know.'

'Jolly good, I like a good war story,' say I before thinking. Damn.

'It was an exposé.'

'Of what?'

'D-Day. He thought men were just led to the slaughter. It was terribly mismanaged.'

This sets me thinking. Governments can be quite touchy

when it comes to things like this. I wonder if poor Chuck wasn't in above his head.

'How many people knew about his writing, Doctor?'

'Elizabeth, please. A few of his old pals back in the States. He still kept in touch with them.'

First mistake. If you're working on something that's going to make a president or prime minister look like a clot, it's best you do it quietly. Once it's out, you should be quite safe. But if they can stop you before you get down to the publisher – well, things can get tricky. I lost my faith in politicians a long time ago. It's hard not to when they're sitting in Downing Street with a good sherry whilst you're busy dodging death round every corner.

'I say, would you mind if I had a look at what he's written? It might help us find who did this dreadful thing.'

Dr Starr looks suddenly alarmed. 'You don't think he was killed because of the book, do you? I'd supposed he was the victim of one of these thieves – you know, all the robberies that have been happening around the village. And that poor man at Holly House yesterday.'

Ah, difficult.

'It's hard to say, Elizabeth. But I'm afraid we mustn't discount any possibilities at the moment.'

'Of course. How stupid of me to jump to such a conclusion. You must see the book. It's all in his study across the hall.' She makes to get up.

'No, please don't trouble yourself. I'll go and have a look. As long as you don't mind if I poke about a bit? I realize how insensitive this sounds. But there may be something crucial, and the sooner we see it, the better.'

'I understand. Please, do what you must, Inspector. I never interfered with his work – it wasn't my place. But now . . .' Her voice tailed off.

'Thank you.' I excuse myself and leave in search of Starr's study.

I don't have to find the right room. Deedee appears out of the door directly across from the lounge.

'I say, what are you up to? You won't find the tea in there.'

For a split second, Deedee looks flustered. But she quickly regains her composure. 'Please don't be angry. I was looking for a photograph. It's of the three of us. I didn't want to ask Elizabeth. Just something to remember him by, that's all.' A fat tear meanders down her pink cheek.

I knew it! I remember the look that passed between them yesterday in the Hanging Beggar. Methinks Charles Starr was even more complex than his wife thinks. I'm beginning to think the same of Deedee.

'You and I will speak about this when we get back to the station,' say I in a low voice.

I leave Deedee to get the tea as I go for a rummage in Starr's study.

It's not what I expected at all. Papers are lying hither and yon, books cast about the floor, an overturned waste-paper basket and some folders cast to the four winds. Two drawers are lying open, devoid of contents. Either Chuck was bloody untidy or there's a more sinister reason. Surely Deedee isn't responsible for this?

I dash back out of the room and lean into the lounge.

'I'm sorry, Elizabeth. Can I ask you to help me for a moment, please?'

Dr Starr gets to her feet and follows me from the room. We stand in the study, and she looks about sadly.

'I'm sure your husband didn't leave things like this, Elizabeth.'

'He did. I know I said I didn't interfere. But I tried to tidy up in here a couple of times. He got so angry. We had a very happy marriage, Inspector. These were just about the only times we ever had words.'

'Gosh. He was so well turned out,' I think out loud, then bite my lip.

'I know. It's the strangest thing. I just left him to it after that. I suppose I've always seen the chaos in this room as a mirror of his mind. Or maybe I'm leaning into my psychology lectures at university too much. It's easy to find something that's not really there. But he was troubled by what he'd seen. This could just have been his way of coping.'

Just as well I don't cope like this. My father would have my guts for garters. He inspects my room regularly. He's been looking for signs of debauchery ever since he arrived home early from a holiday in Devon, only to find his son déshabillé with a member of the opposite sex. Goodness, you'd have thought I'd strangled the Archbishop of York.

'What are you thinking, Inspector?' says Elizabeth.

'Just trying to work through things,' I lie. 'Tell me, where did Mr Starr keep his manuscript?'

She closes her eyes against the past tense, and I feel like a real oaf.

'Please forgive me.'

'You have your job to do, Inspector. Never mind me.' Elizabeth walks over to a bureau. Unlike everything else in this room, it's remarkably tidy. 'He always keeps the manuscript in here.' She opens a narrow drawer underneath an old Underwood typewriter that's sitting on an ink-blot pad. 'Gosh!' she puts her hand to her mouth.

The drawer is empty, save for a fountain pen.

'Would he have put it anywhere else?'

'He might.'

I search about, checking drawers and cupboards that aren't already open. There's no manuscript to be seen.

'I don't understand it,' says Elizabeth. 'He was working on it when I arrived back from the surgery at lunchtime yesterday. I put my head in the door to tell him I was home.'

'Your bedroom. Might it be there?'

'I doubt it, but I'll have a look.'

'If you wouldn't mind.'

As I watch her trek up the narrow flight of stairs, Deedee appears from the kitchen with a tray.

'Did you see a manuscript in here when you were poking about for that photograph?' say I.

'No, why should I?'

'What a shambles, eh? I thought he looked like a neat and tidy chap.'

I follow her into the lounge. Deedee puts down a tray of cups, saucers, a teapot, little milk jug, strainer and a small plate of biscuits on the occasional table.

'I know. It's odd, isn't it? I asked him about that once. He just laughed. Maybe it's a symptom of what happened to him in the war. Who knows?'

We sit down and Deedee plays mother. She's handing me my tea when Dr Starr arrives back in the lounge.

'I can't find it anywhere. I've even checked the box room. Though why he'd have put it there, I don't know.' She sits down heavily and bursts into tears. 'Do you think we've had burglars?'

If they've been in the study, who could tell? 'Well, it's gone somewhere,' I say.

Deedee is comforting her as I take a slurp of tea. It's most welcome. I manage to grab a biscuit as Dr Starr gets a hold of herself.

'Can I ask, were you aware that your husband wasn't in the house early this morning?'

'No, I wasn't. I woke briefly at three, so I knew he wasn't

133

in bed. But that's not unusual. He didn't sleep well, you see, Inspector. He always started working early in the morning. It wasn't until Daisy arrived that I realized he was gone. For good, as it turns out.' She starts sobbing again.

I'm mulling it all over with a custard cream when a phone rings. As Deedee is still fussing around Elizabeth, I volunteer to answer. And though it's been an odd morning, it just gets odder.

'Grasby, is that you?' Superintendent Juggers's voice is unmistakable.

'Yes, sir.'

'Get yourself back to the station, quick-smart.'

'York?' say I, thoroughly confused.

'No, not bloody York. Elderby, man!'

'Where are you?' I ask, but the phone's dead.

14

I hurry off, making my apologies to Dr Starr. I've left Deedee with her for company. But I'm strangely troubled by this. I can't see any possible way she could have smuggled Chuck Starr's manuscript from the study, though she looked rather shifty when I confronted her in the hall. And why on earth would she want to? Thoughts of her reaction to this news and how she coped at Holly House when a chap fell down the chimney give me pause for thought.

My goodness, this is turning into a right pickle.

I remember I've left Bleakly with the vicar. But he should be in attendance at the murder scene. It would be bad form to leave the constables from the Village Oafs Division in sole charge of a murder victim and a man of the cloth. He'll be fine.

Back at the station I spy a jolly nice Jaguar XK120 sitting in the car park. I stop the old station Morris beside it and admire its sweeping lines. Surely Juggers isn't cutting about in one of these beauties? I try to picture his bulbous frame plonked in this wonderful machine. I wish I had one – like driving a bloody Renoir.

I enter the station to find a man in a brown dustcoat at the front desk.

'You'll be Grasby,' he says to me.

'Who are you?' I ask.

'Lumley, Martin Lumley.' He reaches out a calloused hand for me to shake. 'I'm the caretaker. They've asked me to fill in here – answer the phone, and the like.' He looks proud to be at the centre of operations in Elderby police station. At least he can speak, which is an improvement on my first encounter here.

'Good-oh,' I say. 'Have you seen a stout chap? About yea tall and broad?' I do my best to approximate Juggers's dimensions with outstretched hands.

'I'm right here, you cheeky bugger.' The voice comes from nowhere. But when I look to my right, there he is, my superintendent. I've never seen Juggers out of uniform before – I barely recognize him, in fact. He's in a dark blue pinstripe suit, with a waistcoat straining at the seams across his formidable gut.

He holds the door open for me and I'm back in the station corridor. There's a strong smell of cigars, not something one expects in a rural police station, but an odour that accompanies Juggers everywhere.

'In here,' he announces without ceremony.

It's my first time in this office. It's much grander than the sergeants' room. There's a large oak desk and thick, black velvet curtains. The decor is a cut above too, with cream walls and the odd photograph of ancient-looking coppers sporting handlebar moustaches dotted here and there. I take a note to commandeer this place. If I survive this encounter with Juggers and a louche-looking man who's sitting behind the desk, a cigarette in a long holder at his lips, I'll move in. He's about my age, perhaps a bit younger. The stranger's hair is slicked back and he's wearing a monocle, of all things. Dressed in an evening suit, minus the bow tie. How odd.

'Do take a seat, Grasby,' he says in between puffs.

He's an old Etonian. You know the type, so sure of themselves it's almost crushing. I recognize him for what he is in much the same way I did young Damnish – Bo Peep or whatever they call the poor lad. I'd bet my last ha'penny on it. Mind you, I'd bet my last ha'penny on just about anything, as you know.

Juggers is sitting beside me now, which is both unsettling and comforting. Much depends on his mood. One could be forgiven for thinking I'm on the carpet for some misdeed or other, but I can't think what I've done wrong. After all, our unfortunate man in the chimney was likely there before I arrived in Elderby. And as for poor Starr, well, what was one to do? Though this chap with the cigarette holder looks like no senior officer I've ever met.

'Now, you must be wondering who I am, Grasby?'

Eh, just a bit.

'Yes, sir. Quite intrigued, I must say.'

'Well, I'm not going to tell you, I'm afraid.'

Oh-oh, it's the slippery mob. I should have known. I came across intelligence officers during the war. I should have recognized the demeanour straight away. Now we're in bother.

'We're in a bit of a fix, if I'm honest.' This mystery man takes another puff of his cigarette.

'Oh?'

'Bloody awkward,' says Juggers, adding to the tension.

'I know you're aware of the incident earlier this morning. Not to mention Damnish's dead man in the chimney. It's bad luck, old boy. Really, it is.'

'The body from Holly House was taken to York mortuary last night, and I've just left Mr Starr's widow – as you know, sir.' I turn to face Juggers, but he's ignoring me.

'Yes, that's the first thing I want to speak about. Did you give anything away, at all?' This toff's voice could cut diamonds.

'What do you mean?'

'Oh – maybe a theory as to what happened to Mr Starr, that type of thing?'

'I haven't got a clue what happened to him, other than he was strangled and stabbed, sir.'

'Does Doctor Starr know this?'

'Not exactly. I didn't think it was appropriate to go into the details of her husband's gruesome death. She's just coming to terms with the fact it's happened, sir.'

'Jolly good. Just the ticket.' He pulls the remains of the cigarette from the holder and stubs it out in an ashtray. 'How did she seem – Doctor Starr, I mean?'

'Very upset.'

'But you didn't mention that it was murder?'

'Well, yes. What's one to say?' A thought crosses my mind. 'In fact, I didn't impart the death message myself, sir.'

'Who did, Sergeant Bleakly?'

This could be awkward. 'It was a young intern.'

'A what?' Juggers looks at me as though I've started spouting Latin.

'A student, sir. Here to learn about policing in England. From Yale University in America, in fact.'

'You sent a slip of a girl to tell a doctor her husband was deceased?' Juggers shakes his head, his face turning that familiar red hue. 'I don't know about the school, but their locks are rubbish. Some bugger broke into my brother's house as easy as catch-your-auntie. He swears by them.'

Poor Juggers hasn't grasped the concept of Yale University, but our slippery chap has. I can see it in his face. Poor Deedee. But one must know when it's time for a piece of pass-on-the-blame.

'I know, sir. I was livid when I found out. I was interviewing the vicar.' I say this to the mystery inquisitor. 'The young woman's been left to run wild about the place. Bleakly doesn't have her under control at all. I'm told she took it on herself to tell Doctor Starr what had happened.'

'He's a solid bloke, is Bleakly,' says Juggers.

'When he's awake.'

'What do you mean?'

'Well, he rather drops off now and then, don't you know?'

Juggers is about to probe the matter of Sergeant Bleakly's narcolepsy, when he's interrupted.

'Never mind about all that now.' Mr X looks at Juggers. 'We'll be able to convince Doctor Starr that this was all a terrible accident. But what about the vicar? Is he a gullible man, d'you think?'

They've found my area of expertize: the clergy.

'I should think so, sir. I mean, vicars tend to be on the airy-fairy side, putting it mildly.'

'So much so that he could be convinced that Mr Starr suffered from some awful medical condition?'

'One where the symptoms are stabbing and hanging yourself? I'm not too sure anyone is that gullible, sir.'

'Don't get smart, Grasby.' Juggers looks as though he's going to punch me in the face.

The man across the desk leans forward. 'Now listen here, Grasby. I'm telling you this in the knowledge that it won't go beyond these four walls.'

'You have my word, sir.'

'What happened here last night is a matter of national

importance. Not only that, but the very safety of the country is at stake. I must ask you to do something that will go against your every instinct as a police officer.'

If he's about to ask me to break the rules, he shouldn't worry too much. It's not something new to yours truly, after all.

'I want you to conduct an investigation into these deaths.'

'I have no problem doing that, sir. Though it's not going to be easy. Mind you, I have a couple of leads.'

'Forget them immediately!'

'Sir?'

'You're going to investigate this case and come to the conclusion that Charles Starr's death was down to entirely natural causes. A rare condition brought on by a mixture of stress and injuries sustained during the war. And as far as the man in the chimney goes, well, we'll just put that down to him being a hapless burglar – paid a heavy price, what? Basically, you can say what you want. You'll be backed one hundred per cent by everyone – the coroner included.'

This takes the biscuit.

'Hang on, sir. Do you mean you want me to go through the motions, when all the time I know it's a lie?'

'Just so, Inspector. Just so.'

Sometimes a chap knows when to shut up and do what he's told. I've never been very good at that, but this is an exception. Though, in order to preserve my own integrity, I feel it's time to put up some token resistance, if only to impress Juggers.

'Well, I must say, this is unexpected. I'm not sure it's my type of thing, to be honest.' I look at my superintendent, who just stares back blankly.

'It's not really a case of you picking and choosing, old boy. I know it's impertinent of me, but it's an order.'

'Damn right it is. You just knuckle down and do what you're told, lad.' Juggers's jowls wobble in agreement.

I ponder this for a moment. 'And the local chaps – what about them? If they're not in on this, they'll soon get suspicious.'

'Don't worry a minute about them. There's going to be a little change in personnel here at the station.'

'Poor Bleakly,' say I.

'He's staying,' says Juggers emphatically. 'Man was with Wingate – he's a hero.'

'Yes, we'll be briefing him too. But he won't know as much as you, so mum's the word.'

'What about Deedee – I mean, Miss Dean?'

'Deedee? I hope you're not becoming overly familiar with that lass.' Juggers actually shakes his fist in my face.

My other interlocutor removes his monocle and rubs his eye wearily. 'She stays, I'm afraid. Just one of these things. But I want you to keep an eye on her.'

'I don't really understand.'

'That's not a first, as we all know to our cost.' Juggers folds his arms.

'Quite simple, old chap. You spend a few days here, come up with some old tosh – believable, mark you – and we wrap things up. Two new constables arrive this afternoon to assist.'

'Aye, special constables,' says Juggers.

'I think we'll need more than a couple of specials to help me here, sir.'

'I don't mean special constables. I mean *special* constables.' Juggers winks at me, which isn't pleasant to witness.

'You mean they'll be chaps like you?' I address the man behind the desk.

'In a manner of speaking, yes. You can trust them implicitly, so don't worry.' He places another cigarette in his long holder. 'I know this goes against the grain for a chap like you, Grasby, I can see that.'

Good, I've done my job well, thinks I.

'You've had a good education, and your service record from the war is exemplary. What school did you go to, old boy?'

'Hymers.'

He makes a face. 'Really, how nice.' But I know he's never heard of the place.

Mr X hands me a piece of card with a number written on it. 'You can call this at any time, day or night, if you have to.' He reaches under the desk. 'You better have this, too.' He hands me a Webley pistol. 'There's a shoulder holster and some extra rounds in the desk drawer. But don't you go off pretending to be the new sheriff in town. For emergencies only, got it?'

'Yes, sir.' I gulp. I'm not keen on guns. Not since I had no choice other than to carry one, that is. 'I must admit to being quite concerned now – as to the safety of Miss Dean, I mean.'

'She can look after herself, I assure you,' says X. 'No need to worry about her. But keep tabs on her. Let me know on that number if she's up to something.' He stands and reaches out to shake my hand. 'Best of British, old boy. I'm sure this service will stand you in good stead, eh, Juggers?'

'Why, of course, sir.'

We watch our mystery man as he makes to leave.

'Can I have a word with Inspector Grasby before we go, sir?'

'Of course, Juggers. I must visit the little boys' room before I drive back down to York. I hope that damnable snow isn't batting again, what?'

When the door closes, Juggers leans into me.

'Now, lad. You listen and listen good, you hear?'

'Yes, sir.' Now I am really getting worried.

'We've both seen these chaps in our days in the army. You know as well as I do, they'd push their mother off a cliff if the situation demanded. Ruthless, they are. Aye, and like as not, they have to be. You do what you've been told and keep your head down. Get this done. But don't trust anyone. I don't care who you think they are, they probably aren't.'

'Sir, I'm beginning to get rather concerned.'

'Me too, lad. Me too.' He pats my shoulder before struggling to his feet. 'Good luck, Grasby.' This is said as though it's the last time he'll see me. 'The last thing I'd do is call that number, by the way. Just a piece of advice.'

'Can I ask a question, sir?'

'Aye, ask what you like.'

'Can I say no to all this and just come back to York with you? Surely one of their own chaps would be more suited to this . . . this calumny.'

'I've no doubt they would. But you're a police officer, folk know you. We're keeping secrets here, and there mustn't be room for speculation. A real detective stands out in the crowd. No room for imitations. And no, you don't have a choice.' He gets to the door and turns on his heel. 'Before I forget, a message from Stubby Watts. He says he tried to tell you before you left, but you rushed off.'

'Yes?'

'When you're going uphill in that Austin, you have to

reverse, got it? Something wrong with the gears, I don't know.'

'Great!'

'You'll be a'right.'

'It's not goodbye, sir, it's au revoir,' I say jokingly.

'Aye, that's the spirit, lad. Goodbye.'

Juggers's demeanour leaves me in the biggest state of funk I've encountered since the Germans were trying to kill me.

Bugger!

15

I must admit that all this cloak and dagger stuff has me utterly foxed. I can't think what on earth they are trying to hide. The simple fact is that two men lie dead. I know one of them was murdered, for sure. And given recent events, doubts as to the fate of the unfortunate chap in the Holly House chimney must now be called into question even more. The problem is nobody will pay the price. I don't know what the circumstances are, but I'm sure Mr X does. For a reason I can't explain, I'm beginning to wonder if he was responsible. The Grasby intuition isn't to be trifled with, you know.

My mind keeps going back to Martha Thornlie and her statement. Did Lady Damnish have a conversation with the intruder? It's a puzzle. But one I must ignore, it seems.

I've heard all this king and country stuff before. In my experience, it usually leads to the pointless deaths of young men and women, and nothing changes. I know I've signed up for this, but I'm not happy about it. I'm astounded that Juggers is complicit in it all. I thought he was as solid as the Rock of Gibraltar. You can misjudge people, you know.

Talking about misjudgement, where on earth does

Deedee fit in? I've been told to keep tabs on her. Why? She's an intern. A well-qualified one, I grant you – but what is it about her I need to watch? Surely the best course of action would have been to dispatch her to Northallerton or some other awful place. For the life of me, I can't understand it. Probably her father's influence, I think. Money talks – even across the breadth of the Atlantic Ocean.

There's a knock at the door. Caretaker Lumley appears, bearing a large tin mug.

'Thought you might need this, sir.' He hands me the tea. 'I've made it army-style. I hope it's to your taste.'

'I should say so. Thanks, old boy.'

Army-style means that the tea is strong enough to stand a spoon up in, with the tiniest splash of milk and as much sugar as can be found. I take a sip, and it's just what I need, even though the exigencies of rationing have affected the sugar content. It's the strangest thing, you know. I used to take three sugars in my tea. Now, on the rare occasions I've been able to enjoy this indulgence, the drink tastes horribly sweet – almost undrinkable. It just shows you: one can get used to anything. But this goes down a treat – it's the shock, don't you know.

'You an old army man, Lumley?' I have to make some small-talk with a chap who brought me a beverage.

'Yes indeed, sir. Both bust-ups. I got a bullet in my shoulder for my troubles.'

'Damn bad luck.'

'In a training exercise, would you believe? Bad enough getting shot by the enemy, never mind your own side.'

'I should cocoa,' I say. But as any soldier knows, training is probably the most dangerous period of your time in the army. Overzealous NCOs combined with raw young lads anxious to make an impression. The whole thing's miserably dangerous from the off.

I note that Lumley is hovering about, shifting from foot to foot.

'Something to say, Lumley?'

'Well, yes, sir. I hope you won't mind if I'm a bit impertinent. But I thought you would like to know.'

'Know what?'

'That chap with the Jaguar motor car, sir. I know him.'

Well, here's a turn up for the books.

'Who is he?'

'He was a young subaltern back at the end of the war. The Right Honourable Twiston Cummins, sir. His father is the Earl of Harpenden. Of course, I recognized him the minute he arrived, though I'm sure he'd no idea who I was. He's filled out a bit, but not much.'

That much is true. This Cummins chap has the build of a salamander.

'What kind of chap is he?'

'You know, sir. Just like any of the gentry. Decent enough to us lads. A bit uppity when things aren't going his way, mind.' Lumley looks into the middle distance, as though he's remembering something.

'Spit it out. There's a good chap.'

'Well, it's strange, sir. But by all rights, he shouldn't be here.'

'Why on earth not?'

'He copped it, sir.'

'Dead?'

'That's the impression I was under. Shot in the bocage, he was.'

'Bloody hell, that sounds painful.'

'You know, the fields with them big hedges in Normandy.

147

We saw him carried off by some Germans, looked as dead as a dodo. I got quite a shock when he appeared earlier.'

'Well, you would,' say I. 'How odd.'

'Gave me a shiver, it did.'

'I don't wonder.'

'Anyhow, I'll leave you to your tea, sir.'

With that, Lumley is off, and I'm left even more puzzled. Everything has suddenly become most perplexing. I'm to conduct a ghost investigation on the orders of a man who is himself apparently dead. Though he was very much alive when he sat in this chair only minutes ago. I can still smell his cigarettes. Some posh brand I vaguely recognize – a very distinctive aroma.

I'm not one for spectres and the like. Though I do remember an incident in York Minster. I must have been about nine or ten. My father was to have an audience with the archbishop. I was told to sit in the minster and pray for my own soul. As far as my father was concerned, I was damned from a young age. It was boring, and after thumbing through a hymn book, I became rather restive. Just as I thought I was about to burst with tedium, I spied an old man standing a few yards away, looking straight up at the magnificent hammer-beam ceiling. I noted that something was off about him. He didn't look right, for some reason – too serene, somehow.

I sat observing him for a few moments, then the temptation to make myself known to him was too much. I put my hand to my mouth and coughed as loudly as I could. The sound echoed around the great church, empty, save he and I. Just after my cough, I heard a door open, and my father appeared. I looked back to where this man had been standing and he'd disappeared – gone, vanished into thin air.

I remember the feeling I had that day. And the events of this morning brought it back vividly. Something that doesn't feel right rarely is. I don't like the manifestation of spectres, no matter how corporeal they appear.

I decide that I need some fresh air to try to make sense of what's going on. I've already seen the east end of the village, so I decide to take a wander to discover what wonders lie to the west of Elderby. I'm halfway out of the door when I remember something: the Webley.

There's a murderer about, after all. This cloak and dagger stuff has left me as jumpy as a young fawn. I feel the familiar oily cold of the weapon. But once I manage to manoeuvre the shoulder holster in place, and slip the handgun in, I must admit to feeling much more reassured, though I'd very much hoped I'd never have to carry such a thing again. Once my jacket is on, there's thankfully no unsightly, telltale bulge to indicate that it's there. It's all to do with the cut, you know.

I set off for a wander, telling Lumley I'm going to have a gander at something important. Doesn't do to let folk know you're slacking.

It's turning into one of these bright, frosty mornings where everything seems new and fresh. The sky is a flawless blue, but there's no heat in the winter sun. I hear corvid cries in the trees as I head back on to the main thoroughfare. Idly, I wonder if Cecil is about. In a few strides – being careful not to slip on the icy footpath – I leave the last dwellings of Elderby behind.

At this moment I remember that poor old Bleakly is still up at the church. Oh well, such is life. He can wander back to the station, if he wants. Though I can picture him lying fast asleep on a pew.

I happen upon a narrow lane. It leads down to a little copse of trees – ash, I think. All bare and twisted, the frost coating their trunks and branches sparkling in the unexpected sunshine. I wander down to have a poke about.

There's nothing I enjoy more than being in woodland; there's something elemental about it. After all, us English were woodland dwellers for centuries, and our Teutonic ancestors were the same. I firmly believe that our blood – our past – shapes us all. If you think about it, birds can fly halfway across the world to where they were hatched. Salmon are the same, taking on all kinds of hardships to make it back to the rivers in which they were spawned. Now, they've not been sat behind some desk and told what to do, how to navigate. No, nothing of the kind. These creatures feel something that drives them on, something going back for generation upon generation.

Oh yes, I always feel at my most secure and content in the woods.

I breathe deeply. It's all here, the scent of the soil, hard in the chill, the way that cold weather smells, bringing back the memory of childhood Christmases, sledging and slipping about on frozen ponds, the hint of coal fires on the air. Yes, this is just the roborative I need. I've always had a good nose. Somehow, this sense triggers the memory like none other. Already, I see my mother busy with the Christmas goose she's about to cremate. When it's ready, my father will carve, swearing under his breath as he goes. No wonder he fell out with old King George. Still, those were happy days.

I take another deep draw of the frosty air. But something's jarring; not a natural aroma, more like cheap cologne, harsh and offensive. The sensation is sudden, but it's there.

A twig snaps, and I turn to face the noise. But just as I do, something solid catches me on the forehead. I feel as though I've been kicked by a horse. I'm stumbling backwards now, the bare woodland swimming before my eyes. I fall back on the root of a tree, hitting my head on the hard-packed snowy ground as I land. I should be scared, but a strange calmness washes over me.

I gaze up. Sunlight is flickering between the cloying dark branches of the trees all around. But something dark looms before me, blocking out this hazy vision. I feel dizzy, and the world slips away.

16

I come to, with a splitting headache. As I'm trying to
focus, I can hear the sound of struggle. A woman cries
out, then there's the rustling thud of quick, heavy steps
fading into the distance. I can hear someone speaking at
my side.

Though it's bloody painful, I manage to force myself up
on one elbow. It takes me a second or two to focus, but I
see a figure dressed in a green skirt and red woollen coat
getting unsteadily to her feet.

'Deedee, what on earth?'

'Thank goodness you're OK.' She breathes a genuine
sigh of relief. 'Just as well I was following you.'

I can see her blue eyes now; her face is etched with
concern.

'I say, what the bloody hell is going on? Why were you
following me?' These words are tumbling from my mouth.

'I was trying to catch up with you when I saw you walking out of the village.'

'Damn it all, did you wallop me?'

'No! The exact opposite.' Deedee's eyes are wide. 'I lost
you in the woods, but then I heard someone call out.'

It's coming back to me now. The hard object against my
forehead, falling backwards, the shadow.

'This guy, I don't know, he was standing over you with a club in his hand. I grabbed a rock and hit him over the back of the head with it.'

'Jolly well done,' say I.

Deedee takes a deep breath. 'I think he was going to kill you, Inspector Grasby.'

My head is still spinning as I try to take in what's just happened. 'Did he take off?'

'Whoever he was, he has a hard head. I know I hurt him, I saw blood running down his neck. He made to go, but I grabbed his leg.'

You should just have let him bugger off, thinks I.

'Did you get a look at him?'

She shrugs. 'No, not really. He was big – tall, you know. He had one of those caps you English like so much. It was kind of hard to see his face. Dark stubble on his chin, short – unshaven. I don't know. It all happened so quickly.'

'A flat cap?'

'That's what they're called, yes.'

It feels like my brain is throbbing now. I put my hand to my forehead. I can feel the slick warmth of my own blood.

'We need to get you some help, Inspector.'

'Yes, I do feel a bit off-colour, to be honest.'

Deedee helps me struggle to my feet. I feel very dizzy, but she's surprisingly strong for a young woman. The dark, skeletal trees of winter are still swimming before my eyes as we take the first few steps back to the village.

Suddenly, something dawns on me.

'Can you use a gun, Deedee? A pistol, I mean?'

'I'm an American, of course I can.'

I produce the Webley that did me absolutely no good at all when I was attacked.

'Golly! Where did you . . . ?'

'Never mind that, this big bounder could still be hanging about. If I should be overcome by this rascal on the way back, you know it's there. Don't hesitate,' say I.

I'm sorry, but if some great lump of a chap with a grudge is out for mischief, it's us against him. We must make bloody sure we prevail!

With Deedee's help, I make it out of the wood and back on to the streets of Elderby. It takes a while, but we return to the police station, yours truly feeling as though I've been run over by a small lorry.

Deedee tries to guide me into Bleakly's lair, but I indicate the door to the plush office in which I met Juggers and this mystery Cummins chap.

'Oh no, nobody is allowed in there, Inspector,' says Deedee. 'Sergeant Bleakly is adamant about it.'

'Bleakly can go to hell!' say I. 'I'm in charge here, not him. And if I'm to run this murder investigation, it'll be done from this office.'

I'm at my worst when I'm not feeling just so. My goodness, it's barely ten o'clock and already I've stared into the eyes of a murdered man, consoled a grieving widow, been given the strangest remit by a member of Her Majesty's security service and my old boss, then, to top it all, been whacked over the head by some mystery assailant. I dread to think where I'll be come dinnertime.

I'm settled back behind the big desk in my new office. 'I need some ice and a couple of aspirin,' I say to Deedee. There's a duck-egg-sized lump appearing on my forehead.

'It's the weather for ice, and I can do the aspirin,' says she. 'I always have some in my bag, just in case.'

She dashes off. No sooner has she gone than Bleakly appears through the door, without even the courtesy of a knock. He brings with him a cold blast from the corridor. He looks me up and down, a gurn on his long face.

'Where did you get to?' he says. 'Anyhow, you shouldn't be in here.'

'I beg your pardon?' say I. 'I'll be where the bloody hell I want to be. Yes, and in future I'll expect some courtesy from you, Bleakly.'

He raises one eyebrow. 'So, that's the way of it, is it?'

'Yes, it damn well is!' I lower my voice. 'Come in and close the door.'

He does as he's bid and stands before me like a great streak of misery.

'Now, listen here, Elphinstone. I've been put in charge of investigating the deaths of Mr Starr and this chap up the chimney at Holly House. I'll expect your full cooperation.' I eye him up, conscious of the fact I've been told he's in on the whole thing – well, part of it, at least.

'What's happened to your head?'

'I was attacked in the woods. I must say, this village appears to be out of control, Bleakly. A man dead yesterday, another murder before breakfast and an assault just after. What on earth have you been doing?'

Bleakly pulls out a chair and sits down on it wearily. 'I spoke to Superintendent Juggers, sir. I know the *position* in which we find ourselves.'

I'm leery here. Juggers and his aristocratic pal were less than specific on Bleakly's involvement. I know he knows something, but how much?

'I swore I'd have nowt more to do with all this cloak and dagger stuff. But here I am, nonetheless.'

'And did Juggers tell you anything else?'

'I know we're to be joined by two new constables. Aye, and that your investigation is to be, let's say, inconclusive.'

155

'They told you that – good.' I relax a bit. At least I have one confederate in all this. 'I must say, it's bloody odd, don't you think?'

'There are a lot of odd things that have happened here recently, sir. Used to be a quiet little place, did Elderby. Now, well, I'm not sure what's afoot. Curtains twitch, strange glances in the street. I get a shiver down my spine sometimes. I'm tired of it all, to be honest.'

Well, this isn't news, thinks I.

'You mean you've been worried about something for a while?'

'Odd things have been happening for the last couple of years.'

'The farm thefts?'

'Not just that. Tales of strangers hanging about. Things happening in the night.'

'What *things*?'

'Lights, noises. Down in the beck, on the fell – all over.'

I try to take this in. I know you'll likely have formed an opinion of me by now, but I'm not stupid. At the end of the war all manner of skulduggery was afoot. Stories of wonder weapons mighty enough to blow up the planet were legion. I heard that Hitler's mad scientists had been scattered to the four winds at the end. This thought sparks off an idea.

'Did you ever think there was something odd about Starr being here – in the village, I mean?'

'I did, as it happens. But whatever brought him here did him no favours. He's on his way to the mortuary in Leeds now.'

'Leeds? Isn't that strange?'

'Aye, it is, a bit. I've never liked intelligence officers, don't trust them. My feelings haven't changed, neither. I think me and thee will have to watch our backs, Inspector.'

So, he met the mysterious old Etonian, too. I wonder if I

should tell him what caretaker Lumley had to say on that front, but decide not to. I don't know what he knows or doesn't know. It's frustrating.

'We have to go through the motions, sir. For the sake of those in the village, so they tell me.'

'Yes, I intend to do that. What do you suggest? You know Elderby much better than I, Elphinstone.'

'We need to get these new bobbies around the place, asking questions and the like. He might have been a stranger, Starr, but he was married to the local doctor. Folk have a lot of time for her. They'll be unsettled.'

'So, we show face, ask questions, poke about a bit. Shouldn't be too difficult.'

'Aye, then hit a six over the stand and out of the ground, and run for the pavilion, sir.'

I'm rather impressed by this cricketing analogy. It exactly sums up what we must do. Make everything look normal, then bugger off. On reflection, though I'd been dreading this subterfuge, it now seems much easier, somehow. There can't be many witnesses to Starr's movements, given the time of night he bought it – perhaps this fishmonger chap, but he shouldn't be a problem. Then there's the vicar. But like most men of the cloth, he'll say one thing on Sunday and question it for the rest of the week. In any case, his evidence to date hasn't been exactly conclusive. The voices he heard could just as easily have been poor Starr rambling in his death throes.

I'm beginning to feel more relaxed.

'Then there's the parish council,' says Bleakly.

'What?'

'Aye, they have a meeting tonight. I've just had your landlady on the phone about it. She's the secretary, you know.'

'The usual bunch of old duffers, I take it?'

Bleakly strokes his prominent chin. 'Well, I wouldn't be so dismissive, sir. For a start, Lady Damnish is the chairman.'

'Chairwoman, surely?'

'No, she's a stickler for tradition. No surprise, given her bloodline.'

'I wondered about that. I mean, Damnish isn't exactly regal, is he?'

'Aye, that he isn't – but she is.'

Confused, I have a veritable barrage of questions to ask Bleakly. But just as I'm about to, the door bursts open to reveal Deedee with a bag of ice and a bottle of aspirin.

17

As Deedee is feeding me the pills and holding the bag of ice to my bonce, Bleakly looks round the office gloomily. 'By heck, I can't tell you the last time I was in this office. Back in Moore's day.' He examines the carpet. 'I've kept the place clean and aired, mark you, but nobody's been in here since he died – until now, that is.' He raises his head and frowns at me.

'Who is this Moore chap?' I ask innocently.

Bleakly bangs the desk with his fist. 'The finest police officer in Yorkshire – aye, and beyond.' His face is suddenly red with anger or excitement. I can't tell which.

'What happened to him, retired?'

Deedee looks at Bleakly out of the corner of one eye.

'He died,' he says.

Deedee coughs and shuffles about nervously.

'I was on a re-rostered rest day.' Bleakly's head is bowed, his voice barely a whisper. 'There'd been some rowdy lads in the Beggar. From Leeds, they were. A bad lot, at any rate.'

'When was this?'

'Nineteen forty-nine,' pipes up Deedee, much to Bleakly's surprise, I see.

'Hard to believe, really. Inspector Moore went on his

own to see what all the fuss was about. Ethel wasn't happy and wanted them out.'

Something about this story is nagging at me, but I can't think what.

'By the time he got there, they'd all left peaceably enough. Moore stopped for a couple of pints – as you do, like. Show face, and all that. Last beer he ever supped,' says Bleakly.

'What happened?' say I.

He looks me straight in the eye. I swear, I see tears in his. 'Well, he left the pub, just at closing time – back of ten. But he never made it home. His body was found in the weir the next day – snagged on the bank.'

'That's not good,' I whisper, not really knowing what else to say.

'It were a tragedy. A fine man, no question about it.'

I'm beginning to realize that Elderby is one of the most dangerous places in England. Not only are top secret matters of national importance taking place, people keep turning up dead – including police officers. None of this is good news for yours truly. I think with a shiver of my very recent encounter in the woods. But this story is ringing a bell. I seem to remember that a police officer was murdered hereabouts, but the memory is vague.

'Did you collar anyone?' say I.

'Everyone blamed the lads from Leeds,' says Bleakly. 'They disappeared into the night. Nobody round here knew who they were or where they were from. Leeds police had a poke around, asked a few questions, but there was nothing.' He sighs.

'But you think differently?'

'I've thrown my fair share of drunk lads out of pubs in my day. But I've always managed back home to tell the tale. There was something fishy about that night. I'll tell you this for nothing, Inspector: there were folk abroad in the dark all round that time. Slinking in the shadows for days, they were. But I saw them. Just like I did this morning.'

I give Bleakly a questioning look.

'What did you see?' says Deedee.

'A car – a strange car, at that. I was on the way to rouse you, Inspector.'

'What was strange about it?' say I.

'Nothing strange about the car. But it wasn't a car from round here.'

'Don't tell me you recognize every car in the village?'

'Yes, I do,' says Bleakly. 'Morris Oxford, it were. I watched it pass through the village but couldn't see the number plate in the dark. Curse of getting old, poor eyesight. There're a few souls on the go at that time of the morning in this village. Poor Mr Starr was always an early riser. They tell me he didn't sleep well after the war. Took walks early to pass the time. I'll wager, if he could talk now, he'd swear he'd never do it again.'

No argument there, thinks I.

'But a strange car sticks out like a sore thumb.'

'Maybe somebody lost?' I venture.

'Lost in Elderby? That's not humanly possible. You'd have to be thick in arm and short in head to get confused on one main road. No, moving slowly, it was. As though whoever were inside was looking for something – or someone.'

'I'm sure we'll come to that in the inquiry.' I glance at the sergeant, then Deedee, who smiles sadly. 'I better have a word with this fishmonger chap. Maybe he saw something too.'

'Whitmore? He'd be in Whitby by that time. But he

might have come across something earlier. He would have been about then.'

'How is Doctor Starr, I wonder?' say I.

'It's so sad,' says Deedee. It sounds sincere, but I just sense something in her manner. 'She's still very distressed. But hey, who wouldn't be? I think she has that stiff upper lip thing going on. You guys set so much store by it. I don't know why.'

I want to tell her about Agincourt, Trafalgar, the Battle of Britain. But I realize that it's hard to sum up our island race, as Winston calls it. It's an approach to life I think people elsewhere will find hard to grasp.

'Anyhow, I better get going. I've work to do. And it's the parish council later. Now, sir, under normal circumstances, I'd answer the questions the committee have about recent events. But since you're here ... Well, it's your place, I think.'

'I suppose so,' say I, dreading the fact I'm going to have to be dishonest with an entire community.

'I'll come with you,' says Deedee brightly.

At first, through my throbbing head, I'm cheered by this thought. Then I remember that I must keep an eye on Miss Dean. But I suppose if she's where I can see her, she can't get up to no good – if that's what's happening, which I doubt. Still, why's she so immovable?

I remove the bag of ice from my forehead, handing it to Deedee.

'I'll put this in the kitchen – in the sink. You can go back and get it if you need it, Inspector,' says Deedee, and makes off with it.

My head is feeling much better now. The combination of ice and aspirin, I don't doubt. But, despite this relief, cold fear is gripping my heart. A dead man in a chimney, an equally dead American and a mysteriously deceased police inspector. Not to mention whoever attacked me in the woods. I'm beginning to discern a worrying pattern. And just who are these dark figures driving through the village and generally haunting the place late at night?

'I'm glad you'll be at this meeting with me tonight, Elphinstone.'

'I have to be there, really. I'm an office-bearer.'

'You mean you won't be on my side?'

'Don't worry. They're a nice enough bunch. Though Lady Damnish can be a bit of a handful. Especially when she and Ingleby start at it.'

'I'd like to know more about her and this Ingleby,' say I.

Bleakly makes to speak, but the phone on my new desk rings.

'It's a Constable Hardy for you, sir,' says Lumley, still on the front desk.

Bleakly slips out of the office as I take the call.

18

As it turns out, Constable Hardy is one of the replace-ments for the previous incumbents, now in Pickering, so I'm told. My goodness, whoever is behind this doesn't hang about. The two new men appear in my new office looking spic and span.

I don't know about you but I'm always critical when I watch films at the cinema with police officers in them. They never quite get it right. It takes time to relax into wearing the uniform. One must be confident, approach-able and officious all at the same time. Only years of actually doing the job can achieve this. Though I'm a poor example of the art, having spent most of my career in plain clothes. When Hardy and Thomas arrive – yes, I'm not kidding – they immediately look out of place in the dark blue. Both are ramrod-straight, their boots polished to a mirror finish, creases in all the right places. These aren't police constables, they're soldiers. It's staring out of them. They're burly chaps too, over six feet the pair of them.

I must confess to being secretly pleased by this develop-ment. Just what you need when you've been attacked is the sight of two stout lads who know what they're about. Though I must keep in mind that they're attached to the slippery mob. I'd swear they've come from Catterick Army

Base. How else could they get here so quickly? They'd never have made it from York in such a short time.

Despite the obvious deceit, I brief the pair as to what's happened and dispatch them round the village to take statements from everybody as to whether they saw or heard anything in the early hours of the morning. Hardy – clearly the spokesman of the two – turns in the doorway.

'Can't think many locals will have been about to see anything at that time, sir.' He salutes me then goes about his business. This tells me that they know the brief, which is perhaps a surprise, but all the better.

So, it has begun, the great investigation that never was.

It's lunchtime, and the duck egg that inhabited my head now looks more like the product of a peahen. Despite swearing never to darken the door of the Hanging Beggar for a pub lunch again, I'm ravenous.

This happened during the war too. Just before an operation, chaps would be mooning about looking sorry for themselves, no doubt thinking this day may well be their last. But not Lieutenant Grasby, oh no. While everyone was eschewing the miserable fodder placed before us as we were about to risk life and limb for king and country, I was eating enough to keep two small armies on the go. I've been lucky. Like my father before me, I never put on as much as a pound in weight, no matter what I eat.

In order to test this theory, I take to the mean streets of Elderby once more, walking at a good clip just in case some bad bugger tries to hit me over the head again. Lunch is the objective.

But the quiet place I witnessed yesterday couldn't be more different. The Hanging Beggar is thronged with folk, all babbling away. Even more disconcertingly, as I walk into the bar this murmur of chat fades away only to be replaced by absolute silence, save for an old boy in the corner who is singing a sea shanty, clearly three sheets to the wind.

'Well, Inspector Grasby,' says Ethel, 'I didn't think I'd see you in here today, I must be honest.'

'A chap must keep his strength up, as I'm sure you appreciate,' say I. All I garner is a blank look from my host and a disgruntled murmur from the patrons.

'What can I do for you?' says Ethel.

'Pint of mild, please,' say I. Well, better to resign oneself to the facts and drink this swill when one has an investigation to avoid.

'Mild's off, I'm afraid.'

I hear a loud collective tut from those assembled. 'Oh. Well, bitter will have to do. A half pint, please.' I hear a mumble of approval. 'And some of your lovely soup, please.'

'Soup's off, too.' Ethel looks round the room. 'Well, you can see I'm having a busy day.'

I end up having to settle for ham sandwiches, the cheese supply also being exhausted. I resolve to find a table, but there's very little room at the inn. So, I have to settle for my little sliver of bar.

'I hope you're making inroads into catching the rogue what did for Mr Starr, Inspector?' This, from a ruddy-cheeked chap with a great belly and braces holding his corduroy trousers up over a checked flannel shirt. 'Well-liked, he were.'

'I'm sure he was. But as you'll understand, I can't say anything about the investigation.'

Suffice it to say, I'm now thoroughly regretting my visit to the pub.

'I heard screaming,' pipes up one chap from the back of the room.

'You did?' say I.

'Aye, about half three this morning. I put it down to animals, likely foxes, maybe deer. But the more I think about it, the more my blood runs cold.'

'Can I ask, why were you about at such an hour?'

'Insomnia. Can't sleep, so I go for a wander now and then in the night.'

'Oh,' say I. But before I can advise this chap to report to the police station and give a statement, another Elderby early riser reveals himself.

'I heard a car – well, some kind of vehicle – travelling at speed, just after four.' This man is thin and grey. He looks to be on his last legs. 'My chickens were making a racket. I thought there was something afoot. That's why I was up so early, before you ask.'

'Running – you know, quick footsteps. That's what I heard.' This from a plump woman sitting at a table. At first, I can only see the top of her head, but the crowd parts and she has her say. 'Outside toilet, Inspector. It's a curse, especially in the winter, thou knows.'

'Don't you have a pot?' shouts a spotty young man.

'I do! But the nature of my bodily function called for something more substantial, if you must know. Not that it's any of your business, Danny Parr.'

'She were having a shit,' says Danny in a low voice to his friends, who giggle at this behind their pint tumblers, as young men do.

A small chap approaches, regarding me through thick spectacles. 'You're the copper what lost his car, eh?'

Damn! 'Yes, but it's back safe and sound now, so no damage done,' say I breezily.

He smiles. 'I heard. Must say, mind, lad what stole it looked remarkably like you.'

This must be Mr Wallington, he of the excellent eye-sight. Dash it all!

'So I believe. Life's odd like that. I could tell you about all sorts of strange coincidences that I've encountered as a police officer.' I let him think about that, then deliver the *coup de grâce*. 'I say, my father has a similar pair of specs. Just like yours, I swear.'

'Oh, aye,' says this sullen busybody. 'What about it?'

'He can't see a damned thing – with or without them on.'

Message received, he returns from whence he came. Good for me, thinks I.

But as I wait for my lunch, such as it is, one customer after another volunteers information on what he or she heard, felt or saw in the hours just before and after poor Chuck Starr's body was discovered. It rapidly becomes clear that just about everyone in Elderby was up and about when they should have been tucked up in bed. This is emblematic of my luck, you know. If I were actively seek-ing witnesses, you can be certain that none would be forthcoming. Ask any police officer. But the moment you're told to sweep things under the carpet, they come out of the woodwork in droves. I have to think on my feet – and quickly.

'Now, listen to me, everyone.' I tap a beer mug with a pen in an attempt to bring the place to order. As a hush descends, I carry on. 'It would appear that the midnight oil burns bright into the wee small hours here in Elderby.' I thought this might raise a laugh, but everyone just stares at me blankly. 'Rest assured, I want to hear from anyone who was up and about and saw or heard something strange early this morning. I'll have my lunch, and after that I'd be grateful if you'd report to the police station and my con-stables will take statements from you all.' Then we'll throw them in the bucket, I want to say. But professional etiquette dictates otherwise.

There are murmurs of disaffection.

'Why don't you bring the bobbies here?' asks Wallington the smartarse. I'm beginning to find him indescribably irritating.

'Yes, why not? I tell you what, if you go home, I'll draw you a bath and warm your slippers by the fire. They'll be ready for when you emerge all pink and clean. I can knock up a decent supper, too. Then we can all have a cosy little chat as to why a man in the prime of his life was murdered earlier this morning in this village, and we've already had a body lodged down a chimney.'

I pause for effect. 'Yes, in *this* village. And none of us has a clue who did it and – more importantly – why.' I let this hang in the air. The good folk of Elderby are treating this as though it's happened at a remove. And though it likely has, it doesn't harm to remind them of their own vulnerability.

'This afternoon at the police station, you say?' says jam-jar specs.

'That's right,' say I, turning my attention to the cloudy half pint of bitter that has been placed before me.

It's quite miraculous, actually. One by one, the pub begins to clear. Drinks are knocked back, and the little bell above the door tinkles like the bells on Santa's sleigh.

Ethel glares at me from behind the bar. 'Well done, Inspector. I was having a right good day until you appeared.'

It doesn't do to ostracize the only landlady about, so I decide to pour oil on troubled waters. 'I understand, I really do. But I want this case solved, Ethel. You're here in the pub day and night. The last thing I want is for you to be in danger. We must find whoever did this terrible thing.'

'You think they'll have a go at finishing me off?'

'How can I say otherwise? At this moment, I have the whole community in my care, so to speak.'

This visual image imprints itself on my mind's eye. I'm a giant dove, the good people of Elderby sheltering under one of my great outstretched wings. It's biblical, I know. But I spent so much of my childhood staring at these things in books, such imagery often plagues me. Sometimes I wonder whether I'm more religiously inclined than my father, and I should be the vicar. Then I remember the gambling, boozing and carousing, and soon disabuse myself of this fanciful notion. Still, I'd never have fallen out with the king.

'You'll need another half, I reckon,' says Ethel, well and truly spooked.

'Make it a pint,' say I. After all, every cloud, and all that.

19

Having managed to put away another pint and an extra sandwich, I feel pleasantly satiated when I leave the Hanging Beggar. I'm passing the baker's shop when I'm summoned from within.

Entering the premises, I must confess the smell makes me hungry all over again. It's the aroma of hot pies, fresh bread rolls and pastry. Wally the baker is behind the counter. He's stooped, with a long droopy moustache, frosted with flour. At the end of the counter is a dog, a red setter. It can only be Bill. Even I must confess he has a lovely coat, and its shade isn't a million miles away from the colour of my own hair.

'What a handsome chap,' I say with a smile.

'I beg your pardon,' says Wally, looking quite befuddled.

'Your dog. Bill's his name, am I right?'

'My goodness, Inspector, but you're a sharp one. Only here five minutes and already know the name of folks' pets. I reckon it's a case of cometh the hour, cometh the man.'

'Sorry?'

'You know, with all that's going on I can't see them leaving Bleakly in charge of a murder, can you?'

Though this is beyond doubt, I must defend my

colleague. 'Oh, I don't know. I think Elphinstone has hidden depths.'

'I'm not so sure. The only depth he manages to reach is deep sleep.' He brushes his hands clean of flour and offers a firm handshake.

'I must say, you have a lovely shop.'

'Thank you. I wasn't sure I'd make a go of the baking. But I'm glad to say it's all worked out well. Been at it fifteen years now.'

'What did you do before?'

'I was a miner. Fourteen years old, I went down the pit.'

'I don't envy you,' say I.

'Nor should you, Inspector. Bloody hell on earth, it is.' He rubs one shoulder. 'Roof collapsed on me. They tried to fix me up, like. But it never worked. When I couldn't work, they threw me on the dole. My father had been a baker and I'd worked with him when I was a lad. He was still alive when I started up. Taught me everything I know. He was proud I was finally carrying on the family tradition.'

There's a tear in his eye. But I'm rather mystified that he'd see fit to call me into the shop just to tell me this. I ask if that's all he wants.

'Oh, no. Not at all, Inspector. I know you'll be a busy man, what with the murders and all.'

He says this as though it's an everyday occurrence.

'It's the vicar.'

'What about him?' say I, dreading he is going to reveal he saw the Reverend Croucher do for Starr.

'He's taken it bad – what happened to poor Mr Starr, I mean. He comes in most days. He's partial to a French fancy, he is.'

'I don't doubt it.'

'Today, though . . . well, he seemed different. Distracted, depressed, if you know what I mean. Bought a loaf and a couple of scones – that were it.'

'No fishes, then?'

'I beg your pardon?'

'Loaves and fishes – never mind.'

'Right, I see.'

Again, I get that blank stare that people seem so adept at here. It's a cross between disbelief and contempt. Mind you, if they were to find out what I'm up to – well, such emotions would be utterly justified.

'Ecclesiastes seven, verse seventeen, he was quoting.'

'Ah. "Be not overly wicked, neither be a fool. Why should you die before your time?" That one?'

'Right clever, Inspector. I'm glad we have a man of the scriptures looking after us.'

'My father is a vicar.'

'And a fine man, I'm sure.'

Well, unless you see him beastly drunk after his dinner every night. But let's not be too hard on the old boy.

'Very pious. A mountain of a man. Theologically speaking, of course.'

'I don't know what it was. But I got the feeling he might do something stupid.'

'The last thing we need is a suicidal vicar, eh?'

'I was hoping you could have a word with him, like?'

'Well, Wally, I am quite busy, as I'm sure you understand. But I want to ask him a few more questions, so I'll take a run over to the vicarage.'

'He's back at the church, most probably, Inspector. Said he was going to spend the rest of the day in quiet contemplation and prayer.'

'Not been a good day for him.'

'Nor Mr Starr, or that poor bugger down the chimney at Holly House, neither.'

'Indeed not. I'll have a word.'

I'm not lying here. I know that I'll have to speak to Reverend Croucher sooner rather than later, if only to try to make him doubt the evidence of his own ears. It would be much better, as far as my new purposes go, if he'd forget what he heard in the early hours of this morning. In my experience, most of the clergy can be persuaded to do anything, given the right incentives. Ah, what a tangled web we weave.

'I better be off,' say I. 'Half the village was up and about between three and four this morning, it seems.'

'I'd take that with a pinch of salt, Inspector.'

'You would?'

'I've not been here as long as many, as I say. But one in, all in, as far as they're concerned.'

'I'm not sure what you mean.'

'People in Elderby – well, they're inquisitive, Inspector. Nobody wants to feel left out.'

'They'll go as far as to give false evidence just to be involved, you mean?'

'Maybe a few fibs, here and there, like. No harm meant, I'm sure.'

'Bloody rogues,' I say. But I'm secretly happy that this might be the case. The last thing I need are too many witnesses.

'Here, take something for a snack. Do you like pies? They're just fresh out the oven.'

'Too kind, Wally.'

'It'll keep you going until parish council tonight. I'll see you there.' He wraps a wonderful-looking mutton pie in a paper bag.

'You're on the council?'

'I am. It pays to be at the centre of power in Elderby, you know. But keep an eye out for Lady Damnish. If anyone is likely to be difficult, it's her.' He taps his nose.

I thank him for the pie and head off. I'm just out of the shop doorway when I collide with a young woman wearing a short blue coat and a matching headscarf. At first, when I apologize, I don't recognize her. But when she speaks, it becomes clear. Martha Thornlie, the chambermaid from Holly House.

'My apologies, Miss Thornlie. Are you having a day off?'

'A half day, Inspector,' she says rather glumly. 'But most welcome,' she adds hurriedly. She's looking about nervously, biting her lip.

'Are you quite all right?' say I.

'No, as it happens, Inspector Grasby.'

'I'm sure what happened must have come as a real shock.'

'Yes, it did. But that's not what's troubling me most.'

'What is it, then?'

'I didn't tell you the whole truth. In my statement, like.'

'Sorry?'

Martha Thornlie looks about again. 'Her Ladyship did talk to that man – whoever he was.' She's almost whispering.

'What did she say?'

'I couldn't hear much, but I did definitely hear Mr Ingleby's name mentioned, and something about her son, young Master Damnish. Am I in trouble, Inspector? I don't think I could face the gaol.'

'You don't have to worry on that score, Martha,' say I. 'But tell me, why did you not mention this to begin with?'

'It were Mr McGill – the gamekeeper. He said it was best to say as little as possible. I hate lying, Inspector. I hope you'll forgive me.' Quickly, head bent into the cold wind, she was off.

It would appear that, despite what I've been told to do, evidence is just falling in my lap. I have the distinct impression that my meeting with the young maid is no coincidence.

Deep in thought, I make my way back to the station. Initially, I was going to brief Hardy and Thomas as to the likely influx of potential witnesses about to arrive. But as I turn the corner, I find a long queue is already developing outside. Brushing aside a few questions from the locals, I dart round to the car park, and, in a flash and magnificent bang, I'm soon back out on the road in my Austin, heading off to see Reverend Croucher.

20

Only when I try to take the incline leading to the church does the car begin to protest. Then I remember Juggers's message from our resident genius of a mechanic, Stubby. So I stop, execute a perfect three-point turn, and am soon merrily reversing up the hill towards St-Thomas's-on-the-Edge. It's still slippery on the road, but I note some good soul has laid some sand. I would have walked here, but with dangerous footpads abroad dedicated to smashing in my skull, the car suddenly feels like a safer haven.

The lights are on in the church, illuminating the stained-glass windows. A small breeze with the hint of the ocean ripples through the bare oak tree beside the car, making the leafless tree branches wave as though they are skeletal fingers set on maleficence. And they're seemingly not alone. Nobody could possibly conceive of the dark deeds taking place in this quiet little place.

I picture Croucher kneeling in prayer. But these prayers will be for himself, not the murdered Chuck Starr. Though, mark you, I'd be a hypocrite to judge him. After all, I'm busy pretending to investigate this terrible crime. More and more, though, my mind is drawn to what is *really* happening. There are so many questions.

The pie is wrapped in its paper bag on the passenger seat. Even though I've had two flaccid ham sandwiches in the pub, I find myself hungry again. As a child it was instilled into me that no food was to be consumed in the old Bentley my father inherited from my grandfather. So, automatically I leave the Austin and stride up behind the church, to the little escarpment where Starr's body was found. It dawns on me what a long day it's been. And it's likely to get longer, with the parish council meeting in the evening. The snow here is well trampled, but by the look of the sunless sky there will be more where that came from.

I'm looking out across the North York Moors when I take my first bite of mutton pie. I prefer cold pies for no other reason than I'm usually too ravenous to wait for them to be heated up. It's very good, one of the best I've tasted. Mining's loss is baking's gain.

Even though I've been staring around blankly, glad of my thick overcoat, I'm conscious of the fact that somebody assaulted me for no apparent reason this very morning. So my senses are on alert for hidden miscreants.

Perhaps because of this heightened state of awareness, something on the grass catches my eye. A cigarette end. I examine it between my fingers. The brand is an exclusive one, and its being pinched at the end brings back my meeting with Juggers and Cummins. I can see the latter nipping the cigarette to place in the long holder. Why a sharp chill runs through me at this point, I don't know. Cummins must simply have taken the time to examine the body *in situ*. But I feel uneasy all the same. I place the cigarette end in the paper bag that once held my pie and head to the church door.

It takes four knocks before I hear the Reverend Croucher's timid voice from within.

'Inspector Grasby, Your Reverence. I'd like another word with you, if possible.'

Croucher opens the great door in a palaver of slipped bolts and old locks.

'I didn't expect to see you again today, Inspector.'

I go in and take a seat in a pew, inviting Croucher to do likewise. 'I just want to clarify things, if I can.'

'What things?'

'The voices you heard earlier – before you found Mr Starr, I mean. Are you absolutely sure?'

'Yes, of course. I wouldn't have told you otherwise.'

'I understand. But as you say, these are thick old walls.'

'No, I'm quite clear. I heard voices.'

'Can I conduct a little experiment, Vicar?'

'What on earth do you mean?'

'I'm going to go outside, close the door and make my way to the back of the church. I'll start speaking, then I'll shout a bit. I want you to be exactly where you were when you heard the voices this morning. See if you can pick up on what I'm saying.'

'Oh, what a bother, Inspector.'

I treat Croucher to my most serious gaze. 'Come on, old chap. A man lost his life here. I owe it to him to investigate as thoroughly as possible.'

'Yes, yes, of course you do. I must apologize. It's been such a dark day.'

Making sure the vicar is primed and ready, I leave the church, pull the big door behind me and walk up to the edge. All the time being careful that nobody is about to knock me on the head. The pistol under my jacket affords some comfort in this.

I take out a packet of cigarettes, light one and take a long draw. Of course, I'm not going to utter a word. But

Croucher doesn't know that. As I smoke idly, my mind drifts back to the new contents of the old pie bag. I remember Cummins saying he had to go to the toilet before he journeyed back down the road. So, I assume they must have visited the crime scene when I was consoling Dr Starr. They certainly hadn't been there before I arrived. Somebody would have mentioned it.

I trudge back and push at the oaken door of the church. Thankfully, Croucher has found the strength not to lock and bolt it again. I see him kneeling in prayer once more, nearer the pulpit this time.

'I say, why didn't you shout, Inspector?'

'I did. At the top of my voice, as it happens. Don't tell me you didn't hear me?'

'No, not a thing,' says Croucher.

I adopt a serious expression.

'What's wrong, Inspector?'

'Nothing – nothing for you to worry about.' I look nobly into the middle distance.

'There's something you're not telling me.' Croucher looks indignant.

I lower my voice. 'It's just – well, just that when we catch whoever killed Starr, it must go to court.'

'I should jolly well think so.'

'I have you saying in the statement you gave earlier this morning that you heard voices – you know, just before you found the body.'

'Yes, you do.'

'My problem is that any good defence lawyer will try to prove that you didn't hear these voices. D'you see my problem?'

'They'll do what you've just done, and I'll be held up as a liar, you mean. Gosh.' Reverend Croucher begins to weep. 'I was so convinced I'd heard voices. I'm telling the truth.'

'Then you must stick to that, Vicar,' say I doubtfully.

'What will people think?'

'They'll think what I'm thinking. You had a terrible shock, your mind played tricks. It happens all the time. No shame in it. It's just . . .'

'Just what?'

'Well, murder trials. There's little room for sentiment. It can get rather tough in the witness box.'

'I could get into trouble. Is that it?'

'It's possible, I'm afraid.'

'In that case, I want to change my statement. Immediately!' Croucher sticks out his chin, tears gone.

And there it is. Vicar dealt with; witness eliminated. QED.

'I'll adjust it and leave out the part where you heard voices.'

'I don't know how to thank you, Inspector.'

'Think nothing of it. As long as justice is served, that's the main thing.'

Croucher looks mightily relieved.

'I say, can I borrow your phone?'

'Of course, you know where it is in the vestry. I'm going to pray for my wretched soul.' He kneels as I head to the phone.

I suppose I should feel wretched – in a way I do. But I'm just doing what I'm told. For the old soldier in me, that's easy. But for the police officer I now am, there are nagging doubts. Not least what I've been told by Martha Thornlie.

The number I dial is almost automatic. I recognize Deborah, one of the receptionists, on the other end of the line.

'Frank, how are things on the moors? You're quite the

celebrity, what with you heading up a double murder investigation.'

'All in the line of duty, Debbie. You know me.'

'Gosh, yes, I do.' There's a hint of rakishness in her voice that I like. I file it away for later.

'Is Juggers about?'

'He arrived about an hour ago. Do you want me to put you through?'

Soon, I'm hanging on, awaiting his master's voice. Thankfully, Juggers doesn't take long to pick up.

'Grasby, I hope you've not made a right royal arse of things already?'

'Not at all, sir. Everything is on track. Just as discussed.'

'Excellent. Now, what can I do for you? I know you must miss me, but you'll have to buck up.'

I know that Juggers can be frivolous now and again. It's just one never really knows when or why.

'Just a quick question to arrange things properly in my mind, sir. In case anyone should ask, that type of thing.'

'Out with it, then.'

'I'm wondering – when did you and Mr X examine the body?' I can't let him know that I know who X really is.

'We didn't. It's in Leeds.'

'This morning, I mean, sir.'

'We met with you. That was it.'

'And Mr X didn't visit the locus – without you, I mean?'

'He picked me up in Northallerton and we drove to Elderby. Then we travelled back to York. Do I have to tell you my every movement, Grasby? Good grief, man, you'd think we killed Starr . . .'

I don't really hear what he's saying now. I have that horrible sinking feeling that I'm knee-deep in something most unpleasant, and the fetid water is rising fast.

21

If he knew, my father would be deeply satisfied that I've managed – yet again – to find myself in a first-class mess. He spotted my tendency to head straight for trouble when I was a child. I must have been about ten when this first announced itself. It was a rehearsal for a nativity play in a musty old church hall. Our Sunday school teacher had stepped out to take Annabel Swift to the toilet for the umpteenth time. Poor Annabel had some kind of bladder issue and was forever wetting herself in class. I often wonder what happened to her in later life.

Anyhow, us bored little boys decided that a quick game of football was in order. Unfortunately, given the lack of a ball, we decided to kick about the old rag doll that was standing in for the baby Jesus in the nativity display. It was innocent enough stuff. But when Miss Paget – a crushingly boring spinster with a lisp – arrived back with Annabel she looked at us in horror. You see, for her, that rag doll had represented Christ, via some unusual process of transubstantiation. She fell to her knees, lifting this bundle of rags from the floor, damning us to the very fires of Hell.

My father made much of having a 'heretic' son. To this day, he'll assure anyone who'll listen that my life is condemned by this one act alone. Though, if you press him, he'll happily tell you of many more of my transgressions. The thing is, I know he doesn't believe this to be the case. But it's a handy moral stick with which to beat me.

Incidentally, Tubby Blake – one of my associates in this terrible offence against religion – is well on his way to becoming a bishop. I shouldn't be surprised if he makes it all the way to the archbishopric of Canterbury. Then, I'll take great pleasure in telling all and sundry he kicked about the baby Jesus. One thing is for certain, our childish, innocent act hasn't weighed him down.

But such is my luck.

I barely notice the drive from the church back to the station. I keep telling myself that the cigarette end I found up on the ridge could belong to any number of people. But in my heart, I know this isn't true. How many folk smoke President cigarettes, after all? My old colonel enjoyed them. His wife used to send him these exclusive smokes as part of a Fortnum & Mason hamper. How the other half live! It's the only reason I was able to identify Cummins' cigarette of choice. It's all rather grim. I just can't get my head round it.

Back at Elderby station there's still a queue of locals keen to offer up their experiences of earlier that day. As I suspected, it appears that the entire population of the village was up and about between three and four in the morning. Not just that, they all heard or saw something suspicious. Wally was right. It's keeping up with the Joneses.

I find Bleakly alone in the sergeants' room, in the process of drifting off to sleep. For once, I can't blame him. It's been a bloody long day. I'm dead beat myself.

'I say, Elphinstone. Up and at 'em!'

His eyes shoot open, and then his malevolent gaze alights on me. 'It's you. I hope you haven't been attacked again. Though part of me wishes you had.'

'Bit harsh, old boy,' say I.

'I don't know what you said in the pub, but you've set the whole village alight. I thought this was all supposed to be – you know.' He taps the side of his nose.

'Anything of note turned up?'

'No.' Bleakly's tone is dismissive. 'I'd wager every last one of them were in their beds. That, or staring at a pot of tea infusing. It's typical of this place.'

'I thought as much. And we're no further forward with the inquiry into Starr's death, either.' My turn to tap my nose.

At this point I feel like telling my colleague about the cigarette end. But something stops me. For the life of me, I don't know what it is.

'I dare say. Ours is not to reason why, and all that.'

There's a shuffling noise behind the door and Deedee appears bearing a tray. Tea and biscuits – the very thing.

'I thought you guys could do with a pick-me-up,' says she. Deedee stares at me for a moment. 'My, you're a quick healer, Inspector. That lump on your head is only the size of a large pea now.'

I've always been a quick healer. Back in my cricketing days, I remember chaps being out for weeks if they caught a fast ball on the fingers. I'd be moping about for a few days, but I was soon back in the nets. One should be grateful, I suppose.

Bleakly takes it upon himself to be mother, and the three of us are soon round the table enjoying the roborative delights of tea. Well, we've got nothing else to do.

'Now, before you head into the lion's den tonight, there are a couple of things you should know,' says Bleakly ominously.

'About the parish council?'

'Oh, aye.' Bleakly and Deedee exchange furtive glances.

'It's a bit of minefield, to be honest – especially when any-thing about law and order is to be discussed.'

'The old story, I suppose. A room full of people who think they know about police work and really know very little.'

'That's true of some of them, but by no means all.'

'Do tell,' say I, dreading what he's going to come out with.

'For a start, there's Lady Damnish. She's a magistrate, you know.'

'Ha! That doesn't mean she knows much about the law. The reverse, more like. In my experience, these country magistrates are all old windbags, mourning the days they had the power of pit and gallows over everyone.'

'She's a lawyer – or was,' says Deedee.

'Oh.' That's put me back on my heels.

Bleakly gives me a knowing look. 'Aye, and she's got a nose like a ferret into the bargain.'

I think back to my meeting chez Damnish, recalling the small, sharp-featured woman. She does look rather ferret-like.

'Then there's Sir Reginald,' says Bleakly.

'Who?'

'He's retired. But he was one of the deputy assistant com-missioners of the Metropolitan Police.'

'Eh?' I'm beginning to become alarmed.

'Not to mention Finan Whales.'

'He sounds like a cowboy!'

'He used to be a copper in Whitby. Retired here because he developed an allergy to the sea air. Least, that's what his doctor said.'

'So, in actual fact the meeting is to be jam-packed with

people who do know what they're on about. Deedee, could you give us a moment, please?'

I need to speak to Bleakly alone, and I'm now wary of the young American. Suddenly it appears as though I could well be under the hammer. It's one thing pulling the wool over a self-interested vicar, but quite another fooling folk that know what they're about. Silently, I curse Juggers and his slippery friend.

'Don't forget our landlady,' says Deedee as she drains her cup.

'Hetty Gaunt?' say I. 'Don't tell me, she's Sherlock Holmes's sister.'

'She can see things.'

'I'm sure. Like that bloody bird flying at her wherever she goes.' I'm worried about those on the council with genuine provenance when it comes to the law. But I'm damned if I'm going to be spooked by Mrs Gaunt and her ridiculous nonsense.

Deedee vacates the room and Bleakly leans into me. 'Don't rush to judgement, sir. That woman has something, you know.'

'Yes, bloody strange taste in décor and furnishing.'

'You may scoff. But don't say I didn't tell you.'

'I expect you to help me out tonight, Elphinstone.'

'I'll do my best. But I can't afford to be too biased. The rest will pick me up on it.'

'Good grief, remember you're a police officer, man.'

'How can I forget? I know all the pressure is on you, what with these deaths. But it doesn't sit well with me, nei-ther. Even though I know it's for king and country, and all that.'

'Queen.'

'I beg your pardon?' Bleakly looks rather confused.

'It's *queen* and country now, Elphinstone.'

'Oh aye, right enough. I keep forgetting that. Just a slip of a lass, too. I don't envy her job. It did for her poor father.'

'I don't know. Old Vicky managed to hang around for a long time.'

'That, she did. But she was a one-off. There won't be a monarch that outlasts her for a long time.'

'I must say, you're a ray of sunshine,' say I.

'I think it's a shame, that's all. It can't be much fun having something you don't expect thrust upon you like that.'

'I know how she bally well feels.'

Bleakly strokes his chin.

'Penny for them?'

'I'm going to tell you something that I shouldn't, sir.'

Oh no! Statements like this usually presage some awful confession. My mind boggles as to what on earth Bleakly can have been up to.

'It's about Lady Damnish.'

'Yes?'

Now I'm dreading him telling me he's involved in some secret tryst with the lady of the manor. While Lady Damnish is no Chatterley, Elphinstone is most certainly no Mellors. I shall refrain from describing the mental pictures passing before my mind's eye at this very moment.

'This chap called Ingleby.'

'Yes, Damnish suspects him of being behind the farm thefts. That's what he alluded to, at least.'

'I don't doubt he did it. There's bad blood between Ingleby and Lord Damnish. Very bad.'

'What's that got to do with the lady of the house?'

Bleakly clears his throat. 'Well, Lady Damnish and Ingleby are connected, so to speak.'

'Oh. Enough said. Thanks for putting me in the picture, Elphinstone.'

He looks at me blankly for a moment. 'No, nothing like that. They're brother and sister, man!'

'I see,' say I. But I must admit to being rather confused. The ways of the heart are many and varied – I should know. But it's a bit rum for chaps to be at odds over marital situations concerning family members. This Ingleby bloke should be delighted his sister's bagged a peer of the realm. Or anyone, come to that. Again, I remember her ferret face.

'There's more to it than meets the eye. Of course, everyone around here knows. But I doubt anyone will have told you.'

'I've only been here since yesterday!' It seems much longer – honestly, it does.

'You brought a storm with you, too.' Bleakly leans forward in his chair. 'Listen – Lady Damnish's father was Lord Elderby. Lived in the old house before it was demolished and Damnish flung up Holly House.'

I'm puzzled by this, and it must show on my face as Bleakly continues.

'The old man – well, he lived life to the full, you could say.'

'A man of vices?'

'Liked a drink, and the ladies.' Bleakly sniffs with distaste. 'Aye, and he was too keen on the horses, into the bargain.'

'Can't hold that against a chap,' say I defensively.

'You can when the money's running out. They say he lost a fortune when the stock market collapsed in the late twenties. Never managed to recover.'

'Oh dear.'

'Any road . . . Damnish makes him an offer to clear his debts. Bails the old man out financially in return for the hand of his daughter.'

'My goodness, that's a bit fifteenth-century, is it not?'

'That wasn't all. He demanded that Lord Elderby renounce his title, and that his children make no claim.'

'And Lady Damnish agreed to this cruel use of her poor father?'

Bleakly nods his head. 'Most young women would have protested. But she could see the writing on the wall. Her father was finished, and the daughter liked the life of a lady and all that went with it. She swapped sides. Her and Ingleby, her brother, have barely spoken since.'

'This Ingleby chap. What's he like?'

'He's a good man. When nobody's listening, folk round here still call him Your Lordship. Most are tied to the estate in some way, farms, cottages, jobs and the like. So, they have to pay lip service to Damnish. But not behind his back.'

'What does he do? Ingleby, I mean.'

'He paints, mostly. He has the farm but leaves that to others. It was part of the settlement between his father and Damnish. His son should stay in Briarside free of charge for the rest of his life and live off the proceeds of the place. Though, as it is, I think he just about makes enough to make ends meet. He sells the odd painting, but not very often.'

'And old Lord Elderby, what happened to him?'

'Tragic, really. Damnish reneged on his promise. Left the old man high and dry, destitute. He were living with his son at Briarside. They found him hanging in the old Salt House up Withernshaw Fell.'

'He killed himself, then?'

190

'Aye.' Bleakly doesn't sound convinced.

'What aren't you telling me?'

'It's just village gossip, sir.'

'Still, indulge me.'

Bleakly sighs. 'It were Christmas Eve in the Hanging Beggar. It had always been the tradition that Lord Elderby bought his tenants a drink to celebrate the festive season. Went back to Elderby's father – aye, and beyond. So, the old boy kept it going, even though he wasn't in the big house, and all the farmers worked for Damnish. So, this night Elderby is buying the drinks when Damnish arrives with two of his henchmen. Puts a wad of money behind the bar and tells the old boy to sling his hook. That his time has gone, and so forth. He said quite a few cruel things, by all accounts.'

'What did Lord Elderby do?'

'That's the thing – cursed Damnish, he did. He told him he'd have a son and that the boy would restore his family name and Damnish would be forgotten.'

'I've met the lad. It's pretty clear he and his father don't rub along too well.'

'That's putting it mildly. It's only Lady Damnish that keeps the young 'un in the house, so they say.'

'Then what happened to Lord Elderby?'

'Three days later he was found dead up in the Salt House. Hadn't been himself over Christmas. He took off for a walk and was never seen alive again.'

'Goodness. This village of yours has its fair share of ghouls and secrets, eh?'

'I'll say. My old inspector was convinced that Damnish had something to do with it all.'

'Why so?'

'He used to go and see the old man. Keep him abreast of

191

what was going on, like. Just before all this happened, Elderby told him that he was working on something that would finish Damnish, sink him for good.'

'But that never happened.'

'No, it didn't. But whatever it was, Inspector Moore did his best to find out.'

'Until he was killed, you mean.'

'Aye, sad to say, you're right. So, after all that, you'll understand that there's much bad blood between Ingleby, his sister and Damnish.'

'As no doubt I'll witness tonight.'

'That's why the parish council is so popular. Folk love to be there to see it all kick off.' Bleakly gets to his feet stiffly. 'Now, I must pay a visit. It's all this tea, you know.' He leaves me to my thoughts.

I must say, though part of me finds it all quite fascinating, my instinct for self-preservation is screaming to the contrary. When I looked for Elderby on the map only a few short days ago, I had no idea what was bubbling beneath the surface of this quiet little village on the North York Moors. It just shows you: never make snap judgements. Good grief, it makes *Wuthering Heights* seem positively mundane.

Then I remember my father's comments about the place. I'm beginning to wonder exactly what he really knows.

22

There's something about a church hall that gives me the shivers. I'm not sure if it's because of my childish indiscretion with that rag doll, or just the general feel of such places. And they're all the same, you know. Peeling paint, faded notices on the wall – in this case some from the First World War. But most of all, it's the smell. It's always that musty odour of decay. I shouldn't be surprised to look under the stage and find a dead vicar or two. It certainly smells possible.

I've arrived early, with Deedee in attendance to assist. It's not what I want, but she's a forceful young woman, and I'm too bushed to argue. Our evening meal was an early, rushed affair, which didn't live up to the delights of the previous evening. Though it's fair to say that the cold mutton and mash was tasty enough. All brought together with a light gravy, it was. I always admire people who can rustle up a decent gravy – it's not as easy as you think.

I asked our landlady if she'd like to accompany us to the hall. Given the circumstances of Starr's unfortunate demise, I thought she'd jump at the chance, but no. She merely stared at me in horror and mumbled something about danger following me everywhere, and that she'd be safer on her own. Bloody cheek! Though, given

Bleakly's firm belief in her powers of prescience, this is a worry.

I'm not too proud to tell her that I'm concealing the Webley underneath my jacket, just for good measure. After my attack in the woods, I'm ready for anything now. It'll take a sharp cove to jump out of the shadows and catch me unawares again. When it comes to preserving my hide, I can be vicious – as a number of Jerry soldiers found out to their cost.

In any case, minus Mrs Gaunt, Deedee provides another pair of eyes as we dash along to the hall. The moon is illuminating the village in an ethereal glow. There's something strange about the moon, too. Or am I just becoming paranoid?

We arrive and make our way into the church hall. They're the heart of our country, you know. There's a row of trestle tables set up at one end, covered in white tablecloths that have seen better days. I count ten places, each with a utilitarian cup and saucer in a fetching green. Apart from Deedee and me, there's only one other person in the hall. He's of the decrepit variety, wearing a beige dustcoat and wielding a large sweeping brush. I quickly conclude that he's the caretaker. Though he looks much as though he could do with a little care and attention himself. I nod civilly to him all the same. He rubs his nose on the back of his hand and purposefully looks the other way. I console myself with the fact that he won't be long for this world.

'Gee, it's all rather quaint,' says Deedee.

'I thought you'd have been here before?' say I.

'No. First time. We're at the epicentre of power in Elderby.'

'Yes, what a prospect.'

I'm still trying to get my head round Deedee's continued

presence in Elderby. Here I am embarking on the cover up of the century and there's a foreign national of dubious provenance in close attendance. They were quick enough to dispatch Colonel Chinstrap and Mrs Mopp, the original Elderby constables – blink and you'd have missed it. But Deedee appears to be a permanent fixture. As much as I tell myself that it's because of her father's money, there's a little niggle in my mind that says otherwise. Though, for the life of me, I can't think what else could be keeping her here.

A tall man in a black suit appears. He seems to be rather unsteady on his feet as he squints at the top table.

'That's Mr Grimshaw, the undertaker,' says Deedee.

'Gosh, he looks as though he has one foot in the grave himself,' say I.

This vision of misery takes in the rest of the place, then turns his gaze on us. He staggers across like a warship limping away from Gallipoli.

'How do?' says Grimshaw.

'Very well, thank you,' say I, paw outstretched. He returns a weak handshake.

'It's a miserable job, you know. Undertaking, I mean,' says Grimshaw, apropos of nothing.

'I don't doubt it,' say I.

'I'm the last person folk want to see, let me tell you. It's a lonely life.'

At this point I'm looking round for something sharp with which to cut my wrists. But Deedee comes to the rescue.

'I think you do a wonderful job. You're like a spirit guide, seeing the dead on their passage to the afterlife. Such an important task. You should be proud, sir.'

Steady on, thinks I.

'Aye, I haven't thought of it like that. I must say, young lady, you're a real tonic. Talking of which . . .' He reaches into his inside pocket and produces a huge hip flask. 'This is just the job for raising the spirits, an' all.'

He offers me the flask. I'm happy to take a good slug, despite already being fed up with his self-pity. Bottoms up!

As I'm knocking back a quick snifter, I notice that he's looking me up and down.

'About the same height as me,' he muses. 'A bit broader in the shoulder, mind.' He nods sagely, as though filing these little observations away for when I pop my clogs.

'Careful, old boy.'

'I'm sorry. It's a force of habit. You can find me in any room sizing up people. I suppose it's like a dentist staring at teeth, or a barber at hair. And let's be honest, the way things are going in this village – well, enough said.'

And with that, he's off. His stride is long and slow, as though he is permanently leading a funeral cortège. It's all jolly stuff.

I hear voices at the door and look over to see Lady Damnish arrive. She is accompanied by an entourage. And she's not dressed down, either. I'm not sure that a tiara and a stole are suitable for a meeting of the parish council, yet Her Ladyship obviously thinks differently. Her long white gloves are also rather ostentatious. It's like a visit from royalty.

There's a small man at her side with fading fair hair. He's ruddy-cheeked and round-faced but carries himself with the confidence of someone who's done well in life. I'd place him in his late sixties.

'Sir Reginald is with Lady Damnish,' says Deedee. 'He's quite a sweetie, really. He did so well in the police. Deputy assistant commissioner. My, that's impressive,' she fawns.

Delighted to hear it, thinks I. More likely an insufferable

toady who has had his nose firmly affixed to every back-side that mattered.

Lady Damnish, I'm told, still enjoys some of the good-will that no doubt attached itself to her late father's *noblesse oblige*. She certainly looks the part. The new queen doesn't stand a chance against this blue-blooded harridan.

The rest of the council stream in now, along with a good crowd. It's as though they've been waiting outside for Lady Damnish to arrive. I recognize Braithwaite the butcher instantly. Wally the baker looks stooped and uncomfort-able away from his pastries, while I barely recognize Bleakly. He's in a lounge suit, his salt and pepper hair slicked back with pomade. He's licking his lips nervously. I note with some irritation that my colleague doesn't spare us a glance. He must know we're here.

'Doesn't Sergeant Bleakly look fine?' Deedee offers.

'If you say so,' say I contemptuously.

A big man dressed in a tweed jacket appears, pipe clenched between his teeth, from which issue clouds of pungent blue smoke. He's of late middle age, with a large, pockmarked face. A less generous person would call him ugly. But as we all know, beauty is in the eye of the beholder.

'That's Finan Whales,' says Deedee. 'He's quite ugly, isn't he? They say he was a champion boxer in his day. Sergeant Bleakly told me.'

I note that Whales has huge hands, with thick, sausage fingers. No doubt he could punch me through a wall. I make a mental note of caution.

Everyone takes their seats, Lady Damnish at the centre of events, a small gavel now in hand. Her tiara sparkles under the hall lights. Sir Reginald is at her side, looking about the hall. His gaze settles on me for a moment. I'm not quite sure what emotion is displayed on his face.

Neutral with a hint of distaste, I think. He clearly knows who I am.

I cast my eye along the row of the great and good of Elderby, sitting ready to interrogate yours truly. Hetty Gaunt, dressed in black from head to toe, is staring purposefully at the ceiling. My goodness, she's not waiting for the arrival of Cecil, is she?

The door swings open and the Reverend Croucher appears, looking flustered. As he takes in the room, his eyes meet mine. He smiles and winks, which is most disconcerting. He's probably thinking about our little arrangement that I change his statement. The poor man thinks he's done himself a favour, when in fact he's sinning his soul. Not that a modern vicar will care about that. Goodness knows what his philosophy really is – certainly self-preservation is high on the list. But I'll never condemn anyone for that. You know me by now.

As everyone settles, it's clear that one member of the council is missing. There's an empty chair at the end of the trestle tables nearest the door.

'How typical.' Lady Damnish frowns. 'I propose we convene immediately.'

'Seconded!' says Sir Reginald, his right index finger raised in the air.

I've given evidence in court more times than I can remember. But for some reason I find my lips are dry and my hands are trembling. I put this down to it being a very long day. But in reality it's my predicament that's making me nervous. Normally – I'll qualify that by saying it isn't universally true – I tell the truth, the whole truth and nothing but the truth in court. But this isn't court, and I have no intention of being completely honest. My country depends upon it, for some reason.

As we're about to begin, the door swings open. A tall, thin man with grey hair at his temples appears. He's wearing a dun jacket with patches on the sleeves and a pullover with a hole at the breast. But there's an air of grandeur about him. Everyone in the council – including Hetty Gaunt – smiles. Apart from Lady Damnish and Sir Reginald, that is.

There's no doubting that this must be Ingleby. As I study his face, I see his sister's sharp features. But, for him, they are arranged in a much more pleasing way. Instead of being bird-like, Ingleby looks grand, aristocratic. Despite his haphazard clothing, he has an air of superiority, at odds with his sister and her tiara that just makes her look as though she's trying too hard.

Ingleby nods his head in an affable fashion at those gathered, then turns and holds the door open. A woman in a long dark coat, her face hidden behind a black veil, steps into the room. There's a collective intake of breath as everyone realizes that this is the newly and tragically widowed Dr Starr. Ingleby shows her to a chair facing the council, where she sits demurely enough. But I notice the white handkerchief in her hand, there to stem the flow of the tears that are bound to come, I don't doubt.

For a moment, Lady Damnish looks to be off her stride. She stares at Dr Starr, her mouth slightly open. But this is just fleeting. Quickly, she gathers herself, bangs the gavel on the table before her and brings the Elderby parish council to order as her estranged brother takes his seat.

23

As I'm called to stand before this august body, Deedee pats me on the back companionably. I find myself glad that she's there, if only for some moral support. Bleakly has still to acknowledge that I'm here, I note. I find this irritating.

I stand before this line of the cream of the village. Both Lady Damnish and Sir Reginald glare at me.

'You are Inspector Frank Grasby, late of the Criminal Investigation Department of York Police, are you not?' says Lady Damnish. Her voice is cut-glass and shrill, but for a small woman is also loud and commanding.

'I am, but not that late,' say I. 'I've only recently arrived in Elderby, and I hope to return to York.'

I know, I can't help being facetious when I'm nervous. I notice one or two members of the council fending off smiles.

'But the fact remains, you're with us now, and you've been detailed to head the investigation into the deaths of the as yet unidentified man who was found in a chimney at Holly House, and that of Mr Charles Starr, correct?' Lady Damnish says this quite dispassionately, without so much as a glance at Starr's widow.

'I am,' say I sombrely.

'Good,' says Lady Damnish. 'How do you intend to go about catching those responsible?'

'Indeed!' pipes up Sir Reginald.

Hello, everybody, I'm here to lie through my teeth, I should say. But I don't.

Instead, I begin: 'Thank you, Your Ladyship. I'm glad to be able to speak to you this evening.' I turn to face Dr Starr. 'And may I express my condolences to you, Doctor Starr, and assure you that I will do my very best to make sense of the dreadful events that took your husband's life.'

You'll note, of course, that the word 'murder' did not cross my lips. How they're going to explain away Starr's death to misadventure or suicide, I don't know. But it's not my problem.

Dr Starr inclines her head a little at this, but under the veil it's hard to see any emotion.

'A sentiment we all echo, of course,' says Lady Damnish, no doubt conscious that she failed to express her and the committee's condolences at the beginning of the meeting. 'You will be aware that my fellow villagers and I find ourselves ill at ease that people have lost their lives in this quiet little place?'

Not so quiet, thinks I. In your fireplace, in fact.

'Indeed, I am. And, at this point, I'd like to reassure everyone that we are taking steps to make sure that nobody in the community is in any danger.'

'But how, Inspector, how?' bawls Sir Reginald.

'Sir Reginald,' say I, as though we're on familiar terms, 'you of all people will know that it would be folly to reveal the measures we have taken in order to assure the safety of the people of the community.' I turn to Lady Damnish. 'Indeed, at this time, I'm unable to reveal any operational details of the investigation. That would be unwise in the extreme.'

'Can't you even tell us who's involved? For instance, I've seen some new faces about the police station.' This voice is that of Elphinstone Bleakly. I don't know what he thinks he's doing.

'Well, of course you'll have spotted some new faces, Sergeant Bleakly,' say I, full of righteous indignation. 'You're their station sergeant.' This garners a giggle from one or two.

'Inspector Grasby,' says Bleakly sombrely. 'You're a young man – comparatively speaking.'

Huh! Younger than you thankfully, you dozy old bugger, thinks I.

'But you'll find that, in life, a man must wear many hats. This evening I wear the hat of the parish council.'

I want to say that he's not wearing a hat at all. But that would be going too far.

'And while I'm under this hat, it behoves me to ask questions that . . .' He hesitates, his eyelids flutter and my heart soars. But no, he manages to remain awake. 'Questions that must be answered.'

'I'm sorry, I address the chair. 'Sergeant Bleakly finds himself in a very awkward position. But I have my orders, and they must be obeyed, regardless of questioning in this place.' My, I'm proud of myself. Just wait until I get my hands on Bleakly tomorrow.

'Bleakly!' shouts Sir Reginald at the top of his voice. 'This won't do, man. D'you hear? This officer has a job to do, as you well know. Discretion is part and parcel of our job.'

My goodness, he thinks he's still a police officer. However, he's on my side, which is both comforting and surprising. But then a sonorous voice booms through the hall, to Sir Reginald's indignation.

'This is a piece of nonsense.' Ingleby is lounging on his chair, a roll-up cigarette between his long fingers. He looks every bit the aristocrat, aloof and slightly bored.

'You will address any comments through the chair!' says Lady Damnish, staring daggers at her brother.

'How appropriate,' replies Ingleby, without the slightest sign of anger. 'I often think it would be as well talking to a chair. I'll get no sense from you.' He puffs languidly.

I'm happy enough at this turn of events. It deflects attention from me.

Finan Whales gets to his feet, turning his cap between his big hands. 'I'd like to offer my services to the inspector. I spent thirty years before the mast as a police officer here in North Yorkshire. I'm sure I can be of assistance. Especially given these dreadful circumstances.'

As long as our inquiries don't take us anywhere near the sea, thinks I.

'I'm sure the inspector will be glad of the help,' says Lady Damnish, casting her beady eye on me.

'Now, it's very generous of Mr Whales to make such an offer,' say I. 'However, I'm sure the committee will understand that it's not in my gift to appoint anyone to the investigation. In a matter so sensitive, I feel sure that my superiors will only wish *serving* officers to be involved.'

I'm being quite circumspect here. This is a murder inquiry, not the village fete. He may be a star of the tombola, but he's not going to further complicate my work. Gosh, it's complex enough. This is a trait I've noticed in retired police officers. No sooner have they divested themselves of the responsibilities of the job, than they're desperate to be back at it again. I used to meet an old cop in a bookmaker's in York from time to time. He was anxious to be retained as a special constable. Beats me why they're like this. I can't wait to draw the pension and be done with the whole thing. Good riddance!

It's time for Sir Reginald to pipe up again. 'If Mr Whales is to be considered, then surely I must take my place in the investigation? After all, I was one of the most senior police officers in the country.' He raises his head haughtily.

This is rapidly turning into farce. I snatch a glance at Dr Starr. Her head is bowed, and even beneath the veil it's easy to see she's upset. No wonder.

It's Ingelby's turn to stand. 'I must protest. We have Doctor Starr in attendance. Please, everyone, respect her feelings. This is monstrous!'

Lady Damnish bangs her gavel. 'May I remind you that I'm chairing this meeting, not you.' She holds his gaze for a moment. It's easy to see the antipathy that exists between them. She continues. 'It is the duty of this committee to impress upon Inspector Grasby the despair we feel at recent events. And urge him to redouble his efforts. Are you in agreement, Grasby?'

'Of course, Your Ladyship. I can assure you that everything possible is being done in order to get to the truth – in both matters,' say I.

I note her pitiless gaze. One thing's for certain: I don't want to cross swords with the chair. There's something of the night about her, as my father would say.

You'd be forgiven for thinking that all these theatrics would be enough for one parish council meeting, but you'd be wrong. Hetty Gaunt holds one hand to her forehead and closes her eyes. I'm waiting for Her Ladyship's gavel to batter the table, or for another cutting remark from Ingleby, but the room descends into absolute silence. Honestly, you can hear a pin drop.

My landlady begins to mumble. It's a deep, unnerving sound that she emits, at odds with her tiny frame.

'Before sunset tomorrow, another will lie dead,' she says.

There's a gasp or two. I look round and Deedee has her hand to her mouth. But good old Hetty's not finished. 'A stranger in our midst will cross to the other side.' She slumps forward, holding her head in her hands.

Every eye is on me. It takes me a moment to work out why. But it's not hard when you think about it. I'm the only stranger here – well, just about.

It's a sideshow, if ever there was one. I'm usually sceptical when it comes to those who flaunt their relationships with the dead. That fortune teller on the pier at Scarborough I told you about claimed to be able to have a chat with any dead relative you wanted. As a younger man, courting a rather fetching girl, I made out that my great-grandfather had been an American Indian. Damn me, in two shakes of a lamb's tail she was up and about hollering like an idiot, shouting for a peace pipe, telling me she was my ancestor speaking through the host. I think these people are charlatans, absolute bounders, preying on others' grief. But even I have to admit that good old Hetty Gaunt has put the wind up me with that growling voice.

At this, Ingleby gets to his feet and makes his way across to Dr Starr. Her shoulders are rolling, and it's clear that she's been upset by the pantomime that is the parish council. Though her sobs are silent.

Ingleby leans over her and whispers in her ear. I see her nod beneath the veil, and he helps the grieving widow to her feet.

Of course, I'm also a sceptic when it comes to gentlemen who come to the rescue of damsels in distress. Dr Starr is most easy on the eye, and a good deal younger than Ingleby,

I reckon. Whatever his marital status, it's easy to see through his good deed for the day. He knows an opportunity when he sees one. Good for you, thinks I. There's something admirable about the cut of Ingleby's jib, I reckon. I'm rarely wrong.

'Please excuse me,' he says to his sister, the chair of the meeting. 'I think what has happened here tonight is an utter disgrace. How dare you!' With that, he takes the widow by her hand and leads her out of the hall.

'Mind you, he's not wrong,' says Braithwaite the butcher. 'Bloody farce, tonight's been.'

'Please keep your opinions to yourself, Mr Braithwaite,' hisses Lady Damnish. 'Though, under the circumstances, I hereby close this meeting!' She bangs her gavel.

'I'm damned if I know what's going on,' says Bleakly, looking round as though it's just another night.

'Right, Deedee,' says I. 'Time for a stiff drink.' I'm not joking, either. We make our way out of the hall and take a short, brisk walk to the Hanging Beggar.

'Are you OK?' says Deedee as we near the hostelry.

'No, I damn well am not.'

'I wouldn't set much store by anything you heard tonight. A lot of old baloney, if you ask me.'

I think for a moment, but I'm too much of a gentleman to give these thoughts voice. After all, good old Hetty said a stranger would die, and Daisy Dean is every bit as much of a stranger here as I am I feel a bit caddish taking comfort in this thought. But heigh-ho, any port in a storm. A chap can take chivalry too far, you know.

Somewhat appropriately, and at odds with the circumstances, I feel something festive in the air. It's the promise of Christmas, good tidings and all of that stuff. Though I've no idea what Christmas will mean for me. There are a few customers in the Beggar, quite a few worse for wear, too. Ethel greets us wearily.

'Inspector. Miss Dean. How did the parish council meeting go?'

'I think it's fair to say that it was eventful for all the wrong reasons,' say I.

'Bunch of old fuddy-duddies, in my opinion,' Ethel replies. 'They don't ever seem to achieve nowt.' She bends down and rubs her knee. 'Mind you, as they say, it's an ill wind, and all that. I've had my busiest day since the fete. I had to get an emergency delivery from the brewery this afternoon.'

We order our drinks. It's true, you know. Nothing interests folk more than tragedy. I suppose it's a bit like gallows humour in the war. They gather together to talk about the dead, thankful it's not them. I've seen it so many times.

'Here, let me buy you and your young lady a drink. Inspector, what do you fancy?'

The voice comes from behind. I turn to face the large figure of Finan Whales. He's smiling broadly. Suddenly I want to be sick. Not because he thinks that Deedee is my young lady, but something else. He's wearing cologne; quite distinctive, it is. I recognize it from this morning in the woods, when someone tried to knock my block off.

24

I damn rationing, I really do. Of course, we'd all like more meat, sugar, and the like. But for me, it's tea. I can't abide to be without it. And this morning, I wake after what can best be described as a fitful sleep to find that Hetty Gaunt – the reason for a portion of my nocturnal angst – has run out of the stuff. Also, I can still smell Finan Whales's cologne, which makes me both angry and a little scared at the same time. Last night he was amiable and polite. So, why did he try to stave my head in yesterday morning? Or does everyone in this corner of North Yorkshire wear the same scent?

Deedee – up and annoyingly as bright as a button, given the amount of whisky she managed to put away last night – comes to the rescue. So, before long I'm sitting in the dark dining room in the guest house knocking back a strong black coffee, some of Deedee's own supply. I'm surprised how good it is. Most of the coffee I've ever drunk has been heavily adulterated with chicory or is just as likely to be the last sweepings from the warehouse. Deedee's brew is as fresh as you like, with that peculiarly invigorating, almost fruity flavour that readies me to face another hard day. Deedee tells me that her fellow Americans can't function without the stuff. I'm beginning to understand why.

Hetty Gaunt, landlady and resident doom-monger,

appears amidst the black-walled gloom. She yawns spectacularly, Cecil squawking on her shoulder.

'I'm right buggered today.'

Charming.

'I suppose talking all that nonsense must take it out of
you,' say I, venting my wrath.

'Whatever do you mean?' she replies.

'Your prophecy from last night – you know what I'm
talking about, Mrs Gaunt.'

She adopts a faraway look. 'Aye, I heard I had an *experience* at the meeting. You never can tell when they'll come.'

'What?' I say, looking at Deedee, who shrugs.

'I don't have a clue what I've said when it happens, you
know. For me, it's just like falling asleep.'

A likely story, methinks. Just another ruse to get people
to believe her.

'I do get feelings – you know, residual, like.'

'No, I don't know.' I'm feeling less than charitable, so the
reply is curt.

'Faces, people, things like that.'

Here we go. My residual face is no doubt imprinted on
her mind's eye.

'Do you remember any of these things from last night,
Mrs G?' says Deedee.

The landlady looks coy for a moment, as though she
wants someone to coax it out of her. A lot of old tosh, if
you ask me.

'Aye, I did see something – while I was in the trance, you
know.'

Bollocks. I nearly say this out loud but manage to stop
myself in the nick of time.

'Please, what was it?' says my impressionable American
intern.

Mrs Gaunt coughs, stares at the wall and sighs. 'I saw the old Salt House up on the fell. It was an awful thing. Death all around.'

'Oh, come on. Get on with it. I've a job to do,' say I. I'm impatient, you see. Especially when I know I'm dealing with a time-waster.

'Just like your father,' she says out of nowhere.

'I beg your pardon?'

'You heard. You're not the first Grasby to lodge in this house, lad.'

I must admit, while I'm astonished that's she's confessed to it, I can't say I'm truly surprised. That sketch in my room bears too much of a resemblance to my dear old pa to be anyone else.

'A young curate, he was.' A broad smile crosses her face.

I'm not sure I'm too keen to hear this bit.

'Oh, how wonderful!' says Deedee, in that over-the-top way our colonial friends across the Atlantic do. 'What a coincidence!'

Hetty Gaunt stares at me. Her gaze is quite off-putting. I feel as if she's boring into my very soul.

'Now, then, lass. You're young, I know. But you'll find that when you get to my age there's a certain order to things. Pieces of the puzzle fit together, and you just can't explain it. Things are meant to be as they are, and that's just the way – stranger or no stranger, Miss Dean.' Though she addresses Deedee, her eyes remain fixed on mine.

I have the strangest feeling. It's as though she's speaking to me without saying a word. It's as though she's somehow communicating on two levels. Suddenly, everything is clear. I'm not the stranger she was talking about. My instincts were the right ones. It's Deedee that's in danger. I can't bear the thought, regardless of my suspicions. But why would anyone want to harm this pretty young woman? And if they did, what would Daddy say?

'I'm not sure I know what you mean, Mrs Gaunt,' says Deedee innocently.

'It's all right, dear. You'll know it when you experience it.' Hetty Gaunt stares at me again. 'In any case, the inspector knows what I mean. Don't you, lad?'

I was right. In her own strange way, she's warning me. But I've no idea what she's warning me of, or what I should do to mitigate this terrible situation. Why do people insist on talking in riddles?

It's now that a little light blinks into life in my head. I'm being seduced by this absolute nonsense. It's only the same self-interested funk I got myself into when witnessing Gaunt's theatrics at the meeting. It's always the same with this type of stuff. It's pernicious, unsettling.

'You knew him well, then? My father, I mean,' say I, anxious to find out and lighten the mood.

'Well enough, lad. Well enough.'

I see the ghost of a lascivious smile play across her thin lips. Or maybe I'm imagining it.

'My mother ran this place in those days,' she remembers. 'I were just a slip of a lass. Your father was glamorous – different from the local lads I'd known up until then. Even if he was a *stranger*.' The last word in the sentence hangs in the air.

I resolve to have it out with Hetty Gaunt. But now isn't the time.

Back at Elderby police station, Deedee volunteers to get a brew on. It's time to gather my thoughts.

Juggers and Cummins want Starr's death swept under the carpet. And yes, initially, I was happy to do it, reckoning that the security of the country was more important. However, since then a number of things are troubling me. The cigarette end is one. Either Cummins was at the locus where Starr's body was found, or somebody else has very expensive taste in cigarettes. Combine that with the fact that somebody attacked me, old Inspector Moore's death, and Mrs Gaunt's dire portents of doom, and I now have my doubts.

But where to go from here?

It's obvious that I'm going to see little in the way of help from the locals. They're far too busy infighting, or imagining they've seen or heard something they clearly haven't, to focus their minds on a murder. Proceedings at the parish council last night spoke volumes. Though I'm interested to talk to Ingleby. He's clearly a man of integrity.

I remove a cigarette from its packet and begin the habitual search for my matches. I usually keep them beside the cigarettes, but I haven't done so today. No doubt distracted by so many problems. I feel weighed down.

I find them in the pocket of my sports jacket. But there's a scrap of paper there, too. I fetch it out, trying to remember what it is. A note scribbled on a piece of paper torn from a lined jotter, or the like.

Go to Withernshaw Fell. Look inside the Salt House.

That's all it says. The writing is small and neat. But the author of the note has gone over each letter four or five times, probably to disguise the hand. I try to work out how on earth this message made it into my jacket pocket. There can only be two explanations: either it was placed there in the crowded pub yesterday evening, or Hetty Gaunt has been doing some clandestine sneaking about in the middle of the night. I remember being surprised this morning to see that I'd hung my jacket on the hook behind the door, and not in the small wardrobe. Such are the perils of intoxication, I'm sad to say. It would have been easy for her to lean round the door of my room when I was in my cups. But equally, it would have been just as easy for Whales to slip it into my pocket as we were being buffeted by drinkers in the Beggar.

When Deedee arrives with the tea, I quickly return the note to my jacket pocket. She's smart as a whip. But I still can't trust her. I remember the red, dirty legs, the furtive look on her face when I bumped into her coming out of Starr's study. Not to mention the fact: why's she here at all?

'Are you quite all right, Inspector?' says Deedee as she places a small tray of tea and biscuits on my desk.

'Bit worse for wear after last night, if I'm honest. One too many, I think.'

'I have the advantage of being a distiller's daughter. I was fed the stuff from being a child. My father swears by the medicinal properties of whiskey.'

'I'm sure he's right. I have an uncle in Ecclefechan who regularly feels absolutely no pain,' say I ruefully.

This is true, of course – my mother's brother. To be honest, we've rather lost contact with him since she died. Or rather, I've lost contact. My father can't bear the man, thinking him a hapless drunk. Still, Uncle Charlie can tell a tale or two, and I always liked him. This, despite his weakness for the bottle. In any case, my father has a cheek. I wonder who put him on the sofa last night after a surfeit of home brew?

'Enjoy your tea. I have some documents to type up.' Deedee disappears in a flurry of clicking high heels and expensive perfume.

Come to think of it, I don't really know what she does. I mean, I know she's an intern, but how on earth does such

213

a person spend the day? Typing is the obvious answer, I suppose.

I take the note from my pocket and stare at it once more. I don't know about her typing, but Deedee is good at making tea. I sip at a cup whilst studying the clandestine message.

There's nothing for it. I must visit the Salt House.

25

Having consulted the map, I note that Withernshaw Fell is the one that looms behind Lord Damnish's Holly House. I've become more and more concerned about this faux aristocrat. I'm neither for nor against our nobility. For me, they've always just been kind of there. But if one is going to be lord such-and-such or lady this-and-that, well, I think it should come with birth. After all, it's tradition; Damnish is about as far away from that as it's possible to be. A barrow boy made good, a fishmonger on the make. Maybe I'm just getting cynical.

I see no buildings marked on the map at Withernshaw Fell, but standards of cartography have slipped in this country over the last few years, and I'm sure map makers were told to be as vague as possible in order to foil invading Germans. It's no wonder I came to grief on the way to Elderby.

I'm scurrying out of the station, hoping not to bump into Bleakly or Deedee. But just as I reach the car park, I hear her calling me.

'Inspector Grasby, where are you off to?'

Now, normally, I'm happy to have a young lady accompany me wherever I go. It hasn't happened often enough in my life. But on this occasion I feel that I must go alone. I suppose Mrs Gaunt's prediction must be weighing on my mind. And some things are best done by oneself.

'I'm off to do some poking about, Deedee. I'll catch up with you when I come back.'

I toy with the idea of jumping into my Austin, but soon abandon that notion given I'm about to tackle a steep incline, and I don't fancy reversing all the way. There's the little Morris Minor police van parked next to my car. In true police tradition, the keys are balanced on the offside wheel. So, off I go.

I'm soon nearing Holly House, blanketed in the snow. Despite what the locals think, it's a good-looking building – in contrast to Damnish himself, an awkward and unprepossessing man. I roll the window down in an attempt to reinvigorate my morning-after head with fresh, cold air. I did have one too many last night, and I'm feeling a little worse for wear.

I can see some dark clouds appearing overhead, and there's a particular feel to the air – fresh and clean – that, for me, always speaks of the winter and all that goes with it. As I emerge from the trees, I see Withernshaw Fell shrouded in snow. A low cloud – clag, as my mother would have called it – hangs over the summit.

Using logic – yes, I can do that – I suppose that this Salt House must be near by. After all, this is the only road up the mountain. It goes so far, then dwindles to little more than a footpath. At least, that's how it's marked on the map.

The steeper the climb, the deeper the snow gets. Though, strangely enough, the road has been cleared. I brush my fingers against the reassuring bulge of the Webley.

The drive and the deteriorating weather remind me yet again of family holidays. Now and then, mainly at the Easter break, we'd head off to Scotland, so that my mother could reacquaint herself with her relatives. My father was never in the best of moods before, during and after these trips. As I've mentioned before, he's not keen on the Scots. I often wonder why he married one. Other things he dislikes about the place are midges, their beer and the Church of Scotland. It's an eclectic list, I know. But he hates all these things in equal measure.

As the road becomes steeper still, I'm reminded of a hike up the Cuillins on Skye. I was just a child – perhaps seven or eight years old. Leaving my mother in Edinburgh with her cousins, my father and I embarked on a journey by train, bus and ferry, which found us on the beautiful isle.

We booked into a cheap B&B, suffered an awful evening meal and even worse breakfast, before embarking on our hike. I was impossibly excited by the whole journey. These hills looked so dramatic that they conjured up images of magical castles, trolls and goblins to my childish mind.

A good way off the summit, we encountered a fellow traveller. Lo and behold, it turned out that he was a minister in the Church of Scotland. After an amiable enough conversation, they began to discuss transubstantiation – as one does when climbing a mountain, I'm sure. As you know, this is for my father somewhat of a bête noire. The difficulty appeared to centre around whether or not the little wafers of bread offered at Communion were really Christ's flesh or not. Now, to me, the answer to this appeared glaringly obvious. They were hard pieces of bread. I'd often seen my father spread a little French cheese on them when he found the loaf he kept in the vestry was rather past its best. But now he was arguing that this bread was in actual fact the body of Christ.

I'd never really considered any of this in a meaningful

way. Yet, here I was, watching two men of the cloth going back and forth like a pair of drunken sailors. When it got to the stage of clenched fists, I must admit I became scared and started to cry. I'm a sensitive soul, you see. Apart from that, being an avid reader of *Boy's Own* adventures, I pictured the Reverend Archibald McCulloch knocking seven bells out of my father and me being abandoned on the hill.

Ultimately, it all ended well. They shook hands and agreed to disagree. But as I spot a stone building higher up on the fell, I remember that day as though it had happened last week; the feeling in my chest is the same mix of excitement and concern. I pull the little Morris Minor van on to the verge, out of sight behind a large bush, and embark upon my visit to the Salt House.

I realize quite quickly that I should have dressed appropriately for this. My brogues are soon slipping on the snowy ground, and as I near the Salt House I feel pinpricks of hail on my face. Fortunately, I manage to find the remnants of an old path. It too appears to have been cleared and offers extra purchase. Soon I'm heading up the steep incline in much better shape. The hail gets heavier. I pull my coat over my head to avoid the battering hailstones.

I enter the Salt House, an austere-looking building that stands tall and stark against the white hill. It's redolent of caves, or some of the bomb-damaged places I found myself in during the war. The walls are cold with frozen damp, the floor hard stone, pitted with icy puddles here and there. It's hard to imagine that any enterprise once took place here. There are few discernible signs of what happened in this building, save for the odd protruding hook, rusted after years of neglect. I examine one on tiptoes. Though it's old, the damned thing is sharp. I feel a prick on my finger and withdraw it quickly, dismayed to see a drop of my own blood amidst the white frost and rust clinging to my hand.

As I explore further, it isn't clear why anyone would want me to come here. It's also obvious that this place is large, with a number of outbuildings. It's like some of the woollen mills one comes across in the most unlikely places in parts of the north of England, isolated and alone in its current state. Much of the structure is little more than a ruin, with a partially collapsed roof and scattered huddles of dressed stone, the remnants of something once great, a place that had meaning and purpose. Soon the hail is pattering on the floor in front of me. When I can go no further, I turn to have another look round the sounder part of the building.

Back under cover, I poke about, trying to find something that would merit the passing of a note. But all I can see are old stones and broken roof timbers. I look down as a large spider meanders across my left shoe.

I'm about to give up when I hear something outside. It's the thud of a diesel engine.

My heart begins to pound. Instantly, I fear I've been brought here for one purpose and one purpose alone – to finish off the job they couldn't do in the woods yesterday morning.

But the more I listen, this engine noise gets no louder. Plus, it seems to be emanating from behind the Salt House, so whatever it is clearly isn't heading towards me. Quietly, I make my way to the rear of this derelict place. Through an open hole where a window once was, I see something quite remarkable.

At the back of the building the fell rises sharply. An area of ground between the Salt House and the fell has been concreted over, and is also miraculously cleared of ice and snow. This may well have been a storage area, or perhaps the foundations of a construction now long gone. I marvel at its size, and the fact that it's invisible from the road.

But that's not all I see.

Bang in the middle of this yard, as I look down, is a white Ford Anglia panel van. I recognize the model immediately, as we have them at the station in York. Apart from its unexpected location, I'm surprised by what this van is doing, or rather that it has such a facility. The engine noise is coming from an extending antenna that is slowly revealing itself from the back of the vehicle. Given the distance I'm viewing from, it must be at a height of around twenty feet and counting.

Only as I'm taking this all in, do I hear the sadly familiar click of metal on metal. Behind me, someone has cocked a pistol.

26

'What are you doing here?' The voice is sharp and to the point. 'Turn round – slowly.'

Let me tell you, being assailed at gunpoint is by no means my favourite way to spend time. And it's happened rather too frequently in my life, for my liking. You'd think one would get used to facing imminent death, but that's never the case.

I do as I'm bid, my hands in the air. I move the way we were taught to in the army – slowly. Yes, this may be a gun-toting maniac intent on blowing you to kingdom come, but it might not be. The basic tactic is to assess every aspect of your situation as it happens. Personally, I think this is a fine thing to say to a roomful of chaps in basic training – but I've found I'm always in too much of a funk to assess anything in such circumstances. I just rely on the old Grasby intuition. You can see why I'm unnerved, I'm sure.

I turn, ready to plead for my life with anything in my possession: money, favours, a tip for the four-thirty at Kempton Park. But lo and behold, the man pointing the handgun at me is none other than Ingleby.

'I thought it was you,' he whispers, lowering the weapon. 'Come on, time to get out of here as quickly as we can.'

This is not the moment for questions, though I have

many. Relieved that I'm not about to be shot, I follow blindly as we hurry back down the slippery path and away from the Salt House. I reckon Ingleby must have at least ten years on me. I'd put him in his early fifties, to be honest. But still, he's as sure-footed as a mountain goat, and by the time we're back on the main road I'm out of breath while he remains suave and unruffled.

'Let's get to the car,' says he.

We crouch along the verge, taking advantage of the cover of the spindly trees and bushes that come our way. Suddenly, just as we near the little police van, he stops.

'Damn!'

'What's up?' say I.

'Up there,' he says, inclining his head forward.

I follow his line of sight, and sure enough, on a rise about half a mile away, I see the figure of a man standing stock still, silhouetted on the skyline.

'Who on earth's that?' say I, squinting into the distance.

'McGill, His *Lordship*'s gamekeeper.' Ingleby spits out Damnish's title. An honorific that should, as far as I can gauge, be his.

'Not uncommon to see such a man knocking about the countryside, is it?'

'No, under normal circumstances it isn't. But, as you've just witnessed, these are – by any measure – less than normal circumstances, Inspector.' He studies the still figure on the hill for a moment or two. 'Come on, let's go back to Briarside. I'm sure you have many questions.'

I'll say! The peril and mystery of this village continues to surprise. What on earth is going on in the deserted factory?

Ingleby directs me up a rough farm track. It hasn't been cleared of snow, so I'm driving very carefully. In the rear-view mirror, I can see Withernshaw Fell is almost obscured by clouds now. As we rattle up this ill-maintained track, the hail starts again, making the van sound like a tin drum. I have to peer through the windscreen to see where we're going.

Soon, we pull into a yard. It's the familiar farm thing, minus one aspect. There's no work taking place here. I normally gag when I'm near anything agricultural. It's odd, really. I was offered beautiful home-made scones and jam at a farm near Malton not long ago. The farmer's son had gone missing, but despite her concern his poor mother had laid on a magnificent spread. Feeling compelled to feast, I did my best. But that smell made my stomach churn. The farmer and his wife happily tucked into the fare, as though the place was as antiseptic as a hospital. I suppose you get used to anything if you're exposed to it for long enough.

Ingleby asks me to stop by a large door. We get out of the van, and he leads me through it and into a long room. It's a shambles. Half-finished paintings and empty frames lie everywhere. The slick concrete floor is a rainbow of colours. The smell reminds me of art class at school, a heady mix of turpentine and pigment.

'I heard you were an artist,' say I, as he heads to a paint-stained sink where a kettle and some old enamel mugs reside.

'Tea, Inspector?'

'Most definitely, thank you. I must confess to being a little shaken up.'

'I'm sorry about that,' says Ingleby. 'I saw you heading for the Salt House through my binoculars. I would have had a word with you last night, but my duty lay with poor Elizabeth. As for the gun – one can't be too careful. Such a terrible thing to happen. But sadly, I'm not surprised.'

'Really? I would have thought that the death of a villager would catch everyone off guard in a small place like this,' I suggest, still not mentioning murder.

Ingleby busies himself at the sink. 'Yes, that would be the normal course of events. But there is dark business afoot in this village, Inspector. Very dark, indeed.'

'Yes, I've rather picked up on that,' I say, meaning it.

'I'm afraid I'm out of sugar. This damnable rationing. I'll wager they have a plentiful supply in the House of Lords.'

I note that this is spoken with no little spite. I put it down to his reduced circumstances. It must be hard to see someone like Damnish swanning about as cock o' the north when it should be you.

'My father rarely attended. But he had a profound interest in military matters, being an old army man. He always tried to be in London for security debates.' Ingleby suddenly looks rueful.

'You must miss him.'

'Oh yes, in my own way. You see, he and I were often at odds. Very different personalities, that kind of thing. My father liked to think he was a bit of a genius when it came to business. Got himself involved in all manner of things that he should have run a mile from. That's how he lost everything, you know.'

'I heard something to that effect, yes.'

'No doubt. It was a scandal. Damnish bullying a peer of the realm out of what was his right. But that's how men like him operate.' He hands me a mug of tea. 'It's Darjeeling. I hope that's to your taste?'

'It is. My father likes fancy tea. He rather put me on to it.'

'Fathers, eh? They mould our lives in so many ways. For good and bad.'

I take a sip of Darjeeling. 'Well, I must admit, I'm

bursting to know what's happening up at the Salt House. Can you tell me?'

'It's a military operation of some kind.' Ingleby's reply is short and to the point. 'Some kind of monitoring equipment, from what I can tell. The place belongs to Damnish, and he's sanctioning it.'

'How do you know?'

'How else could it happen? You saw McGill on the rise. He and his men are like a small private army. They don't do much in the way of tending to game these days. Full-time working on his whims.'

'Maybe the police markings on the van gave them second thoughts?'

'It didn't give them second thoughts when it came to doing away with your predecessor, did it?'

'Are you being serious?'

'Oh, I can't prove it. But it was Moore who put me in the picture. This is the closest place to the Salt House. He used to come here and keep tabs on what was going on, share his thoughts, and so on. He was a good man.'

'I can't imagine why his death wasn't investigated more thoroughly,' say I.

Ingleby shrugs. 'Wheels within wheels, Inspector. The likes of Damnish have many fellow-travellers in the corridors of power, that's for sure. The war turned a lot of heads. Many fear that fascism isn't dead, merely sleeping. A friend of mine thinks Hitler is alive and well in South America. Who really knows? But there are people, like Damnish – treacherous bounders – who imagine Hitler and his army will emerge over the fell at any moment.'

Gosh, the thought of Adolf taking the sun on Filey Beach isn't something that ever crossed my mind. Though, for a good few years my father reckoned that Mr

225

Dickenson, a retired solicitor who lived three doors down the street from us in York, was the Führer in hiding. This theory grew legs when the unfortunate Dickenson was run over and killed by the number 43 bus. My father surmised that he'd been quietly dispatched by the government so good folk could rest easy in their beds, knowing one of the most evil men in history had finally got what he deserved in Potterhill Terrace. The fact that Dickenson was a tall red-headed man who bore absolutely no resemblance to Hitler didn't seem to bother him.

'You seem lost in your thoughts, Inspector,' says Ingleby.

'Just thinking about Hitler,' say I, without elaboration.

'I'm more worried about Uncle Joe.'

'Does he live around here, then?'

Ingleby narrows his eyes. 'No, not my uncle. Stalin – Uncle Joe – you must have heard him called that?'

Damn. My mind is racing, and I've only been half listening to Ingleby. If what he's saying has any validity, I'm in a much worse pickle than I thought. And where should I turn? Of course, the enigmatic Cummins should be the first port of call. After all, I have his number. But I also have one of his cigarette stubs in an old pie bag. I remember Juggers warning about resorting to that call. I'm not sure I can rely on the monocled old Etonian.

Juggers, too. Hitherto I'd have trusted him with my life. But now, can I really trust anyone? The fate of Inspector Moore weighs heavily on me, as does Mrs Gaunt's vision.

'What do you think we should do?' I ask Ingleby.

'I rather hoped you'd have the answer to that question, old chap,' he says.

'Ah, yes. You're right. But what I want to know is, what on earth are they monitoring?'

Ingleby strokes his chin thoughtfully. 'Between you and me, I heard something from an old friend at Boodle's.'

Still frequenting exclusive London clubs, then. It's clear that Ingleby hasn't lost all the trappings of the aristocracy.

'Oh yes, what did he say?'

'They're planning something big round about here. People aren't sure what it is, but the place has been crawling with army top brass over the last few years. Some say it's where we're going to store our atomic bombs. Others that it's to be an intelligence-gathering facility. I can only imagine that this is what Damnish and his Russian friends are interested in.'

'This old pal of yours,' say I. 'How would he come across such information? All sounds a bit fanciful, if you ask me.'

'He was foreign secretary under Attlee for a while. Got the chop over a fling with a dancer. She had magnificent legs – can't blame the chap, really.'

Hurrah for socialism, thinks I. Boodle's is a long way from a pint down the pub. Nonetheless, it's hard to discount information from such a source.

'Aren't you in danger?' I ask Ingleby.

'No, I wouldn't think so. I know too much, you see. And it's all salted away with my chum. If I disappear, he'll blow the gaff, so to speak. I told my sister. She's bound to have passed it on to her handsome husband.'

'Sorry, I got the impression you and Lady Damnish were rather estranged.'

'Most definitely. But it's fun to poke the bear now and again. I'm afraid I can't resist it. Harry is a good go-between.'

'You like your nephew?'

'Yes, a fine young man. He may be Damnish's son, but he's an Elderby through and through. That fat sod won't last for ever. And when he pops his clogs, we'll be restored to what is rightly ours. Not a bloody thing Damnish can do about it.'

'What about your sister?'

'She can go to hell!'

I'm struck by the viciousness of this. Lady Damnish may still be to the manner born, but in the process she made an enemy for life in the shape of her brother. Something tells me Ingleby would make an intractable foe.

'The man they found in the chimney. I'll wager you any money he was from our security services.'

'Are you serious?'

'Absolutely. Caught Damnish by surprise – they had to act quickly. Killed him and threw him down the chimney to make it look as though he was a burglar. Classic stuff.'

'But in that case the cause of death will soon be discovered. And so will they.'

'It'll be covered up by our government. They can't be seen to be sending chaps out to spy on members of the public, and certainly not on a member of the aristocracy, however fraudulent.'

This is starting to make sense. Starr must have been part of this, hence Cummins' arrival. Damn, I'm just being used. I'm furious, but I try not to let it show.

I wander over to a painting on an easel. It's like Dante's vision of Hell, with people running away from an erupting volcano, by the looks of it. But after a few moments the shape of this volcano begins to look more familiar: it's Withernshaw Fell.

'Gosh, I hope this doesn't happen,' say I.

'Do you like it? I paint from the heart, Inspector. This is what I fear. It's an allegory, of course. But you can see the meaning, I'm sure.'

'Will you sell it?'

He smiles enigmatically. 'No, I rather think I'll give it to my nephew as a gift. I'm sure Damnish would like nothing better on the walls of his monstrosity of a house. It'll likely improve the value of the place tenfold.'

'I'm sure.'

Something tells me that, despite his fears about Joe Stalin and his wicked intent, Ingleby is much more interested in seeking revenge for his father and his lost inheritance.

'I better get going,' say I. 'I have a lot to think about.'

'Good luck, Inspector. But be careful. These people aren't taking any prisoners. Poor old Starr paid the price, I'm sure of it. And Moore, too.'

'You think Starr was mixed up in all of this?' I'm trying my hand, even though I've come to a similar conclusion.

'What do you think? An all-American war hero just happens to find himself in a quiet Yorkshire village with all this going on? I don't think so.'

'A spy?'

'The Americans don't trust us, Inspector – and no wonder. The government is jam-packed with chaps who had their heads turned in Oxford or Cambridge before the war, one way or another. The Nazis may be a thing of the past, but that lot are still loyal to Moscow. You'll see, it'll all come out one day.'

I thank Ingleby for his timely intervention and take my leave. On the way out, I see another painting in progress. It's a huge dome; only an outline but eerily familiar.

I depart Briarside, glad to have met Ingleby.

On the way back to Elderby police station, Deedee crosses my mind. If Starr's death is beginning to make sense because of Ingleby's theories, it would explain why the young woman is here. Maybe it's not the influence of a rich daddy. Perhaps she's also working for the American government. But I must be careful to stay within the bounds of things I know to be facts. Ingleby's theories on the dead man at Holly House and Chuck Starr are mere conjecture, regardless of how plausible they appear. And Boodle's – well, honestly.

It's at times like this that a chap wishes he'd sought another career. I always mocked my father for being a man of the cloth. Now I wish it was me standing in the pulpit.

27

I'm no sooner back behind my desk than the door bursts open.

'What on earth have you been up to?' says a harassed-looking Bleakly.

'I'm sorry, Sergeant,' say I calmly, 'I wasn't under the impression that I answer to you. Please forgive me if I'm mistaken.'

Bleakly mumbles something I don't understand.

'In any event, old boy, I don't know which hat you're wearing. Is it your police helmet or the one Lady Damnish gives you to be her lapdog?'

I always think that treachery is the most pernicious sin. To trust someone, only for them to turn on you, cuts to the very core. Following his attempts to hole me below the waterline last night at the parish council meeting, this is how I feel about Bleakly.

'As I said, a man must have boundaries,' says Bleakly with an indignant raise of his chin.

'Not where the law is concerned, Sergeant Bleakly!'

I'm at a distinct advantage here, having probably been carpeted more frequently than any serving officer in Yorkshire. Therefore, I'm intimately acquainted with the methods deployed in such a scenario.

'The body count is accumulating, and you chose to behave like some sea lawyer. Well, I'm here to tell you, Sergeant, you might be in thrall to Damnish and his family, but I have a job to do.'

Bleakly looks at me levelly. 'That's good, then, sir. Because you'll have the chance to tell Lord Damnish that in person.'

'What?'

'He's in my office waiting for you. Not a happy man, let me tell you.'

I think for a moment. I must be careful. And let's face it, I don't have a splendid record with the aristocracy, real or contrived.

'I'd go and see him now, if I were you.' Bleakly inclines his head in a knowing fashion.

'I realize that you've spent your career in the police at the beck and call of your superiors – it's the lot of the uniform branch, after all. But I'm here in a senior capacity. Go and tell His Lordship to come here and I'll speak to him.'

Bleakly shakes his head. 'Whatever you say, *sir.*'

'And watch your tone, Bleakly. Now, cut along, there's a good chap.'

You know, there are certain advantages to a public school education, regardless of the quality of said establishment. One learns how to come the high hand when necessary. I can almost see Bleakly bridle as he turns to go and tell Damnish to attend me in my office. I despise all that upper-class stuff. I'm about as far away from privilege as you can get. But Bleakly has behaved in a way unbecoming of a police officer.

I dread to think how dear old Juggers would have reacted. He'd likely be in the process of a fit, his head ready to launch through the ceiling.

In any case, it's time Elderby's sleepy sergeant learned the meaning of rank. I know that it's partly my fault; I'm too personable and collegiate. But the fact remains, I'm the inspector and he's a sergeant. QED.

As I sit waiting for the arrival of Damnish, I rehearse how to receive him.

Now, Your Lordship, I'm a busy man, so get to the point. Or perhaps: *I say, old chap, this isn't the Middle Ages. I don't pay obeisance to you.*

But the preparation is spoiled when Deedee pokes her head round the door.

'Lord Damnish is refusing to come to your office, Inspector. Says he's going to phone the chief constable, who's a friend of his, apparently.'

Damn him. I'm not in the best of shape when it comes to credit with senior officers, as you know. I'm anxious to avoid meetings with chief constables, thank you very much.

'Please tell him I'm on my way out. So, I'll drop in on the way past.'

As Deedee does as she's bid, I lean back in my chair and light a cigarette. I may have had to give some ground on this occasion, but I'm damned if this glorified fishmonger is going to hold me to account without a wait.

Once I've stubbed out my smoke, had a good stretch and yawned a bit, I decide it's time to face Damnish. I find him in the sergeants' room looking fit to have an embolism.

'Who do you think you are, Grasby?' he rages, his face the colour of a Cox's Pippin.

'I'm Francis Grasby, Inspector of Police. I earned my title, *Lord Damnish.*'

'And what do you mean by that?'

Ha! I've rattled this Billy Bunter already. Good for me!

'Just what I say. You asked me who I thought I was, and I told you. I'd say that's rather straightforward, wouldn't you?'

'Sit down!' he commands.

'No, I'm happy standing, if you don't mind.' I look at my watch. 'Don't have long. I'm sure you understand.'

Lord Damnish points a chubby finger in my direction. 'Now, young man. You listen to me. You've been trespassing on my land. I'll not have it, do you hear?'

'Your Lordship, I'm following a line of inquiry related to the deaths of the man found in your home and Mr Charles Starr. I shall go where I please.'

A sickly smile crosses Damnish's face, and I feel the ground slipping from beneath my feet.

'You and I both know you're here for one purpose, and one purpose only.'

'Sorry?'

'I have many influential friends, Inspector Grasby. And they in turn also have friends – *lots of them*. If I want to whisper something in Her Majesty's ear, it will only take one phone call.'

'I'm sure she'll be delighted to hear from you.'

Damnish bangs the table at my insolence. 'Don't get smart with me! Your job is to pay lip service to an investigation that's really being conducted by people much better qualified than a York bobby. My advice is to do that *job*. Reassure the folk of Elderby that they can go about their business safe in the knowledge that the constabulary has a man on the case who can be trusted. One who can't even manage to close a stable door, mark you.' Again, he smiles sickeningly.

My bluff has been well and truly called. And I must admit to being rather put out that my instructions from

Cummins and Juggers have been made known to this great lump of lard – by whatever means. At the same time, I'm not so naive as to think that wealth and position in society comes without privilege. One must know when to stand one's ground and when to regroup and await another opportunity. But like the westerns, as you're bolting off on your trusty steed, it's good to turn in the saddle and fire a few parting shots.

'Well, Your Lordship, I must confess to being rather surprised by your absurd theories. You know, I often find that those who take such an interest in police matters most likely do so for a reason.'

'What do you mean?'

'Just that. Let's just say, I'm slightly uneasy that you saw fit to lift the phone to one of your many *friends* to find out about an ongoing police investigation.'

'That's as may be. But you know I'm right.'

I decide just to shrug this comment away.

Damnish shifts in his chair and clears his throat. 'In any case, I'm not here just to chew the fat with you.'

'What, then?'

'I want to report a crime – another one, I hasten to add.'

I nod, remove my notebook from the inside pocket of my jacket, and stand poised with my spider scrawl for this revelation.

'Are you ready?'

'I am,' say I.

'Certain objects have gone missing from my home.'

'What kind of objects?'

'Too numerous to mention, Inspector. But suffice it to say, they are worth a pretty penny.'

'I see. Well, I can't investigate a theft when I don't know what's been stolen.'

'There's a list of these missing items at Holly House. But I don't need you to investigate anything.'

'Sorry? I'm not following.'

'I've found the culprit myself. Rather, one of my men did.'

'You have your own private police force?'

'I have staff who, amongst other things, are responsible for the security of my family and our possessions.'

'Ah, Mr McGill.'

'Yes, he and his men. I'm delighted that Ingleby is keeping you so well informed.'

I shrug again. 'Well, who's your suspect?'

'Not a *suspect*, Inspector. The guilty party!'

The arrogance of it all. No doubt some poor maid or footman is about to be blamed for a crime concocted to keep me busy and away from the Salt House. But that's the trouble with those who see fit to take the law into their own hands – they don't stop to think of the consequences.

'Your Lordship, you seem to be lacking in legal knowledge. Here in England, one is deemed to be innocent until proven guilty in a court of law. I'm sure Lady Damnish will keep you right on such matters, her being a lawyer.'

'A mere formality – caught red-handed. And my wife has nothing to do with this.'

'Who is your *suspect*, then?'

'My son, Inspector.'

'I beg your pardon?'

'You heard. My son has been stealing from his own flesh and blood in order to fund whatever it is he gets up to at that school of his. I have him in custody, awaiting your arrival.'

'Lord Damnish, you have no right to hold anyone in custody.'

He ignores this. 'I want you to come with me now. I've had enough of this to-ing and fro-ing, and justice must be done, d'you hear?'

I have to admit, Damnish's discovery is in line with my theory that his son is responsible for the theft from farms belonging to his father. This isn't a surprise. But it's all rather convenient given my observations at the Salt House earlier today.

'I'll attend presently. However, I have a question for you, Your Lordship.'

'Make it quick, Inspector.'

'What exactly is going on at the Salt House? Your property, I note.'

'None of your business. I'm not here to give credence to Ingleby's deluded nonsense. And you would do well to steer clear of him.'

'With the greatest of respect, you still haven't told me what's happening there.'

'A commercially sensitive operation run by my wife. My land – our business. I can assure you that there's nothing illegal going on. And if you continue to pursue it, you can speak to my representatives. Is that clear, Grasby?'

Well, there's a thing. Lady Damnish is running the show at the Salt House. Maybe that's why Ingleby is so irate about it. I must be careful here, regardless of my suspicions and Ingleby's information, for what it's worth.

It's pretty obvious that Damnish has contrived to rid himself of one of his brother-in-law's confederates. He's clearly unconcerned that it's his own son. And if I'm honest with myself, it's quite probable that the younger Damnish has been imprudent and done something stupid. I was no different as a youth, though the war soon knocked any lingering immaturity out of me – out of so many young chaps. I heard some old duffer banging on about the state of the nation's youth the other day, in the pub back in York. 'What they need is another war' – you know the type. If this imbecile had been through what I experienced he'd never have come out with such nonsense. It's a war of the generations, I reckon. It'll end in tears.

Damnish gets up, with no little effort, and stands in front of me. He's a good head shorter, as well as being a couple of feet broader.

'You listen to me, Grasby. You stay away from my business, do you understand?' His voice has changed, more menacing, the broad Yorkshire accent of the working class, not a peer of the realm. I think I'm being offered a proper glimpse of the real man now.

'I'll go wherever my investigations take me, *sir*.' I stand to my full height, looking down on this stout peer.

This moment of confrontation over, Damnish heads to the door and returns to his normal haughty self.

'I'll be waiting for you. Don't be long, Inspector.'

28

I decide to hop into my Austin and have a smoke. I'm damned if I'll be summoned like a lackey. Though the fact that Damnish knows exactly the nature of my mission as far as the murder investigation goes gives me further cause for concern. I know I should call Juggers, but something is stopping me – instinct, I suppose.

A knock on the window from Constable Hardy nearly shifts my heart.

'Sorry if I startled you, sir,' he says, in his military fashion.

'Just thinking on the case, Hardy,' I lie.

'Very good, sir.'

Hardy has that martial trait of saying something with an absolutely straight face, even though he knows it's nonsense. I must admit, in my time in the army I never managed to achieve a neutral expression. I was forever being pulled up by senior officers for what was happening on my face. My father says I was born that way, which is typical.

'What can I do for you, Constable?'

Hardy lowers his voice. 'Quite sensitive, sir.'

'Good grief, man. This isn't the time for some indiscretion! You've only just got here.'

He looks puzzled for a split second. 'No, sir. It's nothing to do with me.' He leans in the open window. 'It's about Miss Dean, sir.'

'I see. Get in and tell me all about it.'

Hardy wedges himself into the passenger seat of the Austin.

'Sir, you know that we were taking statements from villagers – since poor Mr Starr's murder.'

'Of course I know,' say I, rather put out. After all, it was me who started the stampede over useless information following a throwaway remark in the Beggar.

Like the good officer he almost certainly isn't, Hardy produces a notebook from his tunic pocket. 'I spoke to a Mr Jinks, sir. He owns Newbourne Farm, bordering Holly House.'

'Yes, go on.'

'He was rambling away about noises in the night – lots of that from the villagers, sir.'

'Oh, I'm sure.'

'Miss Dean popped her head in to offer some tea. When she left, he smiled and said what a nice girl she was.'

'She is. Nothing suspicious about that, I wouldn't say.'

'Oh, I know, sir. But he went on to tell me how often he sees Lord Damnish and Miss Dean having chats in the grounds.'

I was rather losing interest in the matter until Hardy comes out with this revelation.

'What on earth for?' I blurt out.

Hardy shrugs his broad shoulders. 'I thought you'd be interested to know, sir.'

He squeezes himself out of the car like he's doffing a tight overcoat, leaving me alone with my thoughts. It's Deedee's frozen, snowy feet in the morning when Bleakly came to inform me of Starr's death. This, plus the fact she's here at all. I find myself having a darker thought. Surely young Daisy isn't in league with that great lummox? This is perplexing to say the least. Or have I simply got it all wrong?

Calculating that, there being no hills between here and Holly House, I'll be able to take the Austin, I fire the car into life. Of course, there is the obligatory explosion as it backfires. As a pall of black smoke rises in my rear-view mirror, I pull out of the yard.

The atmosphere at Holly House could not be in greater contrast to my previous visit. There are men with shotguns at intervals on the driveway, eyeing everything and everyone with great suspicion. As I drive up to the front door of the mansion, another of these men ushers me out of the car, and instead of entering the house via the front door I am taken round a corner, to an outbuilding marked 'Estate Office'.

Inside is a little room dominated by a large desk piled with files and papers. Around the walls office cabinets are arranged. To the side of the main desk is a smaller one bearing an Underwood typewriter and the usual assortment of pens, rulers, pencils and other office stationery. The room is musty and badly aired.

'Wait here,' says my unpleasant guide. I'm left alone and, as any police officer worth his salt would do, begin looking at the discarded documents and letters cast across the desk. I taught myself to read upside down when I was a pup. It's something I've never regretted, and a skill I use to this day.

When I hear a heavy tread and familiar voice in the yard, I take a seat. Well, I'm damned if I'll be left standing for this exchange with Damnish.

The door bursts open and three figures emerge from the light into the gloom of the office. Damnish leads the way, while his son troops in behind with McGill holding him firmly by the arm. The gamekeeper looks at me with contempt, in complete contrast to his charge, young Beauregard – Harry – who looks utterly miserable.

As Lord Damnish takes his seat behind the desk, McGill pulls the son behind his father, where he stands, head gamekeeper in close attendance.

'You tell the inspector what you've been up to, Beauregard, and don't miss anything out,' says Damnish, sitting in his chair and looking uncommonly like a Toby Jug.

'Hang on,' say I. 'I'll interview your son, Your Lordship. But I certainly don't require any gun-toting members of your staff present when I do.' I take time to give McGill a haughty look.

'No, you'll hear what he has to say. Then you can do what you like with him, as far as I'm concerned.'

My response is simple. Without a word, I get up and make to leave the stuffy office.

'Where on earth do you think you're going?' says Damnish.

'I'm going to bring my officers to this house and have you and your man here arrested for false imprisonment.'

Damnish splutters fit to burst. 'You'll do no such thing, Inspector!' Sweat is pouring down his face now.

'I want you to leave me with your son – alone. Do you understand?'

Damnish huffs and puffs for a few moments. Eventually, though, he summons McGill and both of them leave the office. Not before he imparts a few words of wisdom to yours truly, of course.

'Get this right, Grasby. Get it wrong and you'll be walking the beat, I promise you.'

This unsettles me for a number of reasons, not least because it encompasses my greatest fears. But I'm not going to be bullied by a fishmonger, no matter how lordly he now appears.

I wait for them to leave, then motion Harry to take a seat. He's still looking pretty down in the dumps, and there's a shadow of a bruise over his right eye.

'Who did that?' I enquire.

'McGill. He's a bloody brute.' Harry lowers his head. 'If my father told him to cut my throat he would, you know.'

'I don't doubt it. What on earth have you been up to?'

A wicked smile passes over Harry Damnish's lips. 'Rebellion, Inspector. Plain and simple rebellion.'

'Against your father?'

'Of course! The man's a fraud. He has no more noble blood than his gamekeeper. In fact, he's every bit as big a bully.'

'But you have, is that it?'

'Yes, as a matter of fact, I do.' He raises his head and suddenly looks uncommonly like his uncle Ingleby. 'I think he killed my grandfather, too.'

'Do you have evidence?'

'No, but it makes sense, doesn't it? The old man disappears and is found dead in his precious Salt House. There are dirty deeds afoot up there, you know, and my father is to blame.'

'This has come from your uncle, hasn't it?'

'What if it has? He's a clever man. He should be Lord Elderby.'

It's obvious that Harry holds his uncle in much higher

esteem than he does his father. Not hard, I grant you. But it doesn't give him carte blanche to steal from his parents.

'What are they accusing you of taking?' say I.

'A couple of old lamps, some Greek plates and a painting.'

'A painting by whom?'

'Oh, I don't know. Some Italian chap.' Harry folds his arms.

'There are plenty to choose from, I suppose.'

'They'll be mine anyway. How can one steal from one-self, Inspector?'

'They may become your property in the fullness of time. But at this moment, they belong to your mother and father.' I pause for effect, staring at the lad before me. Yes, he has spirit, no doubt about it. But like me as a younger chap, I fear it's much misguided.

'What?' says Harry, noting my silence.

'You've been stealing from the farms too, haven't you? Your father's farms, I mean.'

Harry leans his head back in the chair and looks at the ceiling. 'No, I haven't.'

It's time for a bit of cajolery, methinks. In any case, this young man may know things that will be useful to me.

'I'll strike a bargain with you, Harry.'

He searches my eyes. 'What kind of bargain?'

'I'm going to arrest you. Or at least it will *look* as though that's what I'm doing.'

'I don't understand.'

'Things are happening in and around Elderby. Things I can't explain.'

'You should speak to my uncle.'

'I have. But I need to find out more about the Salt House.'

'That grim old place.' Harry shudders. 'I'm not allowed to go anywhere near it. I've heard my father whispering things down the phone when he thinks there's nobody about. I shouldn't be surprised at anything he does.'

'Have you ever seen him with Miss Dean? You know, the young lady who was with me on my last visit.'

Harry visibly cheers up. 'Gosh, she's a stunner, isn't she?'

'She's a pretty girl,' say I, in the understatement of the year.

'And yes, I've seen them together. So what?'

'You've never wondered what they have in common?'

'I've always thought it was police business. I mean, Miss Dean works with the police, doesn't she?'

A doubtful raise of the brow is enough.

'Oh, my! You don't mean they're – they're lovers, do you?'

'I have no idea, Harry. But I want to find out. And for that, I'll need your help.'

'How can I help if you're going to arrest me?'

'I won't really arrest you. You'll be free to come home. Let's say on bail, eh?'

'But not really. In reality I'm your eyes and ears. Is that what you mean, Inspector?'

'Precisely.'

'Good-oh. That's right up my street.'

'Fine. We'll go to the station, and I'll brief you some more. But there's one thing I'll need you to do for me first.'

'Name it!' Harry Damnish is fully invested in my little plan now. Just as I intended.

'You'll have to return everything you've taken.'

'But that's just giving myself away, Inspector.'

'Where there's a will there's a way, young man.'

He looks at me with his head to one side, as though he's utterly foxed by the suggestion. But I'm a big enough rogue myself to note a bit of obfuscation. I know that he gets it.

'I say, would you mind if I smoke, Inspector? My parents are frightful bores when it comes to my imagined vices, you know.'

I reach into my pocket to offer him one of mine. But it's then I have that sinking feeling again.

'Oh, thanks and all that. But I prefer these.' Beauregard Oscar 'Harry' Damnish produces a pack of President cigarettes from his pocket, places one between his lips, and leans across the desk for me to light it.

Dash it all!

'Oh, by the way,' says he jauntily. 'One of our chambermaids has gone missing.'

'Which one?' say I, expecting the worst.

'Martha whatever-her-name-is,' says young Damnish. 'She was a bit giddy, if you ask me. No sign of her this morning.' He smiles carelessly.

He might be of the Elderby line, but he has his father's disregard for the staff.

'Has this been reported? To the police station, I mean.'

'I've no idea, sorry.' He looks momentarily bemused, as though it's the last thing to cross his mind. Which it probably is. He lives in a world where most of the people around him exist only to make his life more comfortable. He'll learn.

I tell young Damnish not to move, and once again seek out his father.

It's with new eyes that I perambulate the corridors of Holly House. From the front, you know you're looking at a big place. But as you're directed hither and yon, down corridors and up stairs, one realizes that it's a vault of a building.

After much huffing and puffing, I find the man of the house: Damnish.

'Custody,' he says with a smile when I tell him of Harry's immediate fate. 'Good. Let him rot for a while. The boy has no idea about the real world. High time he learned.'

I enquire as to the whereabouts of Martha Thornlie. Her furtive words to me in the village are foremost in my mind. I must admit, I trust no one. And it's clear, given the plight of Damnish Junior, that they don't trust each other, either.

'Can I take a look at her quarters?' say I.

'What on earth for? She's only been gone for a morning. Get your priorities in order! But do as you wish, Grasby,' says Damnish.

It's nice that he's getting my name right consistently now. I wonder if he's known it all along, and the whole thing's been an act of subjugation. I don't care, really.

I suppose you'd expect this great place to be divided in two, though these divisions are by no means even. The servants and some land workers live on the top floor. The ceilings are lower there, the carpets threadbare, and gone is the fine art and furniture that garlands the rest of Holly House. There is more than an air of them-and-us; you can almost taste it. I'm following a whey-faced footman, who says nothing despite my trying to engage him in conversation. He shows me into the room and stands outside while I poke about.

Martha Thornlie's quarters are neat, tidy, and smell of lavender. Damned if I know where women get the stuff from. It's everywhere. But the pleasant, ubiquitous aroma aside, there is nothing in the room that makes it feel lived in. No photographs, no personal odds and ends – no clothes in the tiny cupboard that must have served Martha as a wardrobe.

My first instinct is that she's done a moonlighter, as we

call it in the police. But given what's been happening, a cold hand grabs my heart.

It's not the time for assumptions. I make my way back to Master Damnish, being sure to leave word that I should be informed if anyone should hear from Martha. It's just another ball to juggle.

I'm leaving Holly House for the station as another heavy flurry of snow descends upon Elderby. The men with guns are still about, and as I chance to look up, a figure dashes back from a window; the curtains shift; the shadow of a presence. I'm sure that was Lord Damnish. I don't know why, but it gives me a shiver.

29

With the son and heir of the Damnish dynasty tucked away in a small room in Elderby police station, eating biscuits and drinking tea with Deedee, I am in my new office in a right funk. Who'd have thought that more than one person in this village would smoke the distinctive, not to mention expensive, President cigarette brand? The chances against it must be phenomenal. And what's happened to Martha Thornlie?

The former makes young Harry a suspect in the murder of Starr, and by association, as the other body was found at his home, a suspect in the chimney murder, too – neither of which I am really investigating. Once more I must trust my old boss and mentor Superintendent Juggers. But in my own experience of Damnish Junior, he's no more a killer than old Ada the organist, whose only crime was to murder any hymn in my father's last parish. I heard her play the wedding march once and am convinced to this day that her sheet music must have been upside down.

I must call my boss with the latest.

I lift the phone and am about to dial when something stops me. It's just a feeling, but somehow I know there's something wrong. Let me tell you, there's nothing worse than internal strife. I'm torn in two. Part of me marvels at the fact I do and don't trust Juggers now, while the aspect of my personality in charge of self-preservation is imploring me to take care.

After all, do I really believe that Harry Damnish killed Chuck Starr? Is the lad a clandestine madman set on murder and mayhem? No, I don't think he is. But I can't be sure of anything.

I'm still holding the phone in mid-air. I put it down and think. Eventually I decide that, regardless of circumstances, Juggers is my only hope. How could this incorruptible rock of a man possibly be implicated in all this? I place the receiver to my ear, about to make the call. But a distinct click on the line stops me dead.

Replacing the phone back on its cradle, I leave the comfort of my own office and sweep into the sergeants' room. There, somewhat unsurprisingly, Bleakly is fast asleep, his head on folded arms. I pick up the phone beside him, and there it is again, the same click.

Leaving Bleakly to his sweet dreams, I dash to the front office. Constable Thomas, the more taciturn of the pair of woodentops left for me by Juggers, nods in my direction from behind a typewriter. What he's typing, I cannot imagine. He carries on and leaves me to go about my business. Sure enough, when I lift the receiver once more and put it to my ear, there's that distinct click again.

It appears that all the phone lines in and out of Elderby police station are being tapped. By whom, I have no idea. But during the war I was taught to recognize the signs, and furtive clicks on a phone line are a dead giveaway. As unlikely as this seems, it puts the wind right up me, and no mistake.

I must make a decision, and fast. I need somewhere to think; somewhere I'll not be monitored or manipulated.

I turn to Thomas.

'I'm off to have a poke about, Constable Thomas. Keep an eye on young Damnish for me. If his father appears, tell him he's in police custody and therefore incommunicado. Do you understand?'

'Absolutely, sir.'

I'm about to say that if he doesn't hear from me by this time tomorrow, send for the cavalry. But as I think about it I realize that I know not on which side Hardy and Thomas belong. Bugger. This is an absolute mess!

'Oh,' he says, as an aside. 'This came for you.' With obvious military efficiency, he doesn't have to scrabble about on the desk like most proper coppers would. He lays his hands on what he's looking for straight away. 'I found this under the front door when I came in at six.'

Six, methinks. Unless rostered – and he wasn't – you wouldn't see hide nor hair of a real policemen at that time of day.

He hands me a small blue envelope. The missive smells of lavender. When I open the seal, it isn't the rough tear of glue on paper, but a gentle parting. Is this down to poor-quality stationery, the adhesive not sufficient unto its task, or something else? Either way, I'm careful to make no mention of it.

Dear Inspector Grasby,

As I told you outside the baker's shop, I know things what make it dangerous for me to continue work. You know what I mean.

Please don't worry about me. I'll be fine.

But I beg you, don't pass this on to anyone at Holly House. I trust none of them.

Take care of yourself.

Martha

As I make for the car, I'm wracking my brains. Am I sure that Martha Thornlie wrote that letter? The answer must be no. I'd have to find examples of her handwriting. Even then, I couldn't be certain, as she could have been coerced. But the lack of trust is implicit. Did someone steam open the letter and read it before I did?

Then something dawns on me. I start the engine, which for once decides not to backfire. I drive along Elderby Main Street to the bakery and park outside. Ethel gives me a hearty halloo from the Beggar. She's busy with a mop and bucket at the windows. She's wearing a heavy fur coat. No wonder, it's freezing. There's no doubt she's a hard-working woman.

The bell above the door of the bakery rings as I step inside. Wally is behind the counter, hunched over a large cake, which he's cutting into carefully measured slices. The smell of freshly baked bread, pies and pastries is to die for. I'm sure if you could bottle it every shop in the world would treble its footfall. Maybe someone will think about that one day, but I doubt it. Humanity, regardless of the gifts of large brains and ingenuity, lacks an aptitude to do something different.

'Inspector. Are you back for another pie?'

'Yes, absolutely,' say I. As you'll have remembered, regardless of the situation in which I find myself, I can always eat. Though I hadn't thought about my stomach, the offer of one of Wally's pies has me salivating.

'Can I ask you a favour, Wally?'

'Aye, of course.'

'Can I use your telephone?'

'Surely. It's in the office. Just come through.'

Wally ushers me behind the counter and into a very cold room. Against one wall a side of beef and some game birds hang from stout hooks. No doubt pie filling.

'Apologies,' says he. 'Not as much room through here as I'd like.' He points to a small desk upon which sits a Bakelite telephone. 'There you are. Be my guest.'

'Thanks, Wally,' say I. 'This will save me going back to the station.'

I wait until he's back in the shop then call the only person I can trust. The number is so familiar, yet my hands are shaking as I dial. I wait for an age for a reply, but that's what I expected.

'Hello, who's that?' The voice is distant and sounds as though it's emanating from a far-off, ancient being – which I suppose it is, when you think about it.

'How many times have I told you that's not the right way to answer the telephone?' say I.

'Oh, it's you.' I can hear disappointment in the voice.

My father has always had a great suspicion of the telephone. He's never been able to believe that once one replaces the handset back on the cradle nothing further can be heard. Of course, my father has lived his life within the tight bounds of the clergy. And as they still pay the bills, he thinks that he's being spied on by various bishops, archbishops, deans, etc., etc. It's just as well he isn't. Some of the things he has to say about senior members of the Church don't bear repetition. An inquisitive cleric bent on clandestine listening may find out things about himself of which he was hitherto unaware.

'Three of those horses are still missing, you know.'

Damn! Bloody horses again. I'd hoped that they'd have been successfully rounded up by now. Still, how I wish I was standing in Juggers's office instead of the wilds of the North York Moors, facing goodness knows what. Even in front of the chief constable would do. Anything for a return to normality.

'Father, I have to tell you something. It's really important,' say I, earnestly.

There's a loud belch on the other end of the line. 'I beg your pardon. I had a ploughman's lunch. I love pickled onions, but you know they give me terrible wind.'

'Never mind that! Please, you really need to listen.'

'Don't worry, Francis. I know what you're going to say.'

'You do? And please don't call me Francis, you know how I hate it.'

'It's your name,' he replies flatly. 'Though we very clearly spelled it incorrectly, your mother and I.'

'Eh? What do you mean?'

'I wanted to call you Egbert, after my grandfather. But your mother wouldn't have it. The Scotch are funny about English names.'

Good for dear old mum! Egbert – how ghastly.

'Anyway, say what you have to say. But it will explain a lot.'

'Father, you've completely lost me. What on earth are you talking about?'

'It's why you've never married. We had lads at school like that. Nothing to be ashamed of. You are as God made you. You'll find that there will be purpose behind it.'

The penny drops. It should have done long before we embarked on this meandering conversation. After all, I've been hearing versions of this since I was a nipper.

'I'm not a homosexual, Father. I have nothing against them, and think they're treated disgracefully in this so-called civilized country. But I'm not of their number.'

'Denial is a terrible thing, son.'

I want to ask him what he got up to all those years ago with Hetty Gaunt. But time is short, and poor Wally will have a phone bill like the national debt.

'I need a direct number for Mitch, please. I remember a number, but I'm not sure if that will get me straight through to him. As quickly as you can, please.'

If anyone can get me out of this, it's Mitch.

'Now, let me see,' says my father.

He proceeds to do something he's always done on the phone. He wanders away from the receiver, speaking as though he still has it in his hand. I can hear him mumbling something about clocks, the weather, Don Bradman and the Archbishop of Canterbury. These are the words I can make out as he shuffles through the papers, little address books and diaries that live on the table beside the phone.

'Father!' I shout, desperately trying to get him to hurry up. But the background mumble continues.

When I'm about to abandon hope and try again next century, miraculously I hear the clatter of the receiver being lifted, and another loud belch.

'Pardon me. These bloody pickles. I'm sure I've got heartburn coming on.'

'Fabulous. I can't thank you enough.' I reach for my notebook and pen from the inside pocket of my jacket. 'What's his number?'

'I can't find it. But I can give you the number for the greengrocer or the Salvation Army, if you'd like?'

It's at moments like this that I seriously doubt my parentage. Were it not for the fact I so closely resemble this idiot, I'd swear my mother gave in to passion with a passing rogue and I was the result. Sadly, she wasn't that kind of woman, and her contact with passing rogues was limited, to say the least.

'Father . . . Daddy . . . If you hold me in any regard at all, please find this number. I have to go now but call Elderby 323 and leave it with a man called Wally if I'm not about.

Can you do that within the next hour, please? You have no idea how important it is. Promise me you'll do this.'

There's a silence on the phone before he replies. When he does, his voice has lost all trace of the ditherer that I've been conversing with for the last few minutes.

'You're in real trouble, aren't you?'

'I'm in a bit of a fix, yes.'

'How many times have I heard that? Too many, that's for sure. But I'll do this for you. After all, you're the only issue of my loins.'

Though I'm reassured by this new *gravitas*, the thought of my father's loins and my connection to them leaves me slightly bilious. We say our goodbyes. I hope he finds Parsley's number. My dad's best friend coached me at cricket when I was young. A decent cove, and a man with much influence. If anyone can navigate this bloody mess, he can.

I walk back through into the shop, where good old Wally has a pie waiting, neatly wrapped in a paper bag.

'How did thee get on, Inspector?'

'Like all police work, it was difficult,' I lie.

'You were on for a while, right enough.'

I fetch out my wallet. 'For the pie and the phone call.' I hand him some change, more than enough to cover both. It's then that a business card pokes its way out of a corner from under a ten-bob note. Of course! Mitch gave it to me on the night before I left for Elderby. My excuse for not remembering it is that we were all blotto on dear Daddy's home brew.

For a moment, I consider dialling one of the numbers on the card. But something stops me. Instinct is an odd thing, you know. And mine is crying out for me to wait for the old boy to get back with a telephone number I can be sure will get me straight through to the man who may well save my bacon.

'You may get a call from a chap who sounds quite mad, Wally. Don't let that put you off. He'll give you a number. If you could take a note of it for me, I'd be much obliged,' say I, as though there's nothing odd going on. It's a skill, you know.

'Don't they have phones at the police station?' he asks, amiably enough. I do see his point.

'Organizing a bit of a surprise,' say I. It's good to be able to think on one's feet. It's a decent excuse.

I leave him some more money for the calls, and with a warm pie in hand.

My mind is churning as I head back to the car. Ethel must have finished cleaning her windows, as there's no sign of her outside the Beggar. I must admit, I'd happily retreat into its warmth, comfort and the fug of alcohol, but I can't. It appears that I find it hard to obey orders. I should be here, showing face, making all the right noises, but essentially doing nothing. Instead, I find myself doubting my own sanity. What on earth is happening in Elderby? Whatever it is, it's dangerous – just as the chimney man, Chuck Starr, old Lord Elderby and my predecessor would attest. Not to mention poor Martha.

I try to think of anyone I've met here who possesses the qualities I'm in need of – a pillar of the community, if you like. One name and face stands out: Ingleby. I decide to drive to Briarside, his rather chaotic home. But he can be as chaotic as he likes. If he helps me, I don't care.

I'm on the same road that leads to Withernshaw Fell and the Salt House. Big flakes are again falling from a leaden sky. I think what we've seen so far is just a scattering, a harbinger of what's to come. Having had no time for lunch yet, I'm tempted by the pie. Across a field I can clearly see the farm through some trees. I don't know why, but I decide to slow down. Probably it's due to fear of the ever-vigilant McGill and his men. And I have no desire to have another brush with him – a ruffian if ever I saw one.

There's movement outside Briarside. Two people are standing in the yard conversing. I stop the car on the verge and slip out. Initially, I damn myself for never having a decent pair of binoculars. But as it turns out I have no need of them, for the figures in the farmyard are both quite distinctive. The fear that has been gripping my heart for ages now turns into something much more visceral: the desperate impulse to leave, to drive away from Elderby as fast as the car will go and never come back. I look on as the tall, patrician Ingleby leans forward and plants a fraternal kiss on his sister's cheek. Lady Damnish pats his arm and gets into a large black car. It may be an Alvis, but I'm too shaken to identify it properly. Here are these bitter enemies caught in a fond farewell.

My goodness. As I calculate the implications of this, I forget that Her Ladyship must drive this way in order to return to Holly House. Quickly, I throw the Austin into reverse, testing my double-declutching to the limit. A quick three-point turn as sweat pours down my face, and I'm off.

'Dash it all' doesn't do this situation any justice whatsoever.

Time for perspective. I drive to the foot of the incline that leads to St Thomas's-on-the-Edge. I noticed before that there's a snowy little path that winds to the church. Again, it's into reverse and up the hill.

Sure enough, the track eventually takes me to a small coppice of naked trees. I park the car and get out into the

cold, biting air. If you were told once what an English village smells like just before Christmas, you'd remember it.
The wind in my face brings with it the smell of burning
coal and wood from dozens of hearths. But I've always
liked the coldest season of the year. It's a time for mulled
wine and blazing pub fires.

On the surface, Elderby is a picture-perfect place. I don't
think any visitor could help themselves loving it, with its
little lanes, pretty shops – everything wrought in that grey
Yorkshire stone that makes the village look as if it sprang
from the earth by force of nature alone.

As I am now finding out, though, it's a village of secrets,
mystery and death. What else does it have to reveal?

At times like this, I find it's best to distract oneself, in the
hope that an answer will materialize from nowhere. I light
a Craven 'A' and think of Deedee. If she's a wrong 'un, some
kind of agent or whatever, she hides it so well. But that's
what she'll have been trained to do. I wonder about her
and Damnish. What on earth could they possibly have in
common? Why the clandestine meetings? It doesn't make
sense – not at all. Then there's Ingleby and his acid-tongued
sibling. Is it just me or is this just one enormous joke being
played on me for no particular reason? Is someone going
to reveal themselves and shout 'Got you!'?

My world is upside down. I stare out across the winter
fields of North Yorkshire from the famous Elderby Edge,
deep in thought. I remember the extending antenna at the
back of the Salt House; the distant figure of McGill silhouetted on the hill, guarding the place. The aristocratic
Ingleby, his paintings, and the clearly contrived enmity for
his sister. His nephew and the cigarettes that opened the
batting of my new concerns. Cummins, Juggers, the parish
council, Bleakly, Lady Damnish, Dr Starr, the man who

attacked me in the woods, the dead man in the Holly House fireplace. I'm pretty sure I've identified Finan Whales as my attacker, and the man who placed the note in my pocket to attend the Salt House. But why?

I picture undertaker Grimshaw, his tape measure ever at the ready in order to fit a wooden box round another unwilling customer.

The village looks tiny from here. There are few people out and about, and they look small. It's a strange place: a nice, quiet North Yorkshire village, hiding goodness knows what.

I hear voices coming from the rear of the church, where they found poor Chuck Starr. I duck through the trees to my right. I don't want to be seen, so I huddle near the ground, almost hidden by mounds of snow. Two men are arguing, their voices modulating on the cold wind. I feel I should recognize the man who is shouting, but I can't place him. When this happens, it normally indicates a lack of context. I listen hard, at the same time peering through the dark columns of the frosted tree trunks, hoping someone will heave into view.

And one of them does, and I can hardly believe my eyes. It's the Reverend Croucher and he's pointing his finger and shouting at an unseen figure. Though his words aren't clear enough to follow, it's obvious that he's very unhappy. And though I'm more than used to clerical indiscretion – you do become accustomed to it with my father – the language he's using doesn't seem to match with the meek man I've met.

It happens in a split second. There's a crunch of snow behind me. At first I think it's the wind, but when I'm grabbed round the neck by powerful hands, I know that things have taken a turn for the worse.

I've often wondered what it feels like to drown. The desperate struggle for breath, the burning in the lungs, the flickering path to dark oblivion. But as the grip round my neck tightens, I need imagine no more. I'm being strangled.

My world turns black.

30

I'm rather too well acquainted with waking up in a strange place with no idea how I came to be there. Now, I have fleeting moments wondering why my head feels as though it's about to burst, my ankles are burning and my arms are doing a passable impersonation of imminently taking leave of their sockets and going it alone. Generally, the world is painfully out of kilter.

I remember the tight grip around my neck, open my eyes and try to make sense of my circumstances.

Hanging upside down, tied by one's ankles, is not a sensation I recommend. In fact, it's rather unpleasant. This place is dark, really cold and dank. I can hear water dripping on a hard floor. But it's the smell that gives my location away. That strange scent of age, damp, decay and the peculiar odour, the residue of its productive past, that has been left behind after decades. The Salt House is like nothing I've smelled before.

When I crane my neck up – which is most painful, incidentally – I can see my ankles trussed by a short length of rope. It's hanging from a rusting hook jutting from the wall. Looking in the opposite direction, my arms are hanging loose, fingertips only a few tantalizing inches from the grimy floor. I wonder, is it time for my life to rush before my eyes? I recall the marks around Chuck Starr's ankles that I found during my cursory examination of his body. This now appears to be my own fate.

In training, both the police force and the army try to drum in the principle of staying calm under fire. Under no circumstances submit to the funk of fear and desperation. There are techniques that aid this gargantuan feat of self-control: thinking of a loved one, remembering a happy time, picturing a point in the future when you're not hanging by the ankles about to die or whatever.

Whoever thought up this guff – a great expression of which my mother was fond – has never stared death in the eye. No doubt it was someone whose closest experience of danger was sitting in a country house, swigging a glass of good port, miles behind the lines.

I prefer the Grasby method. This consists of whimpering like a babe in arms, damning one's luck and trying not to inadvertently perform any kind of bodily function. I find this makes infinitely more sense than the conceit that all is fine and dandy. My whimper soon turns into a full-blown scream that echoes around the empty stone rooms. But nobody comes to my rescue.

I have the bright idea of trying to arch my body up and loosen the bonds round my ankles enough to allow nature to take its course and for gravity to send me hurtling groundward. However, after a couple of futile attempts at this, all I succeed in doing is almost passing out. My stomach muscles throb like toothache as I fall back hopelessly.

'I'm a police officer. Set me free this instant!' I shout. But only the drip-drip of water serves as a reply. I try to think of something else to wail, but soon realize the pointlessness of it all. Whoever has placed me in this predicament is likely fully aware of who I am and exactly what I do for a living.

Now, I suppose I must just wait for the knife under the ribs like poor old Starr, my warm corpse ready to be stuffed down a chimney.

Absently, I wonder how my father will take the violent death of his only son. Though he's rarely shown it, I'm sure he has some affection for me. I hope it doesn't drive him to the home brew the way the death of my mother did. I know I'm unkind about him, which he deserves. But her loss hit the old boy hard, and he's never been the same.

These passing thoughts over, I decide it's time to scream again.

I'm screaming myself hoarse, making the place ring with desperation, as though some writhing monster is trapped in here, rather than a moderately well-educated detective with uncertain career prospects.

Wait! I hear movement. Yes, the sound of footsteps is growing louder. Is this my salvation?

Unfortunately, when I manage to focus through the gloom, two malign-looking figures appear before me, and the likelihood of rescue seems remote. Let's face it, liberation rarely manifests itself dressed in black dungarees replete with improvised hessian balaclavas, does it?

'Who the devil are you?' say I, to no real end. I mean, they're hardly going to furnish me with their names and addresses before I'm gutted like a fish. But honestly, one struggles to know what to say in such a damned fix.

The answer comes via a sharp punch to the stomach. It's well disguised, and I'm not ready for it. If I could double up in two, I would. But unfortunately gravity prevents this. So, I groan instead, and gasp for breath.

Here I am, two faceless brutes before me, likely intent on having a bit of sport before they consign me to eternity.

I spot a small shaft of light. I have no idea where it's

coming from, but it's the kind of thing one sees in illustrated biblical texts. You know what I mean, heavenly light shining down on a hill, saint, river or suchlike. Equally, I suppose, it looks like the light from a projector at the cinema. But whatever it resembles, I'm emboldened by this little ray of hope and life. It also shines down on one of my torment- ors, and it's now that I notice something that makes me feel even sicker to the old stomach.

Just as the full impact of what I've seen begins to sink in, I receive another sharp blow to the solar plexus. This one is less vicious, but it prevents me from confronting these men with their true identities. Oh yes, I've worked it out.

I'm gasping for sufficient breath to make this revelation, when the discharge of a firearm sounds, echoing through the place like thunder in a steep valley. I must admit, I'm in such a state of flux that I find it hard to make sense of what's happening. My first inclination is that this is yet another part of the torture process that will lead to my cruel demise. However, when I see the men in the hessian masks with ghoulish eyeholes cut into them hurriedly turn to face the weapon's report, I realize they're not responsible.

I hear a muffled voice, and lo, they take off, their foot- steps thudding on the earthen floor.

Regardless of how jaundiced a view I have of my father and the clergy in general, I am a man of faith. As I've said before, it's not of a conventional nature, but it's there all the same. It would appear that I've been delivered from dan- ger. But the identity of my rescuer surprises me.

'Are you a'right, Inspector?' The voice is of the gruff, Yorkshire variety. Before me stand three men, the fore- most of which is picked out in the blessed shaft of watery light. Gamekeeper McGill takes me in without expression.

'Thank you,' say I, my voice almost a whisper.

'Lord Damnish told you to stay away from this place. You should have paid him heed.' McGill turns away. 'Cut him down, lads.'

Before I know it, one man grabs me round the waist, while another hacks away the bonds on my ankles with a vicious-looking knife. I'm placed carefully on the floor, shaking like a leaf and still gasping for breath. McGill holds something to my mouth.

'Here, drink this.'

He helps me pour a modicum of whisky down my throat. When he pulls the hip flask away, I grab it off him and help myself to a good dram, as my mother would have said.

'You can't be that bad, you've still got a fair swallow,' says McGill, to the amusement of his men. 'We heard a scream and wondered what were going on. Just as well we did. Who were that pair?'

'Yes, just as well you came. I can't thank you enough,' I splutter, the heat of the whisky still on my tongue. 'I'm sorry, I have no idea who they were,' I lie.

'Hopefully one of my lads on the hill will spot them.' He rubs his chin. 'Go on, get another down your neck, and we'll get thee to see the doctor.'

'No, no, I'm fine. Don't worry.'

'You've been hanging from the ceiling being beaten. Nothing fine about that in my book. It's like something these damn Nazis would have got up to in the war.' McGill spits on the floor at the mention of them. I must say, this chap's now soaring in my estimation.

'You were in the army, then?'

'Aye, colour sergeant in the Lancs and proud of it. I wanted to stay in, but the wife would have none of it. She thought it were all going to kick off again. I'm not too sure she's wrong.'

The spirit is beginning to work now, and I feel more like myself. Just shows you how wrong one can be about a chap – about many things, come to that.

'What makes her think that?' say I.

'Bloody Huns, isn't it? We should have walled them up in Germany, never set any o' them free.'

It's interesting, I only met a few Germans during the war. In the beginning they were arrogant and boastful. But the ones that weren't drunk seemed downtrodden and fearful. In fact, the captured German soldiers were a much happier bunch. I suppose that's because they were in our charge and not that of the Red Army – and removed from it all into the bargain. But wars are made by kings, politicians, rogues and robber barons. If ordinary people were left to their own devices, we'd all rub along pretty well, I think. My mother used to bang on about a chap called Jock Tamson, but I'm damned if I ever knew what she meant.

'Right, then, if you won't go to the doctor, we'll take thee back to the police station,' says McGill.

I don't have long to think on this. But I do have to make my excuse plausible.

'Listen,' say I. 'Before we do that, I want to ensure the safety of all present at the station. So, I need a favour – another one, if you can muster it?'

When I explain to him that I'm expecting a message to be left at the bakery, we make a plan. Have I at last found someone I can trust? Well, he did save me from my tormentors. However, through bitter experience, I've learned that very little is as it seems in Elderby.

Quickly, I swap clothes with one of McGill's men. I'm wearing an old flat cap pulled well down over my eyes, a rough tweed jacket with patches at the elbows – attendant odour of livestock more than obvious – and a pair of loose-fitting corduroy trousers, held up at the waist by a stout leather belt. The boots I'm given pinch a bit at the toes – I have big feet, you know. But, as I've discovered, much can be given away by one's footwear.

Simply, I must get to speak to Mitch Parsley. Things looked bleak, but I'm free. Though I'm not sure how all this – whatever it is – will be resolved.

Time will tell.

When we leave the place of my captivity, I'm surprised to note that it's not the main part of the Salt House that I've already seen, but rather some kind of large outbuilding, higher on the fell.

'What was this place?' I ask McGill.

'An old store. There are buildings like this dotted all over the place. It were a big concern, thou knows. Elderby were thriving then. My grandfather were one of the last people to leave when it closed down. Heartbroken, he were.'

After being cooped up in my temporary prison, I'm squinting into the moonlight. It's a pleasure seeing it. I've come close to death many times, but that was one of the closer brushes with the end. Silently, I thank God for my deliverance. But much time has passed since I was last conscious.

Looking down from this elevated position, almost directly below us I can see Briarside Farm. I wonder about Ingleby. He painted McGill in a less than generous light, and yet here he is, my liberator. But Ingleby is a liar. I know that now for sure.

'How do you and Ingleby get on?' I ask in that

conversational way police officers deploy when they're try-ing to coax something of importance from somebody without alerting them to the fact.

'He's a bitter man, Inspector. Bitter and twisted. His father threw away his inheritance, and he can't get over it. Likes to pretend that he's not bothered, but he is, trust me. My advice is to steer clear of him.'

'Funnily enough, that's his advice about you.'

'Aye, no doubt.'

Time to try my hand, methinks.

'Tell me. What exactly is happening here? At the Salt House, I mean.'

The gamekeeper regards me with gimlet eyes. 'I have a good job, Inspector. Lady Damnish treats me and my men well. I don't know and I don't ask.'

Subject closed, but he's told me enough. Lady Damnish. Of course, he must answer to them both.

We make our way downhill until we reach a track which leads to the road. I'm still a bit unsteady on my pins. My ankles ache and my back is now protesting. I'm not sure whether my uncontrollable shivering is down to the bitter cold or sheer shock. However, someone has to put an end to whatever is happening here. I'm still astonished that in rural England such apparent lawlessness can thrive unhin-dered by the authorities. And, by the way, I worry that the forces of law and order of which I'm part might well be complicit in something going on in Elderby. It's all really, really rotten to the core.

We get into an old van and head to Wally's bakery.

31

Thankfully, the village is quiet when McGill drops me off outside the shop. Purposefully, I shorten my stride and slouch into the bakery, lest anyone spot me. I think Wally is a solid enough chap. He's always been very helpful to me, and a man can forgive anyone who bakes a pie like the proprietor of this establishment.

'Can I help you?' he says to me formally as I stand before the counter.

'You certainly can,' say I, straightening up and removing the greasy cap from my head.

'It's you, Inspector.' Wally looks me up and down. 'If you've just changed your tailor, I should change back if I were you.'

'Don't worry about that. I'll explain later.'

I probably won't, of course.

'Did you get that message, Wally?'

'I did, as it happens. Mind you, Inspector, I'm not sure how much faith you should place in it. I'm sure that chap on the other end of the phone was away with the fairies. He were busy telling me a tale about Daniel in the lion's den. I know my scriptures, but he insisted on taking me right through it.'

That sounds about right, thinks I. After all, this is my father we're talking about.

'And he left a number?'

'Aye, he did. That's why I've stayed open. I knew you were anxious for it.'

I look at my watch. Gosh, it's almost six. It shows just how befuddled I was when McGill pulled me out of my temporary prison. Despite the dark, I didn't even notice that we're well into the early evening. Hanging upside down unconscious then expecting imminent death will do that to you every time, you know.

'Here, this is the number I was given.' Wally produces a piece of paper from the pocket in the front of his apron. 'He told me to pass on a message, too.'

'What was it?'

'Asked what time he should roast the fatted calf.' Wally shrugs. 'Are you fond of beef, Inspector?' Wally winks at me.

'He's a laugh a minute, isn't he?' say I, by way of an apology for my unhinged parent. 'But thank you for passing it on.'

Bill, the baker's red setter, pads through from the back room and barks.

'He's after his tea,' says Wally.

I apologize profusely for being such a nuisance and ask if I can use the phone once more.

'Help yourself. I've some accounts to be at. Though I must admit, I wouldn't mind getting home in half an hour or so.'

Point taken, I walk through to Wally's back shop. The door to the bakery is ajar, and I can see a mess of flour, tins, pastry cases, ovens and a wooden worktop. The room doesn't look very big, but Wally certainly produces some marvels in it.

I sit behind the desk and dial the number my father eventually managed to find, which tallies with that on Mitch's card. I damn my instincts that told me not to call it earlier. But even I can be wrong once in a while. The call is answered after two rings.

'Hello, Mitch. It's me, Frank.'

'Grasby Junior. It's good to hear your voice. How are things in Elderby?'

I'm so relieved to hear a friendly voice.

'I need your help – advice, at least, Mitch.'

I go on to tell him my stories about Elderby. The dead man in the chimney, Starr's murder, my abduction, the attack in the woods, the antenna at the Salt House, Lord and Lady Damnish, Ingleby, Cummins, Juggers, Moore, old Lord Elderby – the lot.

I must have rushed this out, because there's a silence at the other end of the line.

'Are you still there?'

'Yes, still here. Just working my way through it all. Gosh, what a tale of woe.'

'It is rather, I'm afraid.'

'In every sense of the word, I shouldn't wonder.'

'Definitely,' say I, meaning it.

'Of course, the soundest piece of advice would be to get yourself out of there as quickly as your legs will carry you. But that's easier said than done, eh?'

'The thought has crossed my mind. But personal integrity just won't allow it.'

There we go: brave, reliable Inspector Grasby. A martyr to queen, country and justice. But running away is a tempting thought.

'I've heard whispers, of course. Catterick is full of them.'

'You have?'

'Can't say too much – you know how things are. Some chaps think we have the wrong allies. I've heard rumours of terrible atrocities in the Soviet Union. Uncle Joe, and all that. I'm sure you appreciate that there have always been certain members of the aristocracy who would have preferred to deal with Hitler rather than go through another lot. It seems some of them still do. Bad show, if you ask me.'

I don't suppose the general public will ever know how close the Second World War came to having a very different outcome. I do, because I was there. But this is not the time to relate my part in that buttock-clenching story of near-calamity. Suffice it to say, our boffins just beat theirs to it. But it could have gone either way. Perhaps it's better that it remains a secret. The very thought of it all makes me shiver. Damn, if this is what I'm knee-deep in, no wonder there have been so many dirty deeds.

'Are you listening?' says Mitch.

'Yes, all ears.'

'Of course, the Americans are poking about. They're up to something. My goodness, I heard the other day they have Hitler hidden away in South America somewhere. Balderdash, of course. They have a lot of influence, you know.'

'We were their allies, not the Nazis.'

'Kings of the castle now, young Francis. They want things their way "or the highway." I think that's what they say. Would rather they had control of the whole shooting match. As it turns out, the Russkies are challenging them for global supremacy. The Yanks don't like it. We were just the same before the First World War. It comes with the territory of being the ultimate power in the world. You want to sign off on every bloody thing.'

'In short, we can't trust the Yanks?'

'Spot on, old chap. But that's been the case since 1776.'

Deedee and Starr are passing thoughts.

'You don't think we'd bump off an American agent, do you? If he or she were in the way, I mean.'

'International politics is a dirty business, no question. America is flexing its muscles. We're like the school bully on the floor after taking a pasting from the younger chap. There's much animus on both sides of the Atlantic these days. I should say almost anything could happen, short of full-scale war, that is. But as you know, it'll be done in the shadows. Us, the Americans, the Russians and what's left of the Third Reich.'

'I rather hoped nothing was left of it,' say I.

'Not so. As I've said, there was much support for fascism in some quarters in this country. Despite what you may think, sentiments linger, even after the unthinkable.'

'What about this Cummins chap?'

'I don't know him, but I can find out. You're right not to trust him. You'd think that, just following a war, our country would be united like never before. But not so. There are all manner of cliques, cabals and conspiracies on the go – at a high level, too. But again, it was ever thus. I'm afraid old Winnie isn't up to the job of keeping them all in order any longer. In his heyday, heads would have rolled. Now he's lost the thread a bit, and everyone who matters is on manoeuvres. But I want you to keep me up to speed on what's happening. Remember, I'm only in Catterick. With you in a jiffy, if need be.'

'Damn it all! What am I to do in the meantime?'

'Keep your head down. Hide, if necessary. But find out

as much as you can, any way you can. Thankfully, reason, good sense and decency still prevail – mostly. I shall make representations on your behalf. But we'll need all we can get on what's happening in this Elderly if I'm to muster the troops.'

'*Elderby*, Mitch.'

'Yes, quite so. In the meantime, I wish you good luck. It's a far, far better thing I do, and all that. Must admit, much as I like you, Francis, I never quite saw you in the heroic mould.'

Oh, thanks. Nice to know I'm so disappointing, thinks I.

'You know me, Mitch. Full of surprises.'

'Full of something, old chap.' He laughs wheezily to himself. After a cough or two he recovers. 'Call me any time, but not from the station or phones belonging to those you can't trust. Understand?'

'Yes, I'll do my best.'

'Let's say that if I don't hear from you by this time tomorrow, I'll assume the worst.'

It's the casual way of the English upper classes. You'd think we're talking about a late grocery delivery, not my miserable existence. I know it's not been up to much, but it's all mine and I'm rather proud of having made it this far.

'I shouldn't wonder if there's something posthumous available for a brave lad like you. If the worst happens, of course,' he adds in a rush.

'My father will be proud,' say I sarcastically.

'I should jolly well hope so! Pity it'll take your premature death to engender that in the old boy, but there you are.'

I'm bally well sick of this. I know he's on my side. But I was feeling cheerier swinging from the ceiling and being punched in the stomach. Getting on my toes and seeking sanctuary is becoming a more and more appealing prospect.

'Let's hope he remains disappointed,' say I.

'Indeed. Well, Francis, it's been good to know you all these years. Keep your chin up. I'll beaver away here and see if we can't bring some sanity to all this. Goodbye.'

I'm about to counter this by saying 'Au revoir, surely', or something similarly inane, but the call clicks off and I'm left holding the phone in the back of a bakery shop, feeling utterly miserable. At least things can't get any bleaker, I suppose.

'Inspector, are you finished on the phone?' Wally shouts.

'Yes, just coming.'

As I enter the shop, I'm about to offer my host sincere apologies until I notice that he's standing with his back to me, addressing a third party on the other side of the counter. Wally's not that tall, but being a long-time producer of pies and delicious sweetmeats, and a consumer of same, makes him a better door than a window.

When I do manage to crane my head round Wally, there, with Bill the dog fussing all around her, is Deedee.

'Hello, Inspector Grasby, where on earth have you been? Bleakly has been awake for three straight hours worrying about you.' She's looking me up and down, which is confusing until I realize that I'm still dressed in the gamekeeper togs. That bloody conversation with Mitch has set me on edge. It's easy to experience a certain dislocation under such circumstances.

'How did you find me?' say I more harshly than intended.

'Oh, you know. Round here, everybody knows everything. Ethel spotted you earlier. I figured it was worth a try. Have you taken to baking?'

Deedee smiles at me sweetly. She's a very pretty young

woman – have I mentioned that? But behind her cornflower-blue eyes is steel, the like of which I've rarely seen in anyone, man or woman. This is new and makes my funk level rise yet again.

I express my profound thanks to Wally, then Deedee and I leave the shop and let him go about his evening. I note that she's brought the old police van. But what to say to her?

'Back to the station, Inspector?' says she, getting behind the wheel.

'No. Actually, could you give me a lift up to my car, please?'

'Oh, where is it?'

'Just off a little lane by the church.' I'm replying as breezily as possible here. I don't want her to suspect anything. After all, she's as likely to stick me with a knife as anyone else. Certainly when one bears in mind what Mitch Parsley says.

She drives to the hill that leads up on to the edge. It's then something strikes me, and I pat the right side of my jacket, unthinkingly.

'Damn!'

'Something wrong, Inspector?'

'Oh, nothing,' say I. I've just realized that I've lost my sidearm. But of course I have. I wasn't going to be allowed to keep my pistol when I was left dangling by the ankles, now was I?

Deedee bites her lip.

'What's wrong, Miss Dean?' I think the time for a bit of *gravitas* is long overdue.

'I need to tell you something.' She glances at me as we take the hill, the old engine straining already. 'I know you've heard about me meeting with Lord Damnish. But it's not what you think.'

'Oh, I see.'

'I was doing it for Bleakly,' says she.

'Beggar that,' say I. 'He's old enough to be your grand-father. What's got into you, Deedee?'

She looks confused. 'No, I mean Sergeant Bleakly asked me to strike up a friendship with him. Find out what was going on, you know.'

Ah, I suppose that makes sense.

'I see,' say I, all *gravitas*.

I don't know whether to stick or twist with Deedee. Yes, Mitch and his distant cavalry aside, I need an ally. If I'm right, Deedee could be the very chap – well, woman, but you know what I mean. I can't tell you the number of clever, resourceful and incredibly brave women I met during the war. Too many men made the mistake of underestimating the fairer sex, the Nazis included. They did so at their peril. Mind you, the damned Nazis under-estimated everyone, which turned out to be their Achilles heel. In any event, I sit ready to hear what Deedee has to say. But the echoes of what Mitch said about Hitler being hidden away in the Pampas, or wherever, niggle at me.

'And have you discovered anything?' say I.

'I know he doesn't trust his wife. When you get to know him, it's obvious.'

'Nobody trusts each other here,' say I.

'What do you mean?'

'I'm not sure everything is as it appears. In Elderby, I mean.'

'Shucks, you should have said earlier, Inspector. I'd never have thought it.' She smiles devastatingly.

You know, whatever it is she's about, Deedee would be a tremendous catch. I mean, she's clever, witty, bold. I'm not sure that being almost thirty and still in university is a good idea. But it would be a sad world if we were all the same.

Deedee looks puzzled for a moment. I can almost see her brilliant mind at work.

'This isn't about me working for Bleakly, is it?'

'What exactly is a chap to think? You doing his bidding in such a way. Above and beyond, I say. One wonders why?'

She sighs exasperatedly and shakes her head. 'I've not been entirely honest with Bleakly – with you either, come to that. I had a chat with Reverend Croucher, and he advised me to come clean.'

'The last man I'd take advice from.'

'I took his pastoral advice, that was all. He is a man of the Church, remember.'

It's now that I remember Croucher having strong words with someone at the back of the church, just before I was nearly strangled. The very thought of it makes me feel sore. My poor noggin has taken quite a battering over the last few days, and I'm sure I have broken ribs. I suppose it's adrenalin that's pushing me onwards. I saw that during the war. Chaps with limbs literally hanging off still up and at the enemy.

Suddenly, I'm a tight ball of pain.

'Oh my, what's wrong, Inspector?'

'Nothing. Just say what you have to say, Deedee.'

She looks at me doubtfully but carries on. 'I'm not all I appear, Inspector. It's beginning to make me feel guilty – the deceit, you know.'

'Surely not?' I say with mock surprise.

'To make matters worse, I think I messed up, too.'

'Drive up there into that small clump of trees. My car's there – we can talk,' say I.

Deedee does as she's bid. We sit for a few moments in silence as dark clouds roll in from the east towards the escarpment that guards Elderby. We're in for another spell of snow, by the looks of things.

'Just tell me from the beginning, Miss Dean.' More *gravitas* – well, there's a time and place for everything. Thankfully, the pain in my ribs is easing.

'I work for the State Department, Inspector.' Tears appear in her blue eyes.

A likely story, thinks I. But I let her carry on.

'Chuck – Charles Starr – he wasn't just a war hero living in a little English village, I hate to tell you.'

'Well, I'll be damned,' say I, knowing full well what she's going to come out with next. But it's good to appear to be surprised. After all, who'd guess that young Grasby, horse liberator, punter and bon viveur, could possibly have any idea of what is going on?

'He was in league with the Communists,' she blurts out. 'The Soviets.'

'Eh?' Now I'm genuinely surprised.

'He wasn't reckoned to be a real threat, so they sent me. It's my first job and I've messed up.'

'You were here to keep an eye on him?'

'Yeah, sure was.' There are tears now. She looks utterly convincing.

'What was he up to?'

'He was writing a book. Something that was going to embarrass my government. And yours, I guess. It wasn't hot enough to send anyone more . . . more experienced. I guess that's why he was here. Everyone at home thinks he was – well, deluded.'

'About the war? The book, I mean.'

'Yeah, about the war, and how wonderful the Russians

were, and how we let the senior Germans escape after the game was up.' She grabs my arm. 'But there was more.'

'Really?'

'I shouldn't be telling you this.' She turns away from me, looking out of the driver's side window.

'You've come this far, Deedee.' Time for the friendly approach.

She turns back, a look of alarm on her face. 'He reckoned that something was happening – here in Elderby. Something really bad. I had dinner with him and Doctor Starr. One night, he got a little drunk when Elizabeth went to bed. He just told me – there and then.'

'Do you think he knew why you were here? To keep an eye on him, I mean?'

'No, I don't think so. The war – it got to him, I guess. He was obsessed. Saw threats round every corner.'

And he was bloody right, too. The war got to us all, I assure you. But this isn't the time to nitpick.

'It's not your fault, Deedee. They should have sent someone with more experience to be his nursemaid.'

'At first, I thought he was delusional. But I've seen things – heard about them. Something isn't right here, Inspector. You must have noticed it, even though you've not been about for long?'

When the dead bodies began turning up, I must admit, it raised my suspicions. What kind of oaf does she think I am? I do my best to shrug in a non-committal fashion. But I don't know. I feel rather shaken up, between one thing and another. I damn myself, because she's spotted my hesitation and changes the subject.

'You're in pain. What happened when you disappeared?' There's a tear in her eye.

'Oh, just a twinge,' say I. For a moment, I'm ready to spill the beans – tell her everything. But something stops me. Daisy Dean – if that is indeed her real name – doesn't strike me as being stupid or vulnerable. I remember how she saw off my attacker in the woods. But suddenly, here she is, blubbing like a three-month-old.

'Did you tell anyone what Starr said?'

I don't really know why I'm asking this. It's like enquiring of a man in a mask, striped jumper and a bag with 'swag' written on it if he's about to rob you. He's going to deny it, obviously.

'No, not a soul.' Deedee bites her lip again. 'Only Reverend Croucher, but he's bound by the laws of the Church, right?'

'I'm sure he is. I wouldn't worry about him.'

It's damned hard to sound convincing when you're reasonably sure someone is trying to play you like a fiddle. But while I'm sure she's not telling me the whole truth, elements of what she says about Starr make sense.

I busy myself comforting Daisy. And to be fair, she accepts my words of gentle encouragement with good grace. But who knows what she really thinks of me? Still, one thing must be said. If what she is telling me is just the tip of the iceberg, she's bloody good at her job.

⁂

***

Command and Staff (North)
Catterick Army Base
Catterick
North Yorks. (By Hand)

19th December 1952 CTCS/1004234/52
For the attention: Superintendent A.
Juggers,
York Central Police

MEMO
Military/Civilian regulation, code D 67 B
(12).

Sir,
Please note that the following officer:
Inspector Francis Grasby, must not be
informed **under any circumstances** of the
murder of Sgt D. Maskill, or any results of
his Post Mortem.
 Sgt Maskill died in the course of his
duty working for Her Majesty's Army
Intelligence Corps, on a matter of national
importance.
 This memo is **TOP SECRET** as per the above
regulation.

CC: (Assistant Chief Constable Harold
Ainsworth)
Yours,
M. C. E. Langton (Major)

32

I had hoped that those who saw fit to knock me over the head and string me up would have had the decency to get rid of my unreliable Austin A30. But I was wrong. There it is, amongst the trees just where I left it, resplendent in its inadequacy in the snow.

On closer examination there is no sign of my Webley pistol, though everything else in the car appears to be present and correct – even the map that guided me to this village in the first place. In fairness, though they took my weapon, my tormentors were good enough to leave me my wallet. But, given their identity, so they jolly well should.

'Are you coming back to the station?' Deedee asks.

'Well, no, actually. I could do with a drink, if I'm honest. It's been a bugger of a day.'

'I bet!'

'Though I wouldn't mind a quick chat with Elphinstone. Could you do me a favour and ask him to join me in the Beggar?'

'Sure thing, Inspector.' She flushes. 'You won't say anything about – well, you know.'

'Absolutely not. I have many reasons to thank the USA. I doubt I'd be here if it weren't for the bravery of your countrymen.'

This is no lie. Though I've often found Americans a bit loud, too pushy and more than a little brash, your average GI is as tough as old boots on the battlefield. I spent time in a foxhole with a rugged sergeant from New Jersey once. I was in a pure panic, as you can likely guess. But his funny stories about back home in the Garden State calmed me.

Not more than an hour later, he took a bullet in the forehead trying to save a comrade. I've always felt rather sad about that. But he was beyond brave, without any thought for his own safety. However, that valiant act alone rather epitomizes his country: bold, fearless – indeed the land of the brave. I have the feeling they'll do well keeping our world safe – eventually. Though there may be a bump or two along the road, as is the case now. It's time tired old Blighty handed over the baton. And let's face it, we're not giving it to the French, are we?

I watch Deedee reverse the van then rattle back down the hill. I've asked her not to reveal my whereabouts. I calculate that she's opened up to me a bit, so I will be slightly more forthcoming where she is concerned. It might help, at least in terms of being of some use now and again. There's an old Bedouin proverb about being lost in the desert and accepting any help you are offered. That's my motto from now on. Surely, I can hang on until Mitch gets something fixed up?

I take a small detour past the church, confident that, going downhill, my vehicle should have no problems. The place is in darkness. So, I reckon that whatever Croucher is up to, he's doing it from the safety of his vicarage, or wherever he spends his private time. Do I trust what Deedee told me? Yes, elements of it. It's all so odd. A bit like the Great Game before the First World War. If that's the case, then poor little Elderby must have taken on the role of the Balkans.

Just as I turn away from St Thomas's-on-the-Edge, there's a massive flash of lightning and a positively biblical clap of thunder. By the time I'm at the bottom of the hill, hailstones are pelting down again like little ball bearings.

In a few minutes, I'm approaching the Beggar. I almost park the car on the main road outside but decide not to. Instead, I pull up round the corner behind a van that says 'Bicksbey's Removals. No job too small' on the side. The van is a bright red, and the signage in white stands out starkly.

I know I have only a few yards to dash to the Beggar under the hail. But I'm unarmed and feeling rather vulnerable, so I sprint, holding my acquired cap down over my face. It's as quick as I ever made it between wickets, you know. The sulphurous air, charged by the electrical storm, is fresh in my nostrils. But the night is dark. Proper storms here on the moors are something to behold, I'm told. It looks as though this is my big opportunity to experience one at first hand.

I push the door open and duck into the haven of the public house. I don't expect to see Bleakly here yet. I think it would be fair to say that I've had my share of the unexpected today already, and nothing now, I reckon, can surprise me. But, almost inevitably, I'm wrong. For here, standing at the bar engaging in conversation with a small man whose dungarees are tied up at the ankles with string, is the unmistakable figure of my father. His tall, thin frame makes him look like a prop that's been brought to hold up the low ceiling.

As if by some sixth sense – anything is possible with my father – he turns, just as I'm removing my cap.

'Blending in with the locals, I see.' He takes me in with a beady eye. 'What's happened to you? You look as though you've been hung outside for a week or two.'

Once I've expressed my utter surprise at his presence, I recover enough to offer my dear old papa a drink.

'Whisky, please. Make it a large one, son,' says he inevitably.

Ethel is looking on, all ears. 'Is this your father, Inspector?'

Before I can say unfortunately yes, he pipes up.

'I'd hoped he'd follow in mine and his grandfather's footsteps. But he joined the police instead. As you can see, he's doing well for himself. Look at those patches on his elbows, for example.' He smiles sarcastically.

'He looked better earlier today. I saw him when I was cleaning the windows,' says Ethel before bustling off to get the drinks.

I usher my father over to the table furthest away from the bar, which just happens to be beside the fire. He bids a fond farewell to his new agricultural chum.

'What on earth are you doing here?'

'Can't a father come to his son's aid?' His words are almost lost in the latest disgorge of thunder. The windows are being fairly pelted by big hailstones. The lights in the pub flicker and go out.

'See what you've done? The man up the stairs isn't happy with you,' I chide.

'Don't blaspheme, Francis. Anyone who finds himself in the trouble you're in should keep God firmly at his side.'

'Why do you assume I'm in trouble?'

'I just *assume* it to be your natural state of being. Has been since you were old enough to comb your own hair, after all.'

It always amazes me at the effortless way my father manages to put me down. He doesn't even have to think, it's just there, instantly.

I lower my voice and lean into him. 'Listen, it's not safe here. I want you to finish your drink and get back to York.'

'My goodness, Elderby was the safest place in the world when I was here last. You're about for a couple of days and there's all sorts going on. Your mother had a name for people like you – a Scotch one that I can't remember. I'd call you a Jonah, but that would be unfair to him.'

Ethel appears with our drinks and a candle.

'Why, it reminds you of the war, doesn't it? Quite cosy, I always think.' She deposits the drinks on our table and holds the candle to the fire until it takes light. 'There,' she says, depositing it in a small holder. 'Let the dog see the rabbit, eh?' Ethel departs with a laugh.

'Better place than it used to be,' says my father.

'Of course, you're intimately acquainted with this village, aren't you?'

As though I haven't spoken, he continues. 'Used to be owned by a miserable sod. McGill was his name. Cruel as Josaphat, he was.'

It can't be a coincidence. There surely can't be more than one McGill family in Elderby.

'So, just how do you intend to help me, eh?'

I don't think I've ever seen my father wink, but he chooses to do so now. 'Nobody suspects a man of the cloth of anything.'

'Yes, including being of any practical use.'

'Now, there you are. Just what I expected. If the good Samaritan were to lend you a helping hand, you'd likely leave him for dead in the gutter. I can be your eyes and ears.' He looks round the room, now illuminated by the

288

flickering flame of candles on each table. 'No doubt you've dragooned poor Mitch into taking up the cudgels on your behalf. He has piles. Did you know that?'

It's yet another fascinating fact from the Reverend Grasby.

'Well, thank goodness you told me. I'll make sure I always carry a cushion with me just in case he needs to take a seat.'

My father knocks back his large whisky in one gulp. 'Poison. Where on earth does she get this gut rot? If your mother taught me one thing, it was the appreciation of fine Scotch whisky.'

She taught you a great deal more than that, you ungrateful sod. And there's still rationing on the go, I don't say.

'Whatever your troubles, son, trust that I'll bear the burden with you. A bit like Simon of Cyrene.' He smiles beatifically.

'They forced him to carry Jesus's cross!'

'A mere detail – you know what I mean.'

Thankfully, before we enter into our umpteenth theological debate, the door swings open and there is Sergeant Elphinstone Bleakly. He's dressed in his uniform supplemented by a long, black cape, from which hailstones fall copiously on to the pub carpet. Though I now mistrust everyone, I'm suddenly pleased to see the old boy. He sent Deedee to investigate Lord Damnish. Though I wish he'd shared his misgivings with me.

'It's a bloody rough one out there.' He shakes himself like a dog. 'I feel as bad as you look, sir.'

'Ha!' My father bursts into a fit of the giggles.

'Have I said something funny?' Bleakly enquires.

'I beg your pardon, Sergeant. But the thought of someone calling my son "sir" is quite amusing.'

'My, thank you, Daddy. You're already helping so much.'

They say that sarcasm is the lowest form of wit, but I've never subscribed to such nonsense.

I introduce Bleakly and my father then buy another round of drinks. It soon becomes apparent that Grasby Senior has appeared in Elderby before managing to visit a bank. I'm surprised to note that Bleakly's drink of choice is gin and tonic. I've only ever seen old women quaff the stuff. He tells me that they drank it in the jungle during the war to fight off malaria. Seems he's developed a taste for mother's ruin, and thinks it'll catch on with everyone some time in the future. I'm buggered if I agree with that, and I'm rarely wrong on all things connected to alcohol and horses – well, apart from the obvious.

'Can I speak freely?' says Bleakly, with a glance in my father's direction.

One thing I'll never commend the old bloke for is his discretion. I once became hopelessly constipated when I was a child and had to endure an enema. Do you know, he kept that quiet for four days until the Sunday service, when he wound it into a cautionary tale that ended up involving the saints and apostles. But I'm sure he'll recognize the seriousness of our current predicament and shut up. I nod in the affirmative to Bleakly.

'I've had our man on the phone.'

'Who?' say I.

'The man without a name, that's who.' He nods at me disconcertingly.

I must be getting slow, for I've missed this entirely. 'Tell me what on earth you're talking about, Bleakly.'

He leans in, and my father copies him. We look like Guy Fawkes and his pals.

'Cummins, that's who.'

'I'll be damned,' say I. Of course, now I have a problem. Bleakly doesn't know about the President cigarette butt that could belong to Cummins. Then again, nor does he know that Damnish Junior smokes them too.

'Now, who is this Cummins?' asks my father.

'You'll have to catch up later, Father,' say I.

He shrugs begrudgingly.

'What does he want, Elphinstone?'

'We've to be on our mettle very late tonight, sir. Something on the go, so he says.'

'Does Juggers know?'

'I didn't ask. Cummins is in charge, as I'm sure you'll agree.' Bleakly looks rather surprised by my question. 'We're to stay put and observe in the village, just in case, like.'

Damn. This is all a bit sudden. Can we trust Cummins? I'm not sure. Exactly what is about to happen in Elderby in the early hours of tomorrow morning? I feel as though I'm on the edge of something for which I'm totally unprepared and less than qualified. It's happened before when I came face to face with one of the most evil men in the world. That's for another time, but it was the same sensation, one of alarm at my confusion, and panic at having been exposed to such a circumstance.

'Sounds to me as though you're in above your head this time, son,' says my father helpfully. 'Now, where is the lavatory?'

I watch my wraithlike father make his way to the WC and take the opportunity to speak to Bleakly man to man. 'I'll have to be quick, Elphinstone,' say I.

'Yes, what is it?'

'Hardy and Thomas kidnapped me earlier. Had it not been for McGill the gamekeeper you'd be investigating another murder, I don't doubt.'

291

Bleakly looks at me as though I've sprouted horns. 'Did you see their faces?'

'No, they were wearing masks. You know, sacks with eyeholes, type of thing.'

'So, how do you know it was them?'

'Their boots. How many people go about their business in this village with perfectly bulled black boots?'

Bleakly looks bewildered for a moment, then his expression turns more to one of anger.

'I know, hard to come to terms with, isn't it?'

'I don't know what to say.' He avails himself of a long draw of G&T.

'And we know who foisted them upon us, don't we?'

'Cummins.'

'Precisely.'

'What do we do?'

'I'm working on something. But it'll take time. Meanwhile, we must keep calm and carry on while we get to grips with proceedings. Hold the fort, so to speak.'

'You don't think Starr's death has anything to do with all this, do you?'

'It would be rather strange if it didn't, don't you think?'

'I suppose. But what on earth is Cummins up to?' says Bleakly.

'I don't know. Lumley saw him captured by the Germans. Who knows what the chap's been through or how it's affected him?'

'But it's a coup. A plot against the police, and murder into the bargain. I never thought I'd see the day.'

I look Bleakly square in the eye. 'Come on, old boy. You know the score. Us soldiers don't matter when there's a fight for the greater good – or ill, come to that. Wheels within wheels.'

'And I thought Elderby would be a nice wind-down to retirement.'

'And I thought I'd only have to round up some farm thieves. How wrong can one be?'

My father returns, rubbing his hands together. 'Right, what have I missed?'

'Nothing. Just a bit of police chat, that's all.'

'You can't go back to the station, that's for sure,' says Bleakly.

'I knew it. Suspended again.' My father shakes his head.

'And you can't go back to Hetty Gaunt's tonight, neither.'

I look at my father, who chooses this moment to stay silent and contemplate the wall.

'Of course, under normal circumstances, you could bunk with Mrs Bleakly and I. But these are hardly normal circumstances, are they? To be honest, I'm surprised you've showed your face here in the pub, sir.'

'I've been attacked twice since I arrived, Elphinstone. On both occasions, there was nobody about. They won't break cover and do anything in public.'

'That's why you wanted to speak to me here.'

'Absolutely correct.'

'There's a bright side to all this,' says my father.

'Exactly what is that?'

'I can take your place at Hetty's. If I remember correctly, she's a fine cook.'

Bleakly looks confused, while I look disgusted. With turmoil in our midst, my father sees fit to rekindle what clearly is an old flame.

'He knows Hetty from many years ago,' say I to Bleakly.

'Oh, nice.' The sergeant takes another drink. 'I've had an idea. As to your accommodation problems, that is.'

'Good man. What is it?'

'Mr Powell. He lives on the edge of the village. My wife used to do for him, you know.'

'Lovely,' say I, while my father looks suspicious.

'Do for?' he says.

'Housekeeping, and the like. He was a miserable old swine, but she felt sorry for him. Heart of gold, she has, my wife.'

'Go on,' say I, impatient to find somewhere safe to hide and catch my breath before the dread hour tomorrow morning.

'He died a week or so back. Sad business, really. He'd forgotten he'd put bleach in a whisky bottle. Came home from here and took a great slug. Doctor Starr did what she could, but it was too much for him.'

At this point, one would have expected a man of religion to express sorrow or at least a prayer for the lost.

Instead, 'Silly old bastard,' says my father. 'Must have been a bit wanting up top.' He taps his own forehead.

Ignoring him, I press Bleakly. 'I could stay there?'

'You could. His daughter lives in London. I get the feeling she isn't too bothered what happens to the place. Turned up for his funeral and was off before Croucher had time to say the benediction.'

'Croucher, you say?' says my father.

'The local vicar,' says Bleakly, by way of explanation.

'I see.' My father has adopted a straight-backed, official attitude. No doubt the kind of posture he used to antagonize George V.

'What is it?'

'Just passing thoughts, son. Nothing more.'

I leave my father to it and work out with Bleakly how I'm to get to the deceased Powell's cottage without anyone taking note.

Again, a clap of thunder, this time it's so loud it appears to rock the whole pub. In from this meteorological turmoil appears my landlady, Hetty Gaunt. I must say, framed in the doorway, she looks remarkably untouched by the hailstorm in her black bowler hat and cape. Mind you, the red feather in the hatband is rather bedraggled.

'Hetty,' says my father, a broad smile on his face. He takes to his feet to greet his long-lost – well, whatever she was.

'Cyril. Well, I never. I heard you were in the village, and just had to come here and see for myself.' She beams from ear to ear.

My father strides towards her and does something I've rarely ever seen him do, enfolding Hetty Gaunt in a tight embrace. 'You haven't changed a bit,' he exclaims.

Odd thing to say, really. She looks about seventy now. Must have looked dreadful when she was young, thinks I.

'Please, take a seat at our table.' My father dashes across to a spare chair and forces Bleakly to move closer to me to enable Hetty to sit next to him. Settling her in her chair, my animated pater offers her a drink. 'Are you still on the same poison, Hetty?'

I'm not at all surprised that she drinks poison. After all, there has to be something seriously wrong with a person who decorates her home so.

'Yes, a Bloody Mary, please. A large one, if you will.'

It's easy to see why this pair get on so well.

'Be a good lad and grab Hetty a drink, will you, son?' He says this without taking his eyes off her.

Standing at the bar, I wonder if it's my lot in life to be little more than a vehicle for the peccadilloes of others. While I'm waiting for Ethel to be about her business, I spy something through the hail and snow of the window. It's normally quite hard to see out of an illuminated room into the darkness outside, but with candles the only lights available in the Beggar I can easily make out a figure standing stock still across the road. Worse, he's tall and wearing a police uniform. It's Hardy!

As calmly as I can muster, I pay for the drink – a small fortune, I might add – and take it back to our table. I break into the conversation between my father and Hetty Gaunt.

'Don't move, anyone.' Those assembled round the table look at me with questioning irritation.

'What on earth is it now?' says Bleakly.

'Hardy is outside. He's in front of the butcher's, just standing there.'

'I hope he's got a cape on,' says Bleakly.

'That's not really what I was driving at, old boy,' say I.

'Oh – oh! Of course,' Bleakly has remembered what I said to him about my incarceration at the Salt House.

However, this piece of news has an unexpected effect on the good sergeant. Bleakly yawns, mashes his mouth a couple of times, his eyelids flicker and before I know it his head flops on to his shoulder and he's sound asleep.

'Drinker, eh?' says my father, as charitably as one would expect from a vicar. 'Just topping up, I don't doubt.'

'He has a condition,' says Hetty.

I have a condition, too: I'm terrified. Clearly, Hardy has got wind of my presence at the Beggar. He has the place under surveillance. Not handy, when I have to make a clandestine exit.

I hate doing it, but I shake Bleakly roughly by the shoulder.

33

I manage to rouse the sleepy sergeant from his impromptu slumber. But it isn't without incident. He rushes to his feet, knocking the table of drinks over my father and Hetty Gaunt.

'Get away, you little bastards!' he shouts at the top of his voice, adopting the stance of the pugilist.

I expect the whole place to be in uproar about this. But it appears that the customers of the Beggar are accustomed to Elphinstone's little episodes, so everyone carries on as though nothing at all has happened. Apart from my father, that is.

'This chap is a bloody liability,' he offers, brushing spilt drinks from his jacket. 'Even you'd make a better police sergeant than him.'

'You're forgetting that I'm an inspector, Father,' say I.

'Yes, of course.' He gathers his thoughts. 'Well, you want to get a grip of yourself, Sergeant. Get to a doctor, man.'

'I'll have you know I contracted this affliction in the service of my country.' He faces up to my father in a rather aggressive fashion, which I must admit to finding quite enjoyable – despite the circumstances.

'You have become an irascible old chap, Cyril,' says Hetty Gaunt.

Become! It's clear it's almost a lifetime since she last set eyes on the Reverend Grasby.

It's watching him and Bleakly knock heads like two ageing stags that gives me a pearl of an idea. I look round the bar. There are two younger chaps enjoying a game of cards in the corner.

I amble over. 'Listen, lads,' say I. 'Would you like to make some quick cash?'

Following a short pause they nod enthusiastically, as another crack of thunder rocks the pub.

'It'll only take a few minutes. But you will get cold and hailed upon, unfortunately.'

'How much?' says the brighter of the two.

'Let's say a fiver between the pair of you. How's that?'

He spits on his hand and shakes mine.

I know, all this is costing me a small fortune. But I shall submit my expenses when things get back to normal. It's something upon which I keep a meticulous eye, you know.

I turn my attentions to Ethel. 'Can I use your back entrance?'

She raises her eyes to the ceiling. 'Well, it's all a bit sudden, but whatever floats your boat, Inspector. I'm game.'

She's a card, eh? But I soon establish that a door leads out of the cellar on to a small yard, thence to a back lane. It's the perfect escape route.

'Remember, Ethel. If anyone comes in asking for me – and I mean *anyone* – you haven't seen me, understand?'

'This is all quite exciting,' she replies. 'Though I did prefer your first suggestion.'

I brief my new young pals and hand over a large white fiver. They examine it as though they've never held one before. Which, I suppose, is possibly the case.

Thankfully, when I get back to the table common sense

has prevailed, and relations are back on a friendly footing between Bleakly and my father. The table has been righted and Hetty is busy with the brush and shovel that sit by the fire, sweeping up any stray glass.

'Elphinstone, we have to get out of here,' say I. 'How far away is this cottage you mentioned?'

'A bit more than ten minutes, if we hurry,' says he. 'It'll be hard going, what with the snow and all this hail, mind.'

Right now, I wouldn't care if someone chucked stones at me. I just want to free myself from the scrutiny of Hardy and Thomas. I realize that Bleakly could go and send him on an errand. But now I'm sure the errant constables – if indeed they are police officers at all, which I've always doubted – will go their own way. And our sergeant could find himself in trouble into the bargain.

I brief Elphinstone on my plan. He nods in agreement, as my father rubs his chin doubtfully.

'What's wrong with you?' I ask him.

'You say there're two of these chaps, Dickens and Charles?'

'Yes, there are two of them. And it's Hardy and Thomas. What of it?'

'Didn't it occur to you that if they have one man posted at the front, the other will be round the back?'

Damn! This is something I should have thought of immediately – so should Bleakly, come to that. But you know what kind of day I've had and, to be fair, my colleague has just woken up and nearly ended up in a fight with a vicar. Still, I hate admitting that my father's right – at any time.

'Any suggestions, then?' I ask.

'I'll go round the back. Give me five minutes or so,' says the Reverend Grasby.

'What on earth are you going to do?'

My father fingers his dog collar. 'These sound like a pair of rum lads. But it's amazing what this will do. Nobody wants to be in conflict with the Almighty. Apart from you, of course.'

I must confess to being rather proud of the old chap. It's enough to make a son's bottom lip tremble. But being Scotch, my mother frowned on such open displays of emotion, and it stuck. So, I shake him by the hand and wish him well.

In contrast, though, Hetty flings herself at her old friend, tears spilling down her face.

'Be careful, Cyril. You know where I am.' She wipes her eyes. 'We've only just found each other again. I don't want to lose you, not now.'

This is too much for me. Any gratitude I felt moments ago has now turned to resentment. I hope Thomas staves his head in. It's the Scotch part in me again. Did my mother know about all this business in Elderby? For business, there has undoubtedly been. I chide myself for being so ungrateful. Though I think whatever passed between them did so before her time.

'Yes, don't forget Hetty's waiting, Father,' say I rather sarcastically. The image of this unlikely pairing in the throes of passion as Cecil flies above their heads squawking his displeasure is a hard one to shift, you know.

With that, my father leaves. He ducks under the door at the back of the bar without a glance back.

'He always was a fine man,' says Hetty.

'You'll be able to tell what's going to happen to him? From your soothsaying or whatever it is you do?'

Bleakly grimaces at my remark. Hetty fixes me with her steely glare.

'I'm not worried in the slightest about him. You, well that's another story, lad.' She gets up, grabs her hat and cape, turns on her heel and exits the pub. No doubt to get ready for a more intimate reunion with dear Daddy later.

Bleakly shakes his head. 'I wouldn't mess about with things you don't understand,' says he.

'I haven't understood my father for nearly forty years and I'm still here. Mrs Gaunt doesn't present a problem,' say I indignantly.

I watch her go and check my Omega. 'We'll give him a few more minutes before I send the lads out.'

'Sounds fair enough.'

As with all such things, five minutes seems more like five hours. But it's soon time to dispatch the decoys. I nod to my accomplices, and off they go into the thunder, lightning and hail. Though we're pretending not to look, they do as I instructed. One pushes the other, and soon a very convincing fight breaks out. I watch for Hardy through the window, still and grim in the lightning like an apparition. He's clearly discomfited by this, looking up and down the street, wondering what to be about. But it's obvious, such is the full-on flyweight bout that's now taking place outside the Beggar, that he must do something.

Soon, Constable Hardy, possibly for the one and only time in his life, finds himself doing the real job of a police officer: keeping the peace. As he wrestles with the two smaller men, they turn on him. Plucky lads, I'll give them that.

'Right, Elphinstone,' say I. 'It's time to go.'

The Elderby sergeant is wearing his cape but has forsworn his helmet, which still hangs on the coat stand. 'I'll take the lead, sir. I know where I'm going.'

We make our bid for freedom.

*

Out in the lane it's slippery, the hail adding to the frozen snow on the ground. Just as we make off, another hail shower – heavier this time – begins. It's so bad, I can barely see Bleakly in front of me. And for an older chap, he's going at a fair lick, something I didn't expect. We take a right and we're out in one of Elderby's little byways. I look round but see nobody following us. If Thomas was stationed at the back of the pub, my father has done a good job of removing him.

'This way!' shouts Bleakly, straddling a garden fence.

It's no time to demur, so I follow suit, still marvelling at Bleakly's pace and agility. I suppose you don't survive the Chindits for nothing.

Suddenly, we find ourselves on open farmland. I look across through the trees and can just about make out Holly House. I'm soaked, my eyes are stinging, but I don't care.

Just as things seem to be going well, I watch as Bleakly slips on the slick ground. From my perspective, it's like watching a ballet. It all happens as though time has slowed down. He pivots perfectly in the air, but instead of a graceful landing on tiptoes, he appears to twist his knee and ends up crashing to the ground with a yelp of pain.

I stop over my stricken colleague. 'Can you walk?' I ask, offering him a hand up.

'I can try, sir,' he groans, clearly in much pain.

I manage to haul him up. But it's going to be slow going from here on in.

'How far?' I'm shouting above another clap of thunder.

'Another few hundred yards. But you'll have to prop me up.'

So, with me as a crutch, we scramble along a field, down a small hill and find ourselves on a rough lane.

'Just over there,' shouts brave old Bleakly, wincing in pain.

Somehow, we manage to make it to a place best described as a hovel rather than a cottage. It looks like something out of a Grimms fairy tale, with a sloping roof on a crooked wooden frame. I get to a warped oak door and push. Thankfully, it gives way and we blunder into the cottage. I hate kicking in doors – well, it's beneath me.

It's dark inside, but through flashes of lightning it's clear that we're in a small hallway. I take a guess and drag Bleakly through a door on our left. My instincts have been correct. We're in the lounge. Now, I must take a moment here to redefine that word. The place is a musty mausoleum, with ancient wing-backed chairs, a big brass coal scuttle, anti-macassars over a chaise longue, and even an aspidistra in a tall clay pot. It's like stepping back seventy years. I suppose the unfortunate Mr Powell was very much a man of his time.

In the gloom, punctuated by claps of thunder, I man-handle Bleakly on to the chaise longue, where he props himself up awkwardly on one elbow like a dowager in distress.

'I've given my knee a right twist,' says he, plainly suffering.

'Nothing much I can do for you, old boy, apart from make you as comfortable as possible.'

'Aye, we're in a bit of a fix here, and no mistake.'

'Do you have a light?' I'm damned if I know where my lighter has gone.

Bleakly delves painfully into his tunic pocket under the cape and hands me a rather soggy box of matches. Though this place appears to have electricity, the lightning has taken it out, as it did in the Beggar. Fortunately, there's a big storm lantern perched on a stone grate. I manage to set light to a match, then the wick, and soon we're bathed in a flickering warm light.

'You're quite grey about the gills, old boy,' say I.

'The bloody jungle. I've not been the same since I came back. Bit of cold weather and I'm as stiff as a board. It gets into your bones, you know. Takes twice as long to recover from anything. It's a hellish place.'

I don't doubt it. I heard far too many tales of what the Chindits faced. Bleakly is a fine example of how it ruined men – some mentally as well as physically. Mind you, Elderby isn't exactly a dream, either.

'I don't suppose there's a phone?' say I.

'No. Old Powell would have nothing to do with such things. He had to be persuaded to have electricity. He said it was the beginning of the end. Soon we'd all be connected by one wire – right round the globe. Countries wouldn't mean anything.'

'Clearly off his chump.'

'I don't know. He was a smart old sod, in a way. He knew how to get a bargain.'

Bleakly tries to move, but yelps in pain instead.

I pull a bedraggled packet of cigarettes from the inside pocket of my jacket and offer one to Bleakly.

'I'm not much of a man for the ciggies normally, but there's nothing normal about this, is there?'

I walk over and light a cigarette for him, from which he puffs clouds of blue smoke as is the wont of a cigar- or pipe-smoker going at a fag.

'Tell me about Cummins' orders, Elphinstone.'

Bleakly coughs, rights himself and yawns. 'We're to muster at three a.m. in the station. Then – well, I don't know what he has in store. He were a bit vague on the phone.'

'There's something afoot. That's all you know for sure?'

'It is.'

'He'll be expecting you to be there.'

'He will. It's our job, after all.'

I'm trying to work out how to get a message to anyone in a way that doesn't involve me being exposed to Hardy or Thomas. They'll have realized that I've escaped the Beggar and are bound to be on our tail. Thankfully, only two other people know where we are: my father and Hetty Gaunt. Will they have the sense to come here? That's not guaranteed by any means. My father's always been a bit of a dunce when it comes to anything that doesn't involve the Church. Gosh, he's not been too clever there, either. I was rather surprised when he announced his plan to distract PC Thomas back at the pub. I suppose everyone can be inspired once in their lives.

'They'll work it out, you know,' says Bleakly, as though he's read my mind.

'How I escaped, you mean?'

'Aye, and it won't take them long to work out who your father is, neither.'

'How? Even he won't be stupid enough to tell them.'

'You must be daft. You're like peas in a pod. Well, an old pea and a younger pea. But anyone would know you're father and son.'

I hadn't thought of this. I never think of myself as anything like my father. But the sketch in my bedroom at Hetty Gaunt's says otherwise. As a young man he did look like me. After all, I have the same build and height, even if our hair colour is different. Well, he's as grey as a goose now, anyway.

'You don't think they'd harm him, Elphinstone?'

'Look what they did to you. These blokes don't care. They'll just follow orders. I don't fancy being strung up, let me tell you.'

Another worry. They're piling up and no mistake. Were

it not for my father's precarious situation, I'd have a good mind to stay here and hope for the best. I know I can trust Mitch Parsley. If anyone can sort out this mess, he can. But now I'm concerned that Hardy and Thomas, whoever they are, Communists, fascists or even our own men, will leverage my father to get to me. Though what obstacle Cummins thinks I'll be to their plans, I don't know. It's puzzling.

'We must get a message to Miss Dean,' says Bleakly.

'What do you suggest, smoke signals?'

He sighs, grimacing at the pain in his knee. 'There's a path round the back of the house here. It belongs to a farmer. The farm is less than half a mile away. He has a phone.'

The thunder crashes again as I think what to do. I can't sit tight, that's for sure. And there's no way Bleakly's up to making the trek. Again, by the ghastly familiar process of wrong place, wrong time, I find myself forced to take one metaphorical step forward, volunteering by default.

'Powell was a drinker, wasn't he?'

'A drinker? I've never seen a man able to put away as much booze. He should have kicked the bucket years before he did. Minor miracle, really.'

In the flickering light of the gas lamp, I look round the room for any sign of bottles containing alcohol of any description. I'm not fussy, but I need a stiffener. But there's no cabinets, sideboards or cupboards to be seen.

I take a wander back into the hall. Through one door is a brass bed sporting a bare mattress. The next door along is the kitchen. There's an old range and an iron sink. Some dirty dishes left about are now sprouting patches of mould. I wonder just how much Mrs Bleakly actually *did* for old Powell.

The first cupboard I look in contains some cracked

plates, cups and saucers. The second is like an Aladdin's cave, full to the brim with odds and ends: candles, bicycle clips, an old tea caddy, a hammer, empty bottles and jars, a roll of string, etc., etc. I close it, then something crosses my mind. I open it again, remove the hammer and slide it into my trouser pocket. Well, it's better than nothing if one finds oneself in a tight spot.

The third cupboard bears more fruit. There's a half-full bottle of something with a faded, handwritten label. I must say, though I'd take a glug of elderflower wine in desperation, the green bottle of whisky beside it holds much greater appeal. I open it and swill down a good measure or two. The spirit burns my throat. Only then do I remember how poor Powell died. Following a moment of sheer panic, I soon realize that this indeed is whisky. I take the bottle through and hand it to Bleakly.

'This should keep the pain at bay, old boy,' say I.

'It's not bleach, is it?'

Clearly Bleakly has a cooler, wiser head than I. I assure him it's the real thing, and he opens the bottle and takes a sip or two.

'Right, it's down the lane about half a mile, you say?'

'Not even that far,' says Bleakly.

'What if I can't get Deedee – Miss Dean?'

'Lumley is a good man. Speak to him.'

He's right, of course. I wish Bleakly a fond, if temporary, farewell.

Outside, the hail is a bit lighter, but still enough to batter the living daylights out of you. Frankly, though, I don't feel a thing.

I look round. We're on the edge of a small wood. If there's anyone about, I can't see them. The path is clear. It meanders off into the trees; I take to it at a trot. Goodness me, this is worse than basic training in the army. At least you had your pals about for company and encouragement. And, at that stage at least, there was no danger of imminent capture. I remember with a shudder the horrid feeling of hanging upside down at the mercy of my tormentors in the Salt House.

I read somewhere that the most dangerous place to be during a thunderstorm is amongst trees. But as I'm in as much danger around trees as I am anywhere else, it's of no consequence. Perhaps being struck down by lightning is my fate.

I pick up my pace to that of a long-distance runner. The sooner this is done, the better. The trees have cleared now and I'm back in open farmland. It's quite ethereal, with the moon trying to poke its head through the dark storm clouds. It's a dreadful night. I imagine this is how purgatory may look. It's something I've often thought about. Who knows, we may all be in purgatory at this very moment. It certainly feels like it.

The path rises in front of me, and I'm aware of the hammer battering my thigh. It's as irritating as it is reassuring. I turn round and canter backwards for a moment or two, just to make sure I'm not being pursued. But the coast still appears to be clear.

I haven't participated in any serious exercise for some time, so my legs soon begin to burn with the effort, and I'm wheezing because of my indulgence in cigarettes. What I wouldn't do for the comfort of my unpredictable Austin now. Over the short rise, I can see down into a shallow valley. Bleakly is right: in the distance is a huddle of farm buildings. Soon, I'll be able to summon help. I forge onwards.

My first notion that something may be wrong is the

absence of any animals or the odour of same. No cattle sitting down on the grass to keep it dry, or sheep huddling together for safety. As I near the farmhouse and surrounding barns and outbuildings, nor is there any sign of human habitation. No glow of lamp or the flicker of fireplace. Puzzled, I make my way into the yard. The whole place is a shambles of broken doors, cracked windows and discarded agricultural odds and ends. I stop, leaning my hands on my knees to catch my breath. The hail is still battering against my face.

At first, I'm confused. I wrack my brains to work out why I've been sent on this wild goose chase. Did Bleakly simply get it wrong? Maybe he's not been out this way for a few years. Then I think of the nature of small communities. Everyone knows everyone else's business. There's no way that a family abandoning their farm – their home – wouldn't attract gossip and speculation. Perhaps he simply forgot – after all, he's clearly not a well man, falling asleep on the hoof the way he does. Then a terrible realization dawns. Bleakly distinctly referred to me as being 'strung up', just before I left the cottage. But thinking on it, I didn't tell him that back in the pub. All I said was I'd been kidnapped and mistreated by Hardy and Thomas, whom I'd identified by their highly polished boots. But why send me to the farm?

Almost crying with anger at my own stupidity, I suddenly feel very vulnerable. I begin my race back to Powell's, this time sticking to the verges, using the cover of the treeline, looking, always looking. My jacket over my head serves against the hail, but also as a pitiful disguise. Soon, I'm up and down the rise. Though I stay low when navigating open farmland, crouching, still watchful. The cluster of trees on the way offers merciful cover. But then I picture

309

either Hardy or Thomas hiding behind every trunk. When I near Powell's cottage, I can see the reassuring flicker of lamplight through the worsening deluge of hailstones.

Fear is a funny thing. It's amazing how easily you can persuade yourself that the danger is over – or never existed in the first place. I did just that during the war too often. Maybe I've misjudged the local sergeant; perhaps he really didn't know that the farm was now unoccupied. It's time to stick or twist, and as usual I don't hesitate – after all, this could still be a haven rather than a trap. I burst through the old, warped door and crash into the lounge. But the chaise longue is empty, the bottle of whisky I'd given Bleakly sitting on the floor beside it.

'Elphinstone!' I call desperately. But there is no response.

It's one of two things, I try to tell myself. Perhaps some-one followed us and waited until I took off to grab Bleakly. Could he be the real prey? I sit on the chaise longue and fret. But I know the truth. Sergeant Elphinstone Bleakly is part of all this – whatever *this* is – and I've been betrayed. Worse still, I'm a sitting duck.

Above the racket of hail on the wooden roof – the sky is still lowering – I hear the rattle of an engine. The swing of car headlights flashes through the window, casting shadows across the dilapidated room.

I'm cornered.

34

It's the classic pose we've all seen at the cinema. I'm standing, squeezed behind the door to the ramshackle lounge, hammer poised at my shoulder. This may end up being futile resistance, but I'll be damned if I'm going down without a fight. I must confess to being slightly buoyed by this steely resolve. But it's a human trait, you know. When faced with seemingly insurmountable odds, it's amazing what reserves of strength and courage one can call upon.

I hear the front door being pushed at, then creaking open. Whoever is about to join me – friend or foe – they're anxious not to make too much of a noise whilst being about it. I tense the muscles in my right arm, ready to swing the hammer down on some unfortunate's bonce.

I'm trying desperately to hold my breath, lest it be overheard. This is difficult to do when you're frozen to the very core. Damn, it's a wonder my chattering teeth alone don't betray my position.

I hear a few tentative footsteps up the hall, then they stop. Whoever is out there is busy taking in their surroundings. There's no sign of a torch or any other kind of illumination, so they must be as disoriented as I was when I first happened upon Mr Powell's cottage.

It crosses my mind to make a wild dash out into the hall, swinging the hammer. But if, as I expect, there are two of them this will end up being a futile endeavour and likely get me killed. Hardy and Thomas, whoever they really are, whomever they are really working for, don't mess about. I'll be dead in an instant.

I hear the gentle padding of furtive feet heading towards me. Though I'm shivering, I swear that beads of sweat are dripping down my forehead.

This waiting is agony. My instinct is to scream out, to frighten the opponent half to death, handing me an advantage. But this likely comes from inclinations set deep in our collective past, facing up to some animal or other. It's not the sophisticated approach.

'Inspector Grasby, are you in here?'

It takes me a few seconds to recognize the voice. It's the context, don't you know. If you expect something – even fear it the way I do Hardy and Thomas – deliverance, real or imagined, is grindingly hard to accept.

Still wary, the hammer held above my right shoulder, I reply.

'Deedee, is that you?'

'Of course it is!' She pushes at the door and joins me in the lounge.

My young American friend takes me in with no little horror. After all, to her it looks as though I'm about to cave her head in.

'What on earth . . . It's me.' She backs off instinctively.

'Are you alone?'

'Yes, why wouldn't I be?'

There are a number of answers to that question, but this isn't the time. I lower my arm, letting the hammer fall to the floor. I don't know what it is – maybe the sheer relief – but I enfold Daisy Dean in an embrace, sobbing as I do so.

'You poor thing. What a time you've been having. I'm so sorry.' She sounds like my mother, rather than a nearly thirty-year-old mature student.

I pull back and apologize for my forward behaviour.

'No need to be sorry. That's half the problem with you English. You're so buttoned up that you never express your feelings. In New York – well, it's different.'

'I don't doubt it,' say I.

'But you have to pull yourself together. We're in trouble – big trouble.'

Thankfully, my mind takes this opportunity to start working again.

'How did you know where to find me?'

'Hetty came to me. Gee, she was so distressed. It was hard to make out a thing she said, at first. She was rambling, confused. She even mentioned your father.'

'You haven't spotted him, by any chance?'

'How on earth would I spot him? I've never met the man before. And anyhow, what would he be doing in Elderby?'

I feel a sudden ache in my chest. It's not the same as worrying for one's own safety. This is a much more cloying, almost visceral fear of loss, the very pit of sadness and guilt. Goodness knows, my father and I have had a turbulent past. But I'm all he's got and vice versa. Remember, he walked out the back door of the Beggar to help me. Now – well, who knows what's become of him.

'We have to move quickly. Get out of sight. Make plans, Inspector.' Deedee looks up at me earnestly. 'It's all moved faster than I thought.'

'What has?'

313

'They're bringing in the weapons tonight. By tomorrow they could be on their way to Catterick.'

'Catterick? What on earth . . . ?' say I, truly befuddled now.

'You must have guessed what's going on here? Going on for real, I mean.'

'Well, I know enough to realize that this isn't the place I thought it was, that's for sure.'

'It's a military coup, dammit! They're gathering their forces and then going to the army base. The Salt House will be their HQ. They have infiltrators everywhere. Lots of them.'

Bloody hell, that's the last thing anyone needs. Suddenly, I wish I'd put a bullet in Cummins' head the day I met him. I know this sounds like a beastly thing to do but, as I hope is the case, you didn't have to suffer the horror of it all. Old Sherman was right – war is hell.

'How are they able to get away with all this?' say I. 'He's even brought my boss in on it all. I thought Juggers was the Rock of Gibraltar.'

'It's the way things work in this country.' Deedee sounds almost dismissive. 'Things go through on a nod and a wink – big things. Your aristocracy still has too much sway over everything that happens here. You guys like to think you have a democracy, but that's tokenism. Great Britain is democratic one day every five years. And even then, we all know the place is run by clever civil servants, not hapless politicians. That's just the illusion of power.'

Well, thanks for the lecture. I'm beginning to wish I'd gone to Yale. It would have made a man of me. 'What an awful place Britain is,' say I, feeling more than a little wounded at this American's verbal onslaught against the nation I hold so dear I nearly gave my life for it – often!

'I'm sorry to offend. It's just a statement of fact. Hey, these people exist in the United States, too. It's just harder to beat the system. Though they've tried, trust me.'

'I'm damned if I can work out who's who in all this.'

'You know what's been happening since the end of the war. The Soviet Union has grabbed half of Europe. Some think they won't stop until they have their feet up in one of your London clubs. Until they're the tenants of Belgravia or Kensington, their kids at all your *public* schools that are in fact the least public places in the world. Can you imagine that?'

'That will never happen,' say I. 'Utter balderdash. The day Russians have their feet up in Boodle's, I'll sail for America.'

'Some would say you should book a ticket right now.'

I must admit to becoming less than enamoured at being lectured by this slip of a girl. Though she's right: the Communists have made great strides into many parts of Eastern Europe. Old Winnie isn't happy about it, I know that.

'I won't support the Nazis, Deedee. Look what they did!'

'It's the old story: my enemy's enemy is my friend. Rogue elements in your government and military see the Nazis as the last bulwark against the Communists. They'll rouse Germany again. And best of all – so the story goes – the Nazis will do the heavy lifting against Stalin, while we sit back and watch them. It may be a minority view, but it's not restricted to your country, Frank. Trust me.'

'That's the last thing anyone wants. Bloody mad idea. Like inviting Attila the Hun to dinner – worse!' I try to think of something more chilling but fail miserably. It's all this kerfuffle, you know.

'Tell that to certain members of your elite. Because that's what we're faced with here.'

315

I'll be damned.

Deedee looks round, a puzzled expression on her face.

'Where's Sergeant Bleakly?'

'You mean you don't know?'

'Miss Gaunt told me he was with you.'

'He was.' I think of what to say. But the fact that Bleakly could be on the way with Hardy, Thomas or goodness knows what other thug in tow, means we don't have time for explanations. 'I'll tell you on the way, let's get out of here.' I bend down and pick up the hammer.

'You planning some home improvement?'

'It's all I've got.'

She sighs. 'I can give you something. But the weapons are at Miss Gaunt's.'

'They are?'

'Sure, under my bed.'

I'll be blowed. I've been sleeping along the landing from a small arsenal and known nothing about it. Come to that, I've been in the dark about a few things.

'Time to go. Don't forget your hammer, Inspector.'

I dash in front of her, like the gentleman I am, and open the door. But as I gaze out in the rain, only a few feet away is the powerful figure of Constable Thomas. For a moment, we're both frozen by the surprise of it all. He reacts first, though, rushing at me like a flanker after a tricky winger at Twickenham. Before I know it, I'm bowled to the floor, Thomas on top of me. I'm completely winded, the sheer weight of the brute pinning me down.

Thomas lifts his fist, ready to propel it into my unprotected face. But just before he does, a deafening shot rings out in the narrow confines of the hall.

I'm looking up at Constable Thomas, or whoever he is. The light leaves his eyes, his right arm falls to his side, and he topples sideways off me, a neat gaping hole in his forehead.

I push him off and struggle to my feet. Deedee has a Beretta pistol in her hand. I want to comfort her on having had to take a man's life. It can't be an easy thing for such a young woman. But before I can, she dashes past me, out into the hail and snow, and towards a Humber Super Snipe.

'Come on!' she shouts to me.

It's frightening how quickly one forgets basic army training. I should have been beside her in the car now, rather than standing with my mouth agape like a child. As I finally make a dash for the car, something whistles past my head, then I hear the report of a firearm.

I throw myself into the front passenger seat. Deedee is behind the wheel, her face set, almost lacking in emotion. She pulls away at such speed the passenger door slams shut, almost parting me from my left leg.

I push myself up just in time to see a figure caught before us in the headlights. In this split second, I recognize Hardy, kneeling in a classic shooting pose.

'Get down!' Deedee shouts as she thrusts her foot down on the accelerator.

A number of things happen at once. The windscreen is shattered and I feel the rush of cold air and splinters of broken glass on my cheek. I duck as low in my seat as I can. Something thuds off the car and Deedee cries out. It's not a feminine gasp of surprise, rather a throaty roar of determination.

Given my slouched position, I can't see ahead, but I can feel that the car is spinning out of control on the icy surface. I look up at Deedee as she expertly forces the wheel into a skid, sending the Humber back on a forward trajectory. She's crying out in pain as she does so, though.

I force myself up in the passenger seat and twist to see through the car's rear window. There, picked out in a flash of lightning, is a still figure face down on the muddy lane.

'You ran Hardy over,' say I without thinking.

'Kismet,' says Deedee dispassionately, but with a grimace.

'Are you hurt?'

'Yeah, you might have to take over. The damned steering wheel wrenched my wrist. I think it's broken.'

Still, things could be a great deal worse. We've come within moments of being sent into oblivion by my former constables. Instead, they lie dead, sent to their maker by the remarkable Daisy Dean.

She stops the car, and we swap roles. Me in the driver's seat, her next to me clutching her damaged wrist.

'What now?' I ask, as we take off towards Elderby.

'The church, go to the church,' shouts Deedee.

The hail is still slanting down and an eerie darkness envelops the village, all power cut by the storm, so Deedee tells me. I begin to wonder if the weather is behind this or whether there's another, more sinister reason. I drive up the hill and make for the edge.

'Park round the back,' says Deedee.

I do as I'm bid.

35

Up here on the edge, behind the church, the hail has turned to snow, while the thunder and lightning are confined to the odd distant rumble and flash. However, the wind is beginning to get a bit lively. Gosh, it's rough.

Without a word, Deedee leaves the car. She's holding her left wrist in her right hand, and still clearly in pain. Not that it holds her back any. She's off at a canter, sure-footed in the white stuff.

I'm following on behind like a little dog. I must admit, it gets a bit wearing being one of the supporting actors all the time. It always seems to happen to me. For once, I'd like to get the opportunity to turn the heads and be in receipt of admiring glances. Still, the team is only as strong as its weakest player – or so our sports master used to say back at Hymers. As we dash through the lichgate, though, I wish I hadn't remembered this bon mot. After all, if I'm the weak link, what is to become of us?

Deedee fairly bursts through the big oak doors of the church. My goodness, poor Croucher will likely have a stroke.

I'll find out very shortly, too, for here, standing in the aisle illuminated by the light of one flickering candle on the altar and two storm lanterns, is the Reverend Croucher.

'Croucher, have you got something I can strap this up with?' says Deedee in a less than respectful manner.

'Is it broken?' says he, in a voice that sounds as though it should be coming from someone else. It's deep, authoritative almost. Not at all like the simpering chap I've spoken to over the last few days.

'Maybe, I'm not sure. But I can still use a pistol,' says Deedee.

Right, hang on a second, thinks I. It's time I'm told just what's going here.

'Inspector Grasby, you've survived, I see,' says Croucher before I can ask the question. It's uncanny. I know I'm face to face with the same man, but he looks almost entirely different: taller, broader, his face set in firm determination. His voice is deeper, too; resonant, with a touch of sibilance I hadn't detected before. He might well be Welsh.

'Yes, I'm rather pleased to say that I have,' say I. 'Now, what's all to do here? It's quite clear that you're not the man you led me to believe.'

He's bending down, rooting through a cardboard box at his feet. 'Never mind who I am. Just be ready for a difficult night.'

I've had a rather hard day. And I'll be damned if I'm to be told to mind my own business. I'm a police inspector, you know.

'No, that's not the way things are going to work,' say I. 'Miss Dean is a foreign national and you're supposed to be a vicar. Therefore, the only one of us with any authority here is me. Plus, you lied to me during the course of a murder inquiry and your accomplice here has just killed two men. You'll tell me what's going on or I'll arrest you both.'

'There's gratitude,' says Deedee. 'You save a man's life and all he wants to do is arrest you.'

Croucher produces a piece of cloth. It's patterned like a dress. But whatever it is, he tears it in two and beckons for Deedee to come towards him. From his pocket he brings a little box covered in black leather. He flicks open the tiny latch and produces a hypodermic syringe. Croucher draws some liquid from a vial contained within the leather box, checks it against the light of a lantern and asks Deedee to roll up the sleeve of her sweater. 'This will help, though I can't give you too much. Don't want you falling asleep.' Gently, he injects morphine into a vein in her arm.

'You were in the army, Inspector. You know how things work: you only know what you need to know. And quite frankly, you don't need to know.' He attends Deedee's injured hand, wrapping the cloth expertly round it. 'This may smart a little,' he says to her as he pulls to tighten this improvised strapping. Though Daisy Dean grimaces, she doesn't make a sound.

'In that case, indulge me, Croucher. We all seem to be together in this mess. At least I should know who I'm in it all with.'

Croucher ties a neat knot in the fabric strapping on Deedee's paw. He sighs. 'You'll remember SOE from the war?'

Do I ever! The Special Operations Executive. Home to the bravest, most selfless and most loyal people I've ever met. They worked operations behind enemy lines. Many – very many – lost their lives. Oh yes, and as well as all the bravery and heroics, they were all mad as a box of frogs, to the very last man and woman. Almost bound to get a chap killed if they happened to stray within a hundred yards of you.

'It would be hard to forget SOE,' say I.

'You perhaps won't know, but it was decommissioned in nineteen forty-six,' says Croucher.

'I didn't know.'

'Since Winston came back into power, he's been keen to reinstate it. Of course, there are all the usual objections about him being a clapped-out old warmonger. But that's what they said in nineteen thirty-nine.' Croucher lights a cigarette.

'To do what, exactly?'

'To keep an eye on what's happening, that's what. We all suffered in the war. But some of us came back with very odd ideas.'

That's true. The whole episode became very personal to a lot of chaps I knew. Well, liberating concentration camps, flattened villages, towns and cities where the most dreadful things took place will do that, you know.

'We're talking people like Chuck Starr, I suppose?'

'Poor Chuck,' says Deedee. 'He was a really good man. He just came to the wrong conclusion.' Then she does something that to most would be of little significance, but for me, the mist begins to clear – just a bit. Daisy Dean produces a packet of cigarettes, removes one and puts it to her mouth. She lights it with a Zippo, then gazes at me through the cloud of blue smoke.

'So, you were sent to kill him.'

Deedee looks at her feet. 'That's an operational matter. But no, I wasn't. He got in someone else's way.'

'So, you're not from the State Department, then?'

'I can't say.' She draws on the cigarette again. 'He was giving away secrets to – well, let's just say some really nasty people. We'd tried to bring him home, but he just resigned. We couldn't have him in Elderby. Too much going on. But in the end the job was done for us, Frank.'

I must admit, her calling me by my first name rather puts me off my stride. But I was in a war, and of course I killed men. I'm not proud of it, but it had to be done. I'm no different to many other servicemen and -women who did their jobs to save their country. I nod, whilst desperately trying to work out what's going on.

'I have another question. Then I'll do whatever it is you want me to do,' say I.

'Go on,' says Croucher wearily.

'Why this place? Why Elderby?'

Croucher looks at Deedee. 'You'll have heard of old Lord Elderby – the dead one?'

'Yes.'

'Despite what people say, he was a wicked man.'

'I thought he sounded like a bloody saint.'

'No,' pipes up Deedee. 'He was a fascist.'

'And a very committed one, at that,' says Croucher. 'You know how many nooks and crannies there are along this coast. Elderby is just a quiet little village. Out of the way, of little consequence. And not too far from Catterick Army Base. It's where they're going to begin their revolution.'

I am a little taken aback by this. But I suppose it makes sense. That is, if you accept the fact there is to be a fascist insurrection in our own country. And, to be honest, if one is to embark on such a thing, it's best done away from London and the South East. Elderby is handy for the coast, so coming and going in a clandestine fashion would be relatively easy. And while it's well known that certain members of the ruling classes leaned towards Hitler before the war, it's fair to say things are much worse than I thought, and not just in relation to malcontents. Tales of some of the stuff the Russians got up to in Berlin are enough to make one blanch. And Catterick! I must get word to Mitch.

I return to matters in hand. 'Hence his precipitous fall. Old Lord Elderby, I mean.'

'Winston had his eye on him for a long time. Thankfully, he was tumbled before the whole thing kicked off,' says Croucher.

'And Damnish put in his place?'

'You got it,' says Deedee.

I ponder on this for a second. It's a notion that makes sense.

'Like father, like daughter.'

'I can see why you're a detective, Inspector,' says Croucher. 'I don't know how they did it, but they managed to get young Lady Elderby and Damnish together. She carried on, unaware that everything she was – is doing – was being monitored by her husband. We've been able to bring down so many Nazi stragglers because of her. But I think she's tumbled us.'

'I see,' say I, remembering Martha Thornlie's whispers to me on Elderby Main Street. 'But as all she wanted was to maintain her place in society and keep the flame alive, she'd have married anyone with a bit of cash and a title,' say I. 'And her brother. He isn't what he appears to be, either. And who's the poor chap down the chimney?'

'That was my fault,' says Croucher. If he's sorry about the death of a man, he's doing it very casually. 'We thought our agent had gained her trust. But that obviously wasn't the case.'

'And the chimney? Why did he end up there?'

'To deflect blame on to the man of the house,' says Deedee. 'We had hoped to bug that room – it's where she makes most of her calls. But she was one step ahead, as usual.'

'Well, dash it all,' say I. 'So, it's Cummins. He has to be part of the hierarchy of all this.' I look around. 'No?'

'We haven't got that far, Frank. We know what they want to do, but not who's behind it. I'll say again, this is the trouble with the class system in your country. It's the old school tie: a ready-made network of people in Whitehall, the military, the police – even the legal system. It's all behind closed doors in London clubs and big country houses. We can't crack it,' says Deedee.

Have you ever heard of Lady Winthorpe? I want to say. There's a wrong 'un right from the off. I know we're in the middle of something nasty, but there's never a bad time to muddy someone who's done one a bad turn. Revenge for the horse debacle!

'I have someone in the army I can trust – an old family friend,' say I.

Deedee and Croucher look at each other with blank expressions.

'Who?' says Croucher.

'Lord Parsley – Mitch. He's high up in the Army Intelligence Corps. Straight as a die. I've known him all my life.'

Croucher shakes his head. 'I've heard the name. But we don't *know* for sure. We can only trust those with established bona fides.' He hesitates. 'Even then it's a bit hairy.'

'I got drunk with him just before I came here,' say I.

'Yes, but you must try to grasp our position. We only know what we know.' This new Croucher closes his eyes for a moment. 'Of course, the prime minister could have come down on them all like ants when he retook office. But so many were unprepared to believe him. And he didn't know good from bad. We're learning, though.'

'We've unearthed many others we didn't suspect,' says Deedee.

'Like Bleakly?' say I.

'Yeah, that's a new one. Sorry about that, Frank.'

It's hard to believe that old Elphinstone is a traitor – especially after his loyal service with the Chindits. But who knows what goes on between a man's ears?

'And Juggers – my boss?' I ask.

Croucher shrugs. 'We don't know. Could just be follow-ing orders from above. Or, well – you know.'

I'd bet anything on the old boy being a good egg. After all, not many fascists support Yorkshire County Cricket Club, I'll tell you. And Juggers loves the place. Honestly, this is all quite bizarre. I feel like Alice down the rabbit hole – or wherever she went. I've always hated that story – nothing to hold on to. Now, I'm living it.

I'm startled when the big church door swings open and Finan Whales appears through the gloom, wiping snow from the collar of his woollen coat.

'Quick, grab this bugger!' shouts I. 'He tried to knock me on the head. If it hadn't been for Miss Dean here, I'd be mincemeat!'

First Croucher laughs, then Deedee.

Whales stomps the cold from his feet, looking rather abashed. 'I'm right sorry I had to bang you on the head,' says Whales. 'We didn't want you caught up in all this. To be honest, we didn't know where your loyalties lay.' He gazes at Croucher. 'You've told him, then?'

'Let's say that it has been recently established beyond all doubt that he's not one of them,' says Deedee. 'And if you hadn't worn that cap as a disguise and told me what you intended, Grasby here wouldn't have had go through all that. It was careless stuff, Whales.' Deedee folds her arms, clearly displeased.

Damn, old Whales is on the side of the righteous.

'You did give me a good crack, old boy,' says I.

'We thought it would be enough to frighten off a man like you,' says Croucher.

'I beg your pardon?'

'Well, your police record doesn't show a great deal of

bravery, to be honest, lad,' says Whales. 'We wanted to spare you all this. We knew that things were about to pop. I should have told you, Miss Dean.'

Take a look at my military record, thinks I. But there's more than meets the eye to be found there. Things to which even they could never have access. Regardless of what skulduggery they're up to at the moment. I'll tell you about it another time. Like most people who think themselves to be very clever, they assume that everyone else is rather stupid. A genuinely clever person knows there are always cleverer people around. That's why you rarely hear anything about their intellect. After all, cemeteries are packed to the gunwales with dead heroes who thought they had it smoked.

'This is it? I mean, this is all you have?'

Whales removes a snowy cap with his big paw of a hand.

'All we need, Inspector. This won't be some big show. They'll arrive in four lorries, two men each. There will be a couple of senior men lurking about. It's them we really want to get our hands on. They're here to consolidate their armaments, get everyone together and head for Catterick.'

'Huh, they'll have no luck there. The boys in the garrison will soon show them the right road,' say I. But when I look at each face, it's clear I'm still not getting it. 'All good chaps at Catterick, am I right?' I say doubtfully.

'The fact that that is where the fascists aim to begin means I think it's safe to say that there must be senior officers there who are sympathetic to the cause,' says Croucher. 'In the army, you obey your commander. It's easy to convince men they're doing the right thing.'

I'll be damned. They've thought it all out. The dawning realization brings back an old friend to greet me: fear.

'Why on earth wasn't all this nipped in the bud earlier?' say I.

'The PM felt that it would have been politically reckless to go after them without the damning proof. He has parliament to convince. It's nineteen thirty-nine all over again.' Croucher shrugs.

'Not like Churchill to be so timid,' say I.

'He has to respect the political process these days. No war to justify him dashing about like a prime minister with no boundaries. Winston's an old man, into the bargain. A tired old man. I fear this stint in office will kill him. But he has unfinished business. Once it's done, he can slip away into retirement.'

'Some of which we can tie up tonight?'

'A portion, Inspector. God willing, that is.'

It's strange, but now I see Croucher is a man of faith. I wasn't sure when I thought him a mere vicar.

'OK,' says Deedee. 'Let's make our plan.'

I'm still wondering what 'OK' really means. Bloody Americans have garbled our language something rotten. I'll give it a couple of hundred years before we can no longer understand each other. We arrested a strange old cove in York a couple of years ago. Swore he was from some time in the future. He said that one day everyone would have a screen to look at that would hold the wisdom of the ages. A likely story. Give humanity access to all the knowledge in the world and they'll still manage to turn it horribly awry. But that will never happen, thankfully.

We huddle together – all four of us – and plan. High on my agenda being: where on earth is my father?

36

It turns out that nobody in the church knows what's happened to my brave papa. The last time I saw him, he was ducking into the Beggar's cellar, ready to go and divert a now-dead constable. I assume he must have convinced that thug to give him directions or something. But when I escaped, they surely realized what was really going on? I hope the old man had the sense to make himself scarce afterwards. But knowing him, he could have been parading down Main Street in a red suit with a flashing light. He's not a practical man, you know.

It turns out that these four lorries will arrive via the new road into Elderby, the one I failed to take. Surprisingly, our job is not to stop them, but to let the convoy make for the Salt House, where they will set up base and prepare. At this point, we are to disrupt and confuse, before the cavalry arrives to clean everything up and grab all those responsible.

'Can I ask a question?'

'Yes, Inspector,' says Croucher, clearly the man in charge.

'Why can't the big boys be lying in wait for the weapons? I mean, what are the four of us to do?'

'It's a fair enough question,' says Finan Whales in his deep Yorkshire brogue.

'I know you haven't had much time to get acquainted

with Elderby, Inspector,' says Deedee. 'Folks round here miss nothing. You can bet that they have eyes here and there. We simply can't flush everyone out.'

'And then there's Ingleby,' says Croucher.

'Yes, I've worked him out,' say I.

'Oh, he pretends to hate his sister, hate fascism, and the like. But it's a ruse.'

'He's fed up that he didn't become the next Lord Elderby,' say I.

'Exactly,' says Deedee. 'We can't pin him down. Though he does really hate Damnish.'

I think for a moment, remembering my visit to Ingleby's studio at Briarside Farm. The unfinished painting of the dome I saw as I was leaving. I knew I should have recognized it at the time. But the answer is so obvious now, here in this context.

'He's painting the Kremlin,' say I. 'Big canvas, too.'

Croucher shrugs. 'It's amazing what he'll do to suit his purposes. All done for the benefit of others, Grasby. After all, how many fascists paint that, eh?'

That's wasted time on his part.

'I won't bore you with all the details,' says Croucher. 'But suffice it to say, we're to hide on the fell just above the Salt House. This weather will help. Once the weapons arrive, we make as much noise as possible. We have flash flares, smoke bombs and all manner of devices designed to make them think an army has landed on their heads. I'm assured that will happen as soon as possible, but in the meantime we're all there is. Hopefully, once we're finished, a few traitors we didn't know about will be exposed.' There's a righteous zeal in the erstwhile parson's eyes.

'Which way are our chaps coming from – these reinforcements?' say I.

'They'll follow on at a distance.'

'Aye, we'll manage to trap a few tonight,' says Whales. 'People who shamelessly wear Her Majesty's uniform and are the lowest of the low.' He makes to spit but checks himself in the nick of time, remembering he's in a church.

'And there's the money,' says Deedee.

I pay my taxes, you know. It's dreadful that these bad eggs have contrived to give renegade fascists weapons in the first place. 'At least they've had the presence of mind to bag some money for it,' say I.

'No, you've got that wrong, Inspector. Our conspirators are giving them money. A hundred thousand pounds, we've gleaned from intelligence.'

I must say, it's absolutely bizarre. We spend a whole war trying to subdue these buggers. We drain our economy, lose the Empire, and who knows how many lives. And now we're happily rearming them, and handing out money into the bargain.

We go back and forth on this for a while, a question here, a possible problem there. When I was removed to the quiet little village of Elderby, little did I expect a dead man down a chimney at Holly House, and I could have had no idea that I'd end up in the middle of an international conspiracy. But it's typical of my life. You think you're on a sure winner, but before you know it, it's off home with empty pockets and a bad case of the glums. How well I recognize that feeling.

The time for talking is done. Whales and Croucher and I are lifting ammunition cases into the back of the Super Snipe. Deedee gets a pass because of her hand. The boxes contain our whizz-bangs. It's after nine in the evening before we're ready, snowing like the very Alps outside. Croucher tells us to take it easy – relax.

Deedee is deep in conversation with him under the pulpit, while Whales is lying back on a pew, snoring his head off.

I wish I could display this kind of sangfroid. I'm a jumble of nerves, as is the case before any kind of operation. Whether it's finding stolen goods in the Shambles or taking on what's left of the SS, it doesn't matter. You'd think a chap who hates such things so very much would try to avoid them at all costs. But I seem drawn to these moments like a moth to a flame. And we all know what happens to poor moths. Ultimately, I'm not even sure why I'm here. But I guess that – knowing what I now know – sitting it out isn't an option.

As though someone turns a switch, it's all action. I am handed a pistol of some kind or other and a box of ammunition. I haven't kept up with guns since the war. This one has writing on the barrel that I can't decipher. I think it could be of Slavic origin, but I'm not sure.

Croucher, this man reborn, strides over and hands me a stout greatcoat. I've worn plenty of these in my time – army issue. It's like wearing a herd of sheep on one's back when they're wet. But it's frightfully cold, so I shrug it on over my borrowed clothes. There are a pair of woollen gloves in the pockets. To add to the misery of the falling snow, the wind is blowing a gale too, a bitter easterly.

Croucher, from whom – amazingly – I am now taking orders, has deemed that we should be in position by two a.m. You'll realize by now that, if my father was accounted for, I'd have gone along with all this until the show started then lost myself in the crowd. After all, this is well beyond police business. As it is, I can only assume he's been rounded up, at best. Hardy and Thomas weren't messing about. But neither was Daisy Dean.

Onwards!

37

I'm glad to be paired off with Deedee; I feel rather responsible for her. After all, she undoubtedly saved my life
back at Powell's cottage, and with her injured hand she's
vulnerable – if one can describe a woman who wiped out
two trained ruffians as such. She winces as I'm thinking
this, as though by subconscious affirmation.

Instead of driving through the village, we take the main
road to Pickering in the snow-felted darkness. Remember,
the Pickering road acts like one of these modern bypasses
they're talking about, passing the village but not going
through it. We use the new side road into Elderby – the
one I missed. It avoids unwanted attention. Gosh, it's like
driving on plate glass, not a bump, unlike my first journey
into the village on the old road. It takes us to a little lane
where we park our car for the hike up Withernshaw Fell, to
a spot just above the Salt House. It's freezing now. In the
light of a crescent moon, I can see my breath rising like
some ghostly wraith through another heavy flurry of snow.

'It'll take less than an hour to get in position,' says
Croucher, in his army windcheater as we stand in the elements. 'We're running a bit late, but there should be plenty of
time.'

It might only take you that time, but I'm no Edmund

what's-his-name. You know, the climber chap. I preferred Croucher when he was a meek vicar.

We set off. It's hard going. The snow and hail have made the ground as slick as an ice rink. The biting wind doesn't help, either. But after much effort – and pitiful swearing on my part – we get to a position where the Salt House is a huddle of shadows to our right. It's dark, and we are using tiny torches, barely fit for purpose. We don't want anyone to spot our progress up the fell. But I have my doubts. To any trained observer, we'll stick out like a sore thumb against the white ground. I'm a worrier, as my father never fails to point out. I'm also concerned about Deedee's injury. Not that she's complaining. Such a Trojan.

This is where we split up. Croucher and Whales take the low road, just behind the Salt House. They're stumbling through drifts, carrying an ammunition case between them. Whales is big and strong, but Croucher, though smaller, is no slouch either. How wrong can a man be about a person? Mind you, if he's ex-SOE, he'll know a thing or two about being someone he's not.

'We're here,' says Deedee as we approach a holly bush on a little flat plateau on the fell. It looks like a Christmas tree, snow-laden, red berries just poking through like tiny baubles. It offers a little cover and camouflage, I suppose. We're looking down directly on the back of the Salt House and its many outbuildings. I tell myself that we are utterly invisible to anyone who doesn't know we're here. But I'm still sceptical.

I look at my watch under the dim beam of the torch. It's almost three and we are late, according to Croucher's schedule. This will be a long wait, but it's better to be in position and ready to go, rather than trying to catch up at the last moment.

'Can you help me?' says Deedee. She appears to be fishing under the bush for something with her good hand. I hope it's not a Bren gun. Suddenly I can picture her mowing down men from this position on the hill. I don't fancy that at all. There's no end to this woman's resolve and resource. But I'm getting ahead of myself – as usual.

I feel something and pull. It's a roll of off-white canvas.

'We'll shelter under here,' says Deedee. 'There's enough to sit on, on the snow, and the rest we can drape over ourselves.'

It turns out that this is to be our temporary home, and I'm glad of it. It keeps the wind and chill off a bit and allows us to sit down without literally freezing into place. Good thinking on Whales's part, whom Deedee tells me put it there on a recce earlier in the day. To be honest, I'm worried about what's to come and the whereabouts of my dear father. I fear this may be the Grasbys' last stand.

The Salt House itself is in complete darkness. Not a glimmer of light to be seen. Suddenly, though, the moon breaks through the heavy cloud. Instinctively, we both crouch further behind the bush. I can now clearly see the huge flat expanse where I glimpsed the vehicle with the antenna. I should have recognized a mobile signal intercept station when I saw one. But again, it's all about context. It's something one doesn't expect, like meeting one's great-uncle in a brothel. That would be a huge surprise for me. First, because he was keener on ornithology, and second, he's been dead for ten years.

I can feel Deedee's warmth as we huddle together.

'Is your father really a whisky magnate?' say I.

'He is, as a matter of fact. And before you ask, I did go to Yale.'

'Then you joined American intelligence.'

She gazes at me with mock amusement. 'You mean to say you didn't fall for my little cover story?'

'Not for a second.'

'Then you're far too clever to be a cop.'

'Steady on, old girl. We're not all plodding drunks, you know.'

She laughs. It all feels quite cosy until I remember her expertly placing a bullet between Thomas's eyes and running Hardy over at the height of the hailstorm. Beautiful she may be, but dangerous too – that's not in question.

We chat away about things – life, love, horses. Well, it's fair to say that I do the talking. You can tell, given the subject matter.

I hear a distant rumble and check my watch. It's five minutes before four. I feel as though only five minutes have passed since I last looked. But it's an anomaly. There are three ways to make time fly: drink alcohol, read a good book, or spend time with a beautiful woman.

'Look, it's the convoy,' says Deedee, squinting through a small pair of binoculars she's produced from deep in her pocket.

Sure enough, I can see the lights of vehicles as they progress along the same road that led us here.

But where are our chaps? Hidden away, ready to follow the fascists and come to my rescue, I hope. But before I have time to ask Deedee, lights begin to flicker from within the Salt House. Our tormentors have been there all the time!

'Did you realize they were in there?' say I.

'It kinda makes sense,' whispers Deedee.

She continues to watch as the convoy gets nearer. They're almost at the point where they will turn off and climb the hill to the Salt House. The snow has decided to get significantly heavier. If we stay where we are, we'll be in an igloo before morning.

You know the kind of feeling you get when it dawns on you something is going horribly wrong? In my case, my face prickles then my stomach churns. That happens now, as Deedee subdues a little scream. I follow her line of sight and see exactly what's distressed her. There's another line of wagons on the new road. But they've stopped. I look to the heavens for the answer, and it's obvious. There's been an accident.

'Shit, there goes our cavalry,' says Deedee, less than daintily. She's peering through the binoculars. 'A truck has skidded on to its side on the snow and it's blocking the damned road. Oh, just fabulous!'

'There's another road into the village,' say I.

'I know. Only an idiot would think of using that.' She shakes her head dismissively.

Dash it all.

'So, what do we do now? We'll just have to abandon the whole idea. The four of us can't take them on, after all.' I'm suddenly filled with hope.

But just as these words leave my mouth, something explodes near by and my heart races. As the convoy heaves its way through the snow into the Salt House yard, Croucher and Whales go about their business, flinging whizz-bangs and shooting into the darkness in order for us to appear like a much larger force. We see them crouching, slipping down the hill, anxious not to be pinned down and fired at by anyone in the Salt House.

They're either mad or they don't know that help isn't coming.

'What do we do?' say I.

She bites her lip. 'I'm not sure. But we can't leave them to it. This is a ruthless business, Frank. All our lives are at stake.'

337

Well, I had worked that out for myself.

'And?'

'What do you suggest, Inspector?'

I adopt the thoughtful expression I picked up from my father. It shouts 'This man is thinking deeply' while in fact I'm panicking and trying to work out how to leave as quickly as humanly possible.

'We should be most circumspect,' say I. 'I mean, if Croucher and Whales are captured, it will focus a few minds round the cabinet table, don't you think?'

'I doubt this is being discussed round any cabinet table,' says Deedee. 'This will be off the books. They don't want to publicize the fact that senior members of your military and ruling class are arming fascist insurgents in plain sight and not caring about the consequences.'

As a misdirected whizz-bang flies just over our heads, firing from the Salt House begins. But they're shooting in the dark. And though I can't see it from here, I know Croucher and Whales are heading into the Salt House via windows, away from where our fascists are busy firing at shadows.

'We go now!' says Deedee out of nowhere.

'Go where?'

'Into the Salt House. We can't just leave our friends!'

At this moment, I can think of several places I'd happily go. Unfortunately, the Salt House isn't one of them. And as far as friends go, well, I hardly know them. However, I can't be seen to be a coward. But once you've already done something heroic, it's hard to raise one's game and do it again. You don't know about that bit yet. Another time, methinks.

She's off. Deedee is sliding down the hillside towards it all. I have no choice but to follow suit.

I slip, tumble, fall – by the time I've travelled only a few yards I'm covered in snow from head to toe. Deedee is much more sure-footed. Apart from a couple of stumbles, she's tripping down the fell like a mountain goat, one arm flying out to keep her balance, her bandaged arm pinned to her side.

I desperately hope that we can find Croucher and Whales before it's too late. I'm sure I can persuade them to regroup and try something other than a headlong rush to oblivion.

'They've gone!' Deedee shouts amidst the turmoil.

Of course, I knew this would be the case. It's ironic I survived all that Hitler could throw at me just to die on a Yorkshire hillside. My father will love this, and likely wind the grisly horror of it all into a sermon. If he's still about to write a sermon, I fret.

The place is in an uproar. There are shots, shouts and explosions, which I assume are from our colleagues. At least this indicates they're still alive – wherever they are. But in the great scheme of things, that may not be a good thing for Inspector Frank Grasby.

I have no idea what Deedee thinks she's going to do, but she's prancing down the hill, getting ever nearer to the Salt House. The place is illuminated by bright lights from within and probing torches from without. They're looking for us.

I hear a shot fly past, closer than I'd like. Deedee has disappeared over a low wall leading on to the Salt House. I can now see lorries and men at the rear wall, not far from where I was observing the transmitter parked on the flat expanse of concrete to the rear of the building. That was the day Ingleby pretended to save me. It was a ruse to frighten me off, as was the beating. Elderby isn't a place where you'd naturally trust the community. In fact, I doubt they trust each other. Who knows who is on whose side.

I must follow Deedee. After all, I wouldn't be here if she hadn't saved me. Fair's fair, and all that.

I tumble down the last few yards of snowy fell and get to the wall, my hands like solid blocks of ice. I wonder how Deedee is managing with her bad paw and wrist. Maybe the cold has numbed the whole thing. I'm soon over the wall, scanning the place for danger and Deedee.

I can feel my heart sinking. Only ten yards or so away I see her. She's lying on her back as the tumult goes on all around. But she's still, unmoving. I'm running now, and skid to a stop beside her.

'Deedee!' I yell.

Her head is turned to one side. She looks as though she's in a blissfully peaceful sleep. But her coat is open, and on the fawn jumper she put on to keep warm, a large dark stain is spreading like milk in a cup of tea yet to be stirred.

I grab her wrist, desperately searching for a pulse.

'She's gone, old chap. Dead as the proverbial dodo. I suppose you could say Deedee is a dodo. That's what you call her, isn't it?'

I turn. Before me is Mitch Parsley. He has a camel overcoat draped over his shoulders as though he's off to the opera. 'You didn't make it in time, Mitch,' say I. 'A beautiful young woman has given her life – her future – for this nonsense.' I must admit to being surprised by his poor attempts at humour.

But when I look up at his face, I understand. This man I've known all my life is smiling.

'I say, had a thing for her, did you? Damn shame, she must have copped a stray one. Bad luck.' He reaches into his pocket and produces a packet of President cigarettes.

'Always smoke these things when the heat's on, old boy. A pipe is too cumbersome, and cigars just aren't practical.' He produces a cigarette, igniting it with the flick of a lighter.

I've had many shocks in the last few days, but this is the worst. Through the haze of sadness for Deedee, I realize that Mitch isn't here to save anyone. No, they're stuck in the snow back on the new road. Lord Parsley – who dandled me on his knee, bought me my first decent cricket bat; the man I shared long, boozy dinners with, looked to as something of a touchstone – is a traitor.

I glance at Deedee's motionless body, then, with all my strength, leap towards this monster.

But before I can get near him, I'm dragged off by powerful, unseen hands. Somehow, though, I don't care. Poor Daisy. So much life to live that she'll never see. I lost too many chums back in the war. Young men who should have had wives, girlfriends, children – all sorts. Instead, they lurk in my head like the ghosts they are. Now, my blood is boiling to match my aching heart.

I'm dragged into the Salt House past men unloading ammunition cases from the wagons and bringing them inside. I'm blind with rage. And that is never a good thing, let me assure you.

38

Big arc lights fill the damp, cavernous space that is the Salt House. As I'm pulled along, most of those working pay me no heed. One man, though, stares at me defiantly.

There is a huddle of soldiers standing around talking. They have their backs to me, but one of them is easily recognizable. It's the awkward gait, the sloping shoulders.

'If it's not Elphinstone Bleakly, the traitor,' say I. I'm in receipt of a sharp blow to the head for my pains.

'Inspector Grasby. You're looking rougher than ever.' He turns to one of his confederates. 'Lad was quite smartly turned out when he arrived here. You wouldn't think it, would you?'

I must confess to swearing quite colourfully now. It's not something I do often. But when one is driven hard enough, it's understandable, I think.

'You know they've killed Deedee, don't you, Bleakly?'

I swear, I see him hesitate. The confident smile fades, just for a split second.

'She played a dangerous game for a young lass. She knew what she were doing,' he says.

I'm about to launch into another pointless tirade of abuse when I hear a man scream and more shouts echoing in the big, empty space. Two men are being dragged towards our little huddle. Croucher and Whales. The valiant vicar spots me and nods sadly.

'What have we here? Are these the firework chaps?' It's Parsley's familiar voice again. But the sarcasm is palpable. 'No support coming, I'm afraid.'

'To hell with you!' shouts Whales, getting him a sharp punch to the stomach for his pains, doubling him in two.

'What was it Robert Burns said about best-laid schemes, eh? You must think me very stupid. I assure you, I'm not,' says Parsley.

'You can be as clever as you like. You're still a traitor,' say I.

He turns to me. 'You served in the war, Francis. At any time did you wonder why?'

'For my country.'

'No, old boy. For the Communists, the bloody working man who wants all we have but doesn't have the brains or strength of character to get it for himself. We should have allied ourselves to Hitler and wiped out Stalin. Yes, and the bloody Yanks, too.' He pauses and looks me in the eye. 'When you were a young squeaker I admired your guile and spirit. As much as he tried, your father couldn't make you conform. Seems you've managed to force yourself. One of the herd now, Francis.'

'One of the herd,' say I. 'You can't imagine the weapons you have here will make a difference? The war is over. This farce will soon be done, too – along with you!'

'They saved my life, you know. The Germans, I mean – back in the Great War.' He is walking towards me.

'Pity,' say I.

He's face to face with me now, the smoke from the President cigarette pungent. Before I can do anything, he

343

grabs my hand and thrusts the hot tip of his smoke on to one of my knuckles. Despite myself, I cry out in pain. Hearing one's voice echo round these dark, dank walls isn't fun.

'Last little chunks of pain for you, Francis. I can't say I take any pleasure in it. But you've always been a cocky little sod. Simply, you were in the wrong place at the wrong time. And worse than that, you made yourself unintentionally useful.' Behind him, not looking tired in the slightest, I may add, is Bleakly. He smiles at my distress.

I look on as Parsley whispers to an accomplice. The man, dressed in a green boiler suit, rushes off to do his bidding.

'I hate to break up this little party, but I must be off.' He turns to a straight-backed man by his side. 'Gibbons, what must we do with these – these poor misguided souls, eh?'

'Put them out of their misery, sir.' Gibbons' bearing and barked reply mark him out as a military man like Hardy and Thomas, no doubt about it.

Suddenly, I'm being forced to my knees. I'm about to die, but I'm feeling strangely detached. It's something I've experienced once before, but this time it's even more pointed, real. I see my father's face before my mind's eye, then my dear mother. I should like to be reunited with her again. Then, for some odd reason, I see Bay Rum, a horse I've fancied for a good few years. Well, I'll be damned. It's clear that my poor brain is just trying to soothe me into oblivion with happy images. I had no idea it possessed such hidden depths.

'Any last requests, old chap?' Parsley at least has the decency to smile at me regretfully.

'Yes, drop dead,' say I.

'I rather think you have me mixed up with you. Bit unfortunate, and all that. But you should have done what I said and joined the Foreign Office. I told your father I'd get you in.'

First I've heard of it. Thanks, Daddy.

Gibbons walks towards me, his face expressionless. He removes a pistol from a side-holster and takes a moment to check it for rounds and functionality. He stands above me and takes aim at my unprotected head.

I hear the sharp report of the gun. Do you know, dying is remarkably painless – I haven't felt a thing. Though my ears are still ringing because of the noise. I expect to open my eyes and see my mother, St Peter or a winners' enclosure somewhere.

But no. Despite being temporarily deafened, the sight I see before me is one of utter confusion and panic. Even worse than before. Dark-clad men are swarming from one end of the Salt House. They have guns and there are lots of them. The intent is obvious. Parsley and his cronies are done for, and I'm still very much alive. Somehow, they got through.

'Bleakly, the bags, man!' shouts Mitch, and each of them picks up a leather holdall, as chaos breaks out all around. I note some men look confused and are surrendering. I get the impression they were just following orders and find themselves in the midst of something they don't understand and certainly don't want anything to do with.

I look down. There, at my feet, is Gibbons, my erstwhile executioner, writhing in pain with a bullet to the leg. I look up and Bleakly stares back at me.

'You're a lucky sod, I'll give you that. Hurry up. On your feet, Frank!' He points a revolver at me.

'Come on, Bleakly,' shouts Mitch Parsley, hefting a holdall. 'Bring Grasby!'

I'm pushed and hustled out of the Salt House via a space

where once there was a window, all the time at the end of Elphinstone's pistol. We're back in the big yard now, as the pandemonium inside roars on.

Bleakly thrusts the barrel of the pistol into my ribs, forcing me onwards. It's now, into the cold night, that I remember Deedee. I look across to where she fell, but there's no body to be seen. I convince myself that I'm disoriented, looking at the wrong place. But I know I'm not. After all, this is my third visit to the Salt House.

We reach a car – it's an old SS, now Jaguar, for obvious reasons. We come to a halt before it.

'Get in,' says Bleakly, a mean look on his long face. I do as I'm told, jumping on to the back seat as though absolutely nothing is wrong. It's the opposite, for what I've glimpsed in the footwell makes me want to scream in shock. I supress this instinctive reaction.

Mitch Parsley jumps into the driver's seat, Bleakly beside him in the front of the car. He turns to face me, his pistol still pointed at my head.

'One move, and it'll be my pleasure. You're an over-entitled buffoon.'

'Steady on, Bleakly,' says Mitch. 'I'm rather entitled myself, don't you know.'

We screech out of the yard, Lord Parsley making for the narrow road into Elderby, cleared of snow for their purposes. I'd wondered on my first visit why the Salt House road was in much better nick than the rest of Elderby and its environs.

'Looks like the game's up, for now. We mustn't get caught. The fight goes on. We'll divvy this up on our way.' He nods to the big bags of money.

It dawns on me what's happening. They have the money that was to be given to the fascists. Who knows, this may well be what Mitch intended all along. He's always been a big spender. But how does one really know what's happening – apart from the fact that I'm in a fix again?

'Put down the gun, Sergeant,' says a voice from the back of the car. It's not mine.

39

Deedee has the gun to Parsley's head, the determined look I last saw when she was about to kill Hardy marked out again on her face.

I must admit, when I saw her squatting in the footwell I nearly fainted. I mean, I know she's a talented young woman, but I didn't have her down for self-resurrection.

'Do as she says!' Mitch's head has sunk into his shoulders. It's never a pleasant feeling, having a gun pointed at you.

'What on earth is going on, Deedee?' say I. 'I broke my heart when you were shot. It was bloody convincing – all the blood.'

Though I'm pleased to see that we seem to have come out on top, I'm less sanguine that Daisy Dean saw fit to give me such heartache.

'An old vaudeville trick. It's amazing what fixes a little stage blood will get you out of. And it works. This is the second time I've been thankful for carrying the stuff. Old hustler's trick.'

I'm desperately trying to think of a smart retort, but it won't come. Well, it's been bloody frantic. I'm about to ask what she intends to do, when the car lurches to the left, Parsley having lost control in the snow. I note that Deedee manages to hold on to her weapon as we come to a sudden, crashing halt against something solid.

For a moment or two, everything is hazy. There's a strong smell of petrol, and smoke and steam emanating from the engine into the body of the vehicle.

'Quick, get out!' I'm shouting at the top of my voice.

We've all been rendered slightly insensible by the impact. While Deedee searches for the door handle on her side, I kick my door open and lever myself out of the car. We're in the village. Through the smoke I see a short garden wall. I think Mitch crashed the car on purpose. For a moment I can't see him, and suspect he's been flung through the windscreen. But just as Deedee runs to my side, I see him leave the car and hurry off across someone's front lawn, a holdall in each hand. Curtains are twitching all around, and no wonder.

'We have to get him. We need to take him to Churchill!' shouts Deedee. But just as she does, I hear a crackling noise come from the engine of the old SS.

Elphinstone Bleakly is slumped forward in the passenger seat. Either he's been knocked unconscious or he's having a quick snooze, to which he is prone. Though my mechanical knowledge is scant, I can smell and hear fire. And I know that fire and petrol don't mix – not at all.

'Stand back!' I pull Daisy away from the car to a safe distance.

'Do you think you can get him out?' says she.

I'm about to give this a jolly good try, when there's a sound akin to that of a heavy bag of coal being dropped into a cellar. In seconds, the dark night is illuminated as the car explodes once, then twice, and bursts into flames.

Having been blown to the ground, I force myself on to my feet. I peer at the bright flames through the falling snow, the thought still to rescue Bleakly. But that's not going to happen. It's just too hot.

Feeling jolly sick, as I look on, one after another, the car's tyres pop in the inferno. Windows have been broken all along the road. There's an old man in a dressing gown and nightcap standing on his garden path, his mouth gaping open.

Deedee is back on her feet. 'Come on, we need to find Parsley. He went this way.' She takes off at a gallop, the pistol held tight in one hand like a relay baton.

I must admit, I'm done in. I can't really see the point of chasing the old boy. After all, where's he going to go?

I look round and spot a large van in the light of the burning car. It's the removal van I parked behind before I went to the pub to meet Bleakly. That seems like a lifetime ago. I run over to it. Sure enough, there's my Austin A30 parked where I left it.

I jump in and give silent thanks, noting that, for once, my careless nature has come up trumps. They keep telling me not to leave the keys in the ignition. But there they are. You know, sometimes it pays to ignore others.

Twisting the key, the car instantly backfires with a bang but it sounds positively meek compared with what's been going on for the last hour or so. Though I'm sure the poor folk of Elderby must think that the Blitz is happening all over again. Mind you, I'm not sure this village was blitzed the first time round. As I drive past the burning car that is Elphinstone Bleakly's tomb, I hear my father's voice in my head.

What goes around comes around.

I hate seeing anyone die – friend or foe. But it's the way of things. I'm convinced that evil is punished one way or another. What led this brave Chindit down the path he took with our dear family friend? We'll likely never know. But take that path, he undoubtedly did. I'm sure he'd have watched me die with very little emotion. Mind you, I'm not sure that Cummins wouldn't have done the same, interested only in tidying up the whole thing for old Winston.

People are strange.

When I turn the next corner, there's Deedee caught in the headlights up ahead. She's pelting off like a sprinter. I pull up beside her.

'Quickly, he's headed up the hill to the edge!' she shouts as she jumps in. As I press on, I can see Mitch Parsley picked out in the lights, both holdalls at his side. Running as fast as he can, he looks behind, sees us, and drops one of the bags, no doubt to lighten his load. He takes off up the hill.

I stop the car and lean out of the driver's window. There are lights overhead, accompanied by a regular thud. I've heard this before. Then it dawns on me. It's one of these new-fangled helicopters. I've only seen them once, American Sikorskys, I think they were. Bloody handy things that don't require a runway to take off and land.

'That's how he's going to escape – in a helicopter,' says Deedee.

I begin the process of turning the car round in the road. We're now facing away from the hill.

'What on earth are you doing?' says Deedee, bewildered.

She's forgotten that this car will only reverse up hills. But before I can begin this process, she implores me to let her out of the car.

'I need to get that money. We can't just leave it there.' She's off out of the car again, the stain of the stage blood still spread across her jumper.

Then she hesitates and leans back into the Austin.

'Hey, you're a good guy, Frank Grasby.'

I smile, but this seems odd. Before I can say anything, Deedee is running off to collect the bag of cash. She ploughs through the snow like a horse, raising her knees high, virtually vaulting the stuff.

I see flashing lights pass overhead. Damn!

I reverse the car up the hill towards the edge, the engine whining its familiar protest. It's tricky navigating through the snow, and I nearly lose control a couple of times. But thankfully, I make it.

On my left, St-Thomas's-on-the-Edge is all in darkness. Briefly, I wonder what's happened to Croucher and Whales. But there's no time for that. There's a clearing to one side of the thicket of bare trees. I can see the helicopter hovering above it, clearly the intended landing spot.

I press my foot down on the accelerator. Navigating at speed and in reverse between trees and through the snow. The going, however, becomes too difficult for the car, the snow much too deep. I stop and take off after him on foot, though I've no idea what I'll do if I catch him. I'm not as good at this as Deedee; the snow makes running hard work. Parsley may well still have a weapon, too, and all I have are my wits. I know what my father would say.

Out of the blue, I'm caught in a strong gust of wind. It's pushing me back, and the noise is deafening.

The helicopter is landing. I can see Parsley crouching before it with his remaining holdall. Slowly the racket abates, the aircraft lands, and the blades slow to a stop.

Lord Mitchell Parsley turns and reaches under his jacket, producing a handgun from a shoulder holster.

'You escaped death once tonight, Francis. It won't happen again. Show yourself, boy!' He aims the weapon at me.

'That'll do, sir, if you don't mind.' On hearing the voice, I want to cheer. There, standing by the aircraft, are three men. Two military types in fatigues, and a smaller, more rotund figure. It's Superintendent Juggers.

'I know you all thought you had me fooled, Your Lordship. But I'm a bit long in the tooth for all that.'

I emerge from the treeline.

'Grasby, how glad I am to see you, lad. Though I must confess, that's not always my instinctive reaction when you heave into view. But this was always His Lordship's preferred method of escape. He and Bleakly were more interested in the money than the cause, the greedy buggers.' He stares at Parsley as he's being dragged back into the helicopter.

I could kiss his big pudding face, but decide he'd likely floor me with a swift uppercut to the chin. Meanwhile, Mitch is being subdued in no uncertain terms by Juggers's companions.

'You all right, lad? You've not been injured or owt?'

'No,' say I, desperate to tell him about the whole bloody awful escapade. Of course, I have many questions to ask him, too. But two things prey on my mind. I must find Deedee, of course. But more than anything, I want to know what's happened to my father. Suddenly, there's a great lump in my throat.

'You'll excuse me, sir. Things to do!'

I dash back through the woods and into the car.

40

I must confess to thinking that Daisy Dean would be easy to find. I thought she'd be toiling up to the edge with the holdall. Anxious to come to my aid. But there's no sign of her. I scour Elderby, looking, but she's nowhere to be seen.

I stop and think for a moment. Where could she be? Come to that, where is my father?'

Coming to the conclusion that the place to start must be Hetty Gaunt's, I park outside the guest house with my heart in my mouth.

There it is in all its dark, forbidding splendour. I race up the path and knock at the door. The first thing I hear is Cecil squawking like a mad thing. Then Hetty Gaunt opens the door.

'You look bloody awful,' says she, in her dressing gown. 'You better come in. But you've had your bath for the week, remember.'

'Where's my father?' Rudely, I push my way past her and into the black dining room. There, at the table, beside an almost empty bottle of sherry, is the man who gave me life. He stares back at me, heavy-lidded.

'What a bloody racket. We couldn't sleep,' says the malicious beanpole.

'We?'

'Hetty and I. Who do you think?'

My landlady takes a seat beside him. But Cecil, I note, opts to sit on the Reverend Grasby's shoulder rather than hers. The bird nestles at his cheek, making a contented sound that wouldn't be out of place coming from a cat. My father looks like Francis of Assisi in an old tartan dressing gown.

'You're safe and well. Thank the Lord, Father,' say I.

'The policeman you were worried about showed me on my way. I tried to hold him up as long as I could, but he was preoccupied, son. Still, he clearly didn't catch you, eh?'

'Not for the want of trying,' say I. But it's now even more obvious to me that, all along, Bleakly's plan had been to knock me on the head. After all, he couldn't do it at the station – or even in the village. When I thought I was being smart, I merely played into his hands. But, mercifully, he failed. This reminds me.

'I don't suppose you've seen Deedee, by any chance, Mrs G?'

'Aye, she were here not five minutes ago. Picked up her things and left in a big car. She wanted you to have this.' Hetty Gaunt pushes an envelope across the table towards me.

I open it, feeling suddenly dog-tired. You can't blame a chap. I read her neat, round hand.

Dear Frank,

It's been so nice getting to know you. You're a credit to yourself and the police force in which you serve. A real English gentleman.

I'm sorry I had to split without saying goodbye. But who knows, our paths may cross again. I really hope they do.

I've left something for you in my room. I know your instincts will be otherwise but ignore them. Use this wisely – not gambling on horses – and make a life for yourself. You deserve a wife and kids, a family. Go make it happen, Inspector!

Yours, always,

Deedee x

P.S. Remember, nobody knows about the money. It's free cash. Have no doubts, everyone needs a break sometimes.

I leave my father, Hetty and Cecil in the dining room and take to the stairs.

The door to Deedee's room is lying ajar. I bound in, and sure enough, there it is, the holdall full of money.

I sit on the bed; her perfume still hangs in the air.

Dash it all!

AUTHOR'S EPILOGUE

GPO TELEGRAM
FROM FORWARD COMMAND (CATTERICK) – STOP –
TO W S CHURCHILL – DOWNING STREET – STOP:
ELDERBY OPERATION SUCCESSFUL – STOP –
ROUNDING UP STRAYS – STOP – MORE WHEN
AVAILABLE – STOP:
YOURS CUMMINS – STOP.

And there we have it. It's an odd place to end, I admit. But it seems quite appropriate, somehow.

The events of that night in Elderby put an end to any notions of a fascist rebellion in England or anywhere else, come to that. Churchill, his long job done, as predicted, retired to live into great old age. Though, in subsequent years, folk looked on with no little concern as the Soviet Union expanded to occupy most of Eastern Europe. In the end, it's the usual thing; one does one's best and hopes for the same. But I dread to think how it will all pan out in these days of nuclear weapons everywhere.

There will be more about Arthur Juggers in these memoirs. The same goes for my father, and the magnificent Daisy Dean – yes, and Hetty Gaunt, too.

As for Croucher, Whales and the rest – I never saw them again. Though I know they survived that snowy night at the Salt House.

Lady Damnish and her brother, Ingleby, were arrested for conspiracy to murder. Though it was never established who killed the man in the chimney at Holly House, I now know he was an MI5 operative who died when a needle pierced the back of his neck and thence into his brain. Though it seemed impossible at the time, I wouldn't be surprised if Her Ladyship did the deed herself. They thought they'd planted an agent who had her trust, but she was at least two steps ahead of them.

Charles Starr, it seemed, did his bit then got in the way. He drank too much and was a liability, so paid the ultimate price. His death was recorded as 'Misadventure'. I never heard any more of his wife, Dr Elizabeth Starr. I've often wondered how much she knew.

You know, I bumped into Martha Thornlie in York six years ago. She was a bit plumper, but I recognized her immediately. She told me she'd seen Her Ladyship before, talking to a man in the grounds a couple of times in the days prior to the events at Holly House. She did the right thing getting out of the way. I reckon that she wanted to tell me as little as possible at the time, without letting me miss the point. Fear is a dreadful thing – as you've witnessed.

With his wife rotting in gaol, and the scandal of it all still tainting him, Lord Damnish – though he'd done the right thing for his country by exposing his wife and brother-in-law – spent most of the rest of his life in the South of France. He died a dozen years later of a stroke, and his son took the title of Lord Damnish. Harry, or whatever his name is now, has tried repeatedly to change his title to that of Lord Elderby. I doubt he'll ever succeed.

By all accounts, he's gradually reduced his father's fortune to a much smaller sum. But that's the way it goes. Fathers and sons, eh?

Brave Chindit Elphinstone Bleakly was buried quietly, the cause of his death explained away as a car accident. Though he should have been brought to justice, with the whole thing being hushed up, he was left free of any damaging association. It doesn't do for the public to lose faith in the police, you know.

In fact, it is as though none of it happened. The incident at the Salt House appeared in the papers as a fire, contained miraculously by the snow. I received a quiet commendation for the nebulous enough 'services to the crown'. Also, I was assured that I'd never have to worry about walking the beat on Hessle Road again.

As for Elderby – well, it's still there, of course. In a fit of nostalgia, I took to the North York Moors a year ago or so, in my new Morris Marina. The village was exactly the same, not changed a bit. And though I took a turn into the Beggar, there was no sign of Ethel behind the bar. I stayed for one drink and left, though not without the events of those few days near Christmas 1952 coming to mind.

Ultimately, people lost their lives, others were ruined – and for nothing. Our old friend Lord Mitch Parsley, freed by the cover-up, decided to emigrate to Canada. Like Bleakly, no blame attached itself to him. Though he died less than a year after the events I describe. No doubt a grubby deal was done: information in return for his freedom. They said he'd fallen drunk from a balcony. But I have my doubts. It's odd to be betrayed by someone you've known so well. He'd have watched me die without a care. I don't grieve.

What about the money, I hear you say?

Well, that's another story. One of many I'm busy writing down for posterity or beyond.

Frank Grasby
York, March 1975

ACKNOWLEDGEMENTS

I'd like to thank all at Transworld, especially my editor Finn Cotton and copy-editor Lorraine McCann. Moving publisher is a bit like the first day at a new school, and they have made the transition very easy.

Thanks as always to my dear wife for putting up with a man whose mind is frequently elsewhere in some plot or other.

To my friends, who never fail to cheer when times are tough – you know who you are.

And so many thanks to my ebullient agent Jo Bell, of Bell Lomax Moreton, for her boundless enthusiasm and encouragement.

Thanks to the Police and Prison Museum in Ripon, North Yorkshire.

Lastly, thanks to the Yorkshire side of my family. My late mother was born in Hull, my grandfather Cyril Pinkney was from Sutton, then a village on the outskirts of the city. Because of them, I have an abiding love of the county, and have visited so many times it's hard to number.

Denzil Meyrick is from Campbeltown on the Kintyre Peninsula in Argyll. After studying politics, he enjoyed a varied career as a police officer, distillery manager, and director of several companies. He is the No.1 bestselling author of the DCI Daley series, and is now an executive producer of a major TV adaptation of his books.

Denzil lives on Loch Lomondside in Scotland with his wife Fiona and cats. You can find him on Twitter @Lochlomonden, Facebook @DenzilMeyrickAuthor, or on his website: www.denzilmeyrick.com